D0466062

King of Storms

Other Books by Amanda Scott

KNIGHT'S TREASURE

LADY'S CHOICE

PRINCE OF DANGER

LORD OF THE ISLES

HIGHLAND PRINCESS

THE SECRET CLAN: REIVER'S BRIDE

THE SECRET CLAN: HIGHLAND BRIDE

THE SECRET CLAN: HIDDEN HEIRESS

THE SECRET CLAN: ABDUCTED HEIRESS

BORDER FIRE

BORDER STORM

BORDER BRIDE

HIGHLAND FLING

HIGHLAND SECRETS

HIGHLAND TREASURE

HIGHLAND SPIRITS

THE BAWDY BRIDE

DANGEROUS ILLUSIONS

DANGEROUS ANGELS

DANGEROUS GAMES

DANGEROUS LADY

THE ROSE AT TWILIGHT

King of Storms

NEW YORK BOSTON

The characters and events in this book are fictitious. Any similarity to real persons, living or dead, is coincidental and not intended by the author.

Cover design by Diane Luger
Book design by Giorgetta Bell McRee

Warner Forever
Hachette Book Group USA
237 Park Avenue
New York, NY 10017

Warner Forever is an imprint of Warner Books.

ISBN-13: 978-0-7394-8603-0

Printed in the United States of America

To Jeanne Rose Fontana Lower (Mills College '39), and to Ray Lower, *in memoriam*, for their generous support through the years, access to their wonderful library and knowledge of all things Sinclair, and for introducing me to Donal Sean.

A man's greatest strength can likewise be
his greatest weakness.

— Origin Unknown

Prologue

England, near the Scottish Border, October 1378

Rain pelted down hard in the dark night, making it nearly impossible to see but covering other sounds as the lone Scotsman in soaked breeks, boots, and leather jack-o'-plate moved up behind the third English sentry in the clearing, clouted him on the head hard with a stone, and eased him to the muddy ground just as he had done with the other two.

As the Scot, Sir Giffard MacLennan, moved swiftly to untie the first of the captives, the man said, "Be it really yourself, Captain?"

"Aye, sure," Giff said. "Who else would it be?"

"There be dunamany more English about, sir, and they ha' sent for reinforcements from Carlisle," the other muttered.

"Then we'd best get back to the *Storm Lass* quickly, so help me set these others free. There were nine of us. Are the others all here?"

"Aye, sir. They willna ha' taken the *Lass*, will they?"

"If they did, I'll hang whoever let them get close enough," Giff said, helping him up. "Now, be quick. The men still with the ship will be waiting for us."

The others were soon free, and as the nine men hurried back along the marshy track toward Solway Firth, one said, "How did ye slip free, Captain?"

Giff shrugged. "They hadn't counted us, and in that thunder-pelt that let them creep up on us, it was only a matter of seizing my moment when it came."

With audible amusement, the other asked, "What sort of a moment was it?"

"When that great bolt of lightning dazzled everyone and thunder boomed all round us, shaking the very earth. I stepped back then between two bushy shrubs and went to ground. Did anyone other than you lads even miss me?"

"Nay, although some did hope they had caught the king o' storms."

Giff chuckled. "We'll keep mum now lest they have others hidden to watch for us. I'd as lief we not all end up prisoners in Carlisle Castle."

"Aye, sir, I thought sure we were goners."

"Nay, you should know I'd not let that happen," Giff said.

A quarter hour later they reached the rise overlooking the firth, near Bowness village. "Where be the *Storm Lass*, then?" one of the men asked.

"Where we left it, yonder, but under the shrubbery," Giff said, pointing as he gave a low whistle and received an answering one from a nearby wood.

On the sound, men emerged from the wood and began flinging away the branches that had covered the fourteen-oared Isles galley.

"We'll launch her and put out the oars quietly," Giff said

as his men moved into position. "No need for sail. We can easily make Powfoot Bay before the tide turns. Then we'll find the others at Brydekirk and get dry again at last."

The *Storm Lass* was soon in the water, her banner flying high and her oarsmen at their oars. Men from Galloway to Cape Wrath and beyond knew the *Lass* by her red banner with its single puffy black cloud.

The storm still pelted, blew, and churned waves as if the gods had gone mad, but every man aboard had faith that his captain could tame the wildest sea, just as men of old had said that Saint Columba could.

Before they were halfway across, the winds dropped, and shortly before dawn they reached the Scottish coast of the firth and saw breakfast fires already burning.

The rain had eased at last to a near silent drizzle, and their encampment boasted tents, so Giff could look forward to a nearly dry bed and a few hours' sleep.

They beached the galley, and ten minutes later, he found Sir Hugo Robison just stepping out of his tent.

"Good morrow to you, Hugo. Didst miss me?"

"Where the devil have you been, Giff?"

"England," he said. "Thought I'd see what Northumberland has set up to do."

"And?"

"He has five hundred strong and looks to be moving east to cross the Sark."

"Then he's still close, so why did it take you so long to get back here?"

"The bastards captured nine of us."

"Us? *You* fell prisoner to Northumberland?"

"Aye, but only for a few minutes. I stepped away when the moment was right, then followed them and fetched my lads back."

"And you expect what for this feat?" Hugo demanded. "Applause?"

"Sakes, I thought you'd be glad to see us all."

"If I'm hearing you properly, you risked your life and those of thirty others to have a peek at Northumberland's encampment. They captured you, and now you want me to tell you that you did a good turn because you were lucky enough to get your lads out of the predicament into which your own actions cast them?"

"Well, I don't know that I'd credit luck for any of it," Giff said, "unless 'twas the bad luck of tripping over an English hunting party. Thunder was drowning out their noise whilst the rain was trying to drown us. But then, to have found the right moment and taken it—"

Hugo's fist slammed into his jaw, knocking him onto his backside and effectively ending his explanation.

As Giff rubbed his aching jaw, Hugo said, "Of all the reckless, mutton-headed things you've done, this is the . . . What the devil are you grinning about?"

Still rubbing his jaw, Giff said, "I was just thinking how good it is to be home again. Would it help to know that Northumberland means to meet up with Bewcastle and another five hundred, then to cross Liddel Water at Kershopefoot after luring the Douglas much farther east?"

"Why didn't you tell me all that straightaway?" Hugo demanded.

"Because you put me right off my tale with your questions, I expect."

"Well, you can just sit right there to enjoy the rest of what I have to say to you, because if you get up, I'll put you on your backside again. In the first place . . ."

Giff waited out the storm, admiring—and certainly not for the first time—Hugo's gift for shredding a man's character thoroughly and at length without pausing even once to think of the right word.

The blessing was that Hugo would just as efficiently send someone to warn the Earl of Douglas, and thus they would spoil yet another English attempt to make nuisances of themselves in Scotland.

Chapter 1

Edinburgh Castle Royal Apartments, Tuesday, June 4, 1381

The Earl of Fife, effectively ruler of Scotland, sat comfortably at a table before the fire in his favorite chamber in David's Tower, preparing documents for his father's signature and royal seal. Fife enjoyed ruling Scotland and saw no reason to anticipate anything but that he would continue to do so for many years to come.

Tall and lanky with dark hair and stern features, he wore all black as was his custom, and although well into his fortieth year, he was a fit man and one with few illusions. As great-grandson of Robert the Bruce and third son of the High King of Scots, Fife was politically astute, ruthless, affable—when affability proved useful—and eminently competent. He understood power, wanted more of it, and for the past few years had been taking more and more of it into his own long, slender hands.

Fife knew he was more capable of ruling Scotland than his aging, half-blind, rapidly failing father, the King, or his incompetent, disinterested elder brother, the Earl of Carrick. But, thanks to a foolish notion of Robert the Bruce's that the King's eldest son must succeed him, Carrick was presently heir to the crown.

Before Bruce altered the process, Scottish nobles had chosen their kings. They did not believe, as the English and French liked to pretend they did, that kings were divinely ordained. The King of Scots was merely the preeminent clan chief. He did not possess a royal army or navy but was completely dependent on the goodwill of his nobles to produce ships and men in support of his causes.

Had Bruce not decreed that the eldest son or nearest male kinsman must succeed, no Stewart could have become King of Scots, because too many noblemen considered the Stewarts upstarts. Even their name was new, derived from his father's previous position as High Steward to the King. Robert the Steward had become Robert II only because he had been David II's nearest male kin when David died childless.

But the way in which the Stewarts had come to power did not concern Fife now. The past was the past, and he knew he would be able to control Carrick as easily as he now controlled their father, but he hoped instead to succeed to the throne himself. He knew that leaders of the Scottish Parliament, given a choice, would always support a strong man over a weak one. More importantly, given sufficient cause, they could legally override Bruce's succession order.

The fact was that both his father and brother were too weak to rule a country rife with noblemen who wielded vast power over their clansmen, knew their own minds, and heartily resented any outside authority. Fife believed he had already shown himself strong enough to rule them and that he therefore deserved to be King. What he did not know was how far he would have to go to seize that right.

He believed he was capable of doing whatever he deemed necessary, but he preferred to produce tangible proof of his greater abilities, proof so clear that the leaders of Parliament would be unable to resist it. A year ago, he had thought such proof lay nearly within his grasp. But foully betrayed, he had failed to capture it.

Still, it was his experience that one could always create new opportunities. One merely had to keep one's eyes open to the omens and prepare for eventualities. His new ship, the *Serpent Royal*, was such a preparation.

As he finished the last document, a minion rapped to announce a visitor.

"The Chevalier de Gredin, my lord."

Stunned to hear the name, especially in view of the path his rambling thoughts had taken, Fife nodded permission, pushed the documents aside, and watched narrow-eyed as the chevalier entered and made him a sweeping bow.

Etienne, Chevalier de Gredin, ten years younger than the earl, was more colorfully if not as richly attired, and clearly fancied himself a dashing fellow.

He carried a document with a half-dozen red wax seals appended to it.

Straightening, his green eyes on the earl, he said coolly, "You are doubtless amazed to see me, my lord, but I bring you word from his holiness, the Pope."

"Do you? I thought you'd fled to the north with your tail between your legs."

"But no, my lord, only to learn what I could there. However, with none but Norse ships and those of my host available, it was impossible to communicate with the Pope or with my friends in France. So I returned to the Continent, and I am to tell you now that his holiness still supports your endeavors and means to supply ships to aid you. With your kind permission, I am to remain here with you as his envoy."

"As his envoy or as my hostage?" Fife inquired mildly.

"It must be as you wish, my lord," de Gredin said, kneeling submissively. "We both still seek the same goals, to seize the Templar treasure, return it to his holiness, and to see you take your rightful place as High King of Scots."

Letting him remain on his knees, Fife gave the situation brief thought.

The Knights Templar, having served as the Pope's own army, and protectors of pilgrims to the Holy Land during the Crusades, eventually rose to become trusted bankers to the world and guardians of the world's most sacred and most valued items, and thus had amassed enormous treasure. But at the beginning of the present century they had fallen afoul of Philip IV of France and his tame pope, who named them heretics and forced the disbanding of the hitherto highly respected Order. However, when Philip tried to seize their treasure, he found that it had vanished. The Templar treasure had been missing now for nearly seventy-five years.

Holy Kirk had claimed ownership, and the present Pope, apparently believing that at least a good portion of the treasure had somehow made its way to Scotland, had twice sent men to find and reclaim it—so far, unsuccessfully.

De Gredin was the Pope's man. Therefore, his return was clearly an omen.

Fife's sole interest in the treasure lay in a single item that he believed formed part of it, and that, thanks to an informant, he had reason to believe truly was hidden in Scotland. So if de Gredin and the Pope needed his aid to find the treasure, he could certainly turn that need to his own good. After all, even if they failed to find the treasure, papal support alone might be enough to tip the balance his way when the time came to persuade Parliament that he should be King.

He had no liking for de Gredin, however, and glowered as he said bluntly, "You betrayed me last year. Why should I trust you now?"

Still kneeling, the chevalier held out the sealed document he had brought with him. "Read this, my lord. Then decide what you will."

Holyrood Abbey Woods, Tuesday, June 4, 1381

A faint ring of ripples forming around the hitherto motionless fishing line was the first indication from below of any interest in its neatly baited hook.

Holding the pole gingerly, nineteen-year-old Lady Sidony Macleod stared at the rings as they expanded and multiplied in number. For at least an hour, she had been sitting on a low, flat granite promontory that jutted into the long, narrow loch without seeing a single fish, although the burly, gray-haired gardener who had lent her his pole had assured her the abbey's loch teemed with them.

Now she wondered if she should pull up her line. She did not really want to catch a fish, anyway. She had only taken the pole because it had seemed to lend a greater sense of purpose to her stolen walk than mere escape.

Having a fish as proof of that purpose might be useful, but having to carry one would be a nuisance. Her older sister Sorcha had always carried any they had caught on such expeditions at home.

"Are you sure I'll catch one?" she had asked the gardener.

"Och, aye, m'lady," he'd assured her. "Likely, ye'll catch a fine salmon or trout for your breakfast."

Sidony had found it impossible to refuse so kind an offer, so she thanked him and accepted a small pot of earthworms as well, to use for bait. Then, crossing the three back gardens between Clendenen House and the woods, and slipping through the hedge boundary, she had strolled among the trees, lady ferns, and flowers, finding the ground annoyingly boggy. But soon she had come upon the glassy, dark-green loch, and its serene beauty had drawn her, making her forget the muddy ground.

With gray sky overhead and trees growing to the water's edge, the loch darkened outward from a grayish green color in the center to a raggedy line of black shadows near the shore, where surrounding trees reflected off the mirror-like surface.

The temperature was mild, and the woods seemed unnaturally still. Sidony had followed the loch shore until she had come upon the jutting granite slab. After slogging through muck, the gray-and-white rock looked invitingly dry and clean.

Her boots were heavy with mud, and the hem of the blue kerseymere skirt she wore with its matching tunic likewise bore evidence of her trek. But it was an old dress and not one she cared for. She had put it on to play with her fourteen-month-old nephew, because it would save any finer gown from grubby hands or spills.

Baiting her hook was easy, thanks to similar expeditions with Sorcha near Castle Chalamine, their home in the Highlands. As she pictured the castle and its nearby tumbling burn and dense green shrubbery, a sigh escaped her lips.

She had been away from home for more than a year—too long.

Tears welled at the thought, and one spilled down her cheek just as the pole jerked hard in her hand. Gripping it tight in both hands, she lurched awkwardly upright, trying to avoid falling into the water, stepping on her skirts, or losing the fish.

Larger than she had expected, it did not want to be caught and was fighting so hard that she wished she had not caught it at all and wondered if she could just extract the hook and let it go.

In a similar instance with Sorcha, her older sister had said the fish would die anyway, and might linger in pain for days first. So at last, as it lay flopping feebly on the granite, Sidony picked up a rock and resolutely ended its life.

Staring at the dead fish, she grimaced and looked for a length of ivy she could string through its gills and mouth to carry it. Telling herself that she had been very clever and that she did *not* want to catch another fish, she picked up the gardener's pole in her left hand and turned back toward Clendenen House.

A few minutes later, finding no track, she realized she had lost her way.

Had the sun been shining, she might have been able to tell what direction to go. Sorcha could tell by the sun, although Sidony was not certain how, because she had never thought to ask. She did know the sun set in the west, though, and had watched it go down the previous night, on the Castle side of Clendenen House.

Perched as Edinburgh Castle was on its own craggy hilltop at what she thought was the northwest end of the royal burgh, it was visible from everywhere—everywhere, that is, except her present location, where the canopy was too dense.

She told herself she was just getting an extra bit of freedom and someone would find her eventually if she did not find her own way. The abbey bell would ring for Vespers, and she could easily find Clendenen House from the abbey.

By now people surely wondered where she was, because she had been gone for some time. They might be annoyed that she had not said where she was going, but she had not wanted to wake her sister Isobel or their hostess, or disturb the men, and she had not meant to get lost. It occurred to her then that if someone did come looking for her, she would just get back sooner—if they searched for her. They might not have noticed yet that she was gone. They often did not notice her.

Perhaps someone would hear her if she whistled a little tune.

Ladies were not supposed to whistle, and she was sure the others would condemn such behavior. But the only one of her six sisters presently at Clendenen House was Isobel, who was pregnant again and sleeping soundly.

Sidony did not know many tunes, so she whistled her favorite one over and over. Since whistling was one of her few accomplishments, it did seem unfair that ladies were not to do it. She wondered, as she often did, who made up such rules.

If it were up to her, she would not be so strict.

Just then, to her relief, the abbey bell began to toll, but its reverberations filled the woods with sound. Only as the last echoes were fading was she able to tell that the bell tolled from somewhere to her right.

In the ensuing silence, a horse snuffled.

She opened her mouth to shout, then realized she might be hailing a stranger or even an enemy. Horrid men had once abducted her sister Adela.

Anyone seeking her would call her name. That the rider remained silent indicated a stranger, at best.

Hearing the soft, melodic whistling, the rider had reined in his horse. The tune intrigued him, and he wanted to hear more, but the thickheaded beast he rode, not nearly as well trained as his own mounts, had snorted in protest, making him hope the whistler was no enemy. But although his profession had won him as many foes as friends, few of either would expect to find him in the abbey woods.

Nevertheless, he dismounted, checked to be sure his sword was properly in its scabbard across his back and had not shifted to one side or the other as he rode. Then, looping his rein around a handy branch, he moved toward the whistler with the swift, silent strides of an experienced woodsman, avoiding twigs, puddles, and pebbles as much by long-developed instinct as by looking out for them.

He saw her moments later, a small, slender, but curvaceous beauty with flaxen, almost white, hair hanging in two thick plaits, one forward over her right shoulder, the left one hanging down her back to her hip. The plaits looked soft and smooth. He felt instant longing to touch one, to see if it was as silky as it looked.

She walked tentatively, peering about, but he thought her uncertain rather than fearful.

Her dress was in sad shape, which was a pity, because as beautiful as she was, she would augment any gown. She should wear silk or satin, and have furs and jewels to enhance her beauty, not a large, fresh-caught salmon in one hand and a decrepit fishing pole in the other.

He thought her father should be flogged for letting such a beauty wander unguarded. Still, there she was, and Giff MacLennan was not a man to let opportunity stroll away. He moved closer, stepping on clumps of bluebells to muffle his steps, altering direction to avoid approaching from behind and startling her.

As he drew nearer, he looked down, certain that if he was not looking when she saw him, she would think he had not seen her. He did not want her to screech.

Hearing the change in her footsteps on the spongy ground, he knew she had spotted him. When she stopped, he looked up to find her staring at him, wide-eyed.

Her eyes were beautiful, too, a clear light blue that looked almost translucent. Her lashes, like her eyebrows, were several shades darker than her hair, yet not dark enough that he would call them brown. She gripped the fishing pole tightly in her left hand. The fine-looking salmon dangled from a vine looped in her right.

"Good morrow to you, mistress," he said. "Art lost in these vast woods?"

She nodded, still wide-eyed, her full, soft-looking lips invitingly parted, her round, equally soft-looking, equally inviting breasts rising and falling gently but with increasing tempo inside her bodice. She still had not spoken.

"I can show you the way if you like," he said, flashing his most charming smile. Usually, it drew a responding smile from its target, but she continued to regard him silently and soberly.

"Would you like that, lass, for me to show you the way?"

She nodded again, looking into his eyes in a way that stirred his loins.

Still smiling, he said suggestively, "I would require only small payment from you in return for such a rescue."

He had not thought her eyes could widen more, but they did.

Still she did not speak.

He stepped closer, holding her gaze, wondering if she would step back.

The ground felt springy underfoot, but for once he paid little heed.

She was even more beautiful up close, and she clearly invited his attention.

Sidony could not stop staring at the dark-haired stranger. He wore a leather, steel-lined vest that Borderers called a jack-o'-plate and plain leather boots and breeks, the latter snug around muscular thighs and calves. The sword slung across his back and the dirk shoved down one boot ought to have frightened her, but not for an instant did she mistake him for a Border ruffian.

Not only was his shirt too white, too well made—and of fine linen, at that—but he carried himself with an arrogance one saw only in the landed classes.

He was not the handsomest man she had ever beheld, for his features were irregular, and his nose too aquiline, but something about him fascinated her.

She liked the merry twinkle in his dark-blue eyes, and his voice was as smooth as honey, the sort one could listen to for pleasure. But he was as tall and as broad across the shoulders as Hugo or Rob, and she preferred men who did not take up so much room. Such men tended to loom over one and assume one would do as they commanded. Her brothers-in-law were all such men. She did obey them, though, so perhaps they had cause to expect obedience.

She was still wondering when the stranger was going to tell her what her payment must be when he bent swiftly and kissed her on the lips. To her shock, he put a hand at the back of her head to hold her so he could keep kissing her.

His lips felt soft against hers, then harder, more demanding. He closed his eyes, which was too bad, because they were the darkest blue she had ever seen. Like the water in the loch, they were so dark they looked almost black.

His free arm slipped around her waist, and she knew she should protest, even push him away. But no one had dared do such a thing before, and she found it more interesting than one might have expected—had one had time to expect anything.

Then his tongue slipped between her lips, and she reacted without thought, pushing hard against his chest with both hands, notwithstanding fish or pole.

He let go of her then, stepping back with a look of astonishment. Behind it, she thought briefly that she detected a shadow in his eyes, but it was gone in an instant, replaced by a mischievous grin.

"Why so violent, sweetheart? You'll not deny you enjoyed that." Still grinning, he put his hands on his hips as if he dared her to contradict him.

Anger surged so swiftly that again she acted without thought. Swinging hard, forgetting she still held the fish, she gave him a clout across the face with it before he—or she, for that matter—had time to recognize her intent.

He snapped up a hand in defense and stepped back, but the boggy ground betrayed him and the fish had smacked hard. His left foot lost traction and shot out from under him, and to her horror, he sat down with a splat on bluebells and mud.

She turned and ran, but before she had taken four steps, a hand of iron clamped round her upper left arm, jerked her to a halt, and spun her to face him.

"By heaven," he said, still gripping her arm, his furious face close to hers. "I should put you across my knee to teach you better manners."

Stiffening abruptly, Sidony found her voice at last. "How dare you!" she snapped. "Release me!"

To her astonishment, he did. But the extraordinary dark-blue eyes flashed fire, then narrowed ominously. "What are you doing out here alone, dressed like a common serving wench?"

"I thought you were a gentleman," she said, giving back look for look. "Is this how gentlemen treat common serving wenches? I didn't know."

"Don't try me too far, mistress. I'm a tolerant fellow, but I don't tolerate insolence from anyone."

"Is it insolent to ask such a question?" She raised her chin. "I should think it much more insolent to go about kissing innocent serving maids."

"They are generally not so innocent," he said, grinning again.

"And why is that, do you think?"

He opened his mouth but shut it again, frowning. "I wonder," he said. "You ask saucy questions but look as cool as if you were inquiring about the weather."

"You do not answer me."

"Nay, lassie, and I won't, because either you know why serving maids are usually not so innocent and asked your question to put me in the wrong, or you do *not* know, and are therefore too innocent for me to tell you. Moreover, you did not answer my question, which was more important than yours. And I asked mine first."

"I forgot what it was," she said, although she remembered quite well.

For a moment, he looked as if he might shake her, and to her utter amazement, she anticipated the experience with tingling curiosity.

That sudden awareness sobered her. What, she wondered, could have put such an absurd notion into her head?

With a patient note in his voice that she knew had nothing to do with what he must be feeling, he said, "I asked you what you are doing here alone, dressed like a common serving wench."

"It is bad manners to comment on a lady's dress, is it not?"

She watched with satisfaction as his eyes narrowed again.

He made a sound like a growl, then said, "Look here, are you really lost?"

"Aye, although now that I know where the abbey is—" She broke off, looking around and realizing that in her mad dash for freedom and subsequent capture, she had lost her sense of direction again. "I'm still lost," she admitted.

"Where do you live?"

"I came into the woods from Clendenen House in the Canongate," she said.

"I ken the Canongate, so we can find Clendenen House.

Had you turned the other way and followed the loch shore, you would soon have seen the abbey."

Having no wish to discuss what she ought to have done, she said sternly, "It was wrong of you to take payment for helping me."

"Aye, it was wrong, but I enjoyed it all the same," he said, grinning again.

"Did you? Why?"

Giff shrugged, then stopped grinning, feeling again the unfamiliar guilt she had stirred moments before with her naive question about serving wenches. He was uncertain what stirred it this time, but the sensation was the same. Surely, she had not elicited such a sharp response from his conscience by speaking three words, but she looked so intent, as if his reply would mean something, as if he could hurt her by saying the kiss had been no more to him than any other stolen kiss.

He did not want to hurt her. She had not smiled once, and he wanted to make her smile.

His conscience, which had long remained agreeably inactive, stirred again. That he had not behaved well was as much her fault as his and was surely no cause for this strange unease. He was a man who took adventure and pleasure where he found them, and who rarely counted cost, but with her, he wanted to make amends.

She still waited patiently, without speaking, but he would not cater to her vanity by telling her the kiss was special. She was a beauty, to be sure, and he would not mind growing better acquainted with her, but a man of his sort had little time for dalliance. And he had no time at all to dally with a virginal maid of doubtless noble birth who might expect marriage to come of it.

Therefore, more brusquely than he had intended, he said, "I must get you home, so we'll go this way." As he put a hand beneath her elbow to urge her forward, he added, "Does anyone even know you came into these woods?"

"Aye, the gardener," she said with a little sigh that struck him like a lance's blow, for it told him he had disappointed her.

"What were you thinking to confide in a gardener but in no one else?"

"I had been playing with my wee nephew so my sister could talk quietly with our hostess," she said, surprising him with her calm. "When his nurse took him away for his nap, and I found that Isobel and Lady Clendenen were also napping, I walked into the garden. I didn't expect to meet the gardener."

"It is surely not unusual to meet a gardener in a garden," he said.

"I know, but although he is very kind, I wanted to be by myself. So when he asked if I was enjoying a stroll, I told him I meant to walk in the woods."

"He ought to have told you to stay in the garden," he said severely.

"Doubtless others will agree with you," she said. "But he asked if I'd like to take a fishing pole along, and he was so kind that I did not like to say no, so I did, and I caught this fish. Then I got lost, and you came along just as I thought I'd figured out where the abbey was," she added.

"But why did you want to get away? Was there no one else at Clendenen House with whom you could converse?"

"Oh, aye, two of my good-brothers were there, but they were talking privately and I did not want to disturb them."

"Are they not kind to you?" he demanded, feeling a sudden urge to have words with men so careless as to let this innocent lass walk abroad alone.

Suppressing an urge to smile at his visible displeasure with Hugo and Rob, Sidony said, "They are very kind, sir. But one hesitates to interrupt such men when they talk privately, and I wanted to be alone. You see, I have been in Midlothian for a year now, and sometimes I like to pretend I am back home. Today was such a day."

"So you don't ordinarily live in the royal burgh."

"Mercy, no. I have been staying alternately with three of my sisters. My sister Sorcha and I came to Midlothian when our older sister Adela did. Isobel was already living here, although she had been visiting our sister Cristina before that."

"Look here, how many sisters do you have?"

"Six now. I used to have seven, but Mariota died and now there are only Cristina, Adela, Kate, Maura, Isobel, and Sorcha. They have all married, and in a month, my father is to marry Lady Clendenen. Until he does, though—"

"Your father, aye. Is he here, as well? Did you just hope I'd not meet him?"

"He is at home in the Highlands," she said. "He is a member of the Council of the Isles, you see."

"But I don't see," he protested. "Who is your father?"

Sidony grimaced. "Faith, here we are, walking together

like old friends, and you do not even know my name. Nor I yours," she added pointedly.

"Nay, then, you don't," he said. "I ken fine that you think you ought to, and that the perfect gentleman you mentioned earlier would introduce himself. But I'd as lief you not mention my name to your friends or family, and I do not know yet if you can keep your tongue behind your teeth when you should."

"Very well," she said, thinking that if he did not want to tell anyone his name, he would not want to meet Hugo or Rob, which would be just as well for her. "My father is Macleod of Glenelg, sir. I am his youngest daughter, Sidony."

"Lady Sidony, in fact," he said with a glint of amusement. "I think I am fortunate that your father is *not* in town."

"I do not think he would berate you," she said. "He would more likely be wroth with me for losing myself in these woods."

"Aye, but he might recognize me, lassie. Sithee, I, too, hail from Kintail."

She regarded him with greater interest than ever. "Have you just come from there? Oh, do tell me, has the weather been fine? Are the wildflowers in bloom? But surely, I must know your family, sir. There are not so many, and we know most of them. I do know all the Macleods. Are you a Mackenzie or a MacRae?"

"Nay, lass, not yet. Tell me more of your family first. I ken fine who your father is, but I have been away more than I have been home these past ten years. Where is your mother, and how is it that three of your sisters live here in Midlothian if you are all good Highland lasses? But stay, did not your sister, the lady Cristina, marry Hector Reaganach Maclean of Lochbuie on the Isle of Mull?"

He was frowning again, this time thoughtfully.

She gathered her own thoughts, uncertain of how much he'd want to know. In her experience, men who asked questions wanted brief answers and few details.

"My mother died when I was two, and Cristina is indeed married to Hector the Ferocious," she said, answering the easiest ones first. "The rest makes rather a long story, though. You see, Adela was to marry Ardelve of Loch Alsh, but someone abducted her before she could and brought her here. Sorcha and I followed them, but Sir Hugo came looking for us. Oh, and before that Isobel met and married—"

"Sir Hugo?" His voice took on a new note that silenced her. It did not sound as if he were at all happy to hear Hugo's name.

"Aye," she said. "Sir Hugo Robison. He is my sister Sorcha's husband."

His lips twitched, his eyes took on an unholy twinkle, then he laughed and shook his head. "My sins have caught up with me," he said when he could speak.

"Why do you say that?"

"Because the last time I met Hugo Robison, he knocked me flat, and if he learns how we met, I've little doubt he'll try to do it again."

Demurely, she said, "Hugo is a gentleman, of course, like you. I wonder if he also kisses innocent serving wenches for amusement."

"Sakes, lass, I hope you don't mean to ask him!"

"But my sisters say that if one wants to know a thing, one *should* ask."

He gave her a look probably meant to intimidate her,

but she met it easily, feeling only that tingling anticipation again as she said, "Truly, sir, you need not be afraid of Hugo. Indeed, I cannot think why you need even meet him. When we reach the abbey, I can easily go back the way I came, through the gardens. Then, he need never know that we've met."

Amusement lit his eyes again. "I don't doubt you'd prefer it that way. Indeed, I'm guessing he'll be as displeased with you as he will be with me, will he not?"

"Aye, he would be if we were foolish enough to go to him together. 'Tis for that very reason that you would be wiser to let me go back alone."

"I cannot do that," he said with a wry smile, politely offering his arm this time. "Sithee, in my experience, unpleasant things are best done straightaway. Moreover, your presence may protect me."

Wondering what was going to protect her, Sidony ignored the proffered arm and said dryly, "Before we go any farther, sir, you had better collect your horse."

Chapter 2

The minx had let him walk nearly a quarter mile from where he had left his horse before speaking up, but Giff decided he could not blame her. Moreover, if he were to suggest that she had done so on purpose, she would doubtless point out that he had been the one to urge departure and insist that she had only obeyed him.

And, too, of course, the horse was his responsibility. The kinsman from whom he had borrowed it would certainly think so, and as that man was a powerful Borderer more likely to react to its neglect with temper than with understanding, it behooved him to collect the animal without further ado.

He glanced at the lass, who regarded him with what he believed was her usual calm, making him wonder what else it would take to stir temper or passion in her. She still carried the fish, which looked none the worse for having clouted him. But for all the heed she paid it, it might have been a worthless trinket.

"I cannot leave you here," he said. "You'll have to walk back with me to fetch the beast."

"Doesn't your horse have a name?"

"Likely it does," Giff admitted. "But I haven't a notion what it may be."

"Faith, did you steal it?"

He grinned. "If I had, it would not be the first time. Nay, then, don't frown at me like that. You're too beautiful to spoil your looks with such a grimace."

Her eyes lit as if no one had complimented her beauty until that moment, but before he could wonder at such a nonsensical thought, she looked away, flushing delicately as she said, "You should not say such things to me."

"I imagine you hear such things all the time," he said. "But you are right to remind me of my manners. Hugo will certainly do so."

"How do you know him?" she asked.

"You mean, how does Hugo come to know a horse thief?" he asked dryly.

"Do you really steal horses?"

"Sometimes." He was looking around, hoping he had not misplaced the wretched beast. It was almost unheard of for him to become disoriented, but from the moment he'd laid eyes on the lass, he'd seen nothing but her. It occurred to him that it was a good thing she had not been bait in a trap set by an enemy.

"Stealing is a black sin," she said primly.

"Aye, well, a man does what he has to do. Moreover, I've just come from the Borders, where men don't believe that taking other men's animals is stealing. They call it 'reiving,' and it is just a way of life. If a man needs a horse or a few kine to feed his family, he goes a-reiving. Ah, there he is," he added.

"You sound relieved," she said. "Did you fear you'd lost him?"

"Don't be absurd. A man does not lose his horse."

"But if it isn't your horse . . . If you stole it . . ."

"Look here," he said. "I did not steal this horse. I borrowed it."

She nodded sagely. "I have heard others say the same thing when they were caught stealing. Moreover, when one borrows something, one returns it."

"And so I shall," he said, grinning now. "The kinsman I borrowed it from is the sort who would behave unpleasantly if I neglected to do so."

"Are you afraid of him?"

"Sakes, how you do twist a man's words! Here, I'll put you up on him, so you need not walk all the way back. I hope you aren't afraid of horses."

"Of course not. I have ridden all my life."

"Have you?" He was surprised. "Highland women rarely ride, and the few I've seen who do are not much good at it."

"I am," she said. "However, I have no wish to ride one you have stolen."

"I wish you would stop assuming that I stole this beast," he said curtly as he untied the bay and stroked its neck and nose to steady it.

"You said you did steal him."

"I did not. I said quite clearly, not two minutes ago, that I did *not* steal him."

"Aye, sure, but before that you said—"

"I said only that if I had, it would not have been the first time."

"So you do steal."

He turned to face her, ready to reply in no uncertain

terms, but when he saw that she was regarding him in much the same speculative way that a robin might regard a tasty worm, her light blue eyes sparkling with anticipation, he hesitated. Then, trying to keep his tone as mild as her own, he said instead, "Do you exert yourself to stir coals like this with every man you meet?"

To his surprise, she did not deny that was what she was doing. Instead, she smiled wistfully and said, "I don't meet many men. I have never met one whilst I was out walking like this, or anyone at all like you."

"A thief, you mean?"

She nodded, still watching him with that speculative look, leaving him in no doubt now that she was somehow testing him, even baiting him.

He sighed. "Lass, I don't know what to make of you, but 'tis clear that the sooner I return you to your kinsmen, the better it will be for both of us, so I'll just put you on the horse now," he added, reaching for her.

She stepped back, saying calmly, "No, thank you. I'll walk."

"Don't be foolish," he said more sternly. "I need to let the mud on my breeks dry anyway, and you'll get your boots even muddier than they are now if you walk on through this bog-ridden forest. Moreover, you'll be more comfortable riding."

"I don't think so, but thank you all the same."

"I'm not offering to let you ride to earn your gratitude," he growled.

"But I prefer to walk."

"And I say you will ride." He put his hands on his hips and gave her his sternest look, the look that sent grown men scurrying to obey his orders.

The horse nudged his shoulder just then hard enough to make him take an involuntary step toward her.

Her lips twitched, and the beguiling twinkle in her eyes deepened.

"By heaven, do you dare to laugh at me?" He reached for her again, and although she began to step back, he was too quick for her, catching her arm.

She made a sound in her throat like a gasp, but she did not look away, and when he looked into her eyes again, he saw that the twinkle had vanished. A look of serene expectation had replaced it.

Her tongue darted out to lick her soft pink lips—a blatant invitation.

His hand was tight around her arm, and Sidony stood still, uncertain if she had angered him. He was certainly frowning, and she knew from experience with her brothers-in-law that men did not like women to laugh at them, but she had not been able to help letting her amusement show when the horse pushed him.

He was still looking at her in that odd, measuring way, as if he were trying to understand her or to decide just how to scold her. Doubtless, the latter was the correct interpretation. The men she knew did not react well to defiance, either.

She did not feel defiant. She just did not want to ride his horse, carrying her fish, while he walked alongside or ahead, leading the animal. To do so would feel awkward and put her under even greater obligation to him. Just letting him escort her would prove to Hugo and Rob that her walk in the woods had been foolish, even dangerous.

Then, doubtless, one or the other would forbid her to do it again.

These thoughts flitted through her head as her gaze met his, but a moment later, she saw the look in his eyes alter. And when her mouth went dry and she wet her lips, his look deepened to unmistakable hunger. His grip on her arm tightened.

She swallowed but did not look away. He was going to kiss her again, and reckless or not, she wanted him to. But before she realized his expression had changed again, he caught her round the waist and lifted her onto his saddle.

Quick as thought, careful not to drop her fish, she swung both legs to the other side of the horse and slid to the ground, stepping quickly back, lest it take exception to such treatment and kick or rear. It did toss its head, snort, and take a few restless steps, but he grabbed the bridle and quickly steadied it.

Grimly, he said, "You begin to irk me, lass."

"I am sorry, for you have shown kindness to me," she said. "But I do not want to ride your horse whilst you lead it, or to ride pillion with you. Just think what people would say if we were to proceed up the Canongate so. Everyone would look and gape, imagining all manner of things about us."

"Do you think it will be any different if we both walk?"

"Aye, sure, it will. There can be naught amiss in our having met in the woods and walked out of them together. Faith, if there is, that just underscores how prudent my earlier suggestion was, that I should go back the way I came whilst you ride on to wherever you meant to go."

"So I should not bother to see Hugo at all. Is that your plan?"

"Well, I would not have put it just that way, but it *is* a better plan."

"I warrant you think so, at all events." He shook his head. "Do you imagine that when we meet again, as we doubtless shall, since I will certainly see Hugo, I should just pretend never to have met you before?"

She had not thought about that possibility. "Must you see Hugo?"

"I must, for that is why I came to Edinburgh."

"Oh. But if you rode here from the Borders, why did you not enter the city the usual way, straight up the Cowgate to the High Street?"

"I don't think that concerns you," he said. "What does concern you is that, regardless of what you think of me, I do not take advantage of innocent wenches, particularly noble ones. Nor do I approve of such wenches' wandering about without protection. Most especially," he added, stern again, "I don't approve of women who are kin to my friends doing such things. My father would take a stout switch to any sister of mine who behaved so."

"Have you even got a sister?"

"Aye, two of them."

"Well, you have no right to take a switch to me," she said. "And although Hugo can be very fierce, I do not think he would, either." Another thought, even less welcome, struck her. "You would not suggest such a course to him, would you?"

His demeanor softened reassuringly. "Nay, lass, I would not. But come now. We have dawdled here long enough."

"You won't try to put me on that horse again?"

"Nay, it shall be as you wish," he said. "This time."

The way he said the last two words sent a shiver up her

spine, but she rallied quickly. The chance that she would see much of him after today was slim.

Giff watched as she moved ahead to pick a path through the boggy woods, wondering what it was about her that had made him give in so easily. She deserved a good smack on the backside, if only for her stubbornness, but when she had asked if he would suggest such punishment to Hugo, something deep inside had recoiled at the thought of anyone striking her.

"Do you mean to stride ahead of me all the way?" he asked.

She hesitated, looking back. "Promise you won't try again to make me ride."

"I have already said I will not," he reminded her. "My word is good."

She nodded. "Very well, then; I'll walk beside you if you prefer."

They walked so in silence, but after she had looked up at him for the third time as if she meant to speak, then looked away again, he said, "What is it, lass? Have you more that you want to say to me?"

She nibbled her lower lip, then looked up again and said, "Not to say, exactly, just to ask you a question. But I should not, I know."

"Ask me anything you like. I shan't mind."

"It is only that the question is most improper. Sithee, I was wondering if you meant it when you said it."

"You will have to remind me of just what I said before I can answer that."

She looked away again. "It is silly, and one should not

care about such things, I know, but when one's thoughts simply fix on something . . ."

"Then one ought to ask the question," he said. His curiosity was increasing by leaps, and her equivocation made him want to shake her. But he sensed that if he grew forceful with her again, he would never learn what had disturbed her, and he wanted very much to know.

She still looked hesitant, so he held his tongue, hoping she was one who could not bear silence without needing to fill it. Nothing in her reaction encouraged that hope, however. She seemed to be thinking, trying to decide what to do, and even his brief experience warned him against showing his impatience.

Reining himself in was a rare experience, but he managed it.

At last, she said, "Do you often say things to women that you do *not* mean?"

"I usually mean what I say to anyone. But you must still tell me what I said."

Color crept into her cheeks, and she hesitated again. Since she had shown no lack of courage before, he suspected it was something he had said about her. But he could recall saying only that she was foolish to have come into the woods alone, and he doubted she could possibly be wondering if he had meant that.

In a tone so gentle he scarcely recognized it as his own, he said, "You can ask, lassie. I'll answer truthfully if I can, and I'll not judge you for the asking."

The look she gave him then was pure gratitude. Then, hastily, blurting the words, she said, "You said I was beautiful. Do you really think so?"

He nearly asked if she was demented, but the intense,

too-anxious look on her face stopped the words in his throat.

Matter-of-factly, he said, "You must know that you are beautiful. Surely, everyone who knows you has told you so."

She shook her head. "No one."

"But that is impossible. You need only a glass to see it for yourself."

"You don't understand," she said. "I have six sisters. People talk about the beautiful Macleod sisters, but most people know only the ones who have gone before me. Cristina, the eldest, is an extraordinary beauty. My hair is pale beside hers, my figure less buxom, and my demeanor far more retiring. When she enters a room, everyone notices her. And people who knew my sister Mariota say that Cristina is but a pale shadow compared to her. I am a shadow to them all."

"Mariota is the one who died," he said, remembering.

"Aye, and Isobel says that whatever they may say about Mariota's looks, her nature was *not* beautiful, but others recall only her astonishing beauty."

"You didn't know her yourself?"

"Nay, I was but a babe when she died. So you see, no one ever thinks of me as beautiful, because my looks are as nothing compared to all the others'."

"But surely, you have been to the King's court. Someone there must have commented on your beauty."

"Nay, for I do not enjoy large gatherings. I went with Sorcha and Isobel to Edinburgh Castle once because my father wanted Lady Clendenen to present me to his grace, but his grace was ill, so we did not stay above half an hour. I'd never heard such a din, though. I don't know how anyone can converse in such a place."

He chuckled, remembering his own brief experience at Stirling. "Half the court is daft and the other half drunk, but most folks find it amusing. And, too, any man who wants to amount to much in Scotland knows he must make his bow there."

"Have you done so?"

Nodding, he said, "I did not like it any more than you did, but I have found my own way to make my mark until I take over my family seat in the Highlands, which I suppose I'll have to do after I've had my fill of adventuring. No one in the west cares much about the doings of the royal court except the Lord of the Isles and those of his ilk who want to acquire as much power as they can. Even they avoid Stirling and Edinburgh and do most of their business at the Isles court instead."

"Is that what you do?"

"Nay, I've not been next or nigh any such doings for years."

"I meant, do you go adventuring?"

"Och, aye, I enjoy that right enough, and presently there are many such opportunities available for a man like me."

"Tell me about them."

"Perhaps another day," he said with a smile. "The abbey lies just yonder, so I expect we'll find Clendenen House nearby, shall we not?"

"Aye," she said, frowning. "Very near."

Too soon, they approached the main entrance of Clendenen House, the home of Ealga, Lady Clendenen, on the south side of the avenue known as the Canongate because it extended from St. Giles Church to Holyrood Abbey.

The stone-and-timber houses flanking the wide road stood close to one another, although nearly all boasted narrow drives leading to stables and deep gardens behind.

On the north side, nearer St. Giles, lay Sinclair House, where Sidony was presently living with her sister Isobel and Isobel's husband, Sir Michael Sinclair. To the northwest, Edinburgh Castle on its craggy hilltop overlooked the whole city.

With four hundred houses and two thousand people, the royal burgh was the largest town Sidony had ever seen, but she had grown accustomed to its bustle and noise. Thankfully, the Canongate remained quieter than the area nearer the Castle, although a cart piled high with wool rattled past on its way to a ship in Leith Harbor.

Sidony's companion tossed a coin to an urchin on the narrow flagway and asked the grinning recipient to hold his horse for him. Then he offered an arm to Sidony, but she paid no more heed to it than before. She wanted no one to suspect that he could be anything more than a casual acquaintance.

The front door of Clendenen House opened before they reached it, and to her relief, Rob appeared in the doorway, rather than Hugo.

"We worried about you, lass," he said, his voice softly husky, his speech slow and measured. However, when his gaze fixed on her companion, Rob's hazel eyes, usually hooded, opened wide.

Before he could say more, a large hand gripped his shoulder from behind, and Sir Hugo Robison appeared beside him, taller, darker, and broader, his displeasure fairly crackling through the air.

Her sisters' husbands all tended to be big men, but Sidony knew only one man larger than Hugo, and that was Cristina's husband, Hector the Ferocious.

She hesitated, eyeing Hugo warily and resisting the urge to look at her companion, to gauge his reaction to Hugo's so-obvious displeasure.

To her shock, the man beside her laughed and said, "Sakes, Hugo, you look ready to eat the poor lass. If you must vent your spleen, man, vent it on me. At least, I can defend myself."

Hugo's attention shifted, but he did not share her companion's amusement. "Wouldst try your skills against mine again, you misbegotten scruff?"

"Aye, and gladly. The last time, you caught me off my guard. That won't happen again."

"The last time, I set you on your backside and put an end to dispute before it had begun," Hugo said. "I'd hoped you'd not require further instruction."

"Just try me, my lad, and we'll see who teaches whom."

He spoke the words softly, but Hugo heard them, for he grimaced and shook his head. Then, to Sidony's profound relief, he said without rancor, "I trust you can tell me the lass suffered no harm at your hands, Giff."

"You know she did not. Do you mean to keep us standing on your doorstep? Sakes, it is not even yours, as I understand it, but Lady Clendenen's. You might also shout for a servant to take the lady Sidony's salmon and clean it to cook for her supper. 'Tis a fine big one, as you can see."

"Aye, we'll go inside," Hugo said, standing aside to let them pass and motioning a gillie forward to take Sidony's fish and the pole. "You can give him that sword of yours, too, Giff," he added.

"That belongs to the old gardener," Sidony said to the gillie as he took the pole from her. "Pray, return it to him with my thanks."

"Aye, my lady," the lad said before turning to receive the heavy sword and scabbard from her companion.

Dismissing the gillie, Hugo said, "It is about time you arrived, Giff. We'd nearly given you up."

"I was in Galloway, so your lads were a good time tracking me down."

"How did you chance to meet the lady Sidony?" Hugo asked evenly.

Rob said, "Let us adjourn to Ealga's wee parlor before we talk more."

The man whom Hugo had called Giff shook Rob's hand and said, "I did not realize you would be here. We are cousins, my lady," he added. "I've a host of Logan cousins, because the earliest MacLennans were themselves Logans who, for one cause or other, removed to the Highlands. But, Rob, are you in this business, too, then?"

"We'll go into the parlor before we talk more," Hugo said firmly.

"Sidony! There you are!"

Recognizing the familiar voice and its note of profound relief, Sidony turned to greet Isobel, who stood atop the stairway on the west side of the small entryway.

Although pregnant with her second child, the fair-haired, gray-eyed Isobel showed no sign yet of her condition and was as beautiful as ever. Sidony saw that Giff was regarding her sister with the same besotted look that most men displayed upon first seeing her.

Oblivious, Isobel said, "But where have you been, dearling? You worried us dreadfully, for you were gone so long. Hugo was just going to go in search of you."

"I did not mean to worry you," Sidony said guiltily. "I just went for a walk."

"But where?" Isobel asked. "And who is this man with you?"

Sidony bit her lip, at a loss for what to say, since she could hardly call him Giff, as Hugo had done. And to admit that she did not know his name was clearly ineligible, and would only make matters worse.

In the silence that followed Isobel's question, the gentleman in question looked pointedly at Hugo, who said, "Forgive me, my lady. Allow me to present my friend Giffard MacLennan of Duncraig. Sithee, he took his training at Dunclathy with my father, and, I might add, delighted in being a great nuisance to the rest of us."

Isobel smiled at the newcomer. "Nonetheless, if that is so, I suspect I should more properly call you *Sir* Giffard, should I not?"

Sidony regarded Sir Giffard with greater interest than ever. If he had trained at Dunclathy, he had learned the same knightly skills as Michael, Hugo, and Rob had. Dunclathy was Sir Hugo's family home, and his father, Sir Edward Robison, was a famous swordsman and warrior with whom only the very best men studied.

Before Sir Giffard could answer, Hugo said, "Isobel is Michael's lady wife, Giff, so take care that you behave yourself in her presence."

"I should not dream of doing otherwise," Sir Giffard said, bowing deeply. "'Tis a great honor to make your acquaintance, my lady."

"How did you come to know my sister, sir?" Isobel asked bluntly.

"I'll explain that to you myself," Sidony said hastily, striving to speak with her usual calm. "I am sure that

Sir Giffard, Rob, and Hugo have much to discuss, so we should leave them to it. I do hope you will forgive me for worrying you so, Isobel."

"Of course I shall," her sister said, giving her a warm hug. But she glanced at Hugo as she did, adding, "Does Sir Giffard stay to supper, sir?"

"Perhaps," Hugo said. Then, as Sidony grasped Isobel's arm and urged her toward the stairway, he added evenly, "I'll talk with you before we sup, Sidony."

"Aye, sir," Sidony said, stifling a sigh. Then, recalling her manners, she turned to Sir Giffard with a downward look and a curtsy to say, "Thank you for your kindness, sir. I trust you have not offended anyone by escorting me home."

Just as politely, he replied, "I am happy to have served you, your ladyship."

She looked up, and as her gaze met his, an urge stirred to remind him that she had required no such service. Aware of Hugo's narrow-eyed interest, she suppressed the urge, made a second curtsy to excuse herself, and followed Isobel upstairs.

Chapter 3

Giff watched the two women hurry up the polished wooden stairway and realized he was hoping Lady Sidony would look back before they disappeared. With half an ear, he heard Hugo tell a gillie to fetch refreshment. Then, except for the hushing of the ladies' skirts and the quick, light taps of their footsteps on the stairs, silence fell until Hugo cleared his throat.

Well aware of the older man's lack of patience, Giff nevertheless waited long enough to draw a breath and let it out before he turned and said, "Let us to the parlor, lads. I am eager to hear what new adventure lies ahead."

He saw the other two exchange glances and was sure Hugo came close to rolling his eyes, but that did not surprise him. Both men were several years older than he was, as Michael was, too, and were already established at Dunclathy when he'd arrived there. They had thought themselves superior then, and although he had soon proven his worth, some of that earlier sense of superiority clearly lingered.

Taking the initiative now, he said, "I was sorry to learn of the deaths of your father and brother, Rob. You are Logan of Lestalric now, are you not?"

"I am," Rob said. "And if you've just come from Galloway, doubtless you bring news from any number of our kinsmen there, do you not?"

"Aye, sure," Giff agreed, recalling that the unnatural beast he had ridden to Edinburgh belonged to one of those kinsmen. "But mayhap this is not the moment—"

"At this moment, Giff," Hugo interjected, shutting the parlor door, "I want to hear how you met Sidony. Surely you do not accost young women in town streets."

"It is worse than that," Giff said, grinning. "You've forgotten her fine fish. I heard her whistling in the abbey woods, and I followed the sound."

The grim look on Hugo's face deterred Giff from mentioning the stolen kiss. He decided to hold that in reserve against a time when he might need a diversionary tactic. Prior experience with Hugo told him such diversion might prove necessary.

Hugo said, "You probably frightened the lass witless."

"I warrant I surprised her," Giff admitted. "But I doubt I'd have scared her witless under any circumstance. Her ladyship keeps a cool head."

"Does she? Why were you in the abbey woods in the first place?"

"Have you seen the main roads?" Giff asked. "Wool carts as far as the eye can see. And sheep! All *baa*ing and leaping over one another, or just leaping when one least expects it. The horse I borrowed takes a dim view of sheep."

Rob grinned. "They do create hazards now and again, I'll agree, but the wool must get to the ships, so I must put up with them more than you did. Sithee, a good bit of the shore of Leith Harbor belongs to me, and those sheep and carts cross my land to get to the harbor. I've even let them put up shelters against the rain when it comes, and some shepherds, especially those with only a cart or two to their name, drive their sheep as far as Lestalric before they shear them."

"That explains seeing as many bald ones as ones still in wool," Giff said.

Hugo's expression indicated a total disinterest in sheep. He peered more closely at Giff and said, "What's that mark on your face?"

Clapping a hand to his left cheek and feeling suddenly eleven again, Giff fought an urge to step back.

"Take your hand away," Hugo said, looking closer yet. "By the Rood, that looks like a smear of fish scales." He glanced at Rob, who was biting his lower lip, rigidly controlling himself. "Does something about this amuse you, my lad?"

"Aye," Rob said unrepentantly.

Hoping to divert them both, Giff said, "I've come all the way from Galloway in just two days, Hugo, so you'll have to forgive me if I've got smut on my—"

He broke off when Hugo put a finger to the cheek in question, rubbed hard, then raised the finger to his nose and sniffed.

Favoring Giff with an enigmatic look, he said, "So that salmon is not just supper. What did you do to warrant smacking with it, Giffard?"

"Sakes, what would make you think such a thing?" Giff demanded.

"My knowledge of you and of the Macleod sisters," Hugo retorted. "You should know that I have the honor to be married to the one nearest in age to Lady Sidony. I own, however, that although my Sorcha would not hesitate to flatten a man who accosted her, it does surprise me that Sidony tried such a thing."

"At least you do me the kindness to assume she only tried," Giff said, ignoring memory of his ignominious descent to the boggy ground as he added glibly, "I fear I mistook her for a serving maid. When I let my error be known, she clouted me. May we sit, Hugo? I've had little sleep these past two days."

"Stay away from her, Giff," Hugo said. "The Macleod sisters may look as high as they like for husbands. Her father and good-brothers will seek one for her who is wealthy, steady, and reliable—not a scapegrace whose byword is 'reck not.'"

"Nay, then," Giff said, smiling again. "Not that I have any intention of taking a wife, however fine, but for MacLennans 'tis 'whilst I breathe, I hope.'"

Hugo shrugged. "If you ask me, it is much the same thing."

"Aye, sure, but 'tis why you sent for me, is it not?" He glanced at Rob. "You keep quiet, sir, yet dare to show amusement. Have you nowt to say in this?"

Rob smiled sleepily. "I can trust Hugo to say all that needs saying, and in my experience, the Macleod lasses are well able to look after themselves."

"Sakes, don't tell me you married one of them, too!"

"The lady Adela."

Giff shook his head. "I trust that all these women have nowt to do with why you sent for me."

"We sent for you because we've a task to undertake that is fraught with peril, and you have a reputation for succeeding at such tasks," Hugo said bluntly. "You'd best succeed with this one, too, because if you fail, all Scotland may suffer for years to come, if not forever."

"You intrigue me," Giff said, pulling up a stool to sit, although Hugo had yet to extend permission. "What is this so-important task?"

When a sharp rap at the door heralded the entrance of the gillie with their refreshments, Hugo murmured, "Have patience."

The lad poured them each a mug of ale, then said, "Her ladyship sent them wee cheese rolls for ye to ha' wi' your ale, me lords, but she did say to tell ye that supper is to be on the table in an hour and that there be roasted lamb and salmon."

Telling him to assure her ladyship that they would not be late, Hugo waited only until the door had shut again behind him before saying, "There are things you need to know, Giff, but first, I trust you still command several good, stout ships."

"Aye, sure, although they won't be much use to you here, as they are all harbored in the west. But, of course . . ."

Looking from one man to the other, he saw from their gloomy expressions that his words were not what they had hoped to hear.

"The first thing you must do is take off that awful dress," Isobel said, looking Sidony over from top to toe as they entered the bedchamber Lady Clendenen allotted to the Macleod sisters when one or more of them visited. "Where is the one you had on when we arrived here?"

"There is no need for me to wear that, either," Sidony said as she shut the door and began to untie the side ribbons of the old blue kerseymere tunic. "With all the visiting I've done this year, I have clothing scattered over three castles as well as here and at Sinclair House. I only put this on to play with our wee William Robert. So I still have at least one other in that kist yonder that is more suitable to wear for a supper with the gentlemen."

"Then we must take it out at once, for I warrant it will need pressing," Isobel said, moving to put her words into action. As she shook out the pale-yellow silk skirt she found neatly folded in the kist and looked it over, she glanced at Sidony with a twinkle. "It won't need much, so are you going to tell me about him now?"

Feeling heat in her cheeks at the thought of describing all that had happened in the abbey woods, Sidony shifted her skirt around so she could untie its waistband as she said, "Should we not send for a maidservant first, and some hot water?"

"No, we should not," Isobel said. "I want a round tale, and I know you won't say a word in front of a servant, so you can use the cold water in that jug on the stand to wash your face and hands, and I'll help you dress. Where are the comb and brush that usually sit on this table?"

Resigned, Sidony found them on a shelf of the washstand that stood between a pair of tall narrow windows overlooking the garden behind the house. Then she undressed to her shift as Isobel shook out the gold-lace-trimmed bodice that matched the pale-yellow silk skirt.

"I think there is a clean shift in that kist, as well," Sidony said.

"There is," Isobel agreed. "What's more, I believe one of the maids must have aired these things earlier. Everything seems quite fresh, so there is naught to delay you in telling me everything now. How did you come to meet him?"

Seeing no way to avoid it, Sidony told her, leaving out only his daring to kiss her and her smacking him with the salmon. If Isobel's eyes narrowed at that point, doubtless it was because Sidony had blushed while explaining that he had wanted her to ride his horse back to Clendenen House.

She was able to indulge that thought only long enough to think it, though, for Isobel said coaxingly, "You are not telling me the whole of it, Siddie. What do you think of him? He is very attractive, is he not? Although not as handsome as Michael," she added loyally but wistfully, as well.

Understanding the wistfulness, Sidony said, "He will be home soon."

"Not soon enough and only because he knows I'll travel to the Highlands for the wedding with or without him," Isobel said.

"You really should not travel alone in your present condition."

"So he says, and I can scarcely blame him whilst I am likely to lose all I eat even without being in a boat on heaving seas," Isobel said. "But that will soon pass, and Michael may still try to make me forgo our father's wedding."

"Mayhap he should," Sidony said, hoping the topic would serve to divert her sister's thoughts from Sir Giffard MacLennan.

"I can handle Michael," Isobel said confidently. "But I don't want to talk about him right now. You still have not told me what you think of Sir Giffard."

Sidony had turned to the washstand and was pouring

water from the jug into the basin. She took a moment to soak a cloth, trying to think what to say.

"Well?" Isobel said encouragingly. "I saw for myself that he has a nice smile. He seems to have a sense of humor, too, and clearly, he does not fear Hugo."

"I cannot decide what I think of him," Sidony admitted without turning. She could think better if she did not have to watch Isobel's reactions. "But if he does not fear Hugo, he cannot know him well."

"Sakes, you don't fear Hugo, do you?"

"Nay, but 'tis nothing like the same thing. He may scold and he may seem fierce enough at times to terrify anyone. Indeed, he terrified me when I first met him, but when I came to know him, I realized I could trust him. His men *do* fear him when he's angry, but although I do not look forward to what he will say to me before supper, I know he won't beat me. I do hope Sir Giffard does not annoy him more in the meantime, though."

"You deserve to hear whatever he may choose to say to you," Isobel said gently. "You cannot imagine what thoughts went through my head when no one knew where you had gone. But I shall let Hugo say all that is necessary. You need not hear it twice. Did you really borrow a fishing pole from the gardener?"

"However did you know that?" Sidony said, turning to face her with profound relief that she did not intend to scold.

"I heard you tell the gillie to return it," Isobel said. "I stood at the top of the stairs for a moment before I came down."

"Eavesdropping," Sidony said wisely. "You should not, you know."

"I rarely do anymore. In troth, I'd got up so quickly

when I heard Rob shout to Hugo that you were home, that I felt dizzy and thought I should wait a minute before I went down the stairs."

"What else did you hear?" Sidony said, uncertain whether to believe in Isobel's dizziness or not. Her sister had few scruples about shading the truth or inventing excuses when she knew her behavior might draw censure.

Isobel shrugged. "Not much. I heard Sir Giffard ask Hugo if he meant to keep you standing on the doorstep, then tease him that it wasn't even his doorstep."

"Hugo said it was about time Sir Giffard arrived, that they had nearly given him up," Sidony said. "Do you know what he meant by that?"

"Dearest, you must stop trying to change the subject," Isobel said. "What difference can it make what Hugo meant? He is not going to share his thoughts with us. Besides, I want to know what you think of Giff MacLennan."

"Mercy, you should not call him Giff, even to me," Sidony said. *Especially to me*, she added to herself, aware of how easily she had spoken her very thoughts to him. If she began thinking of him as Giff, she could guess what would happen next.

"Pooh," Isobel said. "Art afraid you'll call him so when you should not? If that is an indication of what you really think of h—"

"It isn't!" Sidony exclaimed, goaded. Scrubbing her face quickly, she folded the cloth and turned back to say more calmly, "If you are asking if I like him—or more than that, if I could think of him as a possible husband—let me tell you that you should put that idea right out of your head. I know everyone wonders when I'll marry, but Sir Giffard is too much like Hector and Hugo even to consider for that."

"And what, I wonder, can you mean except that both men can be ferocious?" Isobel said with a thoughtful look. "Did you already contrive to make Giff angry?"

"Nay," Sidony said, repressing a memory of the look on his face after she had hit him, and the real fear she had felt, however momentarily, when she had turned and fled, and again when he caught her so easily. "How should I have made anyone angry on such a short acquaintance?"

"How, indeed?" Isobel said with a more searching look. "You are not a good liar, my dear. You should practice more if you mean to do a lot of it."

"We don't have much time, for I warrant Hugo will not keep Lady Clendenen too long from her supper," Sidony said. "Are you going to help me with that skirt?"

"You did make him angry," Isobel said, nodding satisfaction as she moved to hand Sidony first the fresh shift and then the skirt, adding as she donned the latter, "Turn around and I'll fasten it for you."

"Truly, I hope you won't tease me about him," Sidony said as she obeyed. "When I said he was like Hector and Hugo, I meant he gives orders like they do and expects the same obedience, even on short acquaintance. I don't want a man like that, always expecting me to put each foot down as and where he tells me."

"Does he do that?"

"Aye, he does. I told you he wanted to put me on his horse to ride back to Clendenen House. I didn't want to because I knew everyone we met would stare if he led me on horseback through the abbey grounds and along the Canongate, so I declined. But he put me on his horse anyway."

"So he is a strong man," Isobel said.

"Sakes, it doesn't take great muscles to lift me," Sidony protested.

Isobel laughed. "I meant the sort of strength it takes to do what one thinks is right, even in the face of opposition."

"I call it a stubborn determination to have one's own way."

"So what did you do?"

"I swung my legs over and dismounted on the off side."

Isobel's eyes twinkled. "So that's how you made him angry."

"Nay, it wasn't that."

"Still, you did."

"Aye, straightaway, but I am *not* going to tell you about that."

Isobel said no more but turned her attention to fastening the tiny buttons up the back of the silk bodice after Sidony put it on. Her silence did not reassure Sidony, though, because of them all, Isobel possessed the most curiosity. When she wanted to know something, she found out about it, so although she had clearly thought better about plaguing her more now, Sidony knew the respite would be brief.

To forestall further questioning, she said, "He is interesting, and I do like his smile. In troth, I mightn't mind him so much if he were more like Michael or Rob."

"Well, in my opinion, you have not given much thought to marrying anyone," Isobel said. "'Tis just as well that Ealga no longer means to make Father marry off every last one of us before she will marry him."

"Aye," Sidony agreed. "I did fear he might arrange some horrid marriage for me just to get me off his hands, but since Adela's marriage, neither he nor her ladyship seems so concerned about that."

"Aye, for Adela was the real obstruction," Isobel said. "After all, you are not of a decisive nature, but she is."

"I think it was more that she had run the household at Chalamine for years and years," Sidony said. "Even I can understand how Ealga would dislike competing for precedence in her own household. Adela would have continued to make suggestions, too, if not actual decisions, for all that she might try not to."

"Aye, they'll both be happier with things as they are," Isobel said. "Hand me that brush now, and we'll soon show Sir Giffard how well you can look."

"Isobel!" she protested. "Don't say such things! I've told you how I feel, and in any event, he will doubtless soon be returning to the west."

"I doubt that," Isobel said. "After all, Michael and Hugo sent for him."

"They did? He did not tell me that, only that he had come to see Hugo," Sidony added, aware of a surging mixture of unidentifiable emotions.

She had no time to sort them out, though, because Isobel only laughed again and pushed her toward a stool, ordering her to sit and let her brush her hair.

Giff frowned as he waited for either Hugo or Rob to tell him why they wanted ships, but they seemed to prefer staring at each other. They did so long enough to make him feel as if they could read one another's thoughts without bothering to speak.

"What the devil did I say?" he demanded. "You must

have known I didn't bring even the *Storm Lass* when I told you I'd got here in two days from Galloway. The fastest ship before the fiercest wind could not get round the north of Scotland and down to the Firth of Forth in less than a fortnight. As for going south, 'tis just as far, and I'm not fool enough to challenge the English in their own waters."

"Aye, well, we did hope you had access to a boat or two nearer," Hugo said, holding up a hand as he opened the door again, peered out into the entryway, and glanced up toward the top of the stairs. "Forgive me," he said when he had shut it again. "One could wish this door were heavier, but we'll talk quietly."

Nodding, Giff muttered, "Even if I had a ship in Leith Harbor, I'd want a dozen more to escort it if I am to carry an object of value. But the Sinclairs possess the largest fleet of ships in Scotland, Hugo, and not only are you close kin to them, but you and Michael sent for me. Why do we not use his family's ships?"

"Because Scotland is exporting its wool, so the Sinclair ships are all away."

"Even if we could use one, we'd have to disguise it somehow," Rob said.

"Why?" Giff demanded. When neither man answered, he said with a sigh of resignation, "I suppose I can send a rider to Galloway with orders for my lads. It should not take them longer than three weeks to sail here with a sizable flotilla from the Isles, but we should consider what that will suggest to folks here, and think how to ease their fear of such a navy. Your plan cannot be set in motion quickly, though, so three weeks should give us time to work out details, should it not?"

"Sakes," Hugo said, emerging from his thoughts with

a sardonic look. "Don't tell me you've taken to planning, my lad. I doubt you've ever followed a plan in your life even when ordered to do so."

"Now, Hugo, that just shows how little you know me," Giff said in an injured tone. "I can assure you I am all obedience when dealing with the Douglas, who is arguably the most powerful man in Scotland, notwithstanding the King or his ambitious son, Fife. Indeed, with most men of the Douglas's ilk, I—"

"Aye, sure," Hugo interjected. "I've heard your excuses, my lad, and whilst the captain of a ship may claim that a change in weather demanded a change in his interpretation of his orders, the enemy's failure to act as expected is *not* an excuse."

"Is that what you think I do?"

"I know that is what you do," Hugo said. Then, with a shake of his head, he added, "But I'll admit that whatever you do, you usually win through in the end."

"All I do is make decisions without wasting time flinging about for other men's opinions of what I ought to do," Giff said. "That is the trick, you know, being able to make a quick decision and commit to it before the moment to act is lost. And that is what you need, is it not, someone who can act quickly to win the day?"

He kept his tone solemn. The mission intrigued him, and he did not want to anger Hugo, but neither did he want to hear a lecture. His record spoke for itself.

Exchanging another look with Rob, Hugo said, "Aye, that *is* what we need. However, we cannot wait for a flotilla, or even for one ship. The time we have is fast disappearing. Sithee, Fife most considerately occupied himself in the Borders for the best part of this past year, and we'd hoped he would continue to do so long enough for us to arrange the details of our plan without arousing his curiosity. But instead, he has chosen to return to our midst just when we least want him here."

"Aye, well, you'll get no sympathy from anyone in the Borders," Giff said. "Douglas and the others fighting the English there are all warriors far more skilled than Fife. He may be shrewd, but he kens nowt of strategy or tactics and cannot think under pressure, so they're well rid of him. No one was much surprised when he decided to leave just as the English began moving their armies north."

"Are they not still dealing with rebellion in the south?" Rob asked mildly.

"Aye, but it has spread northward," Giff said. "However, we stray from the point. Tell me about this mission of yours."

"First you should know that it involves Templar business," Hugo said. "I trust you remember that your duty to the Order supersedes all others."

"Aye," Giff agreed, more intrigued than ever.

"Many things that affect us have occurred in the past two years," Hugo went on. "We need not discuss them all now, but the safety of an item entrusted to two of our members is in peril. As you know, Templars have long provided safekeeping for items of great value for heads of state and others of wealth or power."

"Aye," Giff said, "including the Templars' own vast treasure until it disappeared from the Paris temple nearly three-quarters of a century ago."

All Scottish Knights Templar knew of that great loss, which occurred when King Philip IV of France, heavily in debt to the Templars, decided that rather than repay the vast sums he had borrowed, he would seize their treasure for himself. To that end, he first took it into his head to destroy the Order's fine reputation with lies of heresy. A devious man as well as an evil one, who had put his own pope at the head of the Kirk and housed him at Avignon, Philip then bullied the man into declaring all Templars heretics. Eventually, still under Philip's thumb and terrified of him, the Pope had issued an edict disbanding the Order.

But Philip had not waited for papal action. In October 1307, he raided the Paris temple and arrested as many Templars as he could lay hands on in France, including their grand master. But his raid on the temple failed in its objective. His raiders found the treasury empty and most of the members gone. Their great fleet, harbored at La Rochelle, had vanished with them.

"One does hear rumors that Templars who came to Scotland when the Bruce offered sanctuary to any who could get here may have brought at least part of the treasure with them," Giff said thoughtfully. "We all know that the Scottish Templars were never disbanded because the Pope had excommunicated Bruce the year before, so Bruce never received the edict. Also, he needed the Templars to help him free Scotland. Still, most folks here believe the Scottish Knights Templar are mythical," he added. "Even most of us Templars don't believe all the treasure tales were true."

"Our Order guards its secrets well," Rob said.

"And must continue to do so," Hugo said. "This does not concern the Paris treasure, Giff. The item we are discussing has never left Scotland. Bruce himself entrusted it to two men, knowing them to be Templars." He hesitated, then added with obvious reluctance, "I should tell you, however, that Fife suspects it lies with the rest of the Templar treasure. He suspects, as well, that the Sinclair family knows the treasure's whereabouts."

"Do they?"

"That is irrelevant. Nor need we discuss it now. My point is that Fife is willing to do whatever he must to find what he seeks. He hopes to win Scotland by seizing it, and he has narrowed his search to a critical point. The object must be moved as quickly as possible now to avoid possible discovery."

"Sakes, man, what is this so-desirable object?" Giff demanded.

"'Tis the most sacred object in Scotland," Hugo replied evenly.

"Well, it must be second most, because the most sacred item to Scots is no longer in Scotland," Giff protested. "The English stole that nearly a century ago."

"Did they?"

A chill shot through Giff, accompanied by a hope so overwhelming that he found it impossible to say what he was thinking without resorting to the language of his childhood, the Gaelic of the Highlands and Isles. "The *Lia Fail*," he murmured.

"Aye," Hugo said. "The—"

He broke off, and Giff heard the distant light tapping sound that had stopped him, and recognized it. One of the women was coming downstairs.

"We'll talk more after supper," Hugo said, moving toward the door again as he spoke. "You'll doubtless welcome time to refresh yourselves before we eat."

On the words, he opened the door, stepped back, and said, "Come in, lass."

Giff stared as Lady Sidony, wearing only pale yellow and gold, stepped into the room with her head high and paused serenely by Hugo.

She was a treasure in and of herself, Giff thought, like an exquisite golden statue come to life.

Chapter 4

Don't encourage Sir Giffard, lass," Hugo said as he shut the door behind the other two, making Sidony wonder if he had meant Sir Giffard to hear the warning.

"I don't encourage anyone," she said.

"True enough," he said. "But you are not always very wise, are you?"

"I did not mean to get lost, sir, or to be away so long."

"You know that is not what I mean. What demon possessed you to wander alone into the abbey woods?"

Although she did not like anyone to be displeased with her, she met his stern gaze without difficulty. "I get tired of being always with other people," she said. "The woods are peaceful and quiet. They belong to the Kirk, after all."

"Even so," he said.

"But who would harm me there, knowing God must be watching them?"

"You left the woods with a man you did not even know," he pointed out.

"But you know him," she said. "Isobel said you sent for him."

"Aye, but you did not know that then." More brusquely, he added, "Or did he dare to impose on you by claiming friendship with me?"

"Nay," she said, remembering. "He told me he had met you, but that only made him more determined to bring me straight back here."

"I see," he said. Whether he did or not, he cast no more blame on Sir Giffard but went on instead to describe her lack of judgment in most uncivil terms.

Sidony listened respectfully, and when he had said all he wanted to say, she said quietly, "I am very sorry to have upset everyone, sir."

"I don't want to hear of your ever doing such a thing again."

"No, sir."

"Good lass," he said, patting her shoulder. "We'll go in to supper now, before Lady Clendenen comes looking for us. I can hear them gathering."

Relieved to have it over, she obeyed with alacrity when he opened the door and gestured for her to precede him.

They found the others in the great chamber with its stone walls and beamed ceiling. The linen-draped table and the dais on which it sat at the south end were smaller than those of other places where Sidony had lived during her year in Midlothian, although the table was still larger than required for the six people gathered there. Nevertheless, the great chamber was comfortable and boasted a fireplace that shared its chimney with the one in the vaulted kitchen below the house. So, although throughout the winter her ladyship frequently grumbled that the chamber was too chilly for comfort, it felt pleasantly warm now.

Isobel began to assure them that she and Lady Clendenen had just arrived themselves, but Sidony's gaze moved to Sir Giffard standing by Rob near the fire. When Giff smiled, she looked quickly away. When she looked again, Rob had engaged his attention to present him to their hostess.

Hugo touched Sidony's elbow, guiding her toward the table.

A narrow screen passage along the east wall contained the buttery and pantry as well as concealing the servants' wall stair to the kitchen and the three upper floors. The dais table bore pewter goblets and platters, polished wooden trenchers at each place, a basket of manchet loaves, and a wine jug. Two back stools occupied each long side of the table with armchairs at head and foot, and a large carving board stood ready for the roast lamb at the pantry entrance.

Two tables for her ladyship's servants occupied space away from the dais.

"We're an odd assortment tonight, are we not?" Ealga, Lady Clendenen, observed as she moved to stand by her chair. "I am very pleased, though, that you all are here with me." A plump, personable woman in her fiftieth summer, she suffered—often vocally—from a lack of height but boasted smooth, fair skin and a ready smile that appeared as she turned to Sir Giffard.

"You may sit at my right hand, sir, if you will," she said. "Rob, dear, take the place beside him. Isobel and Sidony will sit across from you, and Hugo, pray be so obliging as to take the chair at the foot of the table and say the grace-before-meat."

Hugo obeyed without comment, after which everyone took seats. Her ladyship signed to her carver to serve the meat, informed everyone that the fine salmon on the fish platter was the one Sidony had caught, and then added, "Now, my dear Sir Giffard, do tell us all about yourself."

His visibly startled reaction tickled Sidony's sense of humor, but as Hugo was probably still annoyed with her, she hoped her amusement did not show. To her surprise, it was Hugo who intervened, saying, "I doubt you want to know *all* about him, madam. He is as known for daft, impulsive behavior as for aught else. But as Rob may have told you, Giff is here at my invitation, and Michael's."

"No, Rob did not tell me that," her ladyship said with a glance at that gentleman, who seemed interested only in the gillie who leaned past her ladyship as she spoke to fill her goblet with claret. The lad, clearly aware that she was prone to sudden movements, kept a careful eye on her and managed his task without accident. Two other lads moved from place to place, offering bowls and platters of side dishes as the carver piled meat on trenchers his assistant handed to him.

Impulsively, Sidony said, "Sir Giffard comes from Kintail, madam, so we are practically neighbors. Are we not, sir?"

"Faith, do you know him from home then?" Lady Clendenen said as their guest shifted his gaze to Sidony. "I thought you'd met him only this afternoon."

Recalling that little escaped her ladyship's notice, Sidony said, "That is true, but he told me he is from Kintail. Moreover, I have heard the name MacLennan before, although I do not believe we have any living in Glenelg."

"So whereabouts in Kintail *does* your family live, sir?" Lady Clendenen inquired. As he drew breath to speak, she added, "I should tell you, perhaps, that I am most inquisitive. Moreover, I shall be marrying Macleod of Glenelg in just over a month, on July the sixth. And now that I have met you, I shall want to be certain that he has thought to invite your people to the ceremony—unless," she added with a roguish look, "you are sure he will already have done so."

The fleeting shadow Sidony had noted earlier crossed his face again, but Sir Giffard said easily, "I have no notion one way or the other, my lady. I have scarcely been next or nigh my home in a decade."

"As long as that? Do you not get on with your people?"

Their guest looked wary, and Rob said mildly, "She warned you that she is inquisitive, but you'll get used to it if you spend any time in Edinburgh. I have."

"Oh, yes," Lady Clendenen said, nodding to another hovering gillie to serve her from a bowl of steamed cabbage. "I fear I am one whose thoughts tumble out of her mouth as she thinks them. My cousin Ardelve—may his soul rest in peace—was frequently heard to say that I had no acquaintance with tact, and I suppose that may be so. But, in troth, I accept blunt comments as easily as I offer them, so you must tell me if I overstep the mark, sir. I promise you will not offend me by doing so."

Sidony wondered idly if that was true. In her admittedly limited experience, people who prided themselves on plain speaking rarely appreciated it when anyone else spoke plainly to them. She looked sympathetically at Sir Giffard. It could not be easy to reply to such a barrage of questions from a stranger.

But he was smiling and seemed completely at his ease.

Into that brief silence, Isobel said, "You must let me thank you for your kindness to my sister this afternoon, sir. She was fortunate to come upon a friend in the woods, when she might so easily have encountered an enemy."

Sidony shot her an aggrieved look as Lady Clendenen exclaimed, "Mercy, Isobel, do you think enemies lurk behind the abbot's trees? I would not choose to walk there, myself, because the drainage in those woods is so uncertain, but they are as safe as my own gardens, surely."

Sir Giffard said, "I certainly saw no one lurking there."

"Except yourself," Hugo said sardonically. He went on in a more appreciative tone to say, "This lamb is excellent, madam."

"Thank you, but you should not speak as if Sir Giffard had not done us a service, for he has, and Isobel is right to thank him. You have my thanks, as well, sir, and I am sure that Sidony has thanked you, too."

"Aye, mayhap she did," Isobel said, smiling at him. "But I must tell you, sir, that she still fears that, from some cause or other, you may be irked with her."

"Her ladyship need have no fear," he said. "Indeed, my lady, I do not know why you should imagine I was irked at all."

"There is," Rob murmured, helping himself for a second time from the fish platter, "the small matter of this excellent salmon. One feared it might be a bit bruised, but apparently it survived its encounter without injury."

"Survived?" Hugo said with a grin.

Sidony looked down at her trencher, wishing they would all just disappear.

Giff noted her blushes but turned his gaze back to Lady Isobel, who still watched him quizzically. Her expression and the tilt of her head reminded him of a gull perched on a ship's rail, hoping for a scrap. He had no intention of tossing any to her ladyship, but he could not be sure of Hugo or Rob. The latter's comment might not have been intentionally provocative, but if it was, Giff felt certain that he, not the lady Sidony, had been Rob's target. That Rob looked rueful now was plain evidence of that.

He had not expected Lady Isobel to drop the subject, nor did she.

"Does the salmon enter into your annoyance with Sidony, sir?" she asked demurely. "I confess I am as inquisitive as Lady Clendenen."

"Sakes, sir, Isobel is more so," that lady said. "But do answer her. I cannot think how a salmon could enter into a man's ire with a woman unless she stole it from him, and I cannot imagine our Sidony doing any such uncivil thing."

"Nor can I, madam," Giff said. "Her ladyship caught that splendid creature before I encountered her. As to the other, I am not, nor was I then, annoyed with her in any way for any reason whatsoever."

And if that lie perjures my immortal soul, he told himself, *so be it.*

He flicked a look at Lady Sidony, hoping she would reveal some small gratitude for his thoughtfulness, but she stared at her trencher and steadily ate her supper. Her wine goblet remained untouched.

Reinforcing his notion that Rob's provocation had been unintentional, that gentleman tore his attention from his food long enough to introduce a more general topic. Conversation became desultory until some time after they had finished eating, when Hugo said, "I'm thinking we should be on our way soon, lads. We can discuss things more whilst we ride. You can house Giff at Lestalric, can you not, Rob?"

"Aye, sure, and I presume that you will also sleep there."

"I will tonight. Tomorrow I must get back to Hawthornden, though, or soon after I do get there, I'll find my head in my lap."

Giff grinned. "Is your wife so fierce? I own, if she is, I look forward to meeting her."

Hugo grinned right back as he said, "You may hope."

"We should leave, too, Sidony," Lady Isobel said.

"We'll go with you," Hugo said, "and see you safely inside Sinclair House."

"Thank you, but I must first collect Will and his nurse. He's been fussing a good deal of late, so it may take a while, and I know you want to be on your way. One of her ladyship's gillies can easily—"

"We'll wait, lass," Hugo said. "We're not in such a hurry as that. Lestalric is less than two miles away, so take as long as you like with the bairn."

As they all stood, Giff watched Lady Sidony, noting how much quieter she was than the others, and how serene—much more so than the other two women, who seemed to chatter nonstop with each other and with the men.

She held back as everyone moved toward the stair-hall doorway, so he let Rob and Hugo go ahead of him, following the other two ladies. Just as he was congratulating himself on a deft maneuver, however, Sidony murmured that she had forgotten her eating knife and turned back toward the table.

Knowing that Hugo would notice if he followed her, he caught up with the men instead and murmured, "Hugo, whereabouts is the . . . ?"

"Behind us," Hugo said. "Go through the little solar at the southwest corner of this chamber, and you'll find steps leading to the garden. The garderobe is to the east before you reach the shed. You can't miss it."

"Thanks," he said. He half expected Hugo to realize Sidony had gone the same way, but Hugo had rejoined Rob and the two were turning into the parlor as if the lass had slipped right out of their minds.

Wondering if she might be seeking the privacy of the garderobe herself, he hurried to catch sight of her and observed with relief through a window of the solar that she was walking along a path down the center of the garden.

He did visit the garderobe first, as much to keep her from realizing that he had followed her as from a need to relieve himself. Then he strolled into the garden, noting that the sky had cleared of all but a few drifting clouds. The sun had dipped a good portion of its lower half behind the horizon of housetops to the west, splashing its fading rays upward to paint the clouds every shade of pink, orange, and rose.

For a moment, with the sun in his eyes, he lost sight of the lass and wondered if she had dared to slip into the woods again. Then he saw that she had stopped close to a tree at the bottom of the garden to watch the sunset.

When his footsteps crunched on the pebbled path, she turned and soberly watched his approach. The sun's rays gilded her from top to toe.

"I see that I'm not the only one who wanted fresh air," he said when he was near enough to speak without raising his voice.

"You followed me," she said.

He opened his mouth to deny it, to insist that he had come innocently in search of the garderobe and happened to see her. But he could not, so he smiled instead and said, "I did. I wanted to further our acquaintance. Art vexed with me?"

"Nay, although I warrant Hugo warned you to keep your distance."

"Aye, just as he warned you not to encourage me."

She smiled. "You did hear that. I wondered if he meant you to."

"Certainly, he did."

"Are you truly not afraid of him? He has a fearsome temper, as you must know, for you told me yourself that he knocked you down the last time you met."

"He won't do so again," Giff said.

"You sound very confident of that. I must say I am glad you did not tell him why I struck you. And thank you, too," she added, "for not telling Isobel about it."

He frowned. "Would Hugo strike you?"

"He never has, but he does scold rather fiercely. If I were a man, it would be different, though, I'm sure, so I don't understand why you think you need not fear his anger." She tilted her head as she added, "Is it because he sent for you? Why did he, and why did you not tell me that he had?"

"'Tis men's business," he said. "Moreover, it is not my habit to discuss even *my* business with every pretty lass I meet."

Her eyes widened. "Do you meet so many?"

He chuckled. "Dozens a day, but not many who would look as beautiful as you do tonight in that gown. It suits you, lass. You should wear it often."

Color flooded her cheeks. "Why do you say such things to me?"

"Because they are true," he said, gazing into her eyes. Her pupils were enormous, her pale blue irises nearly invisible. As light as they were, they seemed to meld with the whites, fascinating him all over again.

Her mouth was rosy pink and bow-shaped. She dampened her lips—full, soft-looking, enticing lips—and his body stirred lustfully in response.

Sidony did not know what to make of him, but energy crackled from him, making her feel hot and a little dizzy when he stood as close as he was now. Her nerves tingled, and she felt as if she should reach out a hand, but whether to fend him off or draw him nearer, she could not be sure.

He was big, loose-limbed, and broad-shouldered, the sort of man one knew instinctively could protect a woman and do many other things well. And as brash as he was, he seemed to care nothing for what others thought of him, as if he were content to be who he was no matter what anyone said to or about him. He had not even apologized for sitting down in the leather breeks and jack-o'-plate he had worn for two days of riding to have supper with Lady Clendenen—faith, with all of them.

His shirt was white enough to make her nearly certain he must have put on a fresh one not long before they had met, but perhaps he was merely tidy in his habits and had not got it dirty. Even so, he had not mentioned his clothing before dinner or afterward, as most gentlemen would have done under similar circumstances. Nor did he seem bothered by it now.

Another thought occurred to her. Perhaps he had no proper town clothes. Perhaps in Galloway men did not sport finery. But Rob had kinsmen there, and Rob rarely wore anything *but* finery. Of course, she reminded herself, Rob was nearly as wealthy as the Sinclairs. Perhaps Sir Giffard was poor.

She realized with a start that as her thoughts had darted

hither and yon, he had continued to stare at her in that odd, hungry way, making her feel his interest all the way to her toes. She ought to step back, she knew, to put more distance between them, but as the thought entered her head, he reached for her.

His large hands grasped her upper arms, and he drew her gently toward him and kissed her softly on the lips.

"Giff! You out there?"

"That's Hugo," she murmured, recognizing the voice.

"Step behind the tree," he said. "He hasn't seen you."

She obeyed without a second thought. He stood between her and Hugo, and the shrubbery concealed her swaying skirts.

"Aye, Hugo," he called, turning, "I'm here, admiring the sunset." Without turning toward her but lowering his voice considerably, he said, "The sun is in his eyes, so just stand still until he and I go back inside. Then, if he does see you come in, he will assume that you were about your own private business."

"What if he asks you about me?"

"His mind is on other things just now. I doubt that he will," he said, already taking the first step away from her. "Are you ready to leave?" he called to Hugo.

"Aye, I've ordered out the horses, and Rob's waiting out front."

Sidony realized he was likely right in thinking that Hugo had forgotten about her, but she wondered what she would say to Isobel or her hostess if either saw her come in from the garden. She put the thought out of her head to enjoy watching him stride up the pebbled path to the steps. Hugo had already vanished inside.

Counting to one hundred, she went inside to find Isobel

just descending the stairs with her bairn and his nursemaid. Hugo, thankfully, was nowhere in sight.

As the last rays of sunlight slipped below the western horizon, the Earl of Fife led a dozen other riders at a brisk trot along the Canongate from the abbey kirk toward St. Giles and the Castle. Fife wore his customary all-black attire, and the men in his tail wore black, too. They were all well armed and rode fine horses, for the earl had attended Compline at the abbey and had his image to maintain.

De Gredin, riding beside him and wearing far more fashionable clothing as usual, said, "I thought the monks did not allow visitors at their services."

"I attend whenever I choose, whether that cross-grained old abbot likes it or not," Fife said. "He once threatened to excommunicate me when I'd displeased him, but I like Compline, because I can make my confession and the service is short. Moreover, with a dozen armed men waiting for me in his kirkyard, what can he say?"

"What, indeed?" de Gredin said cheerfully. "I am grateful that you have allowed me to stay, my lord. I trust that this time we shall achieve our goal."

"Aye, sure, but we should not discuss that here," Fife said. "You did mention providing ships, though, and I am curious to know how soon they may arrive."

"As I recall, 'tis the season for shipping wool to the Hanseatic countries," de Gredin said. "So I imagine they will arrive soon. With as many vessels as Leith Harbor will see in the next weeks, 'tis an excellent time to add a few more."

"I've had one built for myself," Fife said, switching to

a topic less perilous for others to overhear. "The *Serpent Royal* harbors at Leith. Tomorrow I'll take you to see her, for I doubt that even the Pope has one so fine."

De Gredin expressed eagerness to see the *Serpent*, but Fife paid no heed. Not only did he have his own ship but also the promise of immediate papal aid, rather than the Pope's less certain pledge before to support him only if he helped de Gredin find and return the Templar treasure. If all went well now, de Gredin would help him find Scotland's Stone of Destiny, which was one item to which his holiness could make no honest claim even if it should prove to be part of the treasure. Moreover, if Fife found it, he would have little need of papal support to win the crown.

"I failed to mention earlier how relieved I was to find you were not still in the Borders, my lord," de Gredin said. "Do you intend to return there soon?"

"Nay, for the constant threat there serves to keep the Douglas busy and out of my way here," Fife said in a tone calculated to discourage further discussion. He had brought de Gredin along only because he preferred to keep an eye on him.

"Then I expect you mean to give your full attention to our quest now."

"You talk too much," Fife said, shooting him a look that would have terrified most men. "Practice the virtue of silence."

De Gredin nodded, saying, "Forgive me, my lord. I meant no disrespect."

Fife made no comment. The man's submission did not surprise him. On the contrary, such easy submission was one of the several reasons he distrusted him.

Chapter 5

At the abbey end of the Canongate, Giff, Sir Hugo, Rob, and Rob's armed tail, having seen the ladies Isobel and Sidony safely inside Sinclair House, had returned the way they had come and were approaching Holyrood's gates.

Casually, Hugo said, "Giff, my lad, if you want to stop and complain to the abbot about the overlarge trout in his loch, I warrant he'd hear your grievance."

Giff glanced into the dusky yard, thinking of his muddy breeks. "I might ask instead why the devil he doesn't do a better job of draining that bog-ridden place."

"Go right ahead," Hugo said, grinning.

"I ken fine that you don't think I'd do it," Giff said. "But I just might."

Chuckling, Rob said, "Not now, you fashious bairn. Not only is my lord abbot likely to fine you for trespass, but Fife is out and about."

"Is he indeed?" Hugo said, looking up and down the Canongate.

"He is," Rob said. "I saw him ride toward St. Giles earlier whilst I waited for you. He was not alone, either. He had six of his men with him, well armed. He has been showing himself rather a lot since his return to Edinburgh."

They turned north at the abbey gates and exited the royal burgh to follow the track toward Lestalric and the burgh's official harbor at the village of Leith.

When they were beyond the slightest opportunity for anyone else to overhear them, Rob said in a crisp tone wholly at odds with the sleepy one to which Giff had grown accustomed, "Fife had another companion, Hugo, riding right beside him."

"Did he?"

"Aye, 'twas our old friend de Gredin."

The grim note in Rob's voice made it clear that he did not like de Gredin.

"Should I ken more about this fellow?" Giff asked.

Measuring his words, Hugo said, "He is the chevalier Etienne de Gredin, some sort of kinsman to Lady Clendenen."

"Don't make too much of that," Rob warned. "She is kin to nearly everyone who is anyone in Scotland and France, even to me, but I don't trust the man, distant kinsman or none. No more should you."

"I don't think I am any connection to either of them," Giff said, then reconsidered. "Except that you and I are cousins, so I expect . . ."

"You see how it is," Rob said with a smile.

"At any event," Hugo went on, "de Gredin grew up in France. His father was Scottish envoy to the French court, and the chevalier apparently encountered men there who persuaded him that the Templar treasure rightfully belongs to the Holy Kirk. We've dealt before with de Gredin and at least one other of his ilk. Such men believe that God favors their quest and will forgive them any sin they commit in His service, and will even reward them in heaven if they die serving Him."

"Well, they all sound a bit daft to me, and I don't trust any man I don't know," Giff said. "But is there more than his regrettable beliefs about the treasure and the Almighty's supposed support to make you distrust de Gredin?"

"His present apparent friendship with Fife, for one," Hugo said. "They had a falling-out last year, a serious one, and de Gredin applied to Henry Sinclair for aid."

"What sort of a falling-out?" Giff asked.

"Sithee, when Fife tried to arrest Adela, de Gredin intervened."

"I intervened," Rob said grimly. "De Gredin did make himself useful at one point, but he did nothing before then to keep Fife from dangling Adela a hundred feet above the river Esk and threatening to drop her in when she would not talk to him."

"Aye de mi, he must have terrified her!" Giff exclaimed, truly shocked.

"He did," Rob said. "I suspect that afterward, when he saw that Fife would fail, he wanted to ingratiate himself with us. It worked, too. Henry took him to Girnigoe."

"Henry felt obliged to take him, to get him out of Fife's reach," Hugo said.

With a wry smile, Rob said, "Since de Gredin believes, as Fife does, that the Sinclairs have the treasure, I'd wager he was nobbut a damned nuisance there."

"It was kind of Henry to offer his protection," Giff said. "But why, then, would de Gredin risk facing Fife again? And why would Fife trust him now?"

Hugo looked at Rob, who said, "Because both of them

will exploit anything that takes them a step closer to the goals they seek."

"The main one being to find the Templars' mythical treasure," Giff said. When his companions did not reply, he went on thinking aloud. "Plainly, Fife is a menace. I heard in the Borders that men who merely annoy him have a habit of disappearing, whilst others die suddenly and violently."

"That is true," Hugo said. "Rob's father and brother were two of them."

"Sakes, I'm sorry, Rob," Giff said. "I did know that."

"We all ken fine what the earl wants," Rob said. "He wants to rule Scotland."

"Aye, sure," Giff agreed. "Yet he cannot think Parliament would support him just because he happened to find that treasure—assuming that it *does* exist."

The other two remained silent.

"Sakes, do you mean to say it does?"

"It does," Hugo said. "You should know that much so that you will treat their determination to find it with greater respect."

"Do *you* know where it is?"

"Nay, we do not," Hugo replied firmly.

"Does Henry?"

"We will refrain from speculation on that point. It is not for us to know."

But Giff's mind had been racing. "Aye de mi," he said. "It is not the treasure at all, is it? Even if Fife could lay hands on it, it would not gain him the throne, because every other nobleman would fear such enormous wealth in royal hands."

Neither of his companions spoke.

"'Tis the *Lia Fail*," he said. "I should have guessed at

once. Sakes, but his standing with Parliament would soar if he could return the Stone to Scotland. But one first has to believe that it somehow carried itself back here from Westminster."

"I told you before," Hugo said. "The Stone never left Scotland."

"You did, aye, but I find that hard to believe," Giff said frankly. "Och, now don't stiffen up like that, Hugo. I don't doubt *your* honesty, just . . . Sakes, man, the thing has been missing now for . . . what? Eighty-five years, is it not?"

Hugo nodded.

"Well, then, do you think King Edward of England, whom the Scots called 'the Hammer,' was such a dafty that he carted off the wrong block of stone?"

"The Abbot of Scone had weeks of warning that Edward meant to seize the Stone," Hugo said. "That abbot, being sensible and a patriot, entrusted it to another as trustworthy as himself, who later told Robert the Bruce. Before he died, Bruce entrusted the Stone's safekeeping to two Templars, demanding their promise not to reveal its location until the Scottish throne was truly safe from English seizure. All Scottish Templars are, of course, bound by that same promise."

"Who were these trustworthy people who aided Bruce and Scone's abbot?"

Rob said gently, "Do you really want to know that just as you undertake its protection? Are you so certain you can keep silent if Fife gets his hands on you?"

Giff thought about that, recalling that the Templars' most beloved grand master had found it impossible to keep silent under torture. Jacques de Molay had even uttered the heretical falsehoods his torturers demanded. To be sure, he had recanted them before they murdered him, but his disavowal had aided no one.

"Nay," Giff said. "'Twould be unwise unless I need to know to succeed."

"You may be sure you do not," Rob said, and Hugo nodded agreement.

"So, where is the Stone now, and how do we move it?" Giff asked.

"We have a plan and several options," Hugo said. "We'll let you see it before we move it, but we must first try to learn what mischief Fife and de Gredin intend."

"Aye," Rob agreed. "Sithee, it is still possible that Fife intends only to glean information about Girnigoe and Orkney from de Gredin and then means to send ships and men there in search of the treasure, believing the Stone lies hidden with it."

Hugo said, "That doesn't fully explain de Gredin's accord with Fife, though."

"Nay," Giff said, "for if Fife has more reason to distrust him than to trust him, why would he heed anything the man says about his time with Henry? I should think he would more likely suspect Henry's hand in any plan that de Gredin suggests."

"Aye, Fife suspects everyone," Hugo said. "He's had minions following us, even during his lengthy excursions into the Borders this past year. They slip in and out of Roslin glen and think we don't see them, because we leave them alone unless they annoy us. But we cannot have them flitting about whilst we move the Stone."

"So the Stone is near Roslin," Giff said.

"Aye, and as soon as we take greater precautions, Fife will know we're up to something," Rob said. "There's Lestalric ahead," he added. "On yonder hilltop."

Giff peered through rapidly fading light and saw a steep hill jutting from a nestlike woodland at its base. He could barely discern the outline of a castle atop it but could determine neither the castle's size nor its features beyond a tower or two.

Moments later, as they passed into the dark woods, Rob said, "I'm thinking the first thing we must do is furbish you up a bit, Giff. The King and his court return to Edinburgh soon from Stirling, which means Fife is likely to remain here, at least for a time. You'd do well to look as if that is the reason you are here, too, until we can arrange all the details for moving the Stone. I hope you enjoy court life."

"I don't," Giff said, but as he did, he found himself wondering if the lady Sidony might decide to attend any court functions. He still wondered how in the world Hugo had managed to forget her existence after supper, as if she had faded from the great chamber like a ghost or one of the wee folk. Realizing that Rob apparently expected him to expand upon his curt reply, he said casually, "Mayhap we'd all be wise to attend court once or twice, to learn what Fife means to do."

At Sinclair House, Sidony had conjured up a similar thought, that she might exert herself to attend court a time or two, to see who else might do so.

Even so, when she and Isobel retired to the ladies' solar after seeing wee William Robert tucked sleepily, if fussily, into his cot, and Isobel suggested that they ought to consider what they still needed to complement their court dresses, Sidony said, "You know I dislike taking part in all that din and revelry."

"It is hardly a place of quiet reflection," her sister agreed, smiling.

"Reflection?" Sidony said with an unladylike snort. "The King's kinsmen behave as if they were raised in a sty, and others want only to outdress and outdrink one another. I don't know why any civil person should want to go."

"One must pay one's respects to his grace," Isobel said seriously. "Recall that Countess Isabella will come to town soon. Doubtless we may look for her to arrive within the sennight, and if you think she will allow either of us to stay at home whilst she attends court, you might just as well think again."

Sidony submitted, knowing that Michael's mother, the powerful Countess in her own right of Strathearn and Caithness, would expect them both to accompany her to the royal court, if only to increase the splendor of her retinue. Isabella knew her worth and considered it far greater than that of anyone in the royal family.

"Will Michael be back in time to go with us, do you think?" she asked.

"That will depend upon how his business prospers."

"You said he was just riding to Glasgow. Surely, he should be back by now."

Isobel shrugged and reached for her tambour frame. "He said he might pay his respects to MacDonald."

"The Lord of the Isles—at Ardtornish? Sakes, I could have gone with him. He might have taken me home!"

"Don't be silly," Isobel said, taking up her needle. "MacDonald is as likely to be at Finlaggan, and even Ardtornish is still a good distance from Glenelg."

"But he might have gone farther. The distance is not so great as that."

"You could hardly expect him to take you with him, in any event, dearling. If he did go to the Isles, 'twas because he had important business there."

"Do you know what business it is?"

Isobel looked directly at her then. "If I did," she said quietly, "I would not tell you. I do not prattle about my husband's business to anyone."

Ruefully aware that she had overstepped, Sidony said, "You are right. I should not have asked such a question."

Isobel smiled. "I'd have asked it myself," she admitted. "But now, what do you think about having our seamstress change the narrow lace on your blue gown?"

Sidony made no further objection to discussing court dresses, but she lent only half an ear to Isobel's plans. Her thoughts had returned to the interesting events of the day and Sir Giffard MacLennan.

The following morning, the Earl of Fife and his entourage arrived at Leith Harbor an hour and a half after Terce. The air felt damp, although no rain had fallen since the previous day's light drizzle, and the sky was dull gray and low.

Reining in, Fife turned up the sable collar of his heavy wool cloak and tugged his hat lower as he faced the choppy gray water of the firth.

"Which one is she?" de Gredin asked, reining in beside him.

"The *Serpent Royal*," he said, pointing at his new ship, riding at anchor near the eastern boundary of the crowded harbor, out of the way of careless helmsmen.

"She looks like some of Prince Henry's newer ships," de Gredin observed.

"I want her to mix in with his when we go north," Fife said. "But pray refer to the impudent fellow as the Earl of Orkney if you must refer to him at all."

"Aye, sure," de Gredin agreed. "'Twas just habit, for Orkney's people in the north use his Norse title. Also, living in France as I did whilst my father was envoy there, one forgets that we Scots have no princes, that our highest rank is your own."

Fife grunted, still gazing at his fine ship. The design he had ordered combined comfort for himself with the best qualities of the speedy, easily maneuvered western galleys. It also included cargo holds fore and aft that were large enough to contain the Stone when he found it, as well as other spaces useful for smaller cargo, equipment, or provisions, albeit none as spacious as more cumbersome merchant ships boasted.

"Tell me more about her," de Gredin invited. "How long is she?"

"Seventy feet, I think, and sixteen oars, as you'll see for yourself in just a few minutes," he said dismissively. His captain and shipbuilder had told him a great deal about the *Serpent*, but not being a sailor or fond of the sea, he remembered little of it. "There," he added, "they have seen us and are manning a boat to fetch us."

Never having learned to swim, Fife detested small boats, such as the coble being rowed now to collect them, and he realized that he ought to have sent orders ahead to tow the *Serpent* to a wharf.

As men scrambled to pull the coble higher onto the shingle, an imp of a lad leaped from it and ran toward him, tousled dark curls bouncing with each step, his baggy sleeves and the short skirt of his saffron-colored doublet fluttering about him.

By the time he reached Fife, one of his soled, roll-topped overstockings had sagged to rippled, untidy folds around his ankle. Without taking his eyes off the earl, he bent to tug up the stocking as he said, "Good day to ye, me lord Fife. Me da' sent me to bid ye welcome. He'd ha' come hisself, he said, only ye did give him orders no' to leave the *Serpent* now till we sail."

As the lad straightened, Fife said with easy condescension, "So you are Captain Maxwell's son, are you? What's your name, lad?"

"Jake Maxwell, me lord." Glancing over the rest of the party, he said, "How many will ye take aboard wi' ye? The wee coble canna carry all these in one trip."

Fife looked at the "wee coble" disapprovingly. Six muscular oarsmen stood with it, and the water in the harbor was relatively calm, but he saw no reason to overburden the boat. He gestured toward de Gredin. "They need take only this man and me. We want to decide what more needs seeing to before the *Serpent* sails. Do you mean to sail with us, Jake Maxwell?" he added with a touch of humor.

To his surprise, the lad said, "Aye, sure, me lord."

"I should think you'd be wiser to bide safely at home with your mother."

"Me mam's dead," Jake said. "Me da's teaching me all he kens so I can be captain of a fine ship m'self one day. Will ye board our coble now, me lord?"

Fife hesitated, eyeing the daunting distance from shingle to ship.

Jake, misreading his emotion, said proudly, "She's a fine vessel, is she no'?"

"Aye, that she is," Fife said. "Lead on, Jake Maxwell,

and tell those men of yours to put their backs into their oars. I do *not* want to be all day about this."

"Aye, sure, sir, I'll tell them," Jake said. Grinning, he ran to obey.

At Sinclair House, Sidony was feeling uncommonly dull. Not only did the overcast sky fail to clear by Friday midday, but during that same time, she had seen no one but her sister Isobel, Isobel's son, and the servants. Any lingering interest in her own or her sister's court wardrobe had vanished, and thanks to her usually entertaining nephew's difficulties with the incipient arrival of a new tooth, not to mention the resultant loss of two nights' sleep for most of the inhabitants of the house, no remedy had yet presented itself to rouse her from increasing languor.

"I wonder why Rob has not been to visit, or Hugo," she said to Isobel as they savored a few minutes of blessed quiet in the ladies' solar after their midday meal. "Recollect that both of them promised to look in often whilst Michael is away."

"Sakes, it has only been three days since we saw them."

"Aye, but mayhap we should ride to Lestalric this afternoon to visit Adela and see for ourselves that all is well there."

"Not today," Isobel said, looking out the window. "It looks as if it might rain, and I should not like to arrive at Lestalric soaked to the skin. Nor is Will likely to enjoy an outing just now."

"Then leave him with his nursemaid," Sidony suggested. When Isobel looked astonished, she said guiltily,

"I'm being pettish, I know, and I'm sorry. But I feel as gloomy as the weather. I just wish *someone* would visit us."

"We'll attend kirk at St. Giles on Sunday," Isobel said. "You'll see nearly everyone we know in town there. And next week, Adela's supper—"

"I don't *want* to wait," Sidony said. "I want to talk to people."

Isobel shot her a shrewd look but said only, "I warrant Ealga would welcome a visit, too. You must not go alone, of course, unless you want to risk Hugo's ire again, but I'll send a pair of gillies with you if you like."

Sidony nearly said she did not want to go but held her tongue, not only because she did not like the tone of the thoughts in her own head but because it had dawned on her that Lady Clendenen had an ear for gossip and always knew what everyone in her extensive orbit was doing.

Accordingly, she summoned a smile and said, "'Tis an excellent idea. I cannot remember when I've let a mood overset me like this one, but with her ladyship, I shall have to behave. Pray, forgive me for being so beastly, Isobel."

"Aye, sure," Isobel said with a chuckle. "And when you see Ealga, be sure to ask her where all our menfolk have hidden themselves."

Nearly certain that Isobel knew it was not *their* menfolk who had sunk her into such a mood, Sidony decided to ignore the chuckle and the look that attended it. As she went upstairs to tidy her hair, she decided that the becoming pink and gray bodice and skirt she had on was presentable enough for a visit to her ladyship.

Twenty minutes later, admitted to Lady Clendenen's private sitting room and welcomed with a warm embrace, Sidony politely let her lead the conversation until Lady

Clendenen mentioned the King's expected return to the royal burgh.

"I swore I did not care about such things," Sidony said. "But I own, madam, I quite long for amusement. Without Michael and the others in and out all the time, Sinclair House has grown dull. Poor Will is teething, too, so Isobel and I have only stolen moments now and again to talk to each other. We expected to see more of Rob and Hugo, but I expect Hugo has gone home by now and Rob . . ."

When she paused, her ladyship said, "Aye, Hugo rode home Wednesday morning, because naturally, his duties at Roslin include arranging for Isabella's journey to town. You have seen for yourself how she travels with her sheets and favorite furniture, as if she forgets how comfortable Sinclair House is. Her cavalcade is always enormous, and 'tis Hugo who sees that it travels safely."

"Did Rob go with him?" Sidony asked. "If he did and Adela stayed at home with tiny Anna, they may be feeling as dull as Isobel and I are."

Lady Clendenen shot her a look much like the one Isobel had as she said, "Rob had not gone anywhere as of this morning, nor yet that charming friend of his, Sir Giffard MacLennan. Rob is furbishing him up to join us all at court. Sir Giffard cannot have brought much baggage, riding here from Galloway as he did."

"No," Sidony agreed. "Mayhap they will be at St. Giles on Sunday."

"Oh, I doubt that," her ladyship said. "Sithee, my waiting woman's niece is in service at Lestalric, and she told my woman that Rob and Giff mean to ride to Roslin later this afternoon, doubtless to assist Hugo. She said they would return tomorrow evening, but I think that is most unlikely, because Isabella likes a large retinue, as much for safety as to display her consequence. If she asks them to stay until she leaves, I expect they will do so."

"Do you know yet just when she comes to town?"

"On Wednesday, I believe."

That life could remain dull for five more days gave Sidony an urge to revert to a childish display of temper, but she managed to suppress it. Taking fond leave of her hostess an hour later, she returned to Sinclair House.

Several ideas occurred to her on the way, none of which would appeal to Sir Hugo, and only one of which she dared hope might appeal to Isobel.

At Sinclair House, she found her sister looking worn out and unsuccessfully trying to comfort her son, who was loudly suffering the discomfort of his teething.

Sidony said, "I'll take him for a time, dearling. You'll come to Aunt Sidony, won't you, Will?" When she held out her arms, the baby tumbled into them and curled tight, shoving his fist into his mouth. "You see?" she said. "Go and rest."

"I'm glad you're back," Isobel said gratefully. "He's been crying almost since you left, and wants nothing to do with his nurse. But he'll always go to you."

Sidony could not boast that she comforted Will, but she walked with him and crooned as he whimpered and sucked his fist. All the while, her thoughts were busy, rejecting one plan after another to devise some amusement for herself. She could not ignore the frequently intruding image of Sir Giffard MacLennan, or that each time it appeared she felt the imprint of his lips on hers again, but she assured herself that she had little interest in the man. She just wanted something more interesting to think about than dealing with teething babies or feminine wardrobes.

Waiting until Will had fallen asleep from sheer exhaustion and Isobel had had time to relax, have her supper, and enjoy a goblet of claret, Sidony said as they rose from the table, "We need a respite, my dear. What would you think about riding to Hawthornden tomorrow morning, to visit Sorcha? I was thinking—"

"Sakes, you weren't thinking at all," Isobel said. "You cannot imagine I'd leave Will when he's feeling so poorly. It is not like you to be so thoughtless."

"I know, and I'm sorry," Sidony said, suppressing a huge surge of guilt. "But much as I love you and Will, and little though I understand it myself, I have been feeling like a captive for days, and I need to breathe. Surely, you understand that. Don't you remember how you used to fly off on a horse after only a day's rain at Chalamine, or two of company? Moreover, I've thought it all out. We can take him with us. You know he likes to ride with us, and it will take his mind off his teeth."

"It is six miles to Hawthornden," Isobel said. "That is too far."

"He'll sleep most of the way."

"Even if he does, he won't sleep coming back, and if we stay overnight with Sorcha, we'll have to stay till Monday, because she and Hugo always attend the services at Roslin, and Isabella would expect us to do so as well."

"I did not think of that," Sidony admitted. "But, with Michael away, even if we did have to stay, we'd have no urgent reason to return sooner. Adela's supper is not until Tuesday, and Sorcha won't mind having us there. Nor will Hugo."

"Oh, yes, they would," Isobel said. "Recall that they have no children of their own yet and that Hawthornden is not nearly as large as Roslin or even Sinclair House. Do you imagine either of them will like hearing Will scream with pain all night, as he has these past two? We'd have to take his nurse, too, and she does *not* look on riding as exercise but as penance for one's sins," she added as a clincher.

An impulse stirred to apologize again and do whatever Isobel asked of her, but Sidony looked at her own hands, clasped in her lap, and said nothing.

"Now I'm the one being beastly," Isobel said. "I should not press you to do more than you like, and I *do* do that—often. I know you'd rather be home in the Highlands, and I know I should not depend on you as much as I do to look after Will. Sakes, you should be enjoying your time here, not playing nurse to my son."

Sidony bit her lip hard to stop herself from saying she hadn't meant a word of it. Never before had she ignored a plea from any of her sisters, and if anyone had asked where she found strength to do so now, or demanded to know what demon had possessed her, she could not have explained.

"You won't want to go to Hawthornden alone," Isobel went on. "But you may take the two lads and ride to Lestalric to visit Adela and Rob. I warrant you do need time away from here, so spend the day if you like. Will may be much better by then, and if he is not, Nurse will do all she can to help me. After all, many mothers look after their children without the aid of nurses *or* sisters, do they not?"

Again, Sidony nearly yielded to her better self. But she knew that if she did, she would not find the strength—not for a long time—to try again to do something just for herself. Nevertheless, she said, "Art sure, Isobel? Truly?"

"Aye, dearest, I'm sure," Isobel said with her usual warm smile.

If Will cried that night, Sidony did not hear him, and all was still quiet the next morning when she put on her moss-green riding dress, took a roll from the kitchen to break her fast, and went to the stable to order her favorite horse saddled.

The two gillies, trained by the imperious countess, her daughters-in-law, and her generally amiable sons not to question any unusual doings of the Sinclair House ladies, saddled horses for themselves when she asked them to and followed her.

She hesitated only for a moment at the entrance to the Canongate. After a glance to the east, and with thanks that Isobel's bedchamber did not overlook the road, she turned toward St. Giles and was soon on her way out of town. After all, Isobel had not forbidden her to go south but had only assumed that she would not.

She maintained a good pace as they crossed the river plain and rode toward the hills beyond it. Enough wool carts, sheep, and ordinary travelers were on the road to ease any fear she might have had that her escort was too small. That was a point Hugo would certainly raise if she were so unfortunate as to meet him. It was an unlikely prospect, though, if he was at Roslin preparing for Isabella's journey.

It occurred to her only then that Sorcha was as unlikely to be at Hawthornden as Hugo was. Since the castle lay just a mile from Roslin, Isabella would doubtless expect Sorcha's help as well as his. Nevertheless, Sidony rode on.

She felt delightfully free, if still a little guilt ridden. The sisters who had gone before her had all put their own wishes above anyone else's at times, but she had rarely done so. Surely, she told herself, it could not be such a sin, just this once, for her to do exactly what she wanted to do without counting the cost.

Half an hour later, they came to the road following the east bank of the river North Esk and began the uphill climb to the eastern rim of Roslin Gorge. Not long afterward, they met a small party of Hugo's men-at-arms. But, recognizing her as a member of the family, they made no objection to her riding on.

Giff had spent a portion of each of the previous three days humoring Rob's resolve to outfit him for an appearance at the royal court. He suspected Rob thought they would attend often until they moved the *Lia Fail*—if their Stone was truly the real one, an assumption that Giff remained unwilling to make before seeing it.

Rob had also accompanied him to Leith Harbor to see if any of the many ships harbored there might answer Giff's requirements and be available for purchase or hire. Rob assured him that cost was not a consideration, and although they had certainly not seen all of them, Giff had seen more than one that might do.

Even so, without knowing his cargo, he felt ill prepared to judge their merits with any degree of certainty. As a result, the two had set out late the previous afternoon for Roslin, learning upon their arrival that Hugo had set guards all along the river gorge to deter unwanted visitors until Isabella had made her departure.

"'Tis as good an excuse as we'll find to post so many guards," Hugo said. "With Fife in town, as he is, we haven't seen much of his men lately, anyway, but I've heard he means to travel north soon, doubtless to annoy Henry."

"As long as he stays out of my way as I sail to the west, I'll see that as a good thing," Rob said.

"Aye," Hugo agreed. "But you'll want to keep an eye out for him as you go. And if that fine new ship of his is sitting in Sinclair Bay when you get there, you're to go straight on without stopping at Girnigoe."

"Is Fife's new ship harbored at Leith?" Giff asked. "What is it like?"

Hugo shrugged. "'Tis something of a mixture of galley and merchantman. Doubtless it is not much good as either—or so we may hope if you run into it."

"Aye," Giff said. "I'd prefer a swift western galley, myself, but as our cargo is unlikely to be small enough to be easily concealed—"

"You'll soon be able to judge for yourself what you'll need," Hugo said.

Thus did he find himself midway through Saturday morning, standing with Hugo and Rob before a tall rock slab in a heavily wooded wedge-shaped glen of the sort that Borderers called a *cleuch*.

Without a word, Rob slid a hand down the near edge of the slab, lingered at the bottom for a moment, then stood, grabbed the edge with both hands, and pulled.

The slab moved, revealing an opening large enough for a man to stand in.

"This way," Rob said as Hugo handed him a lighted torch and turned to ease the huge rock slab shut behind them.

Accustomed to the open sea, Giff strongly disliked enclosed places. But as daylight disappeared, leaving only the flickering torch, rampant curiosity overcame his discomfort as he and Hugo followed Rob along the passageway.

It twisted and turned. The torch flickered wildly as Rob

strode, and Giff realized that the ground beneath them was unusually flat and free of obstacles.

Rob's broad shoulders blocked most of the view ahead, but he stopped at last, held the torch higher, and said, "There, Giff, just yonder."

Realizing the passage had opened to a wider chamber, Giff moved to stand beside him. A chill touched him as he looked in awe at the object Rob indicated.

"Bless my soul," he murmured.

Chapter 6

Giff felt instinctively if not yet logically that he was staring at *Lia Fail*, Scotland's true Coronation Stone.

For one thing, it looked important. It was dark in color, of polished black marble or basalt, and it stood as high as his knees. A foot and a half deep, nearly a yard wide, skillfully carved and gilded, with designs that gleamed eerily in the torchlight, the main block rested on feet that resembled an eagle's talons, but the front corners looked more like legs of a reptile, mayhap those of a lizard.

"Looks devilish heavy," he said, bending to touch it. At the last minute, he hesitated, but when neither Hugo nor Rob objected, he caught hold of an edge with both hands and tried to shift it. "Faith, it weighs a ton."

"Less than a quarter ton, I'd wager," Rob said. "I'm thinking six men can carry it out of here. If those pairs of crook-shaped hooks fixed to each side are as sturdy as they look, they'll easily accommodate two stout poles for transport."

"We've had some cut for the purpose," Hugo said.

"You're certain it's the true Stone of Destiny, then," Giff said, squatting for a closer look. With few doubts now of its authenticity, he stroked the smooth stone, fingering what looked like a footprint carved on the seat, imagining ancient kings about to be crowned, admiring it with much the same sense of awe as he felt.

"Henry said it looks like the Stone depicted in wax seals on ancient charters," Hugo said. "Later ones show a taller throne with the king's feet on a stool. Henry said that's how it must have looked when they began to set the Stone under the chair. He thinks Edward carted off the wrong one only because folks hadn't seen the real one for years. Also, Rob and I heard the tale of its rescue from one we ken fine we can trust."

Still squatting on his heels, Giff said, "Are you going to tell me who it was?"

He had assumed that Hugo would take the lead in everything to do with the Stone, but it was Rob who said, "You'll agree to undertake the job?"

"I will," Giff said. Sakes, he would fight anyone who tried to stop him. "I can do it," he added. "I don't know anyone I'd trust more to protect it."

"Then I expect he should know as much as we can tell him," Rob said to Hugo. "He'll be risking his life, after all, as well as the Stone."

"'Tis your right to decide how much we tell him," Hugo said. "You're the lad who loves secrets and thus the least likely to reveal too much."

Turning back to Giff, Rob said, "The Abbot of Holyrood told me that when news reached Scone Abbey in 1296 that Edward of England meant to take the Stone to England, the Abbot of Scone applied to the Abbot of Holyrood, who at that time was a priest from Lestalric. He agreed to keep the Stone safe if they could deliver it to him before Edward reached Lothian. Holyrood's present abbot served as baillie to our man when England's third Edward threatened Scotland again in 1329. The two priests went to the Bruce, told him of the Stone's presence at Holyrood, and asked him what they should do. The English had already sacked Melrose Abbey, and everyone believed they'd do the same to Holyrood, so Bruce recommended that they confide their problem to a pair of his closest comrades who were Templars."

"If Lestalric contributed the abbot, may one be forgiven for asking if one or both of those men enjoyed a similar connection to your branch of the family?"

With visible reluctance, Rob said, "Aye, my great grandfather, Sir Robert Logan. He was one of those who attempted to carry Bruce's heart to the Holy Land after he died, and died on the way himself. However, he'd passed the details to his son—my grandfather—before he left, and my grandfather passed them on to me."

Giff frowned before saying evenly, "Two other great names are associated with that same mission, others who also died in Spain."

"Aye, the good Sir James Douglas and Sir William Sinclair."

"I won't ask who the other confidant was, for I suspect it is not your secret to tell, but I trust you will forgive me if I make a guess," Giff said.

"The important thing now is to move the Stone beyond Fife's reach."

"Since he suspects the Sinclairs and is already plotting to annoy Henry, I'm thinking you don't want me to take it to Girnigoe or Orkney, so where do you imagine it will be safe? The only man I can think of who is powerful enough to keep it out of Fife's hands is the Lord of the Isles."

"Nay, it must not go to Donald," Hugo said.

"Where, then?"

"To a man known for his trustworthiness, who is also a member of the Order," Hugo said. "You will take the Stone to Ranald of the Isles."

Giff frowned. "I ken fine that Ranald enjoys such a reputation, but you must know that Ranald's loyalty is to his younger half brother. He supported Donald's claim to become second Lord of the Isles when nearly every chief in the Lordship wanted Ranald to claim it for himself."

"He supported Donald because his father willed it so," Hugo said. "But Donald is not a member of our Order. Moreover, he is grandson to the King of Scots and Fife's nephew. The first Lord of the Isles knew of our Order and its purpose. He supported both and strongly recommended against telling Donald, claiming it was not right to burden him with a secret he might feel bound to share with his maternal grandfather. Ranald's mother being a Macruari rather than a Stewart, Ranald does not share that connection to the King or to Fife."

"We can discuss this more when Michael returns," Rob said. "He went to Eigg a fortnight ago to talk to Ranald. But I think we should go now, for I don't like lingering here. Someone may see our lads at the opening of the *cleuch* and wonder if they are really just fishing."

"Have you seen enough, Giff?" Hugo asked.

"Aye," Giff said. "Do you have a plan for getting it out of the gorge?"

"We have several plans, depending on when you can sail. What we need to know is if you anticipate any difficulty loading it onto a ship."

"If you can get it to the ship without a tail of Fife's lads following you, I can get it loaded," Giff said. "I'm thinking we'll want a harbor other than Leith, though, especially if Fife's ship is still harbored there when we're ready to move."

"We'll have a better idea about all that when we find a ship and hear what Michael learns from Ranald," Rob said, clearly impatient to be out of the cavern.

They went back the way they had come, replacing the stone slab and brushing dirt and leaves in front of its base to conceal its presence.

Returning along the narrow creek bed that had brought them to the head of the *cleuch,* they emerged into the river gorge, where the men Hugo had set to watch for trouble put away their fishing gear and mounted their horses.

"Any sign of visitors?" Rob asked them as he swung himself onto his saddle.

"None, my lord," their leader replied. "Leastways, none o' the sort ye'll be meaning. Just one o' their young ladyships riding along the ridge."

"Sakes," Giff said. "How could you tell from here who it was?"

"Beg pardon, sir, but our lads be a-watching the track and wouldna let any other lass through. Ye can see her for yourself, though, yonder." The man pointed.

From where they were on the west bank of the turbulent North Esk, Giff could see the rider nearing Hawthornden Castle from the north on the high, sheer cliff across the river. His distance vision was excellent, and he easily recognized her.

When Hugo uttered a curse, Rob said, "Surely, that is not Sorcha?"

"Nay, she's at Roslin," Hugo said. "But that lass rides

on a man's saddle, as they do, so it is Sidony. What the devil is she doing, riding all this way by herself?"

"Likely, she meant to visit you and Sorcha at Hawthornden," Rob said. "When she learns that neither of you is there, she'll ride on to Roslin."

"If my steward lets her leave without adding more men to her escort, I'll have things to say to him that he won't want to hear," Hugo growled. "Let's go."

Giff was watching the rider, who rode as well as any man he had ever watched on a horse. Turning her head just then, she looked down at them and seemed to check briefly before riding on. Having met Lady Isobel at Clendenen House, Rob's lady at Lestalric, and Hugo's at Hawthornden the previous evening, he knew that at least three of her sisters were very like her in appearance.

Nonetheless, he recognized Sidony easily.

Noting that the other two had mounted, he did so quickly and followed them, wondering what Hugo meant to do. But by the time they reached Roslin, he realized that Hugo's duties there would prevent his leaving for at least another hour.

As the others dismounted, Giff said casually, "As we've still hours left of daylight, I think I'll head back now. The sooner I can find a ship, the better."

Rob favored him with a look of sleepy amusement, but Hugo already had his mind on duties that lay ahead of him, for he said only, "'Tis a good notion. We can discuss all the other details more sensibly once we've assured transport."

Giff left them at once, crossing the narrow land bridge that separated Roslin from the hillside and ridgetop to the east.

The north River Esk flowed in a sharp curve nearly all

the way around the base of Roslin Castle's high promontory, so that to reach its west bank, one rode down the steep slope to the arched stone bridge that crossed it. To follow the river's east bank, one used the higher, more-traveled track along the eastern ridgetop.

Giff chose that route and urged his mount to speed.

Sidony had seen the men down in the river gorge and had easily recognized Hugo and Rob—and Giff MacLennan—by the way each moved. She had checked at the sight of Hugo, but her curiosity stirred, especially as it had seemed at first as if the three had stepped forth from the very wall of the gorge.

To be sure, there was dense shrubbery, an astonishing number of trees, a dip in the clifftop, and a burn spilling across the track into the river North Esk, so one could easily imagine the existence of a wee glen or cut there, or even a waterfall.

Discovering at Hawthornden that Sorcha was indeed spending the day at Roslin, she declined the steward's invitation to await her return. Asked if she meant to ride on to Roslin but having no wish to cast herself in Hugo's path, she said lightly that she would come again another day.

"Sithee, I wanted an excuse to give my pony some good exercise, but I promised the lady Isobel I would return to Sinclair House by suppertime."

"Aye, sure, my lady. I'll just fetch a few of our men to ride back with you."

"Thank you, but I don't need them," she said. "I have my own."

The steward eyed the two young gillies askance. "Begging your pardon, your ladyship, but you should have an escort more suited to your consequence. Sir Hugo would be gey wroth wi' me an I let you go with just that callow pair."

Biting her lip, Sidony stayed at the gate until the steward disappeared into the stable against the inside north wall. But as soon as he was out of sight, she said, "We'll go now. If he wants to send men after us, he will do so, but I have no intention of sitting here whilst they all saddle their horses."

The two lads glanced at each other but made no objection, which pleased her. This new sense of freedom was heady, and she decided that she approved of people who did exactly as she bade them.

She knew Hugo had seen her. Faith, all three men had seen her, but until she had spoken to the steward, she had indulged in the hope that Hugo might think she was Sorcha and voice no objection to her riding on the ridge track. Knowing now that he would think nothing of the sort, she wanted to return to town with all speed.

Urging her mount to a brisk pace, she maintained it until the slope of the track began steeply to descend. Then, aware that all three horses were tired, she slowed, noting as she did that her two companions looked relieved.

A moment later, one of them said, "Beg pardon, m'lady, but there be riders coming up quick ahind us. I reckon they'll be the lot from Hawthornden."

Affecting an air of indifference that she did not feel, she said, "They may come with us if they like. I have naught to say about what they do or do not do."

It took every grain of resolution, however, not to look over her shoulder, although she knew that no Hawthornden man-at-arms would dare to scold her. And thanks to

Isabella's still being at Roslin, Hugo would not be with them.

Even if he had ignored Isabella's presence, Sidony told herself, he could not have ridden to Roslin and on to Hawthornden in time to join the riders behind her. Nor would he come after her to order her home when she was going anyway. But her ride from town had taken over two hours, and it would take as long to return. So if he did come after her, he could still catch her before she reached Sinclair House.

She could hear hoofbeats behind her now, and continuing to face forward became more difficult, but she did not want the men following to think she feared them. She was a Macleod of Glenelg, doing what she wanted to do, and they had no right to stop her.

She had simply taken exercise, had chosen to ride outside of the royal burgh, with an escort, on a road she knew well, in sight of other travelers. To be sure, there were none on the track along the river, but it was Sinclair land. She was quite safe.

"How close are they?" she asked the nearest gillie minutes later when the hoofbeats seemed no nearer.

"They've slowed, your ladyship. I'm thinking they mean to hang back."

"We'll see, shall we? Let us slow down a little and see what they do."

The riders behind slowed as well, and thus reassured, she reined her mount to a walk, to rest it again. If Hugo was coming, he would come, and if he wanted to scold her again, he would do it whether she was on the road when he found her or at Sinclair House. Another scolding was nothing to make a song about.

With that realization, the sense of freedom she had enjoyed earlier renewed itself. Really, it was quite easy when one knew how to manage one's thoughts.

She indulged that satisfying assumption for some twenty minutes before a familiar, curt voice much too close to her abruptly disabused her of it.

Having paused at Hawthornden only long enough to learn that the lady Sidony, upon discovering that her sister was not at home, had turned round and headed back to town, Giff had pressed on. He was not as interested in the steward's rambling disapproval of her ladyship's personal escort as he was in learning what had stirred her to make such a journey in the first place.

Clearly, she had not come to warn of some calamity at Sinclair House. Hugo had not even considered that possibility, and rightly so. Lady Sidony would not have been the messenger to carry such news. A lad riding the fastest horse the Sinclair House stable could produce would have carried it.

As he rode, he found himself wondering about his increasing interest in the lass. Little more than impulse had sent him careering after her, but it was an obvious opportunity to learn more about her. That furthering their acquaintance would irk Hugo provided some added incentive. That by pursuing her now he might enjoy a full hour's private converse with her, provided more.

In general, finding even scant moments of privacy with a young lady was awkward, as trammeled about with concerned kinsmen as most of them were. And certainly, Lady Sidony Macleod possessed a host of concerned kinfolk. To be sure, Rob's apparent recognition of his intent had produced only amusement, but Hugo would fume, and Giff decided it would amuse him to get another rise out of Hugo.

Ten minutes later, he saw riders ahead and muttered a curse, remembering Hugo's confidence in his steward and the steward's fretting over her escort. The last thing Giff wanted was half a dozen men-at-arms who reported to Hugo watching his every move and straining to hear every word while he chatted with her ladyship.

Accordingly, he fell in alongside the group leader.

Noting with approval that Lady Sidony and her two lads were far enough ahead not to hear him, he said cheerfully, "Good day again. Doubtless, you recall seeing me with Sir Hugo and Lestalric this morning, do you not?"

"Aye, Sir Giffard," the leader acknowledged with a friendly nod. "I recall your presence well."

"Then you shall have cause to thank me, too, because I mean to relieve you of your duty to her ladyship. I am riding to Sinclair House and will see her safely restored to the lady Isobel. Her two lads and I will be sufficient escort for the main road, which, as we can see, lies little more than a half mile ahead."

"Aye, sir, but Sir Hugo might expect us to go all the way to town wi' her."

"You may present Sir Hugo with my compliments and tell him I commanded you to obey me," Giff said with a smile. "He has known me from my childhood and will readily cast all blame on me. Sithee, we trained together as knights."

The man nodded. "I did hear that, sir."

"Then there is no more to be said."

The leader hesitated, but when Giff spurred his mount

forward, it was with satisfaction that he heard the other order his men to turn back.

He had noticed that each of the lads with her ladyship glanced frequently over a shoulder but that she did not, so either she was hard of hearing or determined to show no interest in who rode behind her. If she was afraid of Hugo coming after her in a temper, surely she'd have looked back to see if he had.

The two young gillies rode just behind her.

When Giff caught up to them, he said in the tone that customarily gained him instant obedience, "Fall well back, lads. I would speak privately with her ladyship."

Neither questioned his right to be private with her. Although he had expected as much in issuing the order, it confirmed his judgment as to the value of the two as protection for her. Hugo had been right to be annoyed.

He saw her stiffen and knew she had heard his command to the gillies, but she continued to stare straight ahead. The only sign she gave that she was aware of his presence was to lift her chin higher.

Composing his features into a mask of sternness, he urged his pony alongside hers and said, "What manner of madness is this, my lass?"

Still staring straight ahead, she said, "I am no such connection to you."

"And a good thing it is for you that you are not," he said.

She bit her lower lip, but he could not tell whether she did so because she realized she was escaping deserved retribution or to suppress a smile.

"What demon possessed you to do such a thing, and so soon after your escapade in the abbey woods? You must know that you've angered Hugo."

"Sakes," she said, turning to look at him, "do you think to scold me? You have no right to do so, and I shan't listen to a word of it."

"There is no reason that you should," he acknowledged. "But you cannot blame me for being curious about this. Do you frequently invite Hugo's wrath?"

"I don't care a fig for Hugo *or* his wrath," she said, raising her chin higher.

"Well said, but take care, lass. If it comes on to rain with your nose tilted so high, you may drown before you know it."

She turned away, biting her lip again. But this time he had no doubt as to the reason, because a gurgle of laughter escaped as she did.

"That's better," he said. "But I prefer it when you look at me."

She did, and her lips twitched irresistibly as she fought to suppress a smile.

"Why *did* you ride all this way today?"

She hesitated, and he saw that dignified words hovered on her tongue, but then she licked her lips, met his gaze, and said, "To see you."

Sidony could not believe she had said the words she was thinking rather than the carefully planned words she had meant to produce for him. The truth had spilled out without permission, as if the demon he had mentioned earlier had taken control of her tongue.

Heat flooded her cheeks, and no wonder. What he must think of her! So forward, so unladylike—not that he was at all gentlemanly. An image of Countess Isabella stirred in her mind, and she squeezed her eyes shut at the sight, which only made Isabella's presence loom larger within.

Sidony's eyes flew open to see him grinning at her.

Relaxing, she said with a sigh, "I don't know what induced me to say that."

"Mayhap you merely spoke the truth."

"What arrogance!" She looked behind her at last then and saw with relief that the Hawthornden men had gone, and her lads were too far back to hear them.

"Did you send those other men away?"

"I did."

"But they are Hugo's men. Why would they obey you?"

"Men generally do obey me when I give an order. 'Tis a required skill for the captain of a boat." Mischievously, he added, "Only women flout such commands."

"But *why* did you send them back?" she asked, determined not to flirt with him—not, at any event, before he answered her questions.

"Honesty deserves honesty," he said. "I wanted to speak privately with you, and I feared they would persist in riding close enough to overhear us, and would report every word back to Hugo."

"He'll be as wroth with you as he will be with me, you know," she said.

"Worse," he said.

"I keep thinking that any sensible person must fear a man who had knocked him down, but you clearly don't fear Hugo."

"I don't think you do, either," he said.

"Well, no, although I do not like him to be angry. But I doubt he'd strike me, and even if I were somehow to infuriate him to such a course, he would not do me any real harm. The only person who might punish me severely is not in Lothian."

"You must mean your father."

"Aye, for he can be fierce, but his true wrath was always reserved for Sorcha or Isobel. They did try his temper, but I can recall his striking me only once, when I sauced him. Usually, he pays me no heed, and most of the time, Hugo is the same."

"I noticed that, but I find it hard to credit," he said. "When you slipped out into the garden the other night, I expected him to notice straightaway. I did."

She shrugged. "It is always like that for me, with everyone."

"Why?"

She hesitated, wondering if she knew the answer.

"Well?"

She looked at him. "I'm thinking. It is not a question I can answer without thinking a little first, so you must be patient."

"I am never patient. That is the first thing most people learn about me."

"Then you should practice to be more so," she said.

"I am being very patient right now," he said.

She looked at him, saw the truth, and said, "I cannot put it better than to say it's as if they stop seeing me. I don't understand it myself, but I expect it is because I tend to be quiet when others are about. My sisters are all more outspoken. Even the two who are not fractious are strong-minded, and they all speak their minds. I've learned from childhood that if I keep silent, I am less likely to draw their anger or become embroiled in their disagreements."

"Do they have many disagreements?"

"Not now that everyone is grown," she said. "And everyone else is married, too, except me. Before, someone was always telling me what to do, what to think, and what to say. They are all very kind, but when one has six elder sisters, unless one is cursed with a combative nature, one soon stops asserting oneself. I quit trying to do things my own way years ago. Until today," she added with a quick smile.

"I suspect you decided to make that change the day we met," he said.

"Oh, no, for I did not make any decision then. The whole notion simply presented itself—to walk in the woods, that is—and I made no objection."

"But today you made a decision?" He sounded amused, and it rankled.

Still, he was the only man she had ever met who'd expressed a desire to know what she thought, and she wanted to be honest with him.

Accordingly, she tried to explain. "I don't really ever make decisions," she said. "I expect I tried to when I was small, but others always changed them for me, so I fell out of the habit."

"I see."

She looked more closely at him to see if she could tell what he was thinking.

"Faith, you are laughing at me," she said, feeling a surge of disappointment greater and more painful than she had ever felt with anyone before. Turning to look straight ahead again, she said in a rigidly controlled voice, "The main road lies just yonder, sir. It won't be too much longer now."

Chapter 7

Giff's amusement vanished in a flood of remorse. He felt as if he had kicked a puppy—or as he was sure he would feel were he ever so cruel as to kick one. If Hugo did knock him on his backside again, it would be less than he deserved.

So forlorn did she look that he had to bite his tongue to keep from assuring her at once that he had not been laughing at her. But her honesty with him made him want to be equally honest. He doubted that she would accept less from him, and he knew she would not believe a flat denial even if it were the truth.

It certainly was not true. The notion of any woman believing she could not make a decision definitely amused him. Sakes, but they made them all day long and raised an unholy ruckus if a man overrode even one. He had seen that for himself many times since his childhood. His own mother and sisters were prime examples.

Highland women were neither submissive nor particularly biddable. Even female Borderers were more so. And heaven knew that compared to Border lasses, English and French women were as anxious sheep scurrying to obey nipping dogs.

As he continued to watch her rigid little face with its stubbornly jutting chin, he could not doubt he had upset her, but she continued to ride as easily as before, her mount clearly unaware of her emotional turmoil. Her willowy body, softly and beautifully padded in all the right places, moved easily with the horse's motion, and her slim, gloved hands, though gripping the reins firmly, employed them lightly.

His remorse eased, and he had begun to enjoy just watching her when he heard a catch in her breathing and noted a tear welling in the only eye he could see.

Reaching out to touch her arm, he said quietly, "Don't, lassie. I'm a beast to have made you feel so. I'll admit that your words amused me, because I have never met a woman who could not make decisions, or one who would admit such a thing if it were true. But I do believe you speak the truth as you know it. As I think about that," he added, "I wonder what it must feel like, always to do what others bid you and never to decide for yourself what you will do."

"It doesn't feel like anything," she muttered, making no move to keep the tear from spilling down her cheek. "It is just how it is. It is not difficult, you know."

"But what if two people press you to do different things?"

She shrugged. "That rarely has happened. Sorcha is the one closest to me in age, and she and I were nearly always together before she married Sir Hugo. She produced thoughts and decisions aplenty for the two of us. Adela, too, was still at home then, and she usually issued commands to both of us because we always did things together. If Sorcha did not want to obey, we didn't. And if Adela complained to our father, he usually punished Sorcha more severely than me."

"So there are benefits, too," he murmured provocatively.

As he had hoped, she looked at him then, even brushed the tear away.

"I told you it was not difficult," she said. "But perhaps you understand now why the others tend not to think of me much even when I am by myself. They only think of me when they would like me to do something. The rest of the time, they assume I am doing whatever they've told me to do."

He nodded, realizing that was possible, at least where her sisters were concerned. But it was still hard for him to imagine how any man could be in her presence without fixing his attention on her to the exclusion of everything else.

They had turned onto the main road to Edinburgh and increased their pace on the firmer surface before he returned to a detail that had puzzled him earlier.

"Surely the lady Isobel must know as well as you do that your riding alone for such a distance would annoy Hugo. I'm surprised that she allowed it."

Unmistakable guilt turned her face crimson, telling him plainly that Lady Isobel was unaware of what she had done.

Instead of replying to his remark, however, she turned, looked straight at him, and said, "Why were you and the others so far down the gorge? I thought everyone would be helping the countess prepare for her journey to town."

"Everyone does seem much involved in that," he admitted, deciding to allow her a change of subject, albeit not to one that would include a discussion of his activities. "In troth, I see little need for such concern. She is a countess in her own right accustomed to a retinue and outriders to match her vast power. But this journey is no more than eight or ten miles. It seems much ado for such a short distance."

"Aye, sure, but you have not seen yet how she travels," she said with a smile.

He was glad to see it, for it had been absent too long. "How does she travel?"

"With so many of her own goods and furniture that if she were anyone else, one would think she must be removing all she owned to a new house."

He looked to see if she could be jesting, but she was sincere. "Why would she do such a thing?" he demanded. "Surely, Prince Henry keeps Sinclair House well maintained and finely furnished."

She chuckled. "It is magnificent, but she likes her own sheets and the table that stands by her bed at Roslin, and numerous other items. I will say she is making a gift to Adela and Rob of a wonderful inlaid coffer that Rob covets for Lestalric. Also, Lady Clendenen says she is bringing other items to give to the abbey."

"It sounds as if her progress will provide a sight worth seeing," he said.

"Aye, sure, it always does," she agreed. "But you still have not said what the three of you were doing in the gorge."

"We were attending to some business of Hugo's," he said glibly. "I left him and Rob at Roslin, seeing to more of the same."

"Adela will be disappointed that Rob is not returning with you."

"Nay she won't, for he returns tonight. Sithee, he is going to help me find a ship," he added, certain such news ought to divert her from her interest in the gorge.

"Why do you want a ship?"

"'Tis the primary reason I came here," he said. "I'm a boatman by both interest and training. When I find the one I want, I'll sail her home to the west."

"Oh."

He saw that he had disappointed her again but felt no remorse this time. His business, especially his present business, was none of hers.

Sidony rallied quickly, and as their conversation continued casually with intermittent periods of easy silence, her thoughts focused more and more on her companion and her own unpredictable reactions to him.

How, for example, she wondered, had she dared to question his business in the gorge, let alone Hugo's and Rob's? Admittedly, her knowledge of men was sadly limited, but if she knew anything about the creatures, she knew they did not like discussing their business affairs with women. Heaven knew, if one wanted to pitch her father into a rage, one had only to question his actions in *any* regard.

But she wanted to ask Giff why he had not mentioned before that he wanted a ship and seemed so eager now to leave Edinburgh. As that thought occurred to her, another followed. Until just days ago, she would have accepted any opportunity herself to do the same, to return home to the Highlands.

Stifling a sigh, uncertain if it was for herself or because

of his impending departure, she realized he was pointing out the royal burgh in the distance.

Vowing to enjoy what time remained of their illicit ride, she said lightly, "You know, sir, thanks to Lady Clendenen's habit of talking more than she listens, and the ease with which new topics divert her, you still have not told us where in Kintail your home lies. Do you mean to keep that a secret?"

"Nay," he said, with a smile that warmed her all through. "I own, though, I don't seem to think of it so much as home these days, which may be why it is easy to let the subject pass without comment whenever possible."

"But where is it?"

"Duncraig."

"Oh, then I do know it," she said, remembering a formidable dark gray stone curtain wall that looked as if it were an extension of the high seagirt cliff on which it sat. "It sits atop the Kintail coastal cliffs north of Kyle Akin, does it not? Faith, it is as imposing as Dunstaffnage, only higher up and perhaps not as big."

"My father would approve of that description," he said. "He likes to think that Duncraig is impregnable."

"Faith, I should imagine it must be."

"It has suffered its share of attackers, as most of its ilk have. But if we are now to answer unanswered questions, suppose you tell me if Lady Isobel does know where you have been today. I'd hate to reveal something I should not."

With guilty embarrassment, she said, "She does know I rode out of town, because she suggested that I ride to Lestalric to visit Adela. I'd thought I would, too, but then I went the other way. So although I never said I would go to Lestalric, I do know she assumes that I did. I would have told her the truth on my return, though," she added quickly, "even without knowing that Hugo will tell her."

"If you'll accept my advice, tell her at once, before you say something that lets her learn the truth without the benefit of your having confessed it to her first."

She nodded, intending to do just that. But when they arrived at Sinclair House, they discovered that Isobel was not at all concerned about Sidony's activities, because Sir Michael Sinclair had returned home.

If he was surprised to see Giff with Sidony, he did not show it but stepped forward at once with a delighted smile to shake his hand.

Giff greeted Michael with equal pleasure, for he liked him very much and had not seen him for several years. When the two had shaken hands, a beaming Lady Isobel tucked her hand into the crook of her husband's arm.

"How very kind you are to escort Sidony home, Sir Giffard," she said. "I trust you enjoyed a pleasant ride."

"We did, my lady," he said, relieved that she had not mentioned her certain belief that they had come from Lestalric. "But you cannot want to hear about us with Sir Michael so recently home. You must be wishing me on my way again."

"No, indeed, for my eager husband neglected to feed himself on the road and has ridden all the way from Glasgow with only his breakfast to sustain him. So we mean to enjoy an early supper. If you are hungry, you must join us at the table."

He grinned, saying, "I am one who can always eat, my

lady. I shall be delighted to accept your invitation but only if you are certain you want me."

"I insist, for you will want to visit with Michael, and unless you leave now, by the time you return to Lestalric, you may find you have missed supper there."

That was true, and as he had missed the midday meal at Roslin by riding straight on to catch up with Sidony, he was very hungry. So he gratefully accepted Lady Isobel's suggestion that he refresh himself first, as well as her assurance that, since Michael had arrived only a quarter hour before them, they did not even mean to change to more suitable clothing.

"We'll take our supper just as we are," she said, leaning a little against her husband and smiling up at him when he put an arm around her.

"How is Will?" Lady Sidony asked when Isobel had released Michael and he and Giff had moved away toward the stairway.

Giff turned back, curious. She had not mentioned anyone named Will before.

"I think he is better, poor thing," Isobel said. "He has not cried as much today. I was just telling Michael about his teething difficulties when you arrived."

Stifling a grin, Giff followed his host.

Sidony watched them go, trying to think how best to make her confession. Isobel was unlikely to carp at what she had done, because Isobel had often done similar things. But Giff had made Sidony feel guilty about her deception, and there was no getting around the fact that she had certainly deceived Isobel and would continue deceiving her for as long as she let her go on believing what was untrue.

Accordingly, when Isobel precipitated the matter by asking how it was that Sir Giffard had offered to escort her home from Lestalric, she said, "We did not come from Lestalric, I'm afraid."

"No?"

"No." Now that the time had come, she found it harder than expected, so before she could lose courage, she said, "I rode to Hawthornden instead. I did not stay," she added quickly. "And I did take two of the lads, and there were travelers on the road, as well as sheep and carts, and then Sir Giffard, so I was quite safe."

"Were you?" Isobel said gently, too gently for Sidony's comfort.

She felt her face growing hot again. "I know you must be angry," she said.

"Nay, not angry, just disappointed that you would do such a thing. Was Sir Giffard at Hawthornden? Even with two gillies attending you, riding so far was not wise, dearling. But, having gone there, why did you not visit with Sorcha?"

"She was at Roslin," Sidony said. She nearly told her about seeing the men in the gorge, but since she wanted to ask what they might have been doing there and feared that the men might return while they were discussing possibilities, she did not. Instead, she said, "I knew that if I went to Roslin, I'd not get away till much later, and I did not want you to worry."

Giff and Michael rejoined them, and they enjoyed a pleasant meal, but looks passed often between the men and Sidony sensed Giff's impatience, so when Michael pushed away his trencher, his next words, though frustrating, came as no surprise:

"Let us retire to another room with this excellent claret, Giff. I want to hear about all your escapades since last we met, and I've much to tell you, too. We may be late, my love," he added, turning to his wife. "I'll bid you good night now, and you must tell Nurse that if Will wakes in the night, she should soak a twist of cloth in brogac and water for him to suck. That was my mother's remedy for teething bairns and should put him out for the night. I'll wager, in your condition, with three sleepless nights behind you, you'll more than welcome a full night's rest."

"I will, sir," she said, rising as he did and standing on tiptoe to kiss him. Then, on a note of promise, she added, "But be warned that I shall not sleep until you have come to bed, too. Do not let him keep you overlong, Sir Giffard."

"I won't, my lady."

Sidony reluctantly bade both men good night and remembered to thank Giff for escorting her home.

To her surprise, when Michael said he would escort Isobel as far as the main stairs and Sidony moved to follow them, Giff caught her arm.

Bending near so that only she could hear him, he murmured, "They won't want you yet. I hope you've told her ladyship the truth, lass, because I shall have to tell Michael I was at Roslin today. And it won't do, you know, for the two of them to be believing different tales. You're sure to fall in the soup, that road."

"I already told her," she said. "So you may say what you like to him."

"Good lass," he said, his intense gaze putting fire in her cheeks again.

She licked suddenly dry lips.

"Oh, lassie, you should not do that," he murmured, catching her close with one hand, cupping the back of her head with the other, and pressing his lips to hers.

In response, Sidony melted against him, astonished at how warm his body felt against hers and how hard it felt, too. And, this time, when his tongue slid between her lips into her mouth, she made no move to resist. Instead, she let herself savor the astonishing sensations that swept through her body.

When she licked her soft lips, Giff needed no further invitation. Nor did he give a thought to likely consequences. But he had just begun to enjoy himself, had just let one hand slip to the side of one soft breast, when his quick ears warned him that someone was coming, and he stepped quickly away from her.

"For the love of heaven, don't show that face to Michael," he muttered, turning to grab the poker and kneel by the fire.

When he looked up again, Michael was crossing the threshold and the lass had stepped nearer the table, where she toyed with a knife.

Turning now with admirable serenity, she said, "Has Isobel gone up, sir? I did not think either of you would welcome my presence straightaway."

He smiled. "She'll want you now, lassie. Why did you not shout for a gillie to attend to that, Giff?" he asked as Lady Sidony hurried from the room.

"Because I am as considerate as her ladyship is, of course," Giff said, rising. "I thought you and your lady wife would prefer some brief solitude."

"Well, we did," Michael admitted. "I'll just grab the wine jug, shall I?"

He did so, and the two of them adjourned to an anteroom off the hall that likewise boasted a fireplace, doubtless sharing its chimney with the hall fire.

"I was relieved to find you here," Michael said as he drew a table out from the wall to a spot nearer the fire and indicated that Giff should pull up a stool. Fetching another, Michael set down the jug of wine and goblets he'd brought as he added, "I know you said you'd not been in town long, but I hope you've had an opportunity to discuss everything with Hugo and Rob."

"I have and learned that I'd not come suitably prepared," Giff said. "Your message was not specific, sithee, and I was down in Galloway when I got it."

"We couldn't be specific," Michael said, pouring wine. "The matter is—"

"I do know what you want of me," Giff interjected, aware that even Sinclair House might possess too-curious ears. "May we talk freely here?"

"Aye, the doors are solid, and no one has cause to listen. Also, there are no squints here, or laird's peeks," Michael added with a reminiscent smile. "My lass listened to Hugo and me once at Roslin. Due to Henry's last renovation, which included walling off a portion of the hall to make a ladies' solar for my mother, the squint there now overlooks that solar. Discovering it, Isobel let curiosity overcome good sense. Fortunately, she no longer yields to such urges."

Giff's thoughts drifted to Sidony's possible urges, but Michael's voice swiftly recalled him when he said, "Just how much do you know?"

"Everything I need to know, I expect," Giff said. "I'm

staying at Lestalric, but I rode to Roslin with Rob yesterday, spent the night at Hawthornden with Hugo, and today the two of them took me to see my cargo."

"And?"

"If you have people you can trust to move it and load it on a ship, and if you can provide me with enough trustworthy, well-armed oarsmen to man a boat and protect it, I can get your cargo safely to Ranald on the Isle of Eigg. I assume that is still the plan if you were able to speak to him and he will take the responsibility."

"Aye, although I did not tell him yet what he will be protecting," Michael said. "I told him only that it was an item entrusted to us as Templars and that we felt the item would be safer well away from Midlothian."

"If you trust the man so, why not tell him what it is?"

Michael shrugged. "'Expect victory but calculate the dangers and prepare for miscalculation.' Sakes, we heard that or its ilk often enough at Dunclathy. Not that you ever seemed eager to heed such maxims," he added with a reminiscent gleam.

"So you don't trust him completely," Giff said, ignoring the rider.

"I do. But I don't trust circumstance, so I did not tell him everything. Now, as to well-armed oarsmen for your ship, do you not have your own lads?"

"Recall that I rode to Edinburgh from Galloway. If I have to return for the *Storm Lass* and my crew, I cannot be back for at least a fortnight, mayhap as long as a month if weather in the north proves uncooperative."

"That won't do then."

"Nay, and although some Sinclair ships may be closer, Rob thinks they are too well known, although I'd wager we could disguise any ship or galley if we set our minds to the task. It requires only a change of banner or sail for most longboats, although newer ones do tend to display notable variations of design."

"Is that an insurmountable problem?"

"Irritating, perhaps, not insurmountable," Giff said with a smile. "You sent for me, so I presume you will not cavil too much at my methods."

"I need not tell you that we want to do the thing quietly. We had first thought to use well-armed Sinclair ships to transport it but realized we might as well walk up to Fife and tell him what we were doing."

"Aye, sure, but, sithee, keeping the cargo quiet may not require keeping the venture quiet. A grand, noisy procession, if organized well, can conceal all."

Michael smiled. "I suppose Hugo told you that Henry will fund us. So, do what you must, but try to keep us all from being hanged, won't you?"

"Aye, sure. Now, tell me more about your talk with Ranald. Are you sure he won't tell Donald about it?"

"I think he was flattered that we would entrust something to his keeping. I mentioned Donald, and Ranald agreed that he has no duty to tell him aught about the Templars or what they protect, and vowed the object would be safe with him. So he perfectly understands what he has promised. He will know what it is when he takes charge of it, of course, but until then, we'll hold that secret close."

"Aye, sure," Giff agreed.

Michael grinned. "I'm surprised Rob agreed to tell *you* what it is. He keeps his secrets closer than most, Rob does."

"Necessity required it if he wants me to move it."

"I ken that fine, but you don't know our Rob. Were it not that Fife already suspects the general whereabouts of the Stone—and that we Sinclairs have it—Rob would doubtless have fought against moving it at all."

"How did Fife come to suspect such a thing?"

"Pure mischief and a bit of happenstance," Michael said, pouring more wine into Giff's goblet. "As to the first, Rob's older brother liked to make himself important. Add to that the fact that from the day Edward of England carted his stone away, rumors that he took the wrong one have flourished. Rob's father wondered if Logans had had aught to do with that, because Rob's great-grandfather, in particular, was a powerful man and a close friend and battle comrade of Robert the Bruce."

Giff realized Michael did not know how much Rob had told him, so he said, "Rob told me his grandfather informed him of the Stone's whereabouts."

"Good," Michael said. "It is much easier to talk about something if one does not have to concern oneself with betraying confidences. To answer your question about Fife, however, once he began taking over more and more of the King's affairs, virtually ruling Scotland, Rob's brother sought to curry favor with him by suggesting that the Logans—specifically Rob—knew the Stone's location."

"Sakes, did Rob's brother *admit* telling Fife as much?"

"Rob's brother and father both died before we knew about any of this. It was Fife himself who let slip the fact that he'd received such information. Although he does not make good decisions in battle and can be something of a coward, he's a damned devious fellow, is Fife, and a dangerous one. Do *not* underestimate him."

"I won't," Giff said. "Hugo and Rob said that Fife thinks the Stone lies with the treasure and wants to find both. Would that not indicate that he searches for something that would require much more space than any one ship could provide?"

"We think he believes that portions of the treasure lie in sundry places," Michael explained. "He has made no secret of his belief that Henry holds much of it. Indeed, he has built himself a ship with the clear intention of sailing to Girnigoe to confront him. He is unlikely to leave, though, before the King returns to Stirling where, as constable of Stirling Castle, Fife wields his greatest power over him."

"I'd heard that he's already assumed many of the royal duties," Giff said.

"Most of them," Michael said. "At Stirling, his grace is surrounded by Fife's minions. I am more concerned now, though, about this matter of finding a ship for you, because with Fife so near at hand, we may have to move swiftly. Have you seen any vessel yet that may serve the purpose?"

"At present Leith harbors a surfeit of boats, but most are collecting wool to carry south," Giff said. "I did note a few that might serve us, including two French longboats that may have some cargo space and a merch—"

"*French* longboats?"

Giff grinned. "Aye, 'tis unusual, I grant you, but the French can sometimes be as wise as the Scots in recognizing a good idea when they meet one. Another possibility is a Dutch merchantman out of Rotterdam that looks as if she might have speed. I'm more at home on a western galley, myself, but I can captain anything that carries sail—or oars, for that matter."

"Your longboats may not have enough room to conceal the Stone."

"True, so I mean to visit the Dutch ship's captain tomorrow and see if perchance he is also the owner. If not, mayhap I can persuade him to hire out his vessel for a few weeks' time. That would satisfy us, and Fife need never know."

"You should disguise it even so," Michael said. "Not many Dutch sail north, so what would you think of impersonating a Norse ship? Such a ship sailing to Orkney would stir little suspicion at all. Orkney is still Norse territory, after all, and Henry receives Norse visitors two or three times a year."

"That is not a bad option," Giff said.

"It is at least something to consider. Now, tell me just how you came to escort my good-sister today if she was at Lestalric and you rode here from Roslin."

~

At the Castle, the Earl of Fife regarded the cowering minion before him with irritation. "What the devil do you mean, they are up to something?" he demanded. "What are they doing? And take off your hat when you speak to me, Rolf Stow!"

"I dinna ken, m'lord," the wretched Stow replied, snatching off his cap and wringing it between his hands. "But all in a moment, they ha' guards everywhere, both sides o' the gorge. Aye, and down in the glen. I tell ye, summat's up for sure."

"You do interest me," Fife said. "But such meager information serves no one, so go back and learn more. And do not bring me such useless claptrap again. Do you expect me to ride out there myself and ask them what they mean by it all?"

"Nay, m'lord. But Sir Hugo hangs trespassers an they get too close."

"Sir Hugo," Fife reminded him, "does not hold the power of pit or gallows. He controls the guard at Roslin, but he lacks authority to hang anyone, so if you should learn that he has, you need only tell me. The Crown can deal with him."

"Aye, sure, but he doesna give the order. 'Tis the countess wha' does that. And she does hold the power, m'lord, as all ken fine. When the Earl o' Orkney dinna be there, Countess Isabella speaks for him. And for herself, come to that."

"Then do not get close enough to be accused of trespass," Fife snapped. "But find out what the devil they are doing. Now go!"

The man fled, and, frowning, Fife turned to the only other person in the room.

"You know the Sinclairs, de Gredin. What do you make of this?"

Stroking his chin, the chevalier said, "His grace, the King, arrives soon, my lord. Mayhap 'tis only that they prepare to move to town whilst he is here. As I recall, when the countess shifts household, she creates a great stir, so they'd want the area free of rabble. Moreover, I'd wager you are not their only enemy."

"You had nearly a year in Orkney, and you say you saw no sign of the treasure," Fife reminded him. "If it is not there, it must be at Roslin."

"In troth, sir, I saw little of the Orkneys. Save the bishop's palace at Kirkwall, 'tis a vast wilderness of islets. To be sure, Prince Henry—that is, Orkney—means to build a seat for himself there, but we spent most of our time at Girnigoe, which is likewise desolate, as I told you. In troth, Henry could well have the treasure and keep it in either place without a hint of its presence being known to anyone, let alone me."

"You said the same of his great fleet of ships that we hear so much about."

"That is no more than the truth, my lord. I had no opportunity to explore further, nor any desire to. A man could disappear there as easily as a treasure."

"We'll see about that, for I assure you, I mean to explore every inch of his land as soon as my ship is ready and your escorts from the Vatican show themselves. How many ships do you expect his holiness to send?"

"I cannot say," de Gredin said with a shrug. "You want them as quickly as they can get here, and they cannot be as many, so. Think what the English would imagine to see an unknown fleet of ships moving through their waters. To see one or two at a time under Hanseatic banners will not unduly distress anyone."

Fife could not argue that, but he did wish the Pope were sending a flotilla. On the other hand, he was by no means sure he could trust the Pope even now, especially as he himself had not been entirely truthful with de Gredin.

Fife wanted to help de Gredin find the Templar treasure for the Pope, but much more than that did he want to find Scotland's Stone of Destiny.

His informer had told him the Stone never left Scotland, and his London spies had reported that the stone there—the one the English had stolen from Scone Abbey a century before—was naught but an eleven-inch bit of sandstone. He knew from seals appended to ancient royal documents that the true Stone was much larger. If he could return it to Scone, it would provide the Scottish Parliament with clear evidence of his superior worth when the time came to name his father's successor.

He'd said naught of the Stone of Destiny to de Gredin, because he did not like or trust the man. And, in troth, he was beginning to realize that if they also found the Templars' legendary lost treasure, neither he nor Scotland could afford to part with it.

Chapter 8

Sidony's lips were still burning from Giff's kisses as she went slowly upstairs to Isobel's bedchamber. She met Will's nurse leaving the room.

Isobel said, "Come in, dearling, do. Nurse says that Will is still sleeping, but I told her what Michael said to do if the poor laddie wakens. Pull up a stool."

"Nay, for I must not keep you from your bed," Sidony said. "I only stopped in to see if you still mean to attend mass at St. Giles in the morning."

"Aye, sure, with Ealga, and I hope you'll go with us, because Michael says he cannot stay long enough for kirk. The business that took him west involves Rob and Hugo as well, and he says he ought to have gone straight to Roslin to tell Hugo what he learned. But he came here instead, so he leaves at dawn for Roslin. I warrant he'll ask Giff to have Rob meet him here and ride with him."

"Adela won't like that," Sidony said. "Rob was at Roslin today, after all, and it is a long way to go two days in a row. Surely, he can just come and hear whatever Michael has to say before Michael leaves."

"They'll decide that between them, I expect. And the ride is not so long as that. You told me as much yourself only today, did you not?"

Isobel looked tired, and Sidony knew that, despite the early hour and whatever she had said about waiting up for Michael, he expected her to go to bed and likely go right to sleep. Still, the opportunity to ask her opinion about what the men might have been doing in Roslin Gorge might not soon present itself again.

Accordingly, she said, "I warrant Rob won't mind the ride. I was just thinking of Adela. But if I may, I want to ask you about something I saw today."

"Certainly, what did you see?"

Sidony described the scene, taking care to give as much detail as she could, including her brief notion that the men had seemed to emerge from the gorge wall.

"I did not see a track of any sort, although I did see a burn trickling into the Esk from the woods," she added. "What do you think they might have been doing?"

"Faith, how should I know?" Isobel said, reaching to remove the pins from her caul so she could take it off. "Did you ask Giff?"

Sidony grimaced. "He said it was some business of Hugo's, but I expect he just meant he did not want to tell me."

"Most men do not like women who pry, my dear," Isobel said. "You must take care not to let him catch you doing so."

Sidony smiled and said, "Such advice seems odd coming from you. You were always the one so curious as to do almost anything to find out things."

"Aye, sure, but I've no need to do that anymore. Michael tells me nearly anything I want to know."

"Then perhaps you could ask him what they might have been doing."

"Aye, sure, but"—Isobel had been avoiding Sidony's gaze, but she looked directly at her now—"if I did that, and Michael told me what they'd done, I would not tell you, my dear. A good wife does not talk about things her husband reveals to her. If she did, I promise you, he would soon stop telling her anything."

Further questions being clearly futile, Sidony soon bade her good night and retired to the chamber that served as her own when she stayed at Sinclair House. The maidservant who attended her was already there.

"The housekeeper told me her ladyship would retire soon, so I came along to put out your things, me lady, but will ye be going to bed now, too? It still be early."

"I don't know that I shall just yet," Sidony admitted. "But if you will light those candles and fetch my tambour frame, I can do some stitching."

The maid did as she asked, then left her to her task.

As Sidony worked in the glow of candlelight, her thoughts turned back to Giff MacLennan, and her lips burned again at the image that leaped to mind. Abandoning her needle to press two fingertips against her lips, she wondered why her own touch created none of the heat that his lips had sent blazing through her.

She wondered at herself, too, for allowing such a liberty. She had not made the tiniest squeak of protest. And how startled she had been when he had stepped away so abruptly! She had had all she could do seconds later to keep from letting Michael see exactly what had happened and how much she had enjoyed it.

For all the heed she had paid to aught else while Giff kissed her, Michael might have walked up unseen and demanded to know what they meant by it.

She smiled at the image, but thinking of Michael stirred her curiosity again. What *had* they been doing in the gorge? They'd had four men with them, doubtless men who usually rode in Hugo's tail but who, strangely, had been fishing in the river. She had never seen men in Hugo's tail do such a thing before. They were his bodyguard, after all, and rarely diverted their attention from him for any cause.

But they had been fishing!

She wondered if Michael and Giff were still downstairs talking in the parlor and wished briefly that the room they were in boasted a laird's peek as Roslin Castle did. With a sigh, she abandoned that fantasy. Even at Roslin it would bear no fruit, because that cupboard was always locked now.

Nor would trying to listen at the parlor door serve any purpose other than to stir one of Michael's rare displays of wrath. The doors at Sinclair House were heavy and solid, and the servants well trained. If she were foolish enough to put an ear to that door, the first to see her would report it to him immediately.

Candlelight not being as accommodating as daylight for setting stitches, she set her tambour frame aside after an hour and went to the nursery to find Will snuffling a little but otherwise sleeping peacefully, whether from exhaustion or brogac she did not know. On a nearby cot, his nurse also slept.

Hearing voices below as she crossed the stair landing, she paused hopefully but heard no more than Michael bidding Giff a safe ride, and Giff's good night.

Returning to her chamber, she undressed and prepared

for bed, then blew out her candles and was soon fast asleep. If she dreamed, she had no memory of it when she awoke the next morning. But when the maid came to help her dress, she brought the welcome news that the lady Adela had accompanied Sir Robert to Sinclair House and meant to attend mass at St. Giles with them.

In Sidony's opinion, the priest talked too slowly and much too long. Her prayer stool lacked sufficient padding for such a tedious service, and when at last it was over, she leaped up, left her stool for the gillie who had accompanied them to carry back, and hurried outside to breathe in the fresh, faintly salty spring air.

When her sisters and Lady Clendenen joined her, Adela said, laughing, "You wriggled so much in there, I thought you'd fall off your stool."

Sidony grinned, her mood changing at the memory that Adela had left wee Anna at Sinclair House. "Can we go back straightaway?" she asked her in an undertone. "I don't feel much like talking with folks today."

"I agree that we should go soon," Adela said. "I know you must all be eager to see our Anna."

"Unless she is teething," Isobel said with a laugh. "Sidony abandoned me yesterday, saying she'd had enough of screaming babies."

"Faith, Sidony, I thought you doted on the creatures," Adela said. "But pray, don't abandon us today. I feel bereft enough with Rob gone again, although he promised to be home for our supper party even if he has to go right back again."

Isobel said, "Michael and Hugo have to stay at Roslin

to deal with any lingering needs for Isabella's cavalcade. Doubtless, Sorcha will stay with them."

Then, at last, Lady Clendenen asked the question that Sidony had been burning to ask but dared not. "Did Sir Giffard go to Roslin with Michael and Rob?"

"Nay, for he said he had duties here to attend," Adela said, exchanging a glance with Isobel. "He insists on coming to Sinclair House later today, though, to escort me back to Lestalric. I cannot think why he should."

"Nor I," Isobel agreed. "Not when Rob has provided you with a tail as impressive as his own. I hope you invited Giff to join us for supper."

"Aye, sure, I did."

Sidony noted the look that passed between them and wondered at it, but she would not give either the satisfaction of snubbing her by asking what they meant by it. They would snub her, too, especially with Ealga there, and as Isobel had invited Ealga to dine with them before returning to Clendenen House, they would have no time for private conversation until she had gone.

At Sinclair House, they adjourned upstairs to the ladies' solar and chatted about the King's upcoming return to the Castle and Countess Isabella's impending pilgrimage from Roslin until the steward announced that dinner was ready.

At the table, Lady Clendenen said, "You know, I should like to ride out to meet Isabella if the day is pleasant and one of you will agree to ride with me. I am sure she would be pleased to have us join her retinue before she enters town."

Isobel declined gracefully, and Adela said she did not think she was ready yet to leave young Anna for an entire day, but Sidony accepted at once.

By the time Lady Clendenen left, Sidony had come

to think she might have made more of a simple look between her older sisters than it warranted, so instead of asking them to explain themselves, she went to play with her niece and nephew and let her sisters visit together without distraction.

If the children received only half of her attention, it was because the other half was mentally sorting through her favorite dresses for one that was becoming enough to wear to supper.

Leith Harbor

Giff stepped out of the coble that had carried him back to shore after a satisfactory meeting with the captain of the Dutch ship, who seemed perfectly willing to hire out his vessel long enough to suit their purpose. Giff's plan was to take the Dutch ship only as far as Castle Girnigoe, where Michael was certain Henry would provide one of his own to carry the Stone the rest of the way.

"Fife will never get ahead of you if you can hire a ship and get away before he even knows you're going," Michael had assured him the previous night. "The winds are contrary, for one thing, and Fife is a nervous, inexperienced sailor."

"His captain is likely to be an excellent one, however," Giff had replied.

"Aye, sure," Michael said, grinning. "Fife will ever hire the best, but he does not know when to give a horse its head, let alone his captains. He sticks his thumb in everything. And you, my friend, are not known as King of Storms for naught."

Dismissing the Lestalric boatmen who had rowed him out to the merchant ship and back, and shifting his sword to its proper place on his back, Giff paused to look again round the busy harbor before reclaiming his horse from the harbor stable.

Looking again at the wide-bodied Dutch merchantman, he let his gaze drift to the ship Rob had pointed out as Fife's and decided that Michael was probably right. The Dutch ship was eminently seaworthy and would weather rough water well. Fife's vessel, being of newer design and as yet untried by its crew, might prove less capable. If its captain should be an Edinburgh man and lack experience directing oarsmen, he'd be most unlikely to know how best to employ their skills.

Knowing that speculation without facts was pointless, Giff walked away with the intention of returning to Lestalric to enjoy his midday meal and consider what to do about the Dutch crew. He had said nothing to their captain about them but was well aware that the man expected him to hire both the crew and himself.

Giff decided to discuss the problem with the others, but his preference, if Henry agreed, would be to pay the Dutch crew to stay in Edinburgh while a Sinclair crew manned the ship. Hugo had told him that Henry's men at Roslin and at Girnigoe—at least, all who were willing and able—trained both to row and to sail, and would therefore be a far more trustworthy crew than any foreign lot could be.

Male voices raised in anger and a childish shriek close behind him spun him around in time to see several grown men, including one black-clad ruffian with a raised club, chasing a wiry lad of eight or ten summers, who dodged nimbly around and over obstacles in his path as he sped toward Giff.

"Stop that thief!"

The lad saw Giff and abruptly changed course to dodge him, casting a glance over his shoulder at his pursuers as he did.

Leaning sideways, Giff scooped the boy off his feet, kicking and wriggling.

"Lemme down! They'll throttle me! D'ye want t' get me killed?"

"Tether that tongue of yours unless you want to feel my hand," Giff said curtly as he set the boy on his feet, retaining a firm grip on one arm.

"Good, ye caught the wee villain," the first of what had become a string of pursuers said angrily. "Thank 'e, sir. I'll take him now. He's due for a good hiding."

"Are you his father?"

"Nay, but I doubt he's got one, the wee menseless fouter."

"I'm nae fouter, ye sappie-headed puddin'," the lad retorted belligerently.

As the irate man reached again for him, Giff gripped the bony arm tighter and eased the boy behind him as he said, "What is the lad accused of stealing?"

"Yon pie man said he took summat," the accuser said. "I didna see it m'self, but the wee *fouter* clouted me in the cods wi' his elbow as he ran past me."

"He cannot have hit you very hard if you outran those others," Giff pointed out. "More importantly, though, where is the pie man who raised the hue and cry?"

"Yonder," the man growled, jerking his thumb at the gathering crowd.

"Stand away, then," Giff said in a tone that brooked no argument. "I'll attend to the pie man, but I fail to see how this concerns you any further."

The man hesitated, glanced behind him and at Giff again, then moved to stand by the man who had waved the club.

"That's tellin' 'im," the small figure behind Giff muttered.

"You keep silent," Giff ordered, giving the arm a shake without taking his eyes off the men before him. More loudly, he said, "Which of you is the pie man?"

"Here, m'lord," a middle-aged man almost as wide as he was tall said, wiping his hands on his apron as he hurried forward. "An it please ye, sir, the wee scamp made off wi' one o' me fine meat rolls, hot out o' the pan."

Giff silenced a snort from behind him with another shake.

"How much?" he demanded, reaching for his purse with his free hand and raising it to his teeth to unfasten its cord.

The crowd began to disperse, and the pie man, smiling in anticipation of satisfaction, said airily, "Nobbut three shillings, m'lord."

Giff looked at him.

With a rueful shrug, the man said, "Eight pence, sir."

"Still too much," Giff said. "I doubt you charge tuppence for a meat roll, and I don't *know* that the lad stole anything from you. But if he did," he added before the man could voice obvious protest, "you deserve a shilling for your trouble. Moreover, it will teach him a good lesson to have to repay me."

"Aye, sir, that it will," the pie man said, accepting the shilling. "But I hope ye teach him another one afore then," he added with a minatory look at the culprit.

"I may, at that," Giff said, casting a glance around to see that most of the men who had joined the chase had walked away. Only the disgruntled one who had led it and his club-bearing companion were still in sight, but they seemed to be chatting amiably together and paying no heed to anyone else.

Giff turned to face his captive.

"Ye gave that mowdiewort a whole shilling!" the lad said indignantly. "If ye think I'm paying ye back any such addlepated sum, ye'd best think—hey!"

Giff lifted him off his feet and held him so they looked eye to eye. "Not another word if you don't want that hiding right now."

"Right then, I'm mum, so ye can put me down. But ye should ken fine that ye're actin' a right bangster."

Stifling an impulse to laugh, Giff said, "I'm no bully, and I'll put you down, but if that is your notion of keeping mum, you should know it is not mine."

Black-lashed hazel eyes twinkled at him, but the lad kept quiet until he was on his feet. Then his gaze shifted past Giff, and he exclaimed, "Look out, ahind ye!"

Suspecting a ruse that would allow the young scoundrel to escape, Giff might have ignored the warning had a trusted sixth sense not raised the hairs on the back of his neck. As it was, he turned, shoving the child out of the way, just as the black-clad ruffian with the club leaped at him, swinging hard.

Giff's left hand shot up in a slash that snapped its hardened edge against the other's uplifted wrist, blocking the blow. At the same moment, his right fist shot into the ruffian's jaw with all the power of his shoulder and back behind it.

The club flew left, and the ruffian collapsed and took no further interest in the proceedings. But his companion, the lad's erstwhile angry accuser, was moving to take his place when a small figure darted at him, head lowered, and butted him in the same place that the man had accused him earlier of planting his elbow.

The victim bent double, reaching awkwardly for his attacker with one hand while he sought to ease his pain with the other. But, with an agility Giff thought would well serve any man in training at Dunclathy, the lad nipped away out of reach.

The pie man and two others hurried up, the latter taking charge of the unresisting victim of the lad's attack, as the former was saying, "We saw what happened, and we'll gladly take them louts in charge to the magistrate, me lord."

Thanking them and leaving them to attend to both men, Giff turned back to find his small assistant bouncing up and down on his toes. "Aye de mi, that's done 'em!" the lad exclaimed. "Ye dunted yours flat onto his hunkers!"

Giff grinned. "Hunkers?"

The urchin returned the grin, showing a ragged gap that large, new front teeth were just beginning, unevenly, to fill. "Aye, sure," he said. "Me da' says I'm no' old enough yet t' say arse."

"Then you should not say it," Giff said.

"I didna!"

Giff raised his eyebrows.

Another grin. "Och, aye, I did, but no' till I told ye about me da'."

"So you do have one, then."

"Aye, sure, don't you?"

"I do," Giff said, sobering. "And if I took something that did not belong to me, he'd give me a thorough hiding."

"Nay, then, ye're too big."

"I was not always so big. Did you take the meat roll?"

The boy's mouth opened and shut again as he eyed Giff's stern face. Then, lifting his chin and squaring his shoulders, he said, "Aye, I did."

"Where is it?"

The twinkle returned as the urchin reached up his sleeve and showed a bare inch of a thick, buttered-crumb-covered meat roll, then pushed it back out of sight.

"Why did you take it?"

"T' see if I could," the lad answered frankly. "Yon greedy lick-penny wha' sells them never asks will ye lick or taste, and I wanted to see what they was like."

"The usual way to do that is to buy one."

"Aye, sure, but for that a man needs gelt."

"And you have none?"

The lad shrugged.

"What's your name?"

He hesitated. Then, in much the same tone as the pie man had used to suggest three shillings for his pie, he said, "Most just calls me 'the wee mannie.'"

"What does your father call you?"

A fleeting grimace gave way to a wide-eyed look. "Did ye ken them louts was a-watchin' ye when ye rowed out to yon Dutchman's boat? I seen 'em m'self, and they was still a-watchin' when your lads rowed ye back t' shore. What did ye want wi' yon Dutchman that interested them so, d'ye think?"

"I cannot imagine," Giff said. Then, deciding that a bit of misinformation floating around the harbor might prove useful, he added, "I've been thinking of traveling north to the Moray Firth. I was just asking him about possible transport."

To his surprise, the lad snorted again and shook his

head. "Ye dinna want t' go north wi' nobbut that great barge under ye. There be rough waters t' sail there."

"And what do you know about boats, Master Long-Wit?"

Rolling his eyes, the boy said, "I ken fine that ye'd do better t' sail wi' me da'. He's going north, and if ye swear t' forget about yon addlepated shilling and promise no' t' tell 'im about the meat roll, I'll ask 'im will he take ye with us."

"So which boat does your father captain?"

"Yonder, wi' the oars a-standing up and the tall mast." He pointed.

"That boat belongs to Lord Fife," Giff said, eyeing him sternly.

"Aye, sure, the *Serpent Royal*, but me da's its captain all the same. 'Tis why they call me the wee mannie, though me true name be Jake Maxwell. But if ye ken nowt o' boats, ye'd no' had understood that about mannie," he added kindly.

"The wee captain is what that means," Giff said. When his companion's face fell, he added, "Do you really think he might provide space for a passenger?"

Smiling again, the boy said, "An ye agree t' me terms, I could take ye to 'im, and ye could put that notion to 'im yourself."

"I won't tell your father, but neither will I agree about the shilling," Giff said. "You deserve to repay the full amount, and I mean to see that you do."

Jake eyed him measuringly, then sighed. "I'll do it, then, someday," he said. "Although I dinna ken how."

"You'll think of something," Giff said. "Shall we go see your father now?"

"Aye, sure, the boat's yonder on the shingle, and our lads will take us."

"Pull out your meat roll," Giff said as they headed back toward the water.

"Why should I?"

"Aren't you hungry?" Giff drew out his knife. "I'm going to miss my dinner, so I thought perhaps you would like to share yours."

"Aye, sure," Jake said, flashing his grin. "I got a mutton bridie, too, in me poke. And a fine currant scone for a sweet."

"A feast, in fact," Giff said dryly as the boy pulled the poke from his breeks and showed both the pastry-wrapped bridie and the scone. "You acquired those the same way you acquired the meat roll, I presume."

"Aye, sure, and still warm, but since ye promised no' t' tell me da'—"

"Oh, *I* won't do that," Giff said. The emphasis in his tone brought the youngster's head up and put a questioning look in the limpid hazel eyes.

"You're going to do that," Giff told him cheerfully as he cut the roll. When visibly tensing muscles told him the lad was on the brink of fleeing, he added, "Unless you're afraid, of course. A man takes responsibility for his actions."

Indignant again, Jake said, "I dinna fear nowt!"

"Good lad," Giff said, putting the knife away and extending half of the meat roll to him. "Here's yours. It smells delicious."

"It ought to, for a whole shilling," Jake muttered, adding in a tone that revealed a lack of eagerness now to row out to the *Serpent*, "That's our boat, there."

Chapter 9

At Sinclair House, determined to reveal no hint of the eagerness she felt to see Giff again, Sidony played with a clearly more comfortable Will and a cooing Anna until their nurses announced that it was time for their supper.

Changing to the pale green, lace-trimmed dress and matching slippers she would wear for supper, Sidony tried to occupy herself with her needlework but gave up after wandering thoughts had twice caused her to prick her finger.

Leaving her door ajar and checking more than once to see that her hair and the simple white silk net and veil that covered it were perfectly in place, she waited only until she heard her sisters' voices on the landing before hurrying to join them. As they went downstairs, the steward opened the front door to admit Giff.

Following the others, Sidony paused on the last step with one hand on the newel post and turned to face their guest as he crossed the threshold.

"Welcome, sir," Isobel said with a smile as he entered.

"I'm glad you are able to join us. I hope your quest was successful."

"Completely successful, my lady, thank you," he said, his gaze meeting hers briefly before moving past her to encounter Sidony's. He smiled then.

"I trust our people provided you with a good midday meal," Adela said.

"Unfortunately, madam, due to my own tardiness, I missed dinner at Lestalric."

"Oh, dear, then you must be nigh starved by now!"

"Nowt of the sort," he said, grinning at her. "I dined on half of a very tasty meat roll clad in crisp, buttery crumbs, half a mutton bridie made by someone with a hand for light pastry, and half of an excellent currant scone."

Speaking as one, Sidony and Isobel said, "Why only halves?"

"He can tell us after we sit down," Adela said. "If the food is ready, it would be an offense to the cook to leave it standing whilst we chatter here."

Adela's reputation for household management being legendary in Edinburgh, it did not occur to the others to debate the point. She and Rob had turned Lestalric Castle from a long-neglected warren into such a welcoming home that members of Scotland's elite clamored for invitations to their frequent supper parties.

On the thought, Sidony said, "Did you say Rob will be back for your supper?"

"I did," Adela said as they reached the dining parlor. "He promised he would, but he will likely have to return early Wednesday to join Isabella's cavalcade."

"Take Michael's chair, Giff," Isobel said, gesturing toward the head of the table. When they had said the grace-before-meat, she nodded to the servants to begin serving, then said, "Now, Giff, tell us your tale."

He did so, proving himself an entertaining storyteller and making them laugh more than once in the process.

"What happened when you met Jake's father?" Sidony asked.

He smiled. "Captain Wat Maxwell is a good man, I think. Young Jake introduced me as if I had been a lord, but as he did not know my name—it not having occurred to him to ask—he could not give it. So I introduced myself and was much surprised, I can tell you, to learn that Captain Maxwell had heard of me. But when his son confessed his sins, he told him they would talk later and sent him off. If I've taken his measure, the lad had a few painful minutes coming to him."

"What did you think of Fife's ship?" Isobel asked.

He shot her another look even more speaking than the one Sidony had noted before, and said, "'Tis a good one. Hoists more sail than most men would carry on a boat that size, but she should handle much as a galley does, despite a higher, heavier stem and stern. The central area is similar, and she can carry fifty oarsmen with benches for eight oars on each side. Moreover, she boasts a stern port for loading cargo like some merchant ships. As to Maxwell, I'd say he knows what he's doing."

This time it was Adela and Isobel who exchanged glances.

About to demand to know what the others were keeping from her, Sidony saw that Giff was watching her. So, instead, she asked him a question that had been puzzling her since he'd told his story. "Why did those two men attack you, sir?"

He shrugged. "Likely, they mistook me for easy prey."

She held his gaze. That anyone could think him an easy victim with his sword slung across his back, as she was sure it must have been, was ludicrous. He walked as if he owned the world even without the sword.

With a frown, as if her question had stirred him to think, he said, "Young Jake did say he'd seen them watch me go out to the Dutch vessel and back."

"Someone may have set them to watch you," Isobel said.

"But why?" Sidony asked.

"Sakes, I don't know," Giff said, then added ruefully, "I should not speak to you so, my lady. Indeed, I would make amends. The afternoon has turned sunny. Will you do me the honor of strolling with me later through the gardens?"

She looked at Isobel, who nodded, then held her breath. But when Adela remained silent, she said, "I would like that, sir, but I would like it even more if you would answer my questions."

Before he could reply, Adela asked what news he had about English activity in the Borders. "Rob heard that Fife is at outs again with Douglas."

"How did he hear that?" Giff asked.

"News travels with the wool from the Border monasteries," Adela said.

"Moreover, if we have heard it, you may be sure the word will soon be all over Scotland," Isobel said. "Certainly, the Lord of the Isles will know."

"How?"

Sidony looked at him in surprise. "Why, you should know that we hear everything in the Isles, sir. Our sister Cristina married the good-brother of the Lord High Admiral of the Isles, who is the best-informed man in all Scotland."

"Aye, he is," Isobel said. "Lachlan Lubanach has informants everywhere. Little happens anywhere in Scotland that escapes his notice."

This fruitful topic provided discussion until they had finished their meal. Standing to leave the table, Giff said, "Will you want a cloak, Lady Sidony?"

Her ladyship having disclaimed any need for her cloak despite the thin fabric of her skirt and bodice, Giff ushered her from the dining parlor to a door leading out to the gardens behind the house. As they passed her sisters, Lady Adela murmured, "Do not disappear out there, sir."

Flashing her a smile, he said, "I have no intention of doing so, madam. But if you are in a rush to return to Lestalric, you need only tell me and we will go at once."

"Nay," she said with a fond look at Sidony. "I'm in no hurry."

Outside with the door shut, Giff put a hand under Sidony's nearer elbow and guided her toward a more distant path. Several windows overlooked the garden.

"You are very quiet," he said.

"I want to know something, but I doubt you will tell me."

He chuckled. "You cannot know until you try me."

"Very well, then. What secret do you share with Isobel and Adela?"

"What makes you think I share any secret with them?"

"The way you looked at Isobel when she asked if your day had been successful. And again, when she asked what you thought of Fife's ship."

"You are observant, lass. Anything more?"

"Aye, sure, the way Isobel and Adela looked at each other when you said Fife's Captain Maxwell knows his business. Each time it made me feel as if one of you might soon order me off to bed so the grown-ups could talk."

"That was unkind of us," he said, shifting his hand from her elbow to her shoulder and pausing on the pebbled path to face her. "Do you want to clout me again? I ken fine that you've no fish in hand this time, but . . ."

That drew a smile at least, but she said, "Will you tell me what the three of you know that I do not? Or do you not trust me?"

"Sakes, lass, how can I know if you are trustworthy till I know you better?" When she stiffened, he added hastily, "In troth, you know much of it already."

"What do I know?"

"I told you I was looking for a ship and would return west when I found one. Thanks to their husbands, your sisters knew I'd had my eye on one in the harbor and was to ride to Leith today to see about hiring or purchasing it."

In the fading light, her eyes were little more than enlarged black pupils in colorless pools, yet he thought he had never known anyone with eyes so clear or a gaze so steady or so intense.

"I see," she said. "But why did Isobel care what you thought of Fife's captain, and why did they look at each other so when you said he knows his business?"

Impulse stirred to say that was his affair, not hers, but instinct warned him that to make a greater mystery of it would just inflame her curiosity.

"I cannot speak for your sisters," he said, shoving a hand through his hair. "But we have heard that Fife built his ship primarily to make trouble for Henry."

"Do you know what sort of trouble?"

"We can guess," he said, wondering how hard she would press him and trying to think what he could say that would not be a blatant snub or untruth.

To his surprise, she nodded and said, "I expect Fife's intent must be plain enough then, but doubtless we should say no more about that."

A nervous tickle stirred in his mind. "Why do you say that?"

Her eyes widened. "Sakes, I did suppose that you must be wholly in Hugo's and Rob's confidence, and Michael's, too. Are you not?"

"I am, but I do not know why you should assume that."

"Because Hugo and Michael sent for you."

"Aye." The tickle had become a tingling chill and was spreading. "So . . . ?"

"So one must suppose," she went on matter-of-factly, "that Fife seeks whatever you and the others found in the gorge, and that you mean to transport it to Girnigoe or somewhere more distant on your journey to the west."

Giff fought to think. If she had not guessed it all, she had guessed enough to be dangerous. If she knew still more . . . "Does this supposing of yours also suggest to you what that object might be?"

"I should think it must be some part of the treasure."

As he fought to avoid revealing his shock, she added, "If Fife wants to lay hands on it, he will certainly make a nuisance of himself. Have you considered that the man in black who attacked you with the club might be Fife's man?"

He had not considered that. He was still struggling to stay calm when what he wanted to do was to shake out of her everything she knew and how she had come to know it.

Instead he said, "Why do you suspect that the man serves Fife?"

"Why, because you said Jake Maxwell had seen the men watching you, and Fife's men do wear black, as he does. Surely you ought to consider the possibility."

He glanced toward the house.

"Come over here," he commanded, drawing her into the shadow of a shrub large enough to conceal them. Then, with his hands on her shoulders, meeting her innocent gaze, he said sternly, "What treasure are you talking about?"

She raised her chin but made no effort to free herself. Nor did she reply.

Impatient now, he gave her a shake. "Tell me."

"Mayhap I should not have mentioned it. I think I should say no more."

Gripping her shoulders hard enough to make her wince, he said, "Then I'll carry you straight to Roslin, and you can explain this to Hugo, Rob, and Michael."

"You wouldn't!"

"Oh, yes, sweetheart, I would. I certainly would."

Sidony's heart pounded. She believed him, but she could not decide what to do and wished she had never mentioned the treasure. She had not expected to make him angry, and that she had done so stirred mixed emotions. To a degree, she wanted to placate him, but she found his anger oddly exhilarating, too—so exhilarating that she experienced a curious whim to see what would happen if she defied him.

The result, inevitably, was silence.

"Well?"

"You are bruising my shoulders."

He released her, but he still stood much too close.

"Step back," she said. "I can't think whilst you're looking about ten feet tall."

"I'm not moving," he said. "Which is it to be, to tell me or them? And don't think I won't just pick you up, put you over my shoulder, and take you to the stables whilst I saddle my horse—or that your sisters could stop me."

She shook her head. The more he urged her to decide, the harder it was to think, let alone to make a decision.

"Tell me what you know about the treasure," he said curtly.

That, being less encompassing, was easier. "Just that Hugo, Michael, Rob, and Henry—and you, I suppose—are guarding one. Also, that Fife wants it."

"Who told you?"

She hesitated. That was harder to answer, but when he frowned, she said, "No one did, really."

"Don't take me for a fool. Someone told you."

"No, sir. That is, no one told me intentionally," she added hastily when he gripped her shoulder again. "I just heard them talking."

"So you listen at doors, do you?"

"I do not!" she said. "They forget I'm there. Even if they remember, they just lower their voices, but I have quick ears. And they soon forget again, anyway."

"Who is it that you heard?"

Shrugging, she said, "Different ones at different times." Ticking them off on her fingers, she said, "Isobel, Adela, and Sorcha, of course, but also Michael and Henry." She thought a moment. "I don't think I've ever heard Rob or Hugo—"

"How the devil could you have heard such things from all of the others?"

"I told you, they forget I'm there. You know they do. You've made comments yourself about how they do."

"That was when you disappeared into the garden at Clendenen House soon after you'd angered Hugo, not when you were in the same room with them all."

"Aye, sure, but they forget whether I'm there or not there. They often make me feel as if no one can see me. I know they don't mean to, but—"

"Of course, they don't," he said. He looked angrier than ever, but strangely, his tone was gentler as he said, "Who else have you told of this treasure, lass?"

"Why, no one," she said, surprised.

"No one at all? Why did you not talk openly about it with your sisters?"

"Sakes, sir, I still remember the time I repeated something I'd heard my father say when he forgot I was within hearing. He skelped me so hard I could not sit comfortably for a sennight. I was eight. One does not forget such a lesson."

"Evidently, one also learned to keep as quiet as a mouse when folks were talking secrets."

"Aye, sure, because people get just as angry being reminded, as if it were my fault they'd forgotten me. And, too, of course, one does like to know things."

"You're sure you haven't said anything about this to anyone else?"

"Who?" she asked. "I would never tell the servants, and in troth, it is better that my sisters not realize how much I have heard them say over the years."

"Better for whom?" he asked, arching his eyebrows.

But he was no longer so angry, and she felt enormous relief.

Smiling back wistfully, she said, "I just meant that I'm no prattler. You are the first person who has seemed much interested in what I have to say. Now and again, the others ask my opinion of something they have chosen to wear or to serve for guests to eat, but even then, they usually just expect me to say that whatever they have chosen is wonderful and perfect for the occasion."

She expected him to dismiss that observation, but he did not.

"We'll walk a little farther, I think," he said. "I have more to say to you, and although your sisters might think nowt of it if they look out once and don't see us, if we stay out of sight for long, they will send someone to search for us."

"Aye," she said. "I heard what Adela said to you."

She was not sure she wanted to hear what he would say to her, though.

As they walked, he said soberly, "The others will have to know about this."

"All of them?"

"The result will be the same whether it is one or all," he said. "Any of the men would be bound to tell the others, and likely they will all speak to their wives. You must prepare yourself for that."

She nibbled her lower lip. "Michael may understand, and mayhap Henry, but Hugo won't, nor Rob. They'll think Sorcha and Adela were careless."

"Sakes, lass," he said impatiently, "they were *all* careless, the men, too."

"Aye, sure, but *they* won't see it that way. They are much more likely to blame me and my sisters."

"If they do, they do," he retorted callously. "That is simply the consequence of your actions and your sisters' actions."

"How like a man," she said scornfully. "Why is it when women do something, it is a fault deserving punishment, but when men do it, it is still the women's fault?"

"Is that the way you think it is?" He sounded amused.

"Don't laugh at me! Far too often, that *is* the way things are."

He faced her, stopping her in her tracks. "If you believe that," he said, "then you should take more care to keep out of the path of your kinsmen's displeasure."

"I did not do this on purpose! Moreover, although I see that you believe you are obliged to tell them I know, surely you need not tell them *how* I know."

"So you would have me lie to them?"

"You don't have to lie."

"Then, what would you have me say that would *not* be a lie when they ask how you came by this knowledge of yours?"

"Oh, well, I do perceive the difficulty when you put it like that, but you *will* explain to them how it came about, will you not?"

"I'm going to explain something to you, my lady," he said grimly. "You say you did not do anything on purpose, but you did. You made a purposeful choice to remain right where you were and listen to those conversations."

"But I couldn't just—"

"Of course you could," he said ruthlessly. "You are not a child's rag doll that has to remain where it is dropped until someone moves it. You are a young woman with a will of her own. Had you acted as you should, you'd have made your presence known the instant you knew the others did not intend their conversation to reach your ears. That's the plain truth whether you want to hear it or not."

"You don't understand!"

"I do understand. You have persuaded yourself that you can't make decisions, that you do what you do because of the expectations, actions, or wishes of others . . ."

"But—"

". . . when the truth is that you make choices the same way anyone else does," he went on. "Every choice is a decision, whether you choose to call it one or not."

Her face felt hot, and tears sprang to her eyes. "Do you really think that?"

"I know it, and I'll prove it to you," he said, woefully oblivious to her distress. "Tell me again how you came to ride to Roslin Gorge yesterday."

"Just as I told you before," she said, dashing an arm across her eyes so she could see him better, then wishing she hadn't, because he looked grim again. "I was going to go to Lestalric as Isobel had suggested, but when I reached the roadway, it just seemed better to go the other way. So, you see, it really wasn't a decision at all."

Hoping she had explained it clearly, she tried to read his expression but could detect no hint in it of acceptance.

Giff was doing his best to keep his temper. He could see that she believed what she said, and he knew he had already been hard on her, but he had come to realize that the others in her family had failed her abysmally by not recognizing what she thought of herself—and them—and correcting the errors long before now.

To that end, he said bluntly, "You did not, actually, tell

me even that much before. You changed the subject several times, in fact, to avoid answering that question. And now that I hear your answer, I can understand why. I had thought you honest—more honest than most, in fact—but now I wonder."

This time the tears that welled up spilled over, but he ignored them as he had earlier. It would not do to let them affect him now, or he would fail to make her see what he was certain she could see if she'd just let him explain it to her.

She was biting her lip, struggling to control herself, and he recognized signs of incipient breakdown. That would not do. Hoping he had judged her mettle accurately, he said evenly, "If you cannot control your emotions sufficiently to continue this discussion, perhaps we should go back inside."

To his relief, her chin came up and she glowered at him. "Say what you will then, sir, although you have already made your low opinion of me quite clear."

"Don't be a fool," he snapped. "If that were true, I'd not waste my time trying to make you understand the error in your thinking."

She dashed her sleeve across her eyes again and sniffed so much like a child that he nearly put an arm around her to reassure her. He resisted and had his reward a moment later when she wrapped herself in dignity and looked straight at him.

Accusingly, she said, "You just told me you think I'm dishonest."

"I did not," he retorted, casting another look at the house and wondering how much more time they would have. "I said I'd noted your honesty. But do you expect me to believe you gave your horse its head yesterday and it just wandered of its own accord up the Canongate, onto the Cowgate, and all the way to the Roslin road?"

"Of course not. But when I realized what I'd done, I just thought that since Isobel would not expect me until supper, it would not make any difference if I rode to Hawthornden to visit Sorcha and . . . and perhaps see you again."

"But even now, you are suggesting that you did not think any of that until you had already turned toward St. Giles instead of Lestalric," he said. "So, try this tale of yours again, lass. Why did you turn toward St. Giles in the first place?"

"I just . . ." She grimaced, then visibly remembered something. "I saw Lady Clendenen's woman talking to one of the gillies on the front step," she said. "I . . . I was afraid they would tell her ladyship they'd seen me and I'd have to stop and talk. I like her very much," she added hastily. "But I did not want to talk to anyone. So I suppose I did make a choice. I see that now, but at the time, I did not think it out. I just acted, and I never thought again about seeing them until now."

He nodded, satisfied. "Now, tell me, if you rode on to see Sorcha or me, why did you turn tail when you did see me with the others in the gorge?"

"I did not turn back because I'd seen you. You know perfectly well that I rode on to Hawthornden. But then I discovered Sorcha had gone to Roslin, and having seen you with Hugo and Rob in the gorge, I thought I'd have to go there to see you, too. But . . ." She paused, then added uneasily, "Well, there was Hugo, but also if I wanted to get back for supper, I had no time for that."

"Decisions, every one," he said gently. "You see?"

"If decisions are just choices, then I do," she said. "I'm not sure that is all there is to them, though. I tend to think of more momentous occasions and the way Sorcha and the others act when they make decisions about what I am to do."

"I understand that," he said. "But you need to understand that just making choices, which *are* decisions, nearly always affects other people. You must face up to that straightaway, too, because as you have realized, some of those people are going to be angry with you—and rightly so."

"Must you tell Isobel and Adela now, before you tell their husbands?"

"I am not going to tell Isobel or Adela," he said, remembering that he had already said nearly the same thing that day under very different circumstances.

She reacted much as young Jake had, heaving a sigh of relief as she said, "Thank heaven. I know Michael and Rob will tell them soon enough, and they will be as angry with me then as they would be now, but at least—"

"No, lass," he said. "You must tell them, and without delay, because if you put it off, you will subject them to what you face, but without benefit of warning."

She looked stricken but rallied quickly. "I ought to have thought of that," she said. "How could I not? Have I grown so selfish that I now think only of myself?"

"Much less so than anyone else I know," he said. "Put your chin in the air again, lass, for I prefer it so. And then we'd better go in before they look for us."

"Aye, we'd best get it over," she agreed.

They went to the solar, where they found both sisters sitting cozily near the fire. Giff watched Sidony, expecting her to hesitate with the moment of truth at hand.

But she walked straight in, leaving him at the threshold.

"Did you enjoy your stroll?" Adela asked.

"I have something to say to you, to confess," Sidony said bluntly.

"Mercy, what?"

"I know about the treasure."

Giff bit his lip to stifle his amusement. He knew what was coming, and just as he'd expected, Isobel and Adela both turned accusing glares on him.

Eyes shooting sparks at him, Isobel said, "Giff, surely *you* did not tell her!"

"No, he did not," Sidony said. "You did."

Chapter 10

Monday dawned bright and sunny with white clouds hurrying free from the west, their shadows skimming over houses and gardens along the Canongate.

Walking in the Sinclair garden after breaking her fast, Sidony imagined that she could detect the scents of Highland thyme and heather on the wind. For once, though, she was not wishing she could waft herself homeward. She was thinking of her walk the evening before with Giff MacLennan, and wondering how a man so maddening, so quick to criticize, could occupy her thoughts as much as he did.

Her thoughts produced no answer.

By midmorning, although the wind still blew from the west, the clouds had slowed their journey eastward and begun to collect and to darken ominously.

When Sidony and Isobel sat to eat their midday meal, the sky had darkened so that a gillie quickly lit candles, finishing as rain began to pour down outside.

Isobel had scarcely said a word all morning, but she

sighed as she looked out the window and murmured, "Truly dismal, is it not? I hope this is not one of those storms that lingers for days. It would spoil Adela's supper tomorrow."

"Are you still angry with me?" Sidony asked quietly. Both Isobel and Adela had been angry the previous evening, but in Giff MacLennan's presence, neither had said more than to ask what she had meant by saying that they had revealed the treasure's existence to her. After Sidony had explained and a fuming Adela had left with Giff for Lestalric, Isobel pleaded a sick headache and retired to her bed.

With only her own thoughts for company, and knowing that the men would be even angrier than their wives, Sidony had enjoyed little sleep.

Now, she waited anxiously for Isobel's reply.

But Isobel helped herself to salmon fritters offered by one of the two lads attending them and said nothing. When the meat was on the table, she dismissed both gillies, assuring them that she and the lady Sidony would want nothing more.

When they had gone, she said, "I'm not angry, Siddie. Not with you. If I am vexed, 'tis with myself. I just wish I knew what Michael will say when he returns."

"He does not ever seem to get angry with you," Sidony said.

"Perhaps not, but when he is displeased, he can make me feel like the lowest form of creation with just a word or two. And this will displease him exceedingly."

"Giff said it was my fault, that I should have spoken up to remind you of my presence as soon as I realized you were saying things you did not mean for me to hear. But, by my troth, Isobel, I am not certain I ever knew that. For as long as I can remember, my whole family has talked of private things without heeding my being within earshot. I did realize that this treasure is a subject I must not mention to anyone else, and you all taught me long ago that I'd suffer for talking out of turn. But, otherwise, no one has ever seemed to mind."

"I know," Isobel said. "I can even recall one such discussion betwixt Adela, Sorcha, and me in the ladies' solar at Roslin, and I'm nearly certain now that you were stitching by the fire at the other end of the room. We spoke quietly, and you usually seem wholly oblivious to our conversations, but clearly, you do hear them."

Relieved that Isobel seemed to understand, Sidony nodded. "Often, I *was* oblivious. But even when I wasn't, I did not think I was doing wrong."

"Well, Adela will probably feel as I do, but Sorcha may be angrier, because Hugo will be. I doubt he will understand at all how such a thing could happen. Also, Sorcha will not so quickly agree that we are as much to blame for this, if not more so, for having developed the discourteous habit of talking as if you were not there."

"I've never minded," Sidony said. "Even as a bairn, I just wanted to be near everyone, to know what you were doing. I do hope you are right about Adela, though, and that she can make Rob understand that I'd never betray your secrets."

"I agree that you would not knowingly betray a confidence," Isobel said. "But as to never speaking out of turn, you did speak of this with Sir Giffard."

"Aye, sure, but I could see that he already knew about it. I repeated no details or anything specific that I'd overheard any particular person say."

"That will help, I think," Isobel said. "At least, it will

with Michael, because he will always listen first and judge afterward. I cannot say about the others. Rob will be home tomorrow, though, and I warrant Giff will tell him as soon as he arrives. His reaction will help us judge how angry the others are likely to be."

Sidony grimaced. "I'd not have told Giff anything, but I knew they'd found something in the gorge last year, and I'd seen him there with Hugo and Rob. Then he talked of danger from Fife and looking for a ship to sail west, so I was nearly certain that whatever they'd found must be part of the treasure."

"And you said as much to him, I expect," Isobel said dryly.

"Aye, but only after he'd pressed me and said he was in their full confidence. But when I mentioned it, he wanted to know who had told me, and he . . . he threatened to throw me over his shoulder and take me to Hugo and the others. And Hugo hasn't even had a chance yet to vent his feelings about seeing me yesterday. Heaven knows what he'll say or . . . or do to me, when he learns about this."

Isobel shook her head. "After so many years weathering Sorcha's stormy temper, you rarely seem to let anyone's ranting daunt you—even Hugo's. So don't tease yourself about it now. What comes will come soon enough of its own accord." She added with a wry smile, "I'll try to follow that good advice myself, if you will."

"Aye, sure," Sidony said. "I know such storms of temper soon blow over, but I own, I won't mind if this rain keeps them all away for just a while longer."

Giff was soaked to the skin and not happy about it. He generally enjoyed the vagaries of weather, but in his opinion, no day that had begun so well ought to have clouded up and rained on him as heavily as it had.

He had ridden the coast to Portobello, seeking the safest, most suitable place to load the Stone onto the Dutch ship, but he was unsure yet how he and the others could achieve that. More often than not, he beached his ships, and to be sure, this one boasted a stern port and oars. But although one could back a galley with ease, only a fool would try to beach a ship as large as the *Zee Handelaar* stern first.

He continued to ponder the problem as he rode back to Lestalric. Could they just tie up at a public wharf and load the Stone as ordinary cargo?

What if Fife and his lads strolled up as they were loading?

Being a man who would dare anything within reason, Giff decided that he would doubtless think of something, but he knew the others would prefer a less audacious plan. They tended to put caution first, but he knew that to succeed, a man had to seize opportunity when it arose or risk losing it.

Rob would know more when he returned tomorrow for Adela's supper. Rob was no seaman, but Michael was a fine one, and Hugo had experience, too, enough with Henry's ships to understand the logistics of loading. Henry himself was the finest Sinclair seaman, but he was at Girnigoe and his ships were off carrying wool.

There also remained the problem of the Dutch captain and crew. Giff had told the captain he had cargo but not what it was, nor would he. But to inform the Dutch crew that he did not require their services would doubtless lead to trouble, especially as he would need them until he could exchange them for Sinclair men. And he could scarcely make that exchange in Leith Harbor with Fife watching.

Weather was also a concern, although experience told him the current storm, damp and annoying as it was, would soon blow itself out. By late afternoon, it had, and the sunset was spectacular, turning the waters of the firth the color of blood.

Later that evening, as Fife was reviewing some royal accounts, a minion entered, bowed, and said solemnly, "Beg pardon, your lordship. Rolf Stow be here to report, sir, and the Chevalier de Gredin be waiting, as well."

"Tell them both to come in," Fife said. De Gredin knew of his informant, and it would do no harm to keep him apprised of Stow's reports. In fact, it would make the chevalier more confident of Fife's trust, and the more confident he became, the more likely he was to make a mistake if he was going to make one.

The chevalier entered first and made his flourishing bow with Stow following obsequiously in his wake, cap in his hand this time.

"Have you learned aught of interest, Rolf Stow?" Fife demanded.

Tugging his forelock, Stow said, "Aye, m'lord. Countess Isabella were to come here Wednesday, but because they be a-moving the wool from abbeys in the south and she fears the roads will be too crowded, she means to come Thursday."

"Faugh, is that all you've learned? Nothing more?"

"Only that she'll take the river path whilst her carts take the high road."

"What of the men? What are they doing?"

Rolf wrung his cap. "They go about their business, m'lord, as ever they do. Sir Hugo be taken up wi' the countess's demands, finding carts and wagons enough for all her lumber. She needs a train o' them, as all ken fine."

"She does," Fife said. "But if they try to move something other than wool, I want to know what it is. You go straight back tonight, so you won't be missed."

When Rolf had gone, de Gredin took up a position by the fireplace and said, "A train of carts and wagons should cover nearly anything one wanted to move."

"Never fear. I mean to see every one of those vehicles searched. Likewise, I want every wool cart approaching Leith Harbor searched as well. But what I want to know from you is how soon those papal ships can get here."

"Soon, sir," de Gredin said. "But I do have a piece of information for you."

"What is it?"

"I set two of my lads to watch a knight called Giffard MacLennan after I learned they had seen him entering Clendenen House with one of the Macleod sisters. He apparently met with Hugo Robison and Robert Logan, and has spent his time since then looking at and even visiting ships in the harbor. Yesterday morning he spent more than an hour aboard a Dutch merchantman called *Zee Handelaar*."

"Do you suspect that MacLennan is captain of a ship now in the harbor?"

"Nay, for by all accounts he did not sail here, although he is said to be a skilled man with boats. My guess is he is either looking to buy a ship or hire one."

"You interest me," Fife said. "Tell your lads to keep a good watch on him."

"As to that, I must put others to the task," de Gredin said with a grimace. "Those two are in the Tollgate, having been haled before a magistrate for some incident at the harbor. It took time to find them, which is why I tell you this only now. They'll keep silent, though, and I did not mention your name to them."

"At least you show some sense, but pray, do what you must to find out what the devil this MacLennan is up to."

When de Gredin had gone, Fife sat thinking for some time. He was as sure as he could be that the Sinclairs and Logan knew the whereabouts of the Stone and had known since the previous year. It had been Logan's own brother, after all, who had boasted that Logan knew how to find it, and Fife had believed he could force Logan to tell him. But his plan had failed, and the only ship to leave the harbor for the north or west then was Orkney's, with de Gredin aboard. Afterward, Fife had set a permanent watch on Leith Harbor and all ships loading to go north.

De Gredin had helped with the earlier search until Fife had threatened the lady Adela Logan, when de Gredin had basely betrayed him. Had he seen aught unloaded at Girnigoe that might lead him to the Templar treasure, Fife doubted that de Gredin would want to share that information unless he had to.

So, he needed Fife for some reason, and it began to look as if the Sinclairs and their friends had something of import now that they wanted to move in secrecy.

Sidony and Isobel rode to Lestalric Tuesday morning, arriving well before midday. The only remaining signs of Monday's downpour were myriad puddles and a sea of tents erected along the shore of Loch End, north of Lestalric's hill, to protect hundreds of bales of wool awaiting the short journey to ships that would carry them to the Low Countries and beyond. Riding up the steep track to the castle sprawled across the hilltop, they enjoyed a fine view of the tents.

Sidony stared, never before having seen such a sight, but Isobel said only, "That must be wool from one of the Border abbeys. Michael said it was on its way."

She explained more, but Sidony was only half listening. She did not care as much about wool as she did about learning if Giff was at Lestalric. Surely, he would be, with Rob due to return, if only to tell him that she knew about the treasure.

Except for servants, the first person they saw was Adela, who hurried down the main entrance steps to welcome them as they rode into the forecourt.

Her smile was reassuring, but as she and Sidony hugged each other, Sidony murmured, "I'm sorry for vexing you, Adela. I hope—"

"Hush," Adela murmured back. "I know how it is. 'Tis only that Rob lives in dread of betraying secrets. But I can assure him you won't betray this one."

"Perhaps," Sidony said doubtfully. "But what of Hugo?"

"Sorcha will manage Hugo," Adela said confidently. "In any event, Hugo and Michael won't arrive until tomorrow, with Isabella, and Hugo knows you are no prattler. But Rob comes today, and he does not yet know you so well."

With that, Sidony had to be satisfied. Inside, she looked for Giff only to hear Adela say he had ridden out early without saying when he meant to return.

Giff had left Lestalric soon after rising, determined to meet Rob on the road. It had occurred to him that with the lady Adela's sisters arriving that morning and heaven knew how many noble guests arriving throughout the afternoon for her supper, he and Rob would find no other good opportunity for private speech.

However, Rob had made a late start from Hawthornden, where he had spent the night with Hugo and Lady Robison, and the Edinburgh road was crowded in both directions with shepherds, *baaing* sheep, nipping herd dogs, and carts of wool drawn by horses, oxen, or braying mules. So Giff did not meet Rob and Rob's usual tail of a dozen armed men until a mile or so south of the river North Esk's track.

"Has the road been this busy all the way from town?" Rob asked him.

"Aye, so I hope your ties to the abbot are such that we may ride through his woods. I want to talk to you without having to shout over this din."

Rob grinned. "As I recall, even without any ties to the abbot, you rode through his woods just over a sennight ago."

"Aye, sure, but sithee, I was alone, not leading a dozen armed horsemen to trample his woods into pulp. In troth, I was sure enough that you'd respect them today that I took the main road with fair certainty that I'd not miss finding you."

Rob nodded and turned to the captain of his tail. "We'll turn off on the abbey track at the foot of Arthur's Seat. You and the lads can carry on through town, for I am as safe on the abbey grounds as on my own."

The captain acknowledged the order, and they soon reached the narrow, muddy, little-used track. Noting deep puddles on the track and nearby landscape from the recent rain, Michael said, "I hope you've good cause for this diversion, Giffard, my lad. Our horses are like to flounder in this devilish bog."

"I want to discuss things without risk of interruption or the odd listener," Giff said. "Lestalric will be teeming with guests."

"I warrant I could find us a place quiet enough to talk," Rob said.

"Aye, sure, but not without stirring remark. And, too, I've something to tell you that you won't like." Ignoring Rob's frown, he explained that the lady Sidony knew about the treasure, adding before Rob could make the same error that Isobel and Adela had, that she had known for some time.

"But how?"

When Giff had done his best to explain, to his surprise, Rob nodded and said with a grimace, "I ken fine how that can happen. One has only to recall how easily folks talk about private affairs in front of their servants, as if they were sticks of wood. I've learned things myself that road. And, as one of the family, Sidony does have a knack for fading from one's awareness when she chooses not to draw notice."

Giff did not think Rob had ever endured a position as a servant, but he did know that as a younger son at odds with both his father and older brother, Rob had done any number of things to support himself before inheriting Lestalric. One such thing was to act as captain of Hugo's tail for some years. Thus, certain members of the nobility unaware of his hard-earned spurs might have treated him disdainfully.

Giff eyed the other man narrowly, trying to gauge the state of his temper.

Rob met his gaze, grimaced, and said, "I was thinking we'll have to take care who the lass marries. Keeping secrets is devilish hard work in any situation, but it seems well nigh impossible after others in one's family come to know about them."

"Tales of the treasure are rife throughout Scotland," Giff reminded him.

"Just rumors, though," Rob said. "And the people who spread them are not involved in protecting the treasure. We are. Moreover, the item we aim to secure now is of personal importance to the Logans and Sinclairs, because its location was passed directly to Henry and to me. So, although the Order is involved, we are directly responsible for its safety."

"The lass kens nowt of the Stone," Giff said. "She does, however, believe I'll be carrying a portion of the treasure with me when I sail."

"Then we must not tell her more," Rob said. "The Abbot of Holyrood does not let its name pass his lips. Adela and I decided we should do the same. Mayhap she remembered that much and passed the advice to Sorcha and Isobel. Sithee, the three of them all learned about it, one way or another, from their husbands."

"Have you determined when it is to go aboard the ship?" Giff asked.

"Have you found one?"

"Aye, a fine Dutch merchantman, although one expert did call it a barge." Describing the ship, he told him about Jake Maxwell and his father, and also that Sidony had suggested that the man who had attacked him might work for Fife.

"Then the sooner we move, the better," Rob said. "We can have the Stone in place early Friday morning if we take advantage of this great wool commotion."

Giff assured him that the ship would be ready and asked his advice about the Dutch crew and their captain. "We can hardly let them sail their boat to our meeting place and then just tell them to go about their business."

"I'll discuss it with Hugo and Michael, but we'll have a complete plan before then," Rob said. "I'm returning to Roslin early tomorrow."

"So your lady wife has said. Must you really go just to return the same day?"

"Hugo's been concerned about a possible spy at Roslin for some time," Rob said. "So although the countess has given it out that she travels tomorrow, she will delay one day, using the crowded roads as her excuse. Fortunately, the Leith road will remain crowded all week, because the abbots' wool is coming in, and others will have to wait, because the abbeys take loading precedence over everyone else."

"Why does the countess not wait until all the wool is loaded?"

"Because his grace means to arrive on Saturday from Stirling and she wants at least two days to settle in before then." With a smile, he added, "Also because, as you told Michael, a bit of chaos may prove useful."

"I think I suggested a noisy procession. Have you moved it yet?"

"Let us discuss first where you want us to meet you," Rob said.

"I've two possible sites," Giff said, remembering Rob's reluctance to reveal details until absolutely necessary, and accepting the change of topic.

He described the sites, and with Rob easily recognizing both, they discussed the relative merits and chose the one nearest the road along which the Stone would come. By the time they had settled the details, they were approaching the castle.

Sidony's pleasure when Rob and Giff were in time to take the midday meal with everyone gave way to dismay when Rob announced, despite his wife's gentle protest, that the family and Giff would dine privately, rather than in the hall as usual.

Adela did not argue but asked the steward to set up a table in the solar for them. "Some of our guests are likely to arrive early," she added. "If they want to dine, pray seat them on the dais as we always do."

"Aye, my lady, and how many lads will you require to serve you?"

As she opened her mouth to reply, Rob said, "Send as many as you need to set out our food. We'll serve ourselves."

Adela's mouth dropped open, but at a look from her husband, she shut it and made no objection when he suggested that everyone adjourn at once to the solar.

"Giff has told him," Isobel murmured to Sidony as they followed Adela.

Watching Rob's stern profile, Sidony saw a muscle

twitch high in his cheek. "Sakes, he looks ready to murder someone," she said. "Probably me."

Isobel did not comment, which was just as well, because Sidony's gaze had shifted to Giff. He turned his head just then and smiled warmly, even, she thought, reassuringly. At any event, she felt reassured and warmed all through.

As soon as the table was ready, Rob took his place at its head and gestured to Giff to take the one at its foot. He said nothing until all the platters were in place. Then, dismissing the gillies, he waited only until everyone had taken seats after the grace, then looked first at Adela on his right and Isobel beside her. At last, his gaze moved across the table and came to rest on Sidony. Heat flooded her cheeks.

It was so unusual to see Rob angry that new guilt surged through her. Although she managed to meet his gaze, it took effort to do so, and more effort to resist looking to Giff for another dose of reassurance.

Rob said quietly, "Giff told me what happened. I won't deny that I'm angry about it, but the thing is done, many are at fault, and now we must take good care that the information goes no further. Do you all understand me?"

Before anyone else could speak, Adela said, "Sir, please, she did not—"

His hand closed over hers where it rested on the table beside him, silencing her. "I've no intention of acting the tyrant, my love, so you've no need to defend Sidony. What she should or should not have done—what anyone should or should not have done—is irrelevant now, unless you can think of anything that happened that may occur again." He paused, looked from face to face, and said, "No? Then we need say no more about that for now. I do not speak for

Hugo or Michael," he added, glancing at Isobel. "They are certainly likely to say more."

Sidony drew a long breath and let it out again.

Rob said, "If no one has anything else about this matter to discuss, mayhap someone can suggest another topic."

When no one else seemed inclined to speak, Sidony felt that she somehow bore a responsibility to do so. She said quietly to Giff, "Is it still your plan, sir, to find a ship and sail back to the west?"

"Aye, my lady," he said. "In troth, I have found my ship."

She sighed. "So you will see Kintail again quite soon, will you not? I do so wish I could go with you."

"You will go soon enough," Adela said as she helped herself from a platter of roast lamb that Rob held for her. "Our father's wedding is just weeks away now, so we shall all be departing in a fortnight. Art so eager to leave us, dearling?"

Sidony shook her head. It did seem impractical to wish she could go with him, but she feared that life in Edinburgh after he sailed would seem sadly flat.

Into the ensuing silence, Giff said to her with a disarming chuckle, "I've no objection if you want to come, my lady. One thing that has concerned us all along is Fife's likely interference, but even he should be put off at seeing a woman aboard."

"Now, see here," Rob said, turning that stern look on Giff. "Don't be putting notions in the lass's head. The last thing you want aboard that ship is a female."

Giff's eyes twinkled. "Now think, Rob," he said. "You've all told me what nuisances Fife's lads have made of themselves this past year, and we want to avoid drawing their interest. What if we were to fly a Norse flag and declare that we're carrying a Norse princess to visit Prince Henry at Orkney?"

"Don't be daft," Rob said, but he was grinning, which told Sidony that both men were joking. "Just think of the consequences, Giff. To take her with you, you'd have to marry her. If you didn't, you can be sure that Macleod would order the marriage the instant you delivered her to him if he didn't cut your liver out first."

"Och, well, then I'm afraid it is out of the question, my lady," Giff said, smiling in a way that wrung her heart. "But at least you can't say I was unwilling."

"But you are certainly of an age when most men do seek wives, sir," Isobel said lightly. "Do you never intend to marry?"

"Someday, perhaps," he answered. "I shall inherit Duncraig one day and have to settle to a laird's duties. But until then, I want as few responsibilities and ties to the land as possible, thus to avoid the usual pain and difficulty inherent in such."

Sidony saw the question hovering on the ever curious Isobel's tongue and said quickly, "Faith, I don't want to marry either, nor do I want to sail round the whole of Scotland to get home. 'Twould be dreadfully uncomfortable as well as unseemly."

She could not enter into the spirit of their exchange, but neither had she any desire to hear Isobel pry into matters that Giff did not wish to discuss.

He was regarding her quizzically, but it was Adela who spoke, saying, "Surely, you mean to marry one day, Sidony. As much as you dote on children, you must want a family of your own."

"Aye, sure, I'd like children," she said. "I'm just not sure I want a husband."

"But, my dear," Isobel said, "you must have the one to have the other."

"Aye, and there's the rub," Sidony said. They were all looking at her now, and she wished they would not but knew she'd brought it on herself.

Even so, she did not want to discuss it further. This was not the time, not with Rob silent again and still looking as if he wanted to beat someone, to tell them how much she was coming to dislike being told what she must and must not do.

Rob having announced that he wanted a few words with his wife, the two had disappeared up the stairs when Isobel said, "I mean to take a nap, Sidony, and I'd advise you to as well. It is likely to be late before we sleep tonight, and you will want to be up early to ride with Ealga to meet Isabella."

Sidony was not sleepy, but she knew Isobel needed her rest and could think of no graceful way to insist on staying alone in the solar or in the hall, since her sole companion—other than servants or men-at-arms—would apparently be Giff.

But then he said to Isobel, "If it please your ladyship, I would speak with Lady Sidony before she retires. I owe her an apology for my comments earlier."

If Sidony was surprised, Isobel seemed more so. But with a glance at Sidony, she said, "Very well, sir, I leave her in your care. Pray don't make me wish I had not."

"I'll take care, my lady," he said. But when she had left them, he said to Sidony with a mischievous twinkle in his eyes, "I have something I want to say to you, and I was going to ask you to step back into the solar with me, but doubtless you'd say 'tis too private and tell me to boil my head. So I've a better notion."

The lurking twinkle reminded her of how her sister Sorcha often looked just before leading her into an adventure that, likely as not, landed them both in the suds. Thus, she said warily, "What is this notion, sir?"

"I've seen what a fine horsewoman you are. Will you come ride with me?"

"Now?"

"Yes, now. Lady Isobel will sleep, and Lady Adela will be some time with her husband, so . . ." He grinned, revealing a hint of challenge in his expression.

"But I can't. Think what they would say!"

"The trick is to seize opportunity when it presents itself, lass, because if one loses the moment, it does not come again."

Nor would it, she knew. He would soon be gone.

"Of course," he added, the challenge now in his tone, "if you fear them . . ."

"Don't be daft," she said, adding honestly, "I am more afraid of you."

"Are you, lassie?" Although they were by no means alone, he put a hand to her cheek as he said gently, "You need not be. I'll not harm you."

"No, for I won't let you," she said, more to reassure herself than him. She hesitated until he raised his eyebrows. Then, with a sigh, as if she had not known from the moment he touched her that she would give in, she said, "Aye, I'll go."

She had second thoughts when he urged her straight out to the stables. She had changed from her riding dress to dine but agreed that she had no time to change again, not without risking an end to the whole mad scheme.

"Faint heart?" he murmured.

"No, but I'll likely ruin this dress."

"Not if you use a proper lady's saddle."

She wrinkled her nose, showing him what she thought of that idea, and said, "But tell the lads to hurry. Rob may not stay as long as you think with Adela."

"He'll spend the afternoon with her if he does not want to endure a bedtime lecture later," he said before turning away to order their horses saddled.

"You seem very sure of that," she said when he turned back to her. "I should think it is Rob who will be doing the lecturing now, and Adela who is enduring it."

"Nay, for he must return to Roslin in the morning," he said.

"But is not the countess coming to town tomorrow? Why does he not ride with Lady Clendenen and me to meet her?"

"Doubtless he wants an earlier start than her ladyship," he said glibly, pushing a hand through his hair. "Now, tell me how you learned to ride so well."

"My father taught us all," she said, and although she suspected he had somehow equivocated about Isabella, she responded calmly as he set himself to draw her out.

The lad who saddled their horses also saddled one for himself, thus telling Sidony that Giff had ordered him to accompany them, which surprised her.

Apparently Giff read her thoughts, because as they rode through the gateway, he said, "I'm daring, lass, not suicidal. I don't want Rob or any of your so-protective kinsmen after my blood. The lad will follow but not too closely."

"What did you want to say to me that necessitated this ride?"

For once it was he who hesitated. Then he said, "It did occur to me that I might have offended you with all that talk of marriage. I'd not want to think I had."

Mercy, she wondered, was he going to ask her to marry him? The thought was by no means as distasteful as she had led herself to believe it would be.

"You did not offend me," she said, lifting her chin. "You may recall my saying that marriage is not something I seek just now."

"Why not?"

She tried to think of a clever reply to make him either laugh or wish she did want a husband. The latter thought shocked her so that she resorted to grim candor. "If you must know, I'm tired of people telling me what to do. Husbands always do."

He laughed and said, "I'd feel the same way if I were a lass, so let us just enjoy this stolen freedom of ours. Would you like to see Leith Harbor?"

She agreed readily, ignoring the prick of disappointment at his easy acceptance of her declaration. But the day remained sunny, and the sight of wool being loaded onto one ship after another in the harbor proved fascinating. Not until they turned back toward Lestalric did she realize how much time had passed.

"Rob will murder both of us," she said. "If he does not, Adela will surely flay me with words for this escapade."

"Still, we enjoyed a fine afternoon, lass, and I'll tell you something I've been thinking this past hour and more. I'd like to know you better if you're willing. Mayhap, after you return to Glenelg, I could come and see you sometimes."

"I'd like that," she said solemnly, "if they *don't* murder us."

But it was neither Rob nor Adela who greeted their return but Lady Clendenen, who bustled up to them as Giff was lifting Sidony from her saddle.

"Sakes, where have you been, child?" her ladyship demanded. "I only just arrived, myself, but when I told one of the lads I wanted someone to fetch you to me directly, he said you had ridden out. But to have done so only with Sir Giffard! What were you thinking, the pair of you?"

"Did you want me for a particular reason, my lady?"

"Aye, of course. I wanted to tell you straightaway before it slipped my mind that we need not be in a bustle tomorrow. We can sleep as late as we want, for Isabella means to delay her journey until Thursday afternoon. But now that I think about it, mayhap Rob has already told you."

"No, madam," Sidony said, looking at Giff. "No one told me that."

Chapter 11

If Lady Clendenen noted tension between Sidony and Giff, she paid it no heed. Having made it clear that she did still intend to meet Isabella on Thursday, she waited only until Sidony agreed to leave town with her shortly before noon, then bustled away to her bedchamber to begin dressing for Adela's supper.

The minute her ladyship was beyond earshot, Sidony said accusingly to Giff, "You already knew about Isabella! I *knew* you were keeping something back."

"Did you?" he said in a maddeningly calm way. "I hope you don't expect me to apologize again, for I've no intention of doing so, but I must find Rob at once and tell him about this. He'll say I ought to have asked how she got her information, but doubtless she'd have snubbed me if I had asked. She won't snub him."

"But why should she snub anyone?" Sidony demanded as he hurried her across the yard to the entrance steps. Her cheeks burned with anger, but he—doubtless without any thought for that anger or for *any* impropriety—had put an arm around her shoulders. The enraging part was that despite being furious with him, she enjoyed the warm feeling it gave her. He did not even seem to be thinking about her, though, because he had not answered her question.

"The most likely person to have informed Ealga is the countess," she persisted. "In any event, why should it matter who did?"

"Because only the few of us directly involved were to have that information, which is why I did not tell you. In troth, I doubt I should say any more about it now. That must be for Rob to decide, but I think you should be with me when I tell him."

Gratified, she said, "I do want to be there, but why do you say I should be?"

He looked down at her with his mischievous twinkle. "Because I'll have to confess that I was with you when her ladyship told us. He is less likely to express his feelings to me so vehemently about that if you are there, as well."

Since she knew that he could not possibly be afraid of Rob if he did not fear Hugo, she realized more quickly than she might have that he sought to protect her, rather than himself, from Rob's displeasure.

"He won't like my having learned more about this, will he?"

"This wasn't your fault, lass, and he won't eat you. I won't let him."

They found Rob in the castle's cavernous, oak-beamed great hall, and noting his surprise at seeing them walk in together, Giff thought it best to give him no time to express it. It was a near thing, though, for servants were scurrying about, setting up tables for supper, so they had to wend their way through the congestion.

By the time they reached Rob, he was frowning heavily.

"We need to talk privately," Giff told him. "Yonder by the fire will do."

The frown grew heavier, but Rob nodded. As soon as they had separated themselves from the general commotion, he said curtly, "What is it?"

Giff knew he need state only the bare fact. "Lady Clendenen just told us the countess means to put off coming to town until Thursday afternoon."

"Did she now?" Rob said dryly. "She's gone upstairs, but I'll send someone to fetch her back down to us in the solar. No one else will be there now, because my lady wife is with our daughter, and I believe Isobel is still asleep."

"You should know, too, that her ladyship and the lady Sidony mean to ride out to welcome the countess and come back with her procession," Giff said.

"Adela did mention that," Rob said. To Sidony, he said, "I forgot that you and her ladyship had formed such an intention, but doubtless someone would have mentioned it today, and I'd have found a way to prevent a pointless journey."

"I hope you won't object to our going Thursday," she said.

"Nay, lass, although I expect Hugo will say I should forbid it in view of your curiously unusual behavior these past few days," he said.

Giff, knowing he bore some responsibility for her behavior, suppressed a smile at Rob's tactful phrasing. But the lass raised her chin at both of them and said, "In the past, my sisters have often behaved so. Mayhap I envied their more-enterprising natures and sought to learn how it feels to do as one pleases."

Giff held his breath, but Rob only shook his head and said, "To think I have always thought you the sensible one. Just have a care, my dear, and do not neglect to take an armed escort. The main road will still be gey busy Thursday."

"Thank you," she said. "We won't forget."

"I expect you'll want to go upstairs now to dress for supper," Rob said.

When she hesitated, Giff knew she was weighing her desire to learn more against Rob's likely tolerance for defying a clear dismissal. Well aware that Rob had treated their stolen afternoon with undeserved leniency, he felt only relief when she said she would see them at supper, curtsied gracefully, and walked away.

Rob said grimly, "You may come with me now. I have more to say to you."

Knowing he would not get off so lightly, Giff accompanied him without a murmur but hoped Lady Clendenen would soon obey her summons.

Shutting the solar door, Rob said, "What game is this with Sidony, Giff?"

Giff had been prepared to make the sort of brash response customary for him in such cases. But Rob's mild tone disarmed him, and in that moment, he realized that Sidony, having flung caution to the winds to ride with him, deserved more from him now than a flippant response.

Meeting Rob's gaze, he said, "Before you rip up at me, I should mention that one of your lads rode right behind us all afternoon."

"Even so . . ." Rob paused, remaining silent long enough

to make Giff feel the same disturbing sense of guilt the lass could arouse in him.

". . . I would know your intentions."

"Sakes, I don't know that myself," Giff said. "I've said I have no wish to marry yet, which is true, and she has said the same. But I'll not deny that when the time comes to settle down and produce a family, I may well want her for my wife."

"How magnanimous of you. How delightfully frank."

Giff winced. "I did not put that well, but in troth, I'm no better at this than at courtly manners. I like her more than any other woman I've met. She is not only gentle and kind but intelligent and never coy. One can enjoy sensible conversation with her. She makes me laugh—and I don't mean that unkindly," he added hastily.

Noting the twinkle that had crept into Rob's eyes, Giff felt deep relief, but he knew he must stay on guard. Mild of manner though Rob might be, he was also one of the finest warriors ever trained at Dunclathy and, thanks to years in the Borders, one of the most experienced. Moreover, Giff wanted to keep him as a good friend.

"Sidony is also an innocent maiden," Rob said. "So mind your step, lad, for it is not only her good-brothers you will face if you hurt her, but her sisters as well. You may not know it, but in the end, that could prove the worse for you."

A light rap at the door interrupted them, and when Rob said, "Enter," the door opened to admit Lady Clendenen. The gillie who accompanied her left at once, pulling the door shut behind him.

"Thank you for coming so quickly, madam," Rob said, drawing up a back stool for her and another for himself as Giff moved to stand by the hearth. "Pray, tell us how you came to learn that the countess means to delay her journey to town."

"Mercy, sir, is that why you've sent for me? I feared something dreadful had occurred, especially as Sir Giffard is here with you." She glanced at Giff.

"Forgive me," Rob said, recalling her attention with a smile. "I did not mean to frighten you, but sithee, I am sure that had Isabella intended to send you such a message, she would have entrusted it to me. She did not, and we concern ourselves with her safety, so we did wonder how you chanced to come by that news."

"Is it not accurate, then?"

"On the contrary, my lady, it *is* accurate."

"Well, I heard it at the Castle, where I dined today with the princess Mary."

"I see. Was it the princess herself who told you?"

She frowned. "Do you know, I don't recall who did. There were any number of us—all ladies, you see, and all talking at once, as we do—so talk just flowed. I'm sorry I cannot tell you more, or even hazard a guess as to who may have said what."

"Thank you, madam," Rob said. "Do not concern yourself further about this. You have done nowt but aid us, and for that I am most grateful."

She rose, and Giff went with her to open the door. Smiling up at him as he did, she murmured, "Thank you, sir. I trust you enjoyed your afternoon."

The conspiratorial manner in which she spoke made him grin as he nodded. Then, shutting the door behind her, he turned back to find Rob smiling.

"So the plan marches, does it?" Giff said.

Rob nodded. "It does. I must let the others know, so it's as well I'd planned to leave early, for I dare not draw notice by going now, nor can I entrust this message to a gillie. You just make sure that ship of yours is in place by first light Friday and that you can load her and be away quickly. Our success may depend on that."

"I won't fail you," Giff promised.

For all the attention Sidony paid while dressing for Adela's supper, her maid could have turned her out in rags instead of a becoming pale-yellow sideless surcoat trimmed with bands of colorful embroidery over a gown of mossy green silk.

When the maid had arranged the soft folds of the skirt and linked a silver girdle low on her hips so that it would show through the surcoat's deep side openings, she handed her mistress a looking glass, then settled a green-and-yellow chaplet carefully over her smooth tresses and bent to buckle her shoes.

As soon as Sidony was ready, she went in search of Ealga. Learning from her that she had been able to tell Rob only that she had heard about Isabella's intended delay at the Castle, Sidony wondered if Giff might be persuaded to tell her more.

The supper was excellent, as all Adela's suppers were, but it was also just like all the others of its ilk that Sidony had attended. A din of minstrels' music and chatter accompanied the meal, and afterward musicians played for dancing. But although she enjoyed the dancing, she saw disappointingly little of Giff.

He wore a blue-velvet doublet with jeweled buttons down the front and matching soled hose, all of which she was sure he had borrowed from Rob, and he deigned to join one ring dance. Otherwise he circulated without lighting anywhere and, most annoyingly, paid her no heed aside from a bow and a smile or two. He left before midnight, and she excused herself shortly afterward to go to bed.

Rob left for Roslin before dawn Wednesday and Giff left as well to make final preparations for his journey, so Sidony and Isobel spent the morning at Lestalric with Adela. They returned to Sinclair House late that afternoon and retired much earlier than they had the previous night.

Thursday morning arrived with a brisk wind whistling around the house, and as Sidony donned her riding dress hours later, she saw clouds flying high and low through a gray sky. But the sun peeped through as she and Isobel ate their midday meal, an hour earlier than usual, and despite the wind, the air outside was clear and brisk when she joined Lady Clendenen and their escort of six men-at-arms.

Sidony knew the ride might grow tedious, thanks to Ealga's preference for the boxy lady's saddle that many noblewomen had begun using. Although well lined and padded with sheepskin, it forced her to sit sideways and rocked precipitously with the movements of her horse. It was no wonder, Sidony thought as she rode beside her through town, that her ladyship did not enjoy riding. That she would endure it to meet Isabella only proved how highly she esteemed the countess.

Giff had spent much of Wednesday seeing everything ready for Friday's departure. He had found the *Zee Handelaar* tied to the shorter of Leith's two wharves, its crew efficiently loading provisions. The Dutch captain was not with them at the time, so when he returned in the afternoon, Giff asked him where he had been.

The Dutchman said, "When you travel, *mynheer*, do you not enjoy to see something of places you visit?" When Giff agreed that he did, the other spoke enthusiastically about Edinburgh, then said earnestly, "My men are reliable, *mynheer*. Also, I have the accounts for your provisions if you would care to see them now."

Finding them satisfactory and having funds that Rob had given him for the purpose, Giff nodded, saying, "I'll pay you half of this amount now, as we agreed, and the rest when we have loaded our cargo Friday morning, before we sail."

The man hesitated, so Giff said, "Recall that I shall also pay you half what we agreed for you and your crew then, too, the rest when we reach our destination."

Although neither captain nor crew would go north, Giff had bargained in good faith, knowing the Sinclairs and Rob would honor all promises he made for hiring the ship. Its men would share a generous sum for doing little, so he was sure they would see it as an excellent bargain unless, of course, he and the others failed to persuade the Dutchman, when they put their own men on as crew, that they were not stealing his ship. Certainly, the man was confident enough, because he shook hands warmly before they parted and he returned the *Zee Handelaar* to its mooring.

Giff returned then to Lestalric, took fond and formal leave of his hostess after supper, and arose early Thursday morning to carry his own gear to the ship. He intended to sleep aboard to be certain that all remained in order until they sailed.

The wind blew, chilling the air and warning of heavier weather to come.

Passing through the tiny, bustling village of North Leith, he emerged onto the shore of the harbor, seeing only then that the Dutch ship had gone.

The ride to meet Isabella was proving longer than either Sidony or Ealga had anticipated, for they had reached the turn onto the track along the river North Esk without seeing any sign of the countess's cavalcade.

"She must have started out much later than we'd expected," Sidony said.

"Aye, well, mayhap sheep and wool carts still obstruct even this track, but I expect we'll find her soon now. This wind is becoming a nuisance, though."

Sidony agreed, and they rode on for another half hour before she noted with a worried glance that her companion was flagging. "Are you unwell, madam?"

"I do wish you and your sisters would just call me Ealga," her ladyship said querulously. "By law, I shall be your mother in less than a month."

"I think you must be very tired," Sidony said. "It cannot be comfortable or easy to ride in a way that makes you fear being flung to the ground at any moment."

"No, it isn't," her ladyship agreed. "But I owe a duty to Isabella, and one does not shirk one's duty. I just wish we knew how much longer she will be."

"If you will consent to rest here for a time, out of the wind, I can ride on until I catch sight of them. The track is dry and my pony nimble, so it should not take me long to find them and ride back to tell you where they are."

Lady Clendenen agreed with obvious relief. "But you must not go without taking at least two of our men with you, my dear."

Since they had six in their escort, Sidony laughed. "They may come if they can keep up, but should I not see you made comfortable first?"

"Mercy, no, just go. The other men will look after me, and the sooner you find Isabella, the sooner I shall be comfortably at home again."

Needing no further encouragement, Sidony urged her mount forward and gave it a touch of heel, exhilarating in the faster pace. Moments later, she looked over her shoulder to see two of their escort riding after her.

Chuckling, she urged her mount to a faster pace. The men would not scold her, and unless she ran right into Isabella or Hugo, no one else would, either.

The track had been steep as it led to higher ground from Edinburgh's alluvial plain, but it eased now to a gentler incline through shady woodland that did not tax her mount in the least. When the woods thinned, she knew the path would soon run nearer the cliff edge at the deepest part of the gorge, so she slowed a bit.

Soon she could see the turbulent river below, and in the distance, the tall, square tower of Hawthornden thrusting through thick-growing trees. The castle was still some distance away, because the gorge did not run straight. The track would soon head into the woods again to avoid having to follow each bend in the river.

Abruptly, she had a long view of the west bank deep in the gorge and saw riders on the path there with banners waving that she recognized as the Sinclairs'. She recognized the slender countess astride her white mare among the leaders.

Having traveled with Isabella's cavalcade the previous year, Sidony knew they had followed the track she was on now. The one down in the gorge was narrow and not frequently traveled. Nor was it suitable for the carts and wagons that usually carried Isabella's astonishing amount of baggage.

Although Sidony felt a little annoyed at what was clearly a change in route, she knew she could not blame Giff or Rob for not telling her. Neither man could have expected that she and Ealga would have to ride so far to meet Isabella.

Noting a single oxcart piled high with canvas-covered contents following the riders, and deducing that it doubtless accounted for their snail's pace, she saw no other baggage vehicle, only laden sumpter ponies in a string.

Knowing that she and Ealga could easily return to where the main road crossed the river in time to meet the others, she wondered if Ealga would want to wait for them. On the winding, narrow path, Isabella could well be another hour.

"Mistress!" shouted one of the men who had been following her, as she turned to head back. "There be riders yonder!"

He was pointing, and she realized with shock that he did not mean Isabella's party. North of them on the river track, a larger group of riders approached a curve in the river that would soon bring them into view of the riders from Roslin.

Sidony was nearly certain the banner the newcomers flew was a royal one.

"Sakes, we must warn them!" she exclaimed. But the

cliff was a hundred feet higher than the river path, and she knew they could not hear her shouts above the echoing roar of the water as it tumbled headlong through the gorge.

No one looked up at them, nor could she imagine how to warn them of the danger ahead even if someone did. Only then did it occur to her that no Roslin guards had intercepted her on the way. That Hugo might have called them all off with Isabella on the move made no sense.

A tickle of fear slid up her spine, and when her brain refused to provide a solution, she shifted her gaze to her two men-at-arms, only to see that both were waiting for her to decide what to do.

Gritting her teeth, she told herself it was exactly the sort of hobble that Rob would call a "bubbly-jock" and just what she had meant in telling Giff she could not make decisions. Sorcha, Adela, or Isobel would know what to do. Why didn't *she*?

Then, suddenly, it came to her that the only route possible for Isabella's usual baggage train was the ridge track, and she said crisply, "You two, we're going on. The baggage carts must lie ahead of us, and they will have men-at-arms with them. Their captain will know what to do, but we must hurry!"

Urging her mount to its fastest pace, she fairly flew into the woods, only to round a curve and meet horsemen so abruptly that her mount reared. As she fought to stay in the saddle, the men closed in quickly around her.

The two lads with her did not reach for their swords, nor did she blame them. They were far outnumbered, and the others wore all black and carried the same royal banner as the riders down in the gorge.

To her astonishment, despite their black clothing, their

leader was not the Earl of Fife but the Chevalier de Gredin. His jade-green eyes gleamed as he flashed the smile that she and her sisters had once thought charming.

"My lady, how pleasant to meet you here." Without pause, he flung orders over his shoulder: "Four of you, with me. Two others, ride on and tell his lordship I've means now to force his enemies to tell him what he wants to know if his search proves unproductive. Tell him I will keep it safe for him. You others, go back and slow those carts until the wench and I are well away. Search them again if you must."

"What are you doing?" Sidony demanded. "I'm going nowhere with you!"

"*Mais bien sûr, ma chère*, you will," he said. "Further, you will go quietly, or I'll order your men killed right here. Then I shall tie your hands behind your back and lead your horse myself. Decide quickly which course you prefer."

With the Dutch ship gone from its mooring, Giff had hoped briefly to find her tied again at one of the wharves. But a single question at the first wharf elicited the information that before dawn that morning, its captain had taken on a load of wool from the abbeys and sailed for Bruges with the outgoing tide.

Recalling that the Dutchman had sailed with half of his provisions paid for, Giff winced, recalling the man's hesitation to take the money and seeing it in new light. Recalling then the two louts that had attacked him on Sunday, and Sidony's suggestion that they might be Fife's men, it occurred to him that he might glean some useful information if they were still residents of the Tollgate.

Remounting, he rode back into town.

The wiry, middle-aged baillie at the Tollgate remembered them. "Aye, sure, sir," he said. "But a man did come late Monday night to fetch them away."

Learning that the man wore black was not proof, but Giff was as certain as he could be that Fife, having discovered that the Dutch ship figured in the reel he danced with the Sinclairs, had persuaded the Dutch captain to take a load of wool and go. The plain fact, Giff decided, was that he could waste time railing that the ship was gone and scramble his brains trying to create a message that would tell the others what had happened without giving information to the messenger or anyone who intercepted him—or he could find another ship.

Any number of them still rode at anchor in the harbor, so he got to it at once. Leaving his horse in the harbor stable, he visited ship after ship only to discover that most captains still in port had either already loaded and were awaiting the next tide, or intended to load that day or the next with cargo for which they had contracted.

He even tried the two French longboats, still moored in the harbor. Both captains seemed willing enough at first but asked more questions about his destination and cargo than Giff wanted to answer, with the predictable result that each declined his offer after wasting a good deal of his time.

Near day's end, he remembered how friendly Captain Maxwell had been. Although undeniably Fife's man, Maxwell had struck him as a seaman first. He would know most of the ships and might be willing to suggest one Giff could hire.

Accordingly, knowing he'd be wise to take along something to ease his welcome in case Fife had warned Maxwell against him, he purchased three hot meat rolls and collected from the stable the satchel containing his gear and a jug of heady Isles brogac to take with him. Then he looked for the *Serpent*'s towboat and found it beached in the same place it had been on Sunday, with its oarsmen nearby.

The harbor water was choppier than Sunday, and the wind blew spray at them as the men rowed him to the ship. When they reached it, Giff slung his satchel over a shoulder and went nimbly up the rope ladder and aboard.

Sidony had expected the Chevalier de Gredin to deliver her to Fife. He had been Fife's man when she and others in her family had met him, and despite certain actions of his that suggested opposition to Fife, and a year spent in the north with Henry, she knew that Adela and Rob believed—and doubtless so would Henry—that de Gredin was still as much Fife's man as any of Fife's men-at-arms. And now, here he was proving it by riding under a royal banner and threatening her.

The thought of being handed over to the earl as a prize of war was terrifying enough, especially as de Gredin had said cheerfully that he expected Fife to enjoy questioning her. He had even suggested horrible means that the earl might use, until she shut her ears to him and thought hard about Giff MacLennan instead. If anyone could come up with horrid things to do to Fife and de Gredin, Giff surely could.

Instead of heading back to Edinburgh as she had expected, de Gredin—leading her horse despite what he had said earlier—had abruptly turned off the track and headed over the ridge and down the other side. In time, they came to a cottage, where he dismounted and lifted her from her saddle.

"Two of you, fetch the cart and see to the horses," he said. "I won't be long."

Gripping her arm, he took her inside the empty cottage, where he allowed her to relieve herself in a night pail in a curtained alcove before mixing her a mug of something horrid that he made her drink. She began to grow sleepy, and although she fought it, blackness soon enveloped her.

She awoke, moaning. It was pitch dark, she could hardly breathe, and her head ached so badly that she could not think. She lay on a hard, bouncing surface and heard the rattle of wheels beneath her. Then blackness descended again.

The next time, she awoke to hear neighing and a jangle of harness. Then came a screeching sound and enough dim light to see that she was inside a crate in an open building, a stable perhaps. Someone had pried off the crate's lid. Gulping fresh air, she tried to sit up and realized her hands were behind her, tightly bound.

"Not a word," de Gredin hissed, helping her. "Drink this quickly," he added, putting a cup to her lips and gripping her jaw, tilting the cup's contents down her throat so quickly that she swallowed, choking, sure she would be sick.

Salty air and a glimpse of harbor outside the wide-open doors told her where they were. Hearing male voices approaching, she opened her mouth to scream, saw his fist coming, and knew no more.

Chapter 12

Giff, Captain Maxwell, and Jake enjoyed supper sitting together on two of the oarsmen's benches in dusky half-light, sharing Giff's meat rolls with their two watchmen. Giff shared the brogac in his jug, too, but only with the captain.

Young Jake, delighted to see him, had said nonetheless bluntly, "I dinna ha' your shilling yet. Me da' wouldna pay me for clearing up below."

"Nor should he," Giff said. "How much of a task can it be on a new ship?"

"Aye, well, it gets dirty enough, and there be bundles and barrels and all to shift. Also, there be rat traps to empty when we've been at the wharf. I dinna mind the clearing, nor even yet the scrubbin', but I dinna like rats, dead or no."

Maxwell told his son sternly that he should be thanking Sir Giffard for his supper instead of complaining. "In this wind, I'd no' ha' wanted to make a fire for cooking," he added. "We've a deep enough firepot, but this be gey safer."

Amiable conversation continued, and Giff entertained his hosts with bard's tales of the Highlands and Isles until Maxwell sent Jake to bed and said, "We ha' been sleeping in the aft cabin, sir, and he'll go right off, so come along and bring that jug o' yours. When ye want to leave, I'll hang a lantern to bring the towboat. All my lads but these two sleep ashore yet, and the boat stays wi' them, but they'll see our light."

"Do you know yet when you sail?" Giff asked as he followed him into the aft cabin, where shelf beds, one atop the other, occupied the stern wall and a small table built into a cubby in the steerboard wall boasted narrow benches on either side of it.

"Not long now, I expect," Maxwell said as the two men took seats facing each other. Jake soon scrambled onto the top bed and pulled a quilt over himself.

"His lordship's people ha' been carrying provisions and gear aboard for some days now," Maxwell said. "Some they stowed in the aft hold, some in the fore, and some o' his lordship's effects be in them kists by the door and in a small hold under the wee trap by yon washstand. See you, this be the master's cabin, but Jake admires them shelf beds more than the pallet he sleeps on in my own wee forecastle cabin, and until his lordship comes aboard, I canna see the harm."

"Does his lordship sail with you then?"

"Wi' respect, sir, mayhap I should ken why ye be asking afore I answer ye."

Giff shrugged. "Plain, rude curiosity, Captain, so you can tell me it is none of my affair. I've more tales to tell if you'd prefer them. One of my favorites, which I thought unsuitable for young Jake's ears earlier, is about a Norse king's daughter known far and wide for her talent in the black arts."

"Indeed, your tales amuse me, and your whiskey is very fine," Maxwell said, glancing at the top bed, where all was silent. "What magical things could she do?"

Giff reached for the jug and poured a generous amount in Maxwell's mug and a like amount in his own as he said, "Doubtless the most useful was to fly high above the countryside, so no enemy could hinder her. She proved gey helpful to her father, the King, who often consulted her when his other advisers failed him. But he was jealous of the vast forests of Lochaber, which were finer than his own, so . . ."

Speaking quietly, he drew the tale out, embellishing the way the wench had flown to rain fire on the forests and the lengths to which people had gone in futile attempts to stop her. He lingered over their talks with the wise man who suggested a silver arrow, and by the time he reached the lass's death and her father's sorrow, Jake was breathing audibly and evenly in the top bed, and Giff's remaining audience of one had refilled the mugs twice and was swaying where he sat.

Giff went on to tell him about Deirdre of the Sorrows, initiator of generations of blood spilled because her father had failed to reward a soothsayer. He stopped talking only after Maxwell put his head on the table and began to snore.

Leaving him as he was, Giff went quietly out on deck and looked for the sentries. One slept on a rowers' bench, wrapped in a heavy blanket. The other stood atop the forecastle, looking east into the starlit expanse of the windy firth.

After quietly raising the rope ladder, Giff climbed up to join him. In the wind, the man did not note his approach until Giff was behind him.

"'Tis a fine blustery night, is it not?" Giff said.

The man swung round. "Sakes, sir, ye startled me near out o' me skin!"

"I believe Captain Maxwell told me the other day that two men alone can raise your yardarm and sail," Giff said amiably. "Is that right?"

"Aye, it is," the man said with a touch of pride. "See you, sir, we've pulleys and that to make the sail light as a bedsheet, so I'm thinking one man could do it alone were it no' for the yard being of a mischievous nature. D'ye want I should hoist the lantern, sir, so yon boat will come t' fetch ye?"

"I would first like you to help me put up the sail."

"Och, nay, sir, I canna do that."

"Can you swim?" Giff asked.

"Aye, sure, but—"

Giff heaved him over the side and went back down to the deck to discuss his request with the second watchman.

The Earl of Fife had endured a frustrating day, for despite his certainty that Isabella, the admittedly formidable Countess of Strathearn and Caithness, carried the Stone in her great train of baggage, he had been unable to find it.

He had confronted Isabella himself, but despite the royal banner to which all loyal Scottish nobles owed duty and respect, Isabella had not deigned to dismount from her horse. She had said he might look at anything he liked but to get on with it. If she held him in any respect, Fife had discerned no hint of it.

It was truly a pity, he thought as he gazed morosely at his laden supper trencher, that sons of the King of Scots, unlike royal sons in every other civilized place he could call to mind, bore only the rank of earl and not that of prince.

Isabella's rank equaled his, for she was a countess twice over in her own right. Doubtless, she believed she outranked him, because although he held two earldoms, his had come to him by judicious marriages, not by birthright.

"Forgive me, my lord, if I intrude on your thoughts," the lady on his left said softly. "You have been so silent. I trust you enjoy your usual excellent health."

"I do, indeed, madam," he said, smiling at her. "The day has been tedious, but I look forward to a more entertaining evening."

He could be charming if he put his mind to it. The lady was beautiful and very generous with her charms. And, too, her husband was away and Fife's wife had stayed in Stirling.

He returned his attention to his supper until a royal page came to inform him that the Chevalier de Gredin awaited him in his audience chamber. Murmuring to his beautiful neighbor that duty called him, he left the hall without another word.

Giff shook the shoulder of the second watchman, noting as he did that the shouts of the first had diminished and doubtless would not carry far in a wind that blew them toward the open sea. The chap seemed an able enough swimmer, though, and would certainly raise the alarm as soon as he reached shore.

Giff wondered briefly if he'd have been wiser to kill him, but the man was not his enemy, and it was not Giff's nature to second-guess himself. In his opinion, concern after the fact generally proved useless.

The watchman stretched out on the rowers' bench groaned and muttered, "Leave me be, Geordie, or I'll give ye your head in your hands to play wi'."

"Wake up, lad," Giff said sternly. "You're wanted."

The man's eyes opened, he blinked, and finally, realizing that it was not his mate who had awakened him, sat up rather too quickly and gave his head a shake.

"Beg pardon, sir," he said, beginning to stand but subsiding when Giff put a heavy hand on his shoulder. "Where be the captain?"

"Sleeping," Giff said. "I need your help, though. What's your name?"

"Hob Grant, sir. But where's our Geordie?"

"Busy," Giff said. "Stand up and I'll show you."

The man stood, clearly still groggy but struggling to come full awake.

"Over here," Giff said, indicating the end of the bench nearest the gunwale. "Look yonder. I ken fine there's little light, thanks to the lack of a moon and a sky full of clouds flying before this wind. But do you see that splashing?"

"Aye, sure," the man said.

"That's your man Geordie," Giff said.

"Nay, he'll be forward atop the forecastle."

Giff watched as he looked, then looked back at the erratic splashing in the water halfway to the shore. When he turned back to Giff, his eyes were wide.

"Sakes, sir, we must do summat straightaway! He'll drown!"

"I don't think so," Giff said. "Can you swim?"

The eyes grew even wider. "Nay, sir, nary a stroke!"

"Then mayhap you will be more obliging than your friend Geordie was. I should like you to help me pull in the anchor and put up the sail."

"But, sir, this be the Earl o' Fife's ship!"

"Fife won't mind, for he shan't know anything about it," Giff said. "So, will you help me, or do you want to join your friend?"

"But ye canna sail this ship by your own self, man!"

"I won't have to; I'll have this fine wind and you to aid me."

"Sakes, his lordship will hang us all when he catches us."

"Then we must see that he does not catch us. But we waste time," Giff said. "If you won't help, I must throw you overboard and get on with it myself."

"Nay, then, I'll do what ye say. But should I no' wake the captain?"

"Not yet," Giff said. "I'm thinking we'll want to weigh anchor first."

"Aye, sure, for that'll take the two of us. What o' the tide?"

"It was turning when the abbey bell rang Vespers, so it won't begin to turn against us for an hour yet. Do you know any obstacle betwixt here and the open sea?"

"Sakes, sir, d'ye no' ken these waters?"

Giff grinned. "I know them well enough. I want to know if you do."

"Well, there be nowt to worry us if we keep to the middle once we be in the main channel—well, nowt till we come to the Isle o' May, as ye might say."

"I think we'll see the Isle of May."

"Aye, sure, but if we go too far north, we could run into—"

"We'll be heading south, not north."

"Mayhap we will then, but we must go north till we clear the east sands o' Leith and the Black Rocks. Then there'll be yon rocks at the narrows, sir—Fidra, Craigleith, and the Bass Rock, as well as—"

"All close to shore," Giff said, having no intention of going so far. If all went well, he would move the ship less than three miles in darkness. He was no fool, and he knew his success must depend on the wind's cooperation and that of the tide.

If either shifted too early . . .

But it was useless now to think about that, so he set to work.

Dismissing the page without ordering refreshment for himself or de Gredin, who annoyed him by having brazenly taken a seat near the fire and not rising at his entrance, Fife waited until the lad had gone before saying curtly, "I don't like cryptic messages. What is this mysterious object you say you have found?"

"One infers from such a question that you found no more of value amongst Countess Isabella's belongings than I did," de Gredin said.

"You will stand when you address me," Fife snapped, wondering how far the man would go in his stupid belief that his hostage remained a mystery.

"I pray that your lordship will forgive my rudeness," de Gredin said, getting up at once and making his customary deep bow. "I rode far today and have had naught to eat. But weariness and hunger do not excuse bad manners. I do believe, though, that I have acquired the means to force both the Sinclairs and Logan of Lestalric to share with us whatever they know about his holiness's treasure."

"So, why did you not bring your acquisition here to me?" Fife asked, ignoring de Gredin's characterization of the treasure. Thanks to his own men, he knew the chevalier had captured Lady Sidony, but he had not yet decided what to do about it. Holding her was a risk he was not certain he wanted to take. He was concerned only with the Stone of Destiny, and it was unlikely that a mere lass—and the youngest of the Macleod lot, at that—would know aught about it. Still, she might prove useful as a hostage, which was clearly de Gredin's intent.

"I dared not bring it here openly," de Gredin said with a touch of amusement. "Nor could I think of a way to assure its concealment if I had to cart it through town and enter through the gates of the Castle. By your own order, all carts and wagons must be searched at the gate tower unless you yourself command otherwise, so it seemed safer to conceal it elsewhere."

"You have yet to identify this so-important item," Fife pointed out.

De Gredin smiled. "It is not, precisely, an item, my lord, but a person."

Curbing his temper, Fife remained silent.

De Gredin's smile faded. He said, "'Tis Lady Sidony Macleod, my lord."

"Her father is a Councilor of the Isles, adviser to my nephew MacDonald."

"More importantly, she is good-sister to Sir Michael Sinclair, Sir Hugo, and Lestalric. Not one will risk her safety. They will bargain to protect her."

"You said you had hidden her. How, and where?"

"Aboard ship, but no one aboard knows she is there. She is in the hold, and I gave her a potion to make her sleep through the night. She will be frightened, dazed, and most uncomfortable by morning—just right for questioning, I should think."

"Then your promised ships have come," Fife said, certain de Gredin meant to keep the lass under his own control. That he had not told Fife the ships had come annoyed him. "Where are they?" he demanded. "I trust they are here at Leith."

When the chevalier did not answer, Fife's impatience stirred again. "Well?"

"I pray you will forgive me, my lord," the exasperating man said quietly. "I can scarcely think. Might it be possible for me to get something to eat?"

Fife recognized the tactic, for he employed many such himself. De Gredin clearly thought his prize had given him the upper hand and that it would do him no harm to flex it. Little though Fife wanted to play games, he decided to let him go on thinking so for a time. It would only strengthen his own position later.

Without comment, he shouted for a gillie and ordered the chevalier supper and wine. "He'll have it here," he added.

When he turned back, he saw that de Gredin had sat down on the cushioned settle in the inglenook, and was leaning back with his eyes shut, apparently resting.

Giff watched with satisfaction as wind filled the great square sail and the ship began slowly to move northward. Thanks to a habit of obedience to command and despite his nearly palpable fear of both his captain and the Earl of Fife, Hob Grant proved an able assistant.

They had raised the anchor, and as the *Serpent* was moored well away from other ships, doubtless due to his lordship's fear that one might drift into it, they had been able to trust the tide's northward run to the harbor exit until they could get the sail up. It was a near thing, though, because the wind blew directly from the west, a detail that made Hob Grant question their ability to get safely free of the harbor.

Giff chuckled. "That's our least concern, lad. Can you mind the helm?"

"Aye, sure, but ye'll never look after that great sail on your ownsome."

"Don't you fret about me," Giff said. He had not enjoyed himself so much for weeks. Energy surged through him. If he spared any thought for Sidony, it was only to wish briefly that he could share such a moment with her.

Ordering Hob to the stern, he returned his attention to the sail, which boasted good stout braces, the so-useful lines at the ends of a yardarm with which one could shift it to different angles and thus take full advantage of the wind. The *Serpent*'s yard also boasted a wooden spar to hold the lead edge of the sail when running close to the wind. Although it lay along the deck now, Giff knew from experience that it would prove useful in the treacherous Pentland Firth north of Caithness.

Manning the braces by himself was a task requiring

strength and agility, but he enjoyed it. The task was not as easy as with two, but he was never happier than with a wind blowing hard and a good boat beneath him.

He knew no feeling in the world like skimming over waves at speed, and once on the open waters of the Firth of Forth, with the wind behind them, he had only to set the sail and pray that he did not run too close to shore before he found the spot on Lestalric's eastern coast where the Nidrie burn spilled into the firth.

Even then, the difficulty would be getting the sail down before he was too near for safety yet near enough for the others to reach them quickly and get loaded. He wanted to be well away before Fife came after him.

By no stretch of imagination could Giff make himself believe that the earl would not learn shortly after daylight that his precious ship had vanished from the harbor. Once he did, he would raise a hue and cry. Most ships now in the harbor were foreign, but Giff knew that the wily earl was capable of commandeering one or another to his use, nonetheless.

"I set the rudder, sir, and tied her off," Hob said, freeing one brace as Giff held the other to adjust the sail. "D'ye think our Geordie made it safe to shore?"

"Aye, sure," Giff said. "That lad is a gey strong swimmer."

"Then, will he no' ha' told the others that we're away? Even an he drowned, d'ye no' think our lads ashore might ha' seen we'd gone and followed us?"

"I don't think they saw a thing," Giff said. "One sees little on a night as black as this one. Even when the clouds part, we've no moon above, only stars."

"Aye, sure, but I can make out the shore yonder," Hob said, gesturing.

"We see better on the water," Giff explained. "If they look from the harbor, they'll see the opposite coast more easily than the ships right in front of them, and what they do see there will be a jumble of masts. No lanterns were lit. I noted that particularly, and if the lad who was set to watch for ours is still awake—which I'd doubt—he'll look for the lantern, not a moving ship. Your friend Geordie will have a tale to tell, right enough, but I wager the tale will stir most men to nowt but laughter. You said yourself, Hob Grant, 'tis impossible to do what we have done."

"Aye, sir, but we did it," Hob pointed out.

"Just so," Giff said. "So don't be so quick next time to believe something is impossible. Chances are that if you just seize your opportunity and make up your mind that you can do it, you will. But if you never act, you'll never succeed."

"Aye, perhaps," Hob said. "But me da' would say that what ye did were plain daft, sir. See you, I'd no' say it m'self," he added. "No' till I learn t' swim."

Giff laughed, clapped him on the back, then peered into the distance, trying to decide just where the devil the wee burn he sought emptied into the sea.

Fife had contained his patience and sipped claret, watching his guest through hooded eyes, until de Gredin pushed away the remains of his supper and drank deeply enough to assure Fife that he sought bolstering as much as to slake his thirst.

"Feeling better?" Fife said then.

"You have been quiet, my lord."

"I feel sure that in your own good time you will provide the information I have requested," Fife said coolly.

De Gredin flushed. "I did not mean to be rude. I was famished."

"And now you are no longer so."

"Yes, my lord. So I'll tell you what you want to know, and then we shall go to bed and arise not too early to go have a little talk with her ladyship."

Fife approved that plan, and when he heard what de Gredin had to say, he was glad—as, indeed, he nearly always was—that he had not revealed his irritation. Not that his ire was entirely soothed, for the papal ships had not yet come, and he did not like anyone, let alone those who served him, to be unpredictable.

Bidding his guest good night, he retired, confident that all would go as he wished. But although he slept well, his rest ended abruptly an hour earlier than usual when a trembling page brought him an urgent message from the harbor.

Discovering that the force of the wind lessened considerably when the land mass of eastern Lestalric interposed itself as they rounded the Black Rocks and Eastern Crags to head southeast, Giff decided to tack back and forth along the coast while staying far enough out to run no risk of grounding.

He knew where he wanted to be, but he had not seen the shoreline from the water, and he realized belatedly that he ought to have made opportunity to do so.

As he peered into the distance off the steerboard side, Hob said, "Where be we a-going, sir?"

"'Tis called the Nidrie burn," Giff said. "Do you know it?"

"Nay, sir, but there be dunamany wee burns trickling into the firth right along hereabouts. Will ye ken the one ye want when ye see it?"

"I will, but by the time I find it, our friend Fife may be looking for us."

"The tide will turn again soon," Hob said. "Out here, ye can feel it."

Giff nodded. "Aye, and the sky is growing lighter, so I'm thinking Captain Maxwell may waken soon. 'Tis a pity you've no towboat aboard."

"Aye, well, we do keep one, but ye left it ashore wi' our lads, did ye no'?"

"You keep a civil tongue in your head," Giff advised him dryly.

The two were grinning at each other when a bewildered young voice from the aft cabin doorway said, "Where are we? Me da's still a-snorin' and he looks gey cross, so I didna wake 'im. Where is everyone?"

"Good morning, Jake," Giff said. "We're heading toward Portobello, which you can just begin to see in the distance yonder. And I mean to wake your father myself, so why don't you see what you can find for us to eat for breakfast."

"I dinna want to go below," Jake said. "It be black as death down there, and me da' won't let me light a torch or carry a candle wi' me, lest I set the boat afire. And, too, there'll be a worricow or a boggart down there, 'cause I heard 'im."

"You heard nobbut the wind whistling over the strakes," Giff assured him.

"Mayhap ye'll be right, sir, but it fair shoogled up me internals."

"I've heard that eerie sound myself many times," Giff said, suppressing a smile. "But, sithee, you need not go below. Have you and your father no provisions in that wee forward cabin of yours?"

"Aye, we've bread and ale, but ye'll be wanting more than what we've got."

"Not me," Giff said. "You go and fetch that loaf. It will do us all just fine and your da' will be glad of the ale." To Hob, he said, "Shout if you want me. We'll go as far as that black pile of rocks yonder and turn back. I'm thinking the burn we want lies in the bay just there"—he pointed—"but we'll want more light to be sure."

"Aye, then, I'll keep watch," Hob said, nodding.

"Where's our Geordie?" Jake asked as Giff turned toward the stern cabin.

"He went ashore earlier," Giff told him. "Are you going to fetch that bread, or do you want to wait until your father tells you to do it?"

"Nay, I'm going. Just seems odd, is all."

Aware that the situation was odd, indeed, Giff did not look forward to his forthcoming interview with Captain Wat Maxwell. For that matter, he did not look forward to hearing what Hugo and the others would say, although he was confident that once he explained his reasons, they'd accept them. Sakes, they had no choice.

Having sent the page to wake his personal manservant and fetch de Gredin, Fife dressed quickly, then paced while he waited for the chevalier to appear. The minute he walked in, Fife said, "The *Serpent* is gone! What the devil can have happened to it? By God, if you had anything to do with this . . ."

"Gently, my lord," de Gredin said, smothering a yawn. "Neither I, nor those who sent me, would have aught to gain by stealing your ship. Nor would any sane person do so. For one thing, unless your captain is a traitor with no regard for his own mortality, whoever took it had to find a crew. Thus, I'd surmise that the man who sought to hire the Dutch ship somehow guessed we'd got rid of her and thinks he's got even by taking the *Serpent*. I wonder if he knew we had the lady Sidony."

"Or knew where *you* stowed her," Fife snapped.

"As you say," de Gredin agreed. "But, still, someone had to row an entire crew to her in last night's wind and black darkness to sail off with her. I'd say they loaded the goods elsewhere, but I wager they'll be miles to the north by now."

"How many ships do you expect to come here?" Fife demanded.

"At least six or eight, sir, but I don't expect them all for days yet. I suspect you want to stay in Edinburgh long enough to greet his grace when he arrives, anyway."

Angrily, Fife retorted, "Don't be daft. I'm going after those malignant traitors as soon as I can arrange to do so. And when I catch them, the *Serpent*'s own yardarm shall serve to hang every last one of them!"

Sometime in the night, Sidony had stirred, moaned at the pain of cramped muscles and a pounding headache, and opened her eyes. Discerning no difference in the blackness that enveloped her, she decided she was dreaming and shut them.

When she opened them again hours later with the same result, she nearly closed them then, too, before she became aware of her growling, unsettled stomach and a certain rhythmic movement of the world around her.

Memory swept back and with it a fear unlike any she had ever known.

The interview with an angry Maxwell suffering the after-effects of too much brogac having gone as expected, Giff could only be grateful that the good captain proved sufficiently resigned not to rant more at him about what he had done.

Afterward Maxwell remained silent until they had broken their fast and Giff had with gratifying ease found his inlet in the increasing, if gloomy, daylight.

"What d'ye mean to do wi' the lad and me?" Maxwell asked as they set the sail to take them in at a pace that would not run them aground with the incoming tide.

Giff said soberly, "I ken fine what your fate would be, sir, if I were so daft as to put you ashore after making off with Fife's ship. I've no wish to do that, but neither will I keep an enemy aboard with me. My task is too vital to risk it. But I believe you are an honest man. If you agree to go with me and swear an oath to aid me with your matchless knowledge of this ship, I'll willingly take you both along."

Maxwell hesitated long enough to count to ten, then looked at him. "Ye've left me wi' little choice, for I'd no' be able to explain this satisfactorily to his lordship. What's more, we both ken fine that he'd hang the lad alongside o' me and make me watch him swing. But how d'ye ken ye can trust me word?"

"Can I?" Giff asked.

"Aye, sure, but ye've only me Borderer's word for that."

Giff held out his hand. "I'll accept that, but the lad stays with us."

"I'd no' do it, did I ha' to leave him behind. Fife would snatch him up in an eye-blink. Look, sir," he added, pointing. "Someone's launching a boat yonder."

Giff looked and drew a long breath. He'd know soon enough just how much his impulsive decisions about the ship and Maxwell would irk Hugo. The thought brought a reminiscent smile to his lips, but although Hugo was in the first boat that rowed out to meet them as they dropped anchor, he did not ask any questions.

Instead, he said gruffly, "We think Fife has Sidony."

Chapter 13

Giff felt as if Hugo had knocked him flat again.

He could scarcely breathe but fought to subdue his fear as Hugo climbed aboard and drew him away from the others. Although he had not spared more than two thoughts for the lass since leaving Lestalric, he realized seconds after hearing the news that it was because he had settled it in his mind that she was safe where she was until he was ready to find her, persuade her to become his wife, and produce the family he would then be of an age to appreciate. That, he decided, had to explain why he felt now as if Fife had taken someone who belonged to him.

"We've organized men to search for her," Hugo said. "But we've learned little other than that she and Ealga Clendenen rode to meet Isabella's cavalcade, and their journey took them much farther than they'd expected."

"Why was that?" Giff asked, feeling his temper stir. *Who had let her go?*

"We'd split Isabella's cavalcade in two. Her own party and one heavily laden oxcart took the river path. The other, with the rest of the carts and wagons, took the track atop the ridge. As we'd hoped, Fife split his force and searched both."

"So he was well informed. Have you identified his man at Roslin?"

"We have. We'd suspected Rolf Stow and two others, so we gave each of them a significant but unique piece of information. Stow was the only one who knew Isabella would ride through the gorge. Fife stopped her himself, so he knew."

"Not proof positive," Giff said. "But enough. What will you do with Stow?"

"Nothing yet," Hugo said with a grim smile. "He may be more useful if he goes on believing himself secure, especially now that they have Sidony."

"You still haven't said how that happened."

"Because of the oxcart, Isabella's progress was even slower than expected," Hugo said. "We'd added it to give Fife reason to search her party for large items, but Ealga and Sidony, failing to meet her as expected, began to worry."

"So the lass rode on alone to see where they were."

"Not entirely alone," Hugo said, grimacing. "She took two armed men with her. We found them last night on the eastern slope of the ridge . . . both dead."

A cold chill swept through Giff, but he kept his voice even as he said, "So Fife himself did not capture her. Not if he was busy searching Isabella's oxcart."

"That's right. The leader of Fife's party on the ridge was de Gredin. Rob and I rode with Isabella, but my lads with the ridge party recognized him."

"He's the chevalier who spent this past year at Girnigoe with Henry, is he not—the fellow Rob does not think much of."

"None of us does," Hugo said. "As we told you, he is part of a group that is on some sort of a holy crusade to return the treasure to the Roman Kirk. Their warriors are as skilled as any from Dunclathy, and one of them, Waldron of Edgelaw, died last year in his second attempt to seize the treasure. De Gredin admitted to Rob that Waldron was his cousin and that the same group had sent them both, but in believing de Gredin no more than a pale image of Waldron, we clearly misjudged him."

"If he abducted the lady Sidony, he's a villain like any other," Giff said.

"Aye, but a clever one," Hugo said. "He must have given Fife irresistible cause to accept his return, because Fife does *not* tolerate traitors. However, Waldron claimed to speak for the Pope, and Rob learned that the group sent de Gredin to Fife in the first place because they knew Fife wanted to enhance his power and undermine that of other nobles. So, we believe de Gredin survives now because he's persuaded Fife that the Pope will support his claim to the crown. Despite that, the one thing we know is that de Gredin is worthy of no man's trust, least of all Fife's."

"Why did you decide to split the countess's party?" Giff asked to get back to the point. It was always good to know one's enemy, but he wanted to find Sidony.

"Because Isabella can hold her own against Fife. We wanted him to bring as many of his men as possible to search her cavalcade. The oxcart held a big cupboard that Rob has long admired. Its cubbies were full of small items, well wrapped."

"I take it the object of Fife's search was elsewhere."

"It was already on its way here, neatly tucked into a

strong cart, beneath a warm coverlet of wool, in a train of similar carts. Although Fife's men do search every cart on the Leith road, they pay no heed to any heading to Portobello, because no merchant ships can harbor there. And, because of his belief that we were moving it through Roslin Gorge, he'd called in many of those other searchers to help him."

"How did you remove it from its place of concealment?"

"Likewise under wool, which many shepherds transport in huge bales with two poles stuck through. Such loads weigh about two hundred fifty pounds, which is more than a hundred fifty less than our cargo, but our lads are strong and had to carry it so for only a short way before setting it on its cart. It's ready to load now."

"But look here, Hugo, first we've got to find her ladyship!"

"Not you, my lad. You cannot delay, which is why, against every inclination, I have not demanded to know what the devil you meant by stealing this ship and how the devil you managed to do it."

Giff grimaced. "I think Fife got to the Dutch captain, because he sailed yesterday. I needed another ship, so I fed Fife's captain brogac until he passed out, then took his. Doubtless Fife has learned of his loss by now, but . . ." He shrugged.

Hugo chuckled. "I'm sure there is much more to this tale, which you can tell me later, but I'd agree the notion to take it was not altogether daft. It should at least prevent his following you until he can find another ship."

"He may just commandeer one of those in the harbor."

"Concern yourself with that when it happens," Hugo

recommended. "In the meantime, tell me how we are to load our crate. It's gey heavy."

Giff appealed to Maxwell, who assured him that the pulleys and lines at the stern port, used to load cargo from a wharf, could likewise load a crate from a small boat. Informed that the crate was particularly heavy, Maxwell said that if men could row the crate out and help steady it from below as it went up, they could load it.

"My lord Fife particularly requested the stern port," he said. "We used it to load provisions in the harbor, and its pulley system worked well then."

It did so again, and in less time than Giff had thought possible, the heavy crate was safely loaded, forty-eight Sinclair oarsmen had boarded with arms and gear, and Hugo was ready to rejoin Rob in the boat to return to the Lestalric shore.

"We've hung one of our cobles where their towboat was, and given you sea rations but little other provision for this lot, as we'd expected your merchant ship to be fully stocked," Hugo told him. "Do you have supplies enough for the journey?"

"In troth, I don't know," Giff admitted. "The captain said that Fife's men had loaded provisions and gear, and since he would require a crew of forty or more, I'm guessing we must have food other than salt beef, and plenty of water. If I'm wrong, we'll find it all as we do in the Isles, by putting in to shore and hunting for it."

Taking a sizable package that Rob handed up to him with a smile, Hugo gave it to Giff, saying, "Michael and Rob thought you might like a Norse flag and a Sinclair banner to fly. They've also contrived a new name board for your ship, which our lads have hung for you over the one that reads *Serpent Royal*."

"I hope they've not named it *The Devil's Own* or some such thing."

"Nay, to suit your Norse flag, you are now *Ormen Lange*, or *Long Serpent*."

"That was a good notion, the name board, and I thank them for it, but I wish they'd known to bring me more brogac. I gave Maxwell all I had."

"One assumes that you believe you can trust the man," Hugo said.

Giff nodded, smiling grimly. "If I find I can't, I'll hang him. But he gave me his word, and I do believe he is a man of honor."

Hugo shook his hand. "I ken fine that you know what you're about on the water, Giff, but Scotland's destiny rides with you now, so take great care. You are sure to encounter storms ahead of one sort or another."

"Aye, but you know what they call me," Giff said. With sober intensity, he added, "Find her, Hugo. I must depend on you and the others for that, and, I own, even knowing you as I do, it goes right against every instinct to leave you to do it."

Hugo promised they would do all they could, and with that Giff had to be satisfied, knowing well that he could delay no longer.

They were soon under way, and he took the first opportunity to talk to Maxwell. "Now that Fife won't need the aft cabin, I mean to take it for my own use. You'll keep the lad with you, of course."

"Thank ye, sir," Maxwell said. "I've sent him below to help the men stowing the gear. Even on a ship this size, there's little room for a grown man to move about down there without clouting his head on a beam, and most o' your men ha' height."

"Be sure they keep weapons, shields, and any gear they need regularly in their spaces between the benches as they would in a war galley," Giff said. "You'll act as my captain, but you'll consider me ship's master. I want a course set to take us north, but keep us away from the coast for a time. And if you've any notion how we can alter the look of this ship, pray make any suggestion that occurs to you."

"Ye're expecting pursuit."

"Fife will be on our heels as soon as he can be, and he'll be in fine fury."

"He's always said he'd go north, but why should he assume that you will?"

"I cannot tell you the whole, but you ought to know that he seeks something he believes we may have. And he'll do whatever he must to find it."

Maxwell gave him a look, and Giff knew he was wondering about the crate in the stern hold. However, the Sinclair men aboard knew it for Sinclair property and would keep watch. And Hugo would have made sure that none were spies.

"Will you tell me where we're bound, sir?" Maxwell said.

"Sinclair Bay in Caithness," Giff replied, seeing no reason to say more.

Maxwell nodded and went to the helm to give the proper commands.

They had been at sea for some time without incident when Giff saw young Jake pop up from the stern hatchway, his face nearly white. His sweeping gaze found Giff near the mast and, darting around men and over gear in his way, the lad skidded to a halt in front of him, saying, "I told ye we'd boggarts below!"

Suppressing amusement, Giff said, "I do think you

ought to recognize the normal sounds aboard ship by now."

"I do," Jake said indignantly. "I been on ships now two years, since me mam died. I ken fine that the wind be still a-blowin' and a-cryin', for I can hear it, but if it ha' found a way to thump a portion o' the underdeck, as well, I dinna ken how."

"Mayhap you missed a rat or two," Giff suggested.

"Nay, then," Jake said, eyes wide. "It'd be a fearsome big rat!"

"Where, exactly, did you hear this thumping?"

"Astern, it be," Jake said, nodding. "I'm thinking that boggart's in the wee hold under 'is lordship's cabin, 'cause ye canna reach into it from the underdeck. But me da' says I'm no' t' go in that cabin anymore. Nor I dinna want to, any road."

"Show me," Giff said. He recalled the trapdoor Maxwell had pointed out by the washstand in the aft cabin. Doubtless, Fife had wanted his personal provisions close at hand. A jug of whiskey to replace his brogac, or a barrel of wine would be a nice find. One never knew when such a thing might prove useful.

Sidony was growing more uncomfortable by the minute. She had come wide awake this time, and although great commotion had wakened her, she had recognized none of a number of loud male voices. She had easily recognized the motion as that of a galley or ship, but believing that de Gredin had put her aboard Fife's boat, she had feared drawing attention to herself.

For some time now, though, nature's ways had been

making her steadily miserable. She still felt sick from whatever de Gredin poured down her throat, but her more urgent concern was an increasingly desperate need to relieve herself.

She tried to call out, but her throat was too dry. So she pounded the side of her prison with her fists, now bound in front of her. Nothing happened for some time. Then heavy footsteps overhead startled her into immobility. Next came the metallic sound of a heavy latch or bolt being moved. The lid opened up, and dim gray light outlined a dark figure bending to hold it.

"What the devil are *you* doing in there?"

The anger in that welcome, familiar voice shook her, but her need filled her thoughts to the exclusion of all else. She said, "Pray, scold me later if you must, but get me out of here! I . . . I need a pail or something of its ilk, and quickly!"

With relief, she heard him snap, "Jake, fetch a pail! Hurry, but do not say a word to anyone about what we've found!"

Then strong, warm hands caught her under her arms and hauled her out, and she saw to her astonishment as he set her on a sort of shelf bed and began to untie her hands and feet, that she hadn't still been in a box at all. A portion of the floor in the tiny room had folded back from the box-like space underneath.

Giff sat her up and gripped her arms. "How the devil did you get in there?"

"Please, sir, I'm very glad to see you, but if that pail doesn't come . . ."

He strode to the door, saying, "Thanks, Jake, shut this door, and mind, not a word." Then he came back, the blessed pail in hand, as the light dimmed even more.

"Sakes," she said, nearly in tears from the pain and frustration of trying to stand up. "I don't think I can."

His voice was gentle, almost tender, as he said quietly, "Let me help you."

She had no choice, because her hands ached from pounding, and pins and needles shot through her feet when she tried to make them support her.

The procedure that followed was embarrassing and awkward, but all that mattered was finding relief. So she gritted her teeth, let him help, and the relief when it came brought the tears she had suppressed earlier.

Silently, he helped rearrange her clothing. As he did, she realized that the pale light entering the chamber came from a round hole a foot or so wide over a narrow table in a nook, with a hinged shutter latched back on the wall beside it.

He helped her back to the shelf bed, then bent to rub her right ankle. His hands were warm, but his look was stern. "Hugo and Rob think Fife has you."

"He nearly did, I think." Recalling the open hole in the wall and noting another, shuttered one over the washstand against the opposite wall, she said, "May we speak frankly here, or could someone overhear us?"

He followed her gaze and said, "Not through those portholes they won't, for they overlook naught but water. I expect someone could lie flat and hang over the top of the cabin, but not without others seeing him. So tell me how you got here."

She told him what she knew, and was surprised that he already knew that de Gredin had captured her. "But he told his men to tell Fife," she said. "He said the earl would question me. As to how I got here," she added, "I haven't a notion. He forced me to drink some horrid stuff that put me to sleep, and when I woke I was in a stable at Leith Harbor, I think. When he gave me more of the stuff, I was sure he meant to put me on Fife's ship. I don't know how I came to be on yours."

"This *is* Fife's ship," he said, astonishing her but sounding angry again.

"Then how did you learn that I was here?" she asked.

Giff grimaced, thinking how easily she could have ended up in Fife's hands had he not asked Maxwell about finding another ship or had failed to seize opportunity when it beckoned. That her folly and the folly of those who too often ignored her and thus let her do as she pleased had put her in such a dangerous position infuriated him, but knowing that she had been under the floor while he'd been drinking with Maxwell made him shiver. What if she had suffocated or de Gredin's foul potion had poisoned her?

Were she not looking so fragile, so earnest, and so bewildered now, he would have liked to shake her, hug her, or put her right over his knee. Clearly, he would have to make it clear to her that she could *not* wrap him around her thumb so easily.

These thoughts all flitted through his head in the instant before he said grimly, "The plain fact is, I did not know you were aboard this ship and might as easily have taken another one instead. Had I done that, you'd be with Fife right now instead of having to deal with me. Have you any idea what he wanted with you?"

Her eyes widened at his tone, but she said, "De Gredin sent him a message to say he could now make Fife's enemies tell him all he wants to know. If he meant you and the others, he must have thought you'd tell them where the treasure is."

The dim light made her pupils look enormous. She had lost any headdress she had worn, she had a bruise on her jaw, and her hair was in a tangle. But just being near her stirred his body. That she could so easily affect him under such conditions made him angrier with her and more determined to resist her charms, if only to make clear to her how dim-witted she had been to thrust herself into such danger.

"You were a fool to ride so far from town," he said roughly, "and a greater one to ride on alone, leaving Ealga Clendenen alone, as well."

"But I didn't! I had two men with me, and she kept four with her."

"Two men! How many did de Gredin have?"

She looked then as if her own temper were stirring, but her voice was as calm as usual when she said, "I didn't count them. He sent two to report to Fife, kept four with him, and sent the others back to supervise the men with the countess's carts."

"And what do you suppose happened to your two men?"

Sidony felt a chill, and her voice sounded small as she said, "I . . . I don't know. They had no chance to fight, for we were greatly outnumbered. They went back to Isabella's cavalcade with de Gredin's men. Surely, those men would not have harmed them, not with Hugo's men there, too."

His expression had softened, but it hardened again as she said the last bit, and when she paused, he stood over her and began grimly to shred her character in exactly the way she was sure Hugo would have shredded it, had Hugo been there.

She was only sorry that Giff stopped rubbing her ankles. Feeling had returned to both of them, but his rubbing felt good, and she had not wanted him to stop.

Then, with rising irritation, she realized he was just like Hugo and her sisters, thinking he could scold whenever she did something of which he disapproved.

When she had heard enough of it, she interrupted the flow without hesitation to say, "Did I understand you to say that you stole this ship?"

"Aye, and a good thing for you that I did," he snapped and went on scolding.

But she could not allow it to continue, because she wanted to know something more. So, interrupting him again, she said, "What are you going to do with me?"

"I ken fine what I ought to do to you," he growled. "But I'll—"

When he broke off, looking grimmer than ever, and frustrated, she said, "You cannot take me back, because Fife must be looking for you by now. So how long will it take us to get to wherever you are going?"

He said curtly, "About eight hours, I should think."

"Sakes, I had no notion we'd been under way so long! Where are we?"

"Somewhere near the mouth of the firth west of the Isle of May, I suspect."

"Then you must be daft, sir, unless you mean to put me ashore on the Fife coast, and I cannot think you would deposit me in the midst of the earl's own shire."

"I was thinking of St. Andrews. There is a good bay there, and—"

"But St. Andrews is still in Fife," she protested.

"May heaven protect me from educated women," he growled. "Even so, it is also the home of the Bishop of St. Andrews. He can see that you have all the protection you need to get back to Edinburgh safely. In any event, you cannot go with me. Recall that Lestalric said you'd have to marry me first."

"I don't think that can be true," she said.

"Sakes, lass, you're aboard a ship with fifty lusty men. Have you any notion what life can be like aboard such a vessel?"

She shrugged. "It cannot be much different from life aboard any other galley. I have traveled before, sir."

"Aye, sure, to the Isle of Mull to visit your sister."

"And to the Isle of Eigg to see Donald inaugurated as second Lord of the Isles," she said with dignity. "Other places, as well."

"How long have you stayed on any boat during any journey?"

"That is of no consequence," she said.

"I'll wager you've never been aboard even one overnight."

"Isobel was," she said, then realized that fact would not help her.

He said, "Isobel married Michael, though, did she not?"

Falling back to the one factor she knew must weigh with him, she said, "But you don't want to marry any more than I do."

"'Tis exactly why I am taking you to St. Andrews."

Glowering, she said, "I've had naught to eat since mid-yesterday, so if you have finished scolding, do you suppose we might find something to eat?"

He nodded, clearly thinking he had won, and said, "I'll find you something, never fear, but you stay here. I won't have you wandering about in front of all those men. You should be glad I'm turning you over to the bishop," he added, "if only because he'll be able to find you other clothes to wear. You'd have grown sick of this riding dress of yours by the time we reached Girnigoe, I can tell you."

Having made all speed to the Harbor of Leith, Fife stood on the shingle and stared at the space where the *Serpent Royal* had been. His anger had burned from the moment he'd wakened to the dreadful news of its disappearance, but the fury he felt now rendered him speechless.

Beside him, de Gredin stood quietly.

Regarding him with distaste, Fife glanced back to be sure his usual escort was not near enough to overhear, then said, "I wish I could be sure of you. But after your betrayal last year at Hawthornden and your subsequent flight with Orkney . . ."

When he paused, de Gredin said, "I was indeed guilty of a gross act of insubordination when you would have killed Lestalric, my lord. But as I explained before you generously allowed my return to your service, I acted so because you had allowed personal animosity to cloud your customary good sense."

Fife grunted. He disagreed, but this was no time to gnaw that bone again. "And your reason for running away to the north with Henry Sinclair?"

"Doubtless a mistake, but if you will forgive my saying so, I feared you meant to see me dead for my insubordination and believed I'd stay healthier at Girnigoe. I'd hoped, too, to find an opportunity to explore the Isles of Orkney."

"Where you say you found nothing."

"As I said, I saw only the patch where Henry means to build his castle. But Henry and Lestalric are just two of several who must know where the treasure lies."

"Exactly," Fife said.

"You are still thinking you ought to have killed Lestalric, but not only would you have aroused the ire of the King, thus endangering his usual compliance to your will, but you would also have angered Lestalric's friends. The Sinclairs and Douglases are two of the most powerful families in Scotland, my lord."

"The Stewarts hold the throne and are therefore the *most* powerful, surely."

"You and I know better than that," de Gredin said bluntly. "The Stewart name is not yet well respected, and if your nobles go against you, Parliament will go against you. You are politically astute, sir, so I know you are aware of what the consequences would be. My masters likewise understand your predicament."

"Masters? The Pope is but one man," Fife said, eyeing him narrowly.

De Gredin shrugged. "He is indeed, my lord, so I rarely talk with him. His holiness surrounds himself with ministers and councilors just as his grace, the King, does. In the normal course of events, it is his holiness's secretary and others who see his edicts carried out and who communicate his wishes to others, even to me."

"I see."

"I am sure you do," de Gredin said, looking at the water again. "To return to your present dilemma, my lord, one must admire MacLennan, must one not?"

"*Admire* him?"

"But yes, for although we cannot prove it yet, surely it was he who achieved this feat. And if one cannot simply seize victory, it is most helpful to undermine one's enemy, is it not? Certainly, in taking your fine ship, he has done that."

"I disagree," Fife said, fighting another surge of anger and wondering if de Gredin had spoken so merely to provoke him. "As I represent his grace in all things, by stealing my ship, MacLennan has assaulted the Crown. 'Tis why I'll hang him."

"Certainly," de Gredin said. "But first we must catch him, no?"

"First, I must find another ship," Fife said testily. "I shall have to consider again who amongst the nobility on this coast owns a suitable vessel."

"But to learn exactly where he goes one must depart at once, my lord. We both believe the Sinclairs are moving part of the treasure, but MacLennan cannot have loaded anything in the harbor without drawing notice. Even your unobservant lackeys would have noticed if he'd moved the *Serpent* to one of the wharves."

"Aye, he'd have to load somewhere, but I now have no ship to seek him, and I don't know this coast," Fife said. "Do you know where he'd be likely to load?"

"That does not matter," de Gredin said. "Doubtless, he has already loaded and gone. However, the Dutchman told us MacLennan means to sail north, and we do have a ship. In troth, we have two fast longships right here in the harbor."

Chapter 14

The minute Giff left the cabin, Sidony remembered how she had fastened her thoughts on him the previous day to shut out de Gredin's list of horrible methods Fife might use to question her. Picturing Giff then had soothed her fears. Picturing him now as he would be by the end of the day, handing her over to some stern bishop who as likely as not lived in Fife's pocket, made her want to shake him.

The thought of shaking a man a foot taller and many pounds heavier than she was made her smile. Then, as she tried putting weight on her feet again, she wondered how one man could stir so many contradictory feelings in her. Most people she knew seemed relatively uncomplicated, but she did not know from one minute to the next what to make of Giff MacLennan.

He had seen nothing amiss in her ramble through the abbey woods until she had mentioned Hugo. Even then, he had seemed only amused.

He had kissed her, too, three times. The first he had stolen, the others . . .

"Faith, the man is by nature a thief!" She was standing now with no ill effects save some slight dizziness from the motion of the ship added to a lingering sense of confinement in the dimly lighted cabin and a sad lack of sustenance.

Surely, though, he would not expect her to eat alone in the cabin.

Making her way carefully to the door, she opened it and stepped outside.

The helmsman's position was to her right, and oarsmen, two to an oar, rowed rhythmically despite a billowing sail larger than any she had seen before. In the Isles, a galley that carried cargo was called a birlinn, but this was unlike any birlinn she had seen. Not only was the *Serpent* longer, and wider astern, but its gunwales were stepped, higher at stem and stern than amidships—and it boasted two cabins.

The sky looked threatening, darkening under flying layers of clouds. The air felt chilly and damp but was still much fresher than the stuffy cabin.

She saw that they were in the narrowest part of the firth, and seeing an island ahead, she was certain from its high cliffs and the old stone priory atop them that it must be the Isle of May. They were entering the outermost part of the firth.

Seeing Giff coming toward her along the central plank, or gangway, running fore to aft atop the benches, she pulled the door shut behind her and braced herself.

His expression was nearly as threatening as the weather, for his eyes looked stormy, his irises all black, as he stepped down and said, "I told you to stay inside."

"I don't want to," she said, looking away with a mixed sense of shock and delight that once again she'd actually said what she was thinking. "I've been crated up too long and I must breathe. No man on this ship is going to harm me unless . . ." She paused, then looked right at him. "Do you fear you cannot control them, sir?"

"Nay, lass, I don't fear that," Giff said. Her sober expression as she had asked the question stirred his sense of humor, but he suppressed it, not wanting her to think he laughed at her. To be sure, she was a sight. Her green riding dress was rumpled and streaked with dust. Her face bore dusty streaks, too, and he suspected some were the result of tears. For that alone he looked forward to bringing de Gredin to account.

"If you insist on staying outside, we'll sit on that bench yonder," he said, indicating the aft corner opposite the helmsman's post. "Do not suppose you can always manage me so easily, though," he warned. "Remember that I am master of this ship, and a ship's master wields the powers of life and death over all aboard. I will not tolerate insubordination from you any more than from one of my crew."

"I don't think I am insubordinate," she said. "I'm just hungry."

"Well, I've got rolls and salted beef, so come now and sit."

He eyed the men. Despite the strong wind, he had set them two to an oar, to reach open water as quickly as possible. Then, the oarsmen could leave the work to the sail. Those not rowing awaited their next turn by resting in the spaces between benches, known as their "rooms," or pacing to stretch cramped legs or doing chores, such as picking old ropes apart to mix with tar for oakum to caulk the ship's seams.

Two men talked near the forecastle, and Hob Grant stood atop it, clinging to the stempost and the backstay as he watched the water ahead. None looked Giff's way, but he knew that not one man had missed seeing him walk there with her.

Maxwell, having taken the helmsman's post, watched the rolling seas ahead.

"Where's Jake?" Giff asked him.

Maxwell nodded toward the stempost, and Giff saw him kneeling in the "room" of the steerboard-bow oarsmen, near the gangway, with his arms folded on the bench and his chin resting on them. The men seemed content with him there, but if they were not, Giff doubted Jake would notice, because he was intently watching Sidony. Perhaps sensing Giff's gaze, the lad looked at him, and his face reddened.

Giff motioned to him with an index finger.

With visible reluctance, Jake climbed onto the gangway and, easily matching his stride to the ship's motion, made his way toward them.

Giff said quietly to Sidony, "You have that lad to thank for your release, my lady. He feared you were a boggart."

"I must have terrified him," she said. "But I'm glad someone heard me."

"You might thank him for the pail, too," Giff said with a chuckle.

She flushed but said stoutly, "Laugh all you want, sir. If he is Jake o' the Pail, I am even more grateful to him."

"Jake, this is the lady Sidony Macleod," Giff said when Jake reached them.

Scarcely waiting until he had swept off his cap and

made a jerky little bow to her, Jake said, "How'd ye get in that wee hold, me lady?"

"A bad man put me there," she said, smiling. "Sir Giffard tells me that you are the one I have to thank for hearing me pound on the wall."

"I heard, but the noise fair shoogled up me internals, I can tell ye! I thought boggarts had come t' carry us all off. Did ye no' bring a comb wi' ye, me lady?"

Clapping a hand to her hair, she looked at her skirt, then at Giff, clearly not having given thought to her appearance until that moment. "Mercy! How bad is it?"

"Ye look a rare mess, me lady," Jake said without hesitation. "Ye've a gey fine bruise on your gizz, too. How'd ye get that?"

"The same bad man hit me," she answered, glancing at Giff.

Having guessed the bruise was de Gredin's doing, making yet another score to settle with the man, he said evenly, "You're as beautiful as ever, lass, albeit quite the first woman I've ever met who did not think first and always of how she looks."

She grimaced.

"Nay, then," Jake protested. "She canna look so weel as she would wi' her hair combed proper and them muddy streaks washed off her gizz. There'll be a wee basin in the master's cabin, me lady, and if ye dinna ha' a comb, ye can use mine."

"Thank you, Jake," she said with her beautiful smile. "You are very kind."

Giff put a hand on the boy's shoulder and gave it a squeeze. "I, too, owe you thanks for your sharp ears, Jake. You have more than repaid your debt to me."

Jake's eyes grew round. "I dinna ha' to pay ye back?"

"You have done us both a great service," Giff said. Then, sternly, he added, "But don't ever let me catch you stealing again, for you won't just have to make restitution next time. I'll give you a good hiding, as well. Do you understand me?"

"Aye, sir, and me da' said I'd no' ha' me sorrows to seek 'cause he'd give me a rare skelping, too," the boy said soberly. "I'll no' take what isna mine again."

He reached inside his jacket and felt around, producing a broken comb of ordinary bone and handing it to Sidony with another of his jerky bows.

Giff said, "You've no need to—"

"Thank you, Jake," Sidony said, accepting the comb with another smile. "I have not one thing of my own that I am not wearing, so I am doubly grateful to you."

"Ye're right welcome," the boy said. Then looking at Giff, he said, "D'ye swear I'll no' ha' to pay ye back yon cat-witted shilling?"

"Are you calling me a cat-wit?"

"Nay, I'm no' so daft. But to give the meatman a whole shilling *were* daft."

A slender, warm hand on Giff's forearm changed the words about to leave his tongue to a simple, "I do swear it, Jake." But then he turned to Sidony and said, "I was just going to suggest that as Fife's people brought at least some of his personal gear aboard, we may find a comb or brush amongst them."

She tossed her head. "I'd not let a comb or brush belonging to that awful man touch me. Jake's comb will serve me very well."

The lad beamed, and Giff said, "Take yourself off now, Jake. Don't annoy the oarsmen, and tell the men tending the sail that I say they have made the luff too taut and must ease it a bit."

"Aye, sir," Jake said, grinning and running to obey.

"How does he run like that on that narrow plank?" Sidony asked. "I have all I can do just to stand up without grabbing hold of something to support me."

"Jake has lived most of his life on a boat," Giff said, watching as one man at the mast signed to another to help him increase the forward curve of the sail. "I'd wager he has to make greater adjustment to lack of motion underfoot when he's on land. You'll grow accustomed to the motion, lass. That is, you would if you were to stay aboard her long enough," he amended.

Making no response, she tried to smooth her skirt, then said casually a moment later, "How will you know where we are after we leave the firth behind?"

"Do you fear I'll get lost?" he asked, smiling.

Her expression remained serious. "No, of course not. I told you, I have sailed before, and although in most parts of the Isles one can see the mainland or another island, I have seen shores disappear, especially in dense fog. But we always arrived safely at our destination. I just wondered how sailors do that."

Forcing himself to think for the first time in years about how he did things that now seemed instinctive, he said, "We use a compass, of course, but we also observe the color of the sky and the courses of the sun, moon, or stars. When we can see a shoreline, we note identifiable points. One uses the glass to heed passing hours, too, to calculate distance. And one learns to mark the movements of the sea."

She had put a hand to her hair, trying to smooth it, but she paused to stare at him. "Sakes, what does watching the sea's movement accomplish, other than to note if it is rough or calm?"

"A good sailor observes many things. For example, most of the time, the waves all roll the same direction. A sailor can judge his course by them as long as he pays close heed to any changes in their nature. The closer one gets to shore, the more likely one is to encounter crosscurrents and even some that run counter to the incoming swells. Such things can give a man timely warning of hazards."

"But surely, close to shore, there are many dangers that the waves conceal."

"There are, indeed, and to learn of them, most captains carry a rutter, wherein they note details they've learned from experience or from others about every mile of coastline along their routes. They note landmarks, and they measure time, distance, tides, direction, and depth, to name just a few things."

"Do you carry such a rutter?"

"I do on my own ship, and Maxwell has one for our present route, because Fife planned to travel this same way. I can read the waters gey well, too, lass," he added to reassure her. "Sithee, I grew up sailing not just on the sea and sounds near Kintail but on sea-lochs, where conditions of wind and tide are particularly treacherous. Doubtless, you have been on Loch Hourn, just south of Glenelg."

"Aye, sure," she said.

"Its steep-sided glen funnels wind with fearful ferocity in all directions. Sakes, there, the wind can blow hard from behind one minute and broadside or head-on the next. At Dunclathy, we sailed cobles on Loch Earn, which is much the same. Oars help, but a good captain learns to expect such shifts and to read the waves as they change. Such skills prove especially useful in fog, helping one follow the water's motions to shore and beach civilly on sand or shingle without hitting rocks."

As he'd talked, she glanced several times at the oarsmen, fidgeting with her skirt or fussing with her hair, and Giff realized that thanks to Jake's guileless remarks, her newfound self-consciousness was distracting her from their conversation.

He said gently, "You must want to go back inside, lass. Why do you not simply say so? Sakes, you're even shivering!"

She flushed, met his gaze, and said ruefully, "I did not want to give you the satisfaction of telling me that I ought to have obeyed you in the first place."

He chuckled as he got up and offered a hand. When she placed hers in it, he noted how well it fit there. "I'll go with you," he said. "We'll see what my lord Fife has gifted us by way of combs and clothing and such."

Sidony did her best to untangle her hair with Jake's broken-toothed comb while Giff searched through the cubbies and kists that contained what gear the Earl of Fife's men had stowed in the master's cabin. He unearthed several fine shirts that he said cheerfully would augment his wardrobe as well as hers, a silver comb and brush—both of which she rejected disdainfully—a clothes brush, two black doublets, one edged with silver lace, and four pairs of black silk trunk hose, and a pair of boots too small for him and way too large for her that he said Maxwell might like.

"I don't want to wear his clothes," she said.

"You'll not have to," he said. "You will be warm and dry inside the bishop's palace by sundown. I've found a nice, thick wool cloak in this kist, though, that will serve you well if it grows much colder before then."

"I don't want—"

"See here, lass, a comb is one thing," he interjected, looking stern. "But if you think I'll let you freeze from pride rather than be sensibly warm, think again."

Noting that he had left the door open so that it banged against the wall with the motion of the ship, she moved to shut it.

"Let it be," he said. "I don't want more scandal than we can avoid. Except for Jake, his father, and one other, they're all Sinclair men, but I'd not be surprised to learn that even some of them suspect I somehow spirited you aboard myself."

"But how could that be?"

"'Tis enough for them that I've a reputation for acting on impulse and accomplishing the impossible," he said. "So whilst you remain aboard, we'll avoid giving them cause to imagine that we might be doing anything improper."

Sidony left the door alone and tried to ignore its thumps and bangs as the boat rose and fell. She could do nothing about her skirt, bodice, or riding doublet; and her hair was as tidy as she could make it without a veil or caul, but she could certainly wash her face and hands and even a bit more of herself after Giff left.

"Jake mentioned a basin, sir. Have you fresh water aboard other than for drinking, and perhaps a towel?"

"Use what water you need. We can collect more at St. Andrews if we need it. As to a towel and mayhap some soap . . ."

He found both in the washstand cunningly attached to

the wall opposite the shelf beds, just beyond the trapdoor that had confined her below.

"I must go now to talk to Captain Maxwell," he said then, explaining that although Maxwell had been Fife's captain of the *Serpent,* he had agreed to remain with them and to share his knowledge of both the ship and the coastal waters.

"Do you trust him?" she asked as he began to pull the door to behind him.

Pausing, he said, "I think so. He seems to care more for the ship than for any loyalty he has toward Fife. He may prove disloyal to me, too, in the end, but I need his knowledge of this boat and these waters, and I doubt he'll risk the lad's safety."

She nodded, understanding that it would do neither the captain nor his son any good to fall into Fife's clutches after losing the ship to Giff. She understood Giff's need, too, and also that expediency ruled such men more often than compassion did.

However, stealing Fife's captain as well as his ship was sure to infuriate the earl even more, and increase his thirst for revenge. She suspected that such certainty would delight and exhilarate the man who had achieved the feat. But she wondered if such emotions might not cloud his judgment of Captain Maxwell's reliability. With these thoughts for company, she returned to the task of tidying herself.

Despite Fife's fury at the loss of his ship, a more primitive instinct and bitter memory stirred when de Gredin blandly declared that he had two ships in the harbor.

"What do you mean *two longships*?" Fife demanded.

"You first promised me a flotilla of well-armed papal ships. Then you promised six or more, not two!"

"They are merely the first two," de Gredin replied calmly. "Their speed is the very reason they are already here. I expect the others will be along shortly, but it is as well that the two are here now, is it not, because we can follow the *Serpent* at once. Mayhap, if we act swiftly, we can even get ahead of them and lie in wait."

"Do you expect me to climb into a coble this minute and just sail off with you?" Fife asked, wishing he had a navy of his own. "In troth, I do not trust you enough to do any such thing, no matter how badly I want to catch MacLennan."

"Nor would I expect you to, my lord. You will want your own well-trusted men to attend you. We have sufficient time for you to collect them and any personal gear, as well, whilst I give orders to prepare the ships for sailing and arrange to leave word for those others to follow."

"Take care you do not say too much," Fife warned. "The men aboard those ships need know nothing about our purpose. They must simply follow orders."

"They'll obey us," de Gredin said. "In any case, we don't know exactly what MacLennan is transporting. But whatever it is, they've had no time since Isabella traveled to Edinburgh to move it from Roslin, so they must have done that earlier."

"Aye, sure they did," Fife said. "We ought to have examined every wool cart in Scotland, although I haven't a notion how we could have managed such a feat at this time of year. And we did examine every cart or wagon that left Roslin Castle."

"We thought we did," de Gredin said.

"Faugh," Fife said rudely. "You seek a vast treasure, sir,

one you yourself have said filled any number of ships. If, as we believe, the Sinclairs concealed it in Roslin Castle or the gorge, it would take time and many journeys to move it all."

"That only means that whatever they're moving now is but a portion of it. We've no notion when, or even if, they moved the rest. Waldron was sure they had moved some of it, though, and 'tis clear that they are moving something now. If we can follow them, we may learn much more from where they lead us."

"We know they hid something last year, and we came close to learning where," Fife said, glowering to remind him whose fault it was that they had failed.

"That is true," de Gredin admitted without remorse. "But we had only your own belief then, as we do now, that what they guarded was part of the treasure."

Certain, thanks to his own informants, that as far as Scotland was concerned what he sought was the most valuable, most significant item the Templars held, but unwilling to say so to de Gredin, Fife said with a shrug, "If it was not part of the treasure, why keep it so close to home till now or act as they have been acting?"

"As to that, my lord, we'll ask them when we catch them. Might one suggest that a royal banner for our ship may prove useful at some time or other?"

Fife nodded, resenting de Gredin's assumption that he'd go but deciding he'd have to risk it or let him go after MacLennan alone, a quite unacceptable alternative. He preferred taking time to think carefully, to plot the possibilities and risks, before making decisions. But he had no time, and for that matter, he had little choice if he wanted either to lay hands on the Stone of Destiny or recover his splendid *Serpent*.

They had not spoken of the lady Sidony, but there was little need. If she was aboard the *Serpent*, they could do nothing to keep MacLennan from finding her.

Fortunately, the only villain she could name was de Gredin.

Fife decided that such an accusation might well serve his own purpose later better than any more devious plan. He was growing tired of the chevalier.

Although Giff had been to the town of St. Andrews only twice before, he easily recognized the outline of its twin cathedral spires and bishop's palace atop the jutting sea cliff that formed the south tip of the bay. As darkness fell, lights glowed in a wing of the palace and began to dot the shore of the harbor below.

The lass had just come back outside, clearly having slept or otherwise occupied herself in the tiny cabin for the past hours. Seeing her about to step onto the gangway, he strode to meet her and suggested she sit where they had before.

Her eyes widened, telling him that his tone had been brusquer than he had intended, but a recent conversation with Maxwell still disturbed him.

"I ken fine that ye told our Jake to keep his mouth shut about the lass and how ye found her, sir," Maxwell had said, grimacing. "Sage advice, I thought, but he's just told me some o' the lads ha' been talking amongst themselves."

His temper stirred. "Have they, indeed?"

"Aye, but ye canna blame them," Maxwell said. "Nae man amongst them could ha' any notion she came out o' a hole in the floor. Sithee, Jake said nowt when ye found her, because he said ye'd told him straightaway to keep mum."

"That was a mistake," Giff admitted. "But they must know I haven't been with her. You and Jake slept in that cabin last night. Did the lad say aught of that?"

"He'd nae cause, knowing nowt o' what they'd think, but he doesna like their talk, so I thought I'd tell ye afore he puts a foot wrong. Ye'll be setting her ashore here, in any event, will ye no? The bishop will see her safe to her kinfolk."

Although that had been his plan, and although he'd told Maxwell that it was, Giff had stiffened at hearing it on the other man's lips. As he looked into her widened eyes now, he wondered why the plan had suddenly felt wrong. He had no reason to distrust Maxwell yet, certainly not where her welfare was concerned.

Fife was the one he distrusted, and although the town did lie within the earl's domain, St. Andrews was the ecclesiastical capital of Scotland. Its good citizens looked more to the Kirk for governance than to Fife or the King of Scots. But even so, Fife's known political skill made it likely that he'd cultivated strong allies there, perhaps even the bishop. If the bishop mentioned that she was in St. Andrews . . .

She had turned to walk silently beside him to the bench where they had sat earlier and he noted that she had nearly gained her sea legs. She still looked unsteady, but he made no attempt to touch her or to speak to her.

Her silence made him feel uncomfortable, though, and even a bit guilty.

When they reached the bench, he gently touched her arm and said quietly, "I did not mean to speak so sharply to you, lass. I hope you are not vexed."

"No, sir. Is that St. Andrews yonder?" Her voice lacked its usual spirit.

"It is," he said. "Those tall spires are its famous cathedral."

"Will you take me ashore yourself?"

"Of course, but not until I make sure the bishop is in residence and willing to undertake the responsibility for returning you safely to Edinburgh."

"I am sure that is the best plan."

Her still, lifeless voice told him what she really thought but likewise stiffened his resolve. He had a duty to keep her safe, and he could not be sure of doing so on any ship, certainly not one hunted by Fife and carrying such precious cargo.

"Are you hungry?" he asked.

"Doubtless the bishop will feed me. Do you think Fife is following us yet?"

"Perhaps not yet," he said. "But, sithee, he has no other ship of his own."

"He is powerful, though," she said. "He could make someone else bring him here, and he would soon discover that his ship had put into the harbor here."

"Do you fear for the bishop's safety if he aids you, or for your own if I leave you?" he asked, amused at the obvious tactic despite his own lingering concern.

Stiffly, clearly annoyed now, she said, "I doubt even Fife would dare to harm the Bishop of St. Andrews. But what will you tell the bishop about me?"

"Sakes, I don't know. I'll think of something."

"Would it not be better to plan first what to say? You can hardly tell him the truth, that after I was hidden aboard Fife's boat you stole it and found me."

"I shan't mention the Earl of Fife or his boat," he said coolly.

"The *Serpent* is a distinctive boat, sir. I've not seen its like before."

"Your experience is limited, lass. It is different, to be sure, but it shares common traits of many Norse galleys and cargo ships that ply this coast."

"Even so, surely Fife will know his own ship!"

"He might if he were to pursue us himself, although we did hang a new name board. We are now the *Ormen Lange*, so his recognizing her is not a certainty."

Her words did stir him to think, though.

"Sit down now," he said. "I want a word with Maxwell before we enter the harbor. And as we draw nearer, I want you to stay well out of sight, so I'm afraid it must be the wee cabin again then until our course here is clear."

"What will you do when we arrive?"

"Seek an audience with the bishop," he said. "I'll explain that due to rougher seas than usual, this voyage has made you ill and that you therefore want to return to Edinburgh by land rather than travel any farther by sea. How does that sound?"

"You will have to explain my lack of a maidservant or chaperone."

"I'll think of something," he promised. "Are you sure you don't want food?"

When she shook her head, he got up to speak to Maxwell, a few feet away at the helm, saying, "You carry long sheets of canvas, do you not, to drape over the lowered mast for shelter, if needed, when we must remain at sea overnight?"

"Aye, sure, sir," Maxwell said. "'Tis stowed in the forward hold."

"Have some of the lads fetch out enough to conceal the lowest portions of the gunwales and make them look as high as the next level. They'll have to manage without getting canvas in the way of the oars, too, or we'll have to take her into the harbor against this wind under sail alone. I just want to disguise the ship's lines, and it should soon be dark enough, I'm thinking, for canvas to do the job."

"The oarports are low enough, but that can work only until it grows light."

"I mean to be away again as soon my business here is done," Giff said.

A short time later, Sidony watched through the open doorway of the aft cabin as men affixed canvas to make the lowest portion of the gunwale even with the next. Then, furling the sail, they rowed the ship to its anchorage below the town.

She watched as they lowered the coble, and saw Giff climb over the side to get into it. She lost sight of him then until the coble pulled away. Watching it vanish behind another ship moments later, she tried to imagine what he could say to the bishop that would not destroy what little reputation she had left after her ordeal.

"I got ye cheese and hard rolls, me lady," Jake said, abruptly appearing in the doorway. "Will I bring it in to ye, or no'?"

"Bring it in, Jake," Sidony said, deciding she was hungry after all. "Would you like some yourself?" she added when she saw how much he had brought.

"Aye, sure," the boy said, squatting beside her and handing her a roll, then slicing hunks of the cheese for each of them with his eating knife.

Encouraging him to talk to her, she learned some of his history and found him most entertaining. He shifted easily from one topic to another, touching on his mother's death with no more than a shadow flitting across his face at the memory before moving on to how much he enjoyed life aboard his father's boats.

"How did he come to be captain for the Earl of Fife?"

Jake shrugged. "His lordship did tell his men to find the best, and that be me da', o' course. I think he looks like Auld Clootie, Fife does, all in black and that, but when I said that, me da' skelped me good, so I dinna say it anymore."

Suppressing a smile, Sidony said, "I agree that he looks like the devil, Jake, but mayhap you should not say so to anyone but me. He's a gey dangerous man."

"Aye, me da' doesna love him neither," Jake said, chewing around the words. "He says his lordship's a bad example t' set for a lad like me."

"He is that," she said, wondering if his da' thought Giff any better for Jake.

Maxwell appeared in the doorway then and said curtly, "Jake, stay wi' her ladyship and dinna the pair o' ye come out for nowt. Beg pardon for me curtness, m'lady, but there be ships a-coming in, two Frenchies as were in Leith Harbor."

"Surely, we do not fear the French, sir," Sidony said.

"Nay, m'lady, but now they both be flying the banner o' the King o' Scots."

Chapter 15

Having beached their coble on the shingle, Giff and his two oarsmen disembarked, pulled it above the high-tide mark, and set out up the path to the town. Giff had never visited the bishop's palace and knew it had been damaged some years before, but he hoped the lights he had seen meant the bishop still lived in it.

Dusk had turned to darkness, and thanks to the lingering overcast, they had little light beyond the ambient glow of a lantern on a post at the foot of the path.

They met only a solitary young priest out taking the air. He would doubtless return soon, as it was nearing the hour of Compline. Having no notion how many townspeople would be up and about, Giff took the liberty of stopping him.

"Forgive me for intruding on your solitude, Father, but can you tell me where I might find his eminence, the Bishop of St. Andrews, at this hour?"

"He'll be at the cathedral, my son. At the top of this path, turn left along the roadway and follow it round the curve of the cliff. You will soon come to the cathedral close. Doubtless you saw the spires from the sea."

Thanking him, Giff acknowledged that they had. Minutes later, they reached the top of the path and turned as the priest had directed. The shadowy, dark bulk of the bishop's palace lay ahead of them, and Giff eyed it curiously as they passed by. Approaching the cathedral with the palace behind them, he had a clear view down to the sea and saw two shadowy longships nearing the bay from the south.

Memory of the two at Leith stirred a swift reaction.

"Back to the ship, lads, and quickly, but not so quickly as to stir comment."

Their long strides took them swiftly to the harbor path and down it. As they neared the shingle, they met the priest again, coming up.

A notion stirred in Giff's mind, and he intercepted the man again.

The priest showed immediate concern. "You cannot have got lost nor yet found his eminence, my son. Is aught amiss?"

"Aye, Father, and it did occur to me that you may serve our purpose more quickly and spare his eminence the trouble," Giff said glibly. "Can I persuade you to accompany us to our ship for a time?"

"Is this an emergency, my son?"

"It certainly is," Giff said, casting an eye toward the bay's wide entrance, where he could just make out the prow of the lead longship coming into view. "I expect that you have the authority to perform all rites of the Holy Kirk," he added.

"I do," the priest said. He waited expectantly. "Is someone dying?"

"No, sir, but we've no time to spare. Our boat lies yonder."

The priest gave him a look, which Giff met easily enough, albeit fervently hoping the man would not demand more details. He seemed poised on the brink of doing just that, but with a glance at the two tense oarsmen, he nodded instead.

Motioning him on ahead, Giff stopped one of the men. "Can you find your way to Sinclair House from here?" he murmured urgently, pulling out his purse.

"Aye, sure, sir," the man said, taking the money Giff gave him. "But—"

"Go there, and tell Lady Isobel that her sister is safe with me," Giff said.

"Aye, sir, I'll see to that right enough."

Moments later, Giff and the other two were in the coble. By taking one pair of oars himself and carefully keeping other vessels between the coble and the two longships, they returned to the *Serpent* without attracting attention.

By the time the two drew near, Giff's boat had pulled in along the landward side of the *Serpent,* and lads aboard her had lowered the coble's ropes.

Giff saw that the false canvas gunwale gave the ship a much less distinctive profile. Maxwell had also had the lads ship the oars and let down more canvas to mask the oarports. The canvas did not interfere with the ladder, either, because to avoid interference from the oars, it customarily hooked over the first step at the aft end of the gunwale. Even the priest climbed aboard with ease.

Giff, following, expressed his approval to Maxwell as soon as he saw him. "She looks less like a Norse knorr now and more like an ordinary merchantman."

"Thank 'e, sir, but we should keep low as they pass by,"

Maxwell said. "I doubt they'll see our faces, but ye'll no' want to take any risk. I've told the lads to keep low, too, and show only two or three o' theirselves at a time, to look as if we ha' watchmen aboard. But who's this then?" he added, nodding toward the priest, who gazed in fascination at the rowing deck.

"I met him on the way to town and brought him back to gain protection for our passenger," Giff said. "Thanks to these new arrivals, we dare not linger long enough to arrange her return to Edinburgh."

Maxwell frowned. "Mayhap the word of a priest will serve ye . . ."

"It'll take more than words," Giff said. "But I must first persuade her of that."

"Her ladyship and my Jake be in the aft cabin, sir."

"Her ladyship?" The priest was frowning, but Giff ignored him and turned back to Maxwell.

"Here's what we'll do," he said. "They'll beach those two ships, so keep silent until they do. Then we'll sail out of here, heading due east, as if we were a Norse merchant that stopped only to take on fresh water or some such thing."

"See here," the priest said without lowering his voice. "Where is this crisis you spoke of? I shall have to attend to it at once, because I must return for prayers."

"I'm sorry, Father, but I cannot allow that now," Giff said quietly. "And I must ask you to keep your voice down. We are in grave danger and will shortly require both your prayers and your good offices."

"But you've just said you mean to set sail!"

"That's true."

"Where are you going?"

"North," Giff said.

"But you said east! How far north?"

"About a hundred and fifty to a hundred and seventy miles, I should think."

"Bless you, sir, I cannot go so far! I must get back. I came with you only because you said you had an emergency."

"Believe me, Father, this has become a matter of life and death."

"Whose?"

"Mine, for one, when I tell her ladyship why you are here," Giff said dryly.

"Sir Giffard and the two men as went ashore wi' him ha' come back," Jake murmured to Sidony as they waited in her cabin. "But what be they a-doing now?"

The interior was dark, so although she could discern his shape in the half-open doorway, she could see little beyond him.

"Faith, I don't know," she said. She wished Giff would come tell them what was happening, because if the two longships were French but flew the royal banner, surely Fife was aboard one of them. He had shown more than once that he thought the royal banner as much his as the King's to fly. And surely, the King of Scots had not suddenly taken a whim to sail to St. Andrews.

"I could keep low and go ask them," Jake whispered.

"Aye, sure, if you want to risk a skelping," she said, smiling although she knew he could no more read her expression than she could read his.

His response was a soft grunt, but she knew he saw the wisdom of staying where he was. The men she could see were motionless shapes, except the few who wandered from point to point occasionally, to show that they kept watch.

"Did you note watchmen on any of the other boats here?" she asked him.

After thoughtful silence, he said, "I dinna ken they be watchmen, but men do stay aboard ships in harbor. Sithee, most o' them ha' no place else to sleep."

"Then I should think there would be more lanterns."

"Nay, they sleep wi' the dark and rise wi' the dawn. It's no' safe to keep lanterns lit, especially when the wind blows. It'd be gey easy for a fire to start, and fires dinna belong shipboard. 'Tis why me da' willna let me carry a torch or a lantern below. He says it'd be easy for me to drop it, and then, he says, where would we be? Burnt to a crisp, he says. But I'd no' drop such a thing, ye ken."

"I'm sure you would not," Sidony said, repressing a shiver. "But it is better to take extreme care when the consequences can be so dire."

"Aye, sure," he said. "But wait now. I think one o' them men what come aboard wi' the master dinna be ours at all. He looks like a priest o' some sort."

"A priest?" Her stomach knotted. Had Giff brought the bishop to her here? He had said he would take her to the bishop. What if the bishop *was* Fife's man and Fife was right here in the harbor? "Are you sure the man is a priest, Jake?"

"We'll see soon enough," Jake said, still peeking out the door. "Sir Giffard be a-bringing him this way right now."

"Mercy!"

She stood up, tried to shake out skirts she could not see and, realizing the futility of such an effort, abandoned it. Instead, she drew a long breath to steady her nerves and reminded herself of what Giff had said to her in the garden, that she had proven herself as capable as anyone of making decisions.

Squaring her shoulders, she decided that he was right. She would decide for herself what to do.

Then doubt stirred her to mutter, "But can I make him heed me?"

"What's that ye say, me lady?" Jake asked from the doorway.

"Nothing," Sidony said firmly.

"I should talk to her before you do, Father," Giff said as they neared the cabin.

"First, *we* must talk, my son. I must know what you hope to accomplish, and I should prefer to sit whilst you tell me. All this rocking makes me dizzy."

He was keeping his voice down, and Giff thought he had resigned himself to going with them, but perhaps the good father hoped that if he acted quickly, Giff would put him ashore again. Giff did not look forward to telling him he could not do that. The priest was going to Girnigoe. Henry would see that he got home safely, but in the meantime, no one else in St. Andrews knew that they had been there. If they could slip away now, the best Fife could do was guess where they were.

Guiding the priest to the bench where he and Sidony had sat, Giff told him about her abduction and his earlier hope that he might leave her with the bishop.

"But you can still do so, my son. His eminence would keep her safe."

"Nay, for her abductor is a minion of Lord Fife's, doubtless acting on his orders, and it is my belief that Fife means to hold her captive to force her otherwise powerful kinsmen to submit to his wishes. That is why he has followed us here, for it is Fife himself who sails with the royal banner."

"Aye, he nearly always does now, does he not?"

"He does, and by my troth, Father, the only way to protect Lady Sidony now that he is here in St. Andrews is to get her away again as quickly as I can."

"But at what risk to her reputation? Surely, his lordship will not harm her."

"I'm told he once held a woman over a hundred-foot drop into a raging river to force her to talk," Giff said. "He is completely ruthless, and he wants something he believes her family has, so he would certainly use her ladyship to achieve his ends. As I said, I'd hoped to give her into the bishop's care, but as she has already been aboard this boat overnight, I doubt that even that course would serve now."

"His eminence would insist that she marry quickly to preserve her reputation. Indeed, I can counsel no other course. Is this, then, your emergency, my son?"

"It is, although I'd not expected to marry anyone yet. No more does she."

"Do you care for her?"

Giff said, "God help me, I do, and I want nothing more than to protect her."

"Then it must be marriage. 'Tis the only way."

"She won't agree," Giff said. "She knows me for a bad bargain by now, and 'tis true that I'd make her the very devil of a husband."

"You must strive to be a good one," the priest said sternly. "However, I cannot perform any marriage if her ladyship refuses to agree."

"I believe she is persuadable," Giff said. "She would doubtless defy me if I were to command her, but I doubt she will defy you if you can remain firm."

"Do you want me to be firm?"

"Do you know any other way to protect her?"

"Nay, for if she has been overnight on this ship and will remain aboard days longer, since you mean to sail so far north, everyone will assume the worst."

"Then do what you must," Giff said curtly. "I'll take you to her."

"With God's help, it should not take me long," the priest said.

Giff grimaced, wondering what God would think about his having abducted a priest, then decided that if anyone knew about lost moments, the Almighty did.

Sidony stood beside Jake near the doorway and watched them. Giff was frowning, and the man in priestly robes looked somber, although he did not look old enough for such a grave demeanor. He seemed scarcely older than she was.

Both men stepped into the cabin, filling it so that she moved to the corner where the shelf bed met the wall with the porthole and the wee table.

Giff told Jake to go to his father and to keep low as he did. The boy's reluctance to leave was obvious, but he went.

"This priest is from St. Andrews Cathedral, my lady," Giff said. "He would speak with you. As you may have realized, the earl's arrival has made it impossible for me to arrange matters with the bishop. Thus, we have little choice now."

"Faith, I thought *he* was the bishop," she said.

"No," Giff said. "Although, in troth, I've not asked you your name, Father."

"I am Father Adam," the priest said. "My kin hail from Roxburghshire."

"This is the lady Sidony Macleod of Glenelg in Kintail, Father. She is here, as I've explained, through no fault of her own."

Sidony kept silent. She did not want to go with Father Adam any more than she had wanted to go with the bishop.

"I'll leave you to it, then," Giff said. "But you should know, lass, that the course he recommends is what your family would want and that I . . . I have also approved it."

"Is he not to take me to the bishop, then?"

"No one is leaving the ship," Giff said. "We are about to hoist sail."

He left them, and Sidony watched him go, wondering what he had been about to say before, when he had begun so sternly and ended with such a mild statement.

She shifted her gaze to the priest. Feeling renewed confidence tempered by tension, she was curious to hear what he would say.

The silence in the small cabin lengthened as he seemed to study her.

She could hear the rattling thumps of the braces and halyard, the creaking of the yardarm, and then the flapping of canvas as they hauled the sail up.

Father Adam said quietly, "I think you must know the particular course of which he spoke, my lady. 'Tis also the course that I must recommend."

"Did he tell you to recommend it?"

"I can do no less, because there is no other acceptable course for you to take."

"My being here is not my doing," she said, suppressing memory of what Giff had said to her earlier about that, and what Hugo and her father were likely to say. "I fell victim to a villain who stuffed me into one of the holds here, to be—"

She broke off, realizing she was about to say she had been a gift to the Earl of Fife. But without knowing what Giff had told the priest—and certain that he had not told him he had stolen the earl's boat—she pressed her lips tightly together.

"I should prefer to talk outside, in the open, my lady, not only for propriety's sake but to see you a little more clearly as we talk."

"It is better if no one on the other ships sees me here, Father."

He looked out, and she easily discerned his irritation and frustration. After a look heavenward, however, he seemed only resigned. "They have cast off," he said. "I'm thinking that neither of us has much choice now, my lady. You must marry to protect yourself, and I am willing to perform the ceremony."

"Do I truly have to marry Sir Giffard?"

"Is that his name?"

"Aye, Sir Giffard MacLennan. Sakes, sir, did he not tell you?"

"He just insisted that I accompany him. Does his birth match your own?"

She sighed. *Steal a ship, steal a priest; what is the difference?* But all she said was, "His birth does match mine, sir, but he has no wish to marry me."

"Nevertheless, he has accepted responsibility for you by keeping you aboard this boat, my lady, and he has expressed his willingness to marry you. It is therefore meet and right that a marriage between you shall take place at once."

"Must I do anything else if I marry him?"

She felt his shock and was sure he blushed as he said with careful firmness, "A wife must submit to her husband's will in all things."

"But one can have a marriage annulled, can one not?" She had heard that such a thing was possible if a bride and groom failed to couple.

He frowned. "I certainly cannot recommend such a course."

"But it is possible?"

"It is, but only under certain circumstances. If your husband should find that you are not a maiden, for example."

"Or if I refuse to submit to him?"

"That would be a dangerous choice, my lady. Sithee, as your husband, he would be within his rights to force your submission, so you'd do better to refuse to marry him in the first place. I do strongly recommend that you do marry, but I must in good conscience also tell you that, under Scottish law, I am obliged to refuse to perform the ceremony if you express your unwillingness to go through with it."

The decision she ought to make was clear enough. She certainly did not want to marry a man who did not want her. But even as she opened her mouth to tell the priest she would certainly decline, a vision of her father and all the others in her family who would be furious with her, ranting at her, rose up in her mind.

She could have no doubt that, in time, others would

command her obedience, and whether the priest supported her now or not, she doubted she could withstand a direct order from her father. After all, by then, heaven knew how many nights she would have spent aboard with Giff. Word traveled much more swiftly in the Isles than boats did, so she might well return to find herself the object of a truly sordid scandal. Her sister Isobel, after all, having been but one night with Michael and that only to save his life, had had to submit to such a command.

But if she agreed now to marry . . .

Her furious kinsmen faded away at the thought.

~

Giff had kept one wary eye on the two beaching longships and one on the open doorway of the aft cabin as he talked quietly with Maxwell.

When he saw the longships' passengers disembark and begin wending their way up to the town, and their crews moving about on the shingle, making camp for the night, he motioned to his own men to cast off and hoist sail.

Wind soon filled the canvas, and despite a tide on the turn that would soon be strongly inflowing, they made good headway without reaction from shore. He doubted that anyone on the shore or in the harbor paid them heed as they moved east toward the open sea. It was dark enough that when they were well outside the bay they could correct their heading without anyone seeing them from town.

"Could you see just how many went ashore?" he asked Maxwell.

"Looked to be at least eight," Maxwell said. "One were the earl, for sure. Ye canna mistake his figure, nor the proud way he carries himself. D'ye no' think someone will tell him ye were there?"

"We saw no one taking interest in us, and this harbor is not nearly as busy as Leith," Giff said. "But we did walk as far as the beginning of the cathedral close before I saw those longships and noted the royal banner."

"I'd wager someone else noticed ye, then."

"Whether anyone did or not, I mean for us to be well away before Fife thinks to order a closer look at the other boats in the harbor. And if he does nowt else whilst he's here, he'll stay in town long enough to speak to the bishop."

"Aye, after flying the royal banner as he did coming in, there'd be talk if he turned about so quick and left without paying his respects," Maxwell agreed.

"I'm guessing they'll stop for the night. Those ships seem to have full crews and are gey fast, but few French ships come so far north, so I doubt their information about tides, distances, and hazards can be as accurate as what your rutter provides."

"Also, the earl be a nervous sailor, sir. He doesna like small boats, nor he don't want to sail too close to shore. He said once that, rutter or no rutter, where there be one rock poking up, there likely be dozens more lurking underneath."

"We'll remember that," Giff said. "He may also assume that we'd avoid any sizable harbor and stop somewhere each night, even if we remain at sea. But I want to take advantage of this wind if we can now that we know how close he is."

"Beg pardon, sir," Maxwell said. "How d'ye suppose the earl persuaded them French ships to bring him here so quick?"

"I suspect it is the Chevalier de Gredin rather than Fife who is responsible," Giff said. "His father used to be Scottish envoy to the French Royal Court in Paris, so doubtless he has powerful friends there and used their names." *And if that is not the answer*, Giff told himself, *we may be up against a stronger foe than we knew.*

He wished he could hear the conversation in the aft cabin. One minute he hoped Father Adam would persuade her, the next that he would fail. At one point he found himself wondering if he was such a coxcomb that he just wanted her to *want* to marry him despite his own reluctance to enter the married state.

"D'ye think yon kirksman will persuade her ladyship?" Maxwell murmured.

"I don't know what she'll do," Giff admitted. "Tell the lads to take away that canvas from the gunwales now and put out the oars. Use them for the turn, then weigh them, but keep them at the ready lest we should drift too close to shore."

As Maxwell moved to the helm, where he could issue the orders without shouting, Giff made out the priest's slender figure emerging from the cabin.

Something tightened inside him, warning him that he was more concerned about her answer than he'd expected. He went to meet the priest, telling himself he hurried only to spare Father Adam a possible fall on the rolling deck.

"What did she say?" he asked.

"She's willing," the priest said. "But I must tell you—"

"Nay, 'tis enough that she's willing, Father. I'll do what's right for her. 'Tis doubtless time that I thought about raising a family, as I'm sure you will agree."

"As to that—"

"Let's get it done," Giff said. Despite the chilly air, his palms were sweating.

"Now?"

"Aye, sure, or she may change her mind. I don't want to fratch with the lass, so 'tis better to get it done whilst she's willing."

"I cannot say I like this, my son."

"Think, Father," Giff urged. "To arrive at our destination as a married lady will do her more good than to arrive there as a bedraggled lass who has been stuck on this boat for a sennight with only fifty rough men as her companions."

"A good argument," Father Adam admitted. "But, as she is willing, you could just marry her by declaration, albeit without the benefit of blessing."

"I'd not want that unless we had no other recourse," Giff said, wondering why the priest seemed less determined than before but not caring as long as he'd do what they required. "I doubt that such a declaration would preserve her reputation in this instance. Having your blessing would be better for us both, would it not?"

"Aye, then, we'll do it straightaway."

Suddenly nervous, and hoping the priest could not read his expression, Giff said, "Do you know the words of the service?"

"I remember enough to do a proper wedding, my son, but I do think you should know that—"

"Nay, Father, if we're going to do it, let's get to it."

The priest sighed. "Very well, sir. The lady Sidony is waiting."

Giff nodded, and as he did, a most agreeable image of Sidony awaiting him in a proper bedchamber at Duncraig, wearing a thin silken dressing gown and nothing else, with her shiny silver-blond hair spilling down her back, filled his mind's eye. His body stirred, but his lips twisted into a wry smile. A shipboard wedding night was unlikely to be particularly agreeable for either of them.

Sidony heard them before she saw them, and her heart began to pound. What had she agreed to—and with Giff MacLennan?

All very well to assume that he would not force her submission whenever the mood struck him, but what did she really know of the man? Not enough, certainly, to make such a judgment of him, let alone to be depending on it.

He filled the doorway, blocking what little light there had been.

"You've agreed then, lass?" His voice was gentle in the darkness, and it did something to her. Her mouth was dry, but the words came more easily than expected.

"Yes, I have agreed," she said. "I am not sure I should have, but I *am* sure that everyone else would say I must, and I don't want them all ringing peals over me and ordering me to do it after I've created a scandal to last all my life."

"That's good enough," he said. "Come in, Father. We're ready."

"We'll need at least two witnesses, my son."

Giff reached outside the door and pulled Jake to him. "Get your da' and Hob Grant," he said, "and come back with them. Tell your da' to bring a lantern."

At last, with the portholes shuttered, a lantern glowing from a hook in the ceiling, and Hob and the Maxwells squeezed in with them, Father Adam began.

To Sidony's surprise, the ceremony was brief, with only one delay after Giff had recited his vows, when Father Adam asked him if he had a ring for her.

When Giff said no, Wat Maxwell pulled one off his left little finger and said, "It were me wife's, lad, but if ye'd like the use of it until ye can get one for her ladyship, ye're welcome. I'd like Jake to have this 'un for his own lass one day."

Thanking him, Giff took the thin silver ring and with an indecipherable look on his face, gently slipped it onto Sidony's finger.

She stared at it as the priest asked her if she would marry Sir Giffard, and when she had agreed, he proceeded to her vows. When he put special emphasis on the last one, to swear meekness and obedience in bed and at board, she saw Giff smile. *He* had not had to make any such vow, of course. To add to her annoyance, she had discerned no priestly emphasis on any vow that Giff *did* make.

Then, suddenly, Father Adam said, "By the power vested in me by Holy Kirk, I pronounce you husband and wife. You may kiss your bride, Sir Giffard."

Putting the wee silver band on her finger had stirred unexpected emotions for Giff, and the announcement that she was now his wife stirred more. As he gazed at her, his throat felt tight. Despite the fact that she wore what she had worn since he had released her from the small hold, and her efforts to smooth her hair had achieved little by way of its usual tidiness, he felt pride in what he had done.

The suggestion that he might kiss her now without consequence stirred a wish to do so at once. He put a hand under her chin, tilted her face up, and touched his lips gently to hers, smiling when her eyes sparkled in the lantern's glow.

The priest said, "It is customary to announce your new estate to any onlookers, Sir Giffard. We must certainly tell your crew the good news."

"Go and tell them then," Giff murmured. "And close the door behind you."

A moment later, the door shut with a solid click, and they were alone. His earlier fear that his body would fail him in such surroundings proved untrue.

He reached for the fastenings of her riding doublet.

"Please don't, sir," she said. "I agreed to marry you, but that is all."

At St. Andrews, Fife and de Gredin, escorted by all but two of Fife's tail, had walked to the palace and thence to the cathedral to find his eminence, the bishop. The service of Compline being soon over, he had invited them back to his palace for supper and to spend the night, as Fife had expected. He had certainly not wanted to stay aboard the longship all night, for a more uncomfortable craft he had never imagined.

De Gredin had not been enthusiastic about stopping at St. Andrews, but he had agreed when Fife pointed out that if MacLennan had found the girl aboard the *Serpent*, he would want to put her ashore as expeditiously as possible.

And where, Fife had asked, could he be more certain of her safety than with the bishop?

Accordingly, they had finished an excellent supper at the bishop's table and were still enjoying his fine claret when a lackey entered and said, "Beg pardon, your eminence, but a man has come from the harbor with a message for my lord Fife."

Chapter 16

In the cabin, his fingers still on the fastenings of her doublet, Giff stared at his bride. "*What* did you say?" he demanded.

"You heard me," Sidony replied calmly.

"I heard you, but I do not believe my ears," he said, wanting to shake her but lowering his hands to his sides instead. Trying to sound reasonable, lest she feared to couple, he said gently, "Our marriage is not a marriage until we consummate it."

"Nevertheless, sir, I have made my decision."

"This is the devil of a time to find you can make decisions," he retorted.

"You are the one who made it clear to me that I *can* make them," she reminded him. "So I have made this one, and I mean to stand by it. You are also the one who made it necessary by deciding to keep me aboard—twice. You did so when you might have turned back and put me ashore at Lestalric, and again at St. Andrews, when you might have let Father Adam take me to the bishop."

"You did not want to go to the bishop!"

"True, but that does not affect my decision now. I do understand that to stay on this boat puts me in danger of creating a scandal that would embarrass me and infuriate my father and everyone else in my family. But unless you mean to tell the world that I refuse to couple with you, they need know nothing about that."

"Marriage is for life. Do you mean to refuse me forever?"

"I have not decided that," she said, but her gaze slid away from his as she said it, and she did not look at him again. "In troth, sir, you behave much too impetuously for my taste. I do not approve of acting in such haste, on impulse, but you seem to make a habit of it. For now, I would ask that you restrain yourself."

"Look here," he said, beginning to get angry. "Rob, Hugo, and the others would have been gone before we could have got back to Lestalric, and even if we could still have moored safely there, we'd have had no way to get you home with any speed. As it was, Fife was on our heels much sooner than I'd expected."

"I could easily have walked to Lestalric."

"Don't talk foolishness. Those two boats Fife commandeered are faster than ours in every respect. Did you see how many oarsmen they have, how long they are, how little draft they require? Had we delayed, they'd have been on us before we reached St. Andrews. As to our escape there, it was just by a hair that we succeeded. If Fife learns we were right in that harbor, he'll pursue us with even more vigor."

"You should have taken me ashore at once," she said stubbornly.

"This may surprise you," he retorted. "But getting you

home again was not the most crucial thing on my mind. Getting my cargo safely to its destination is more so. You need to understand that."

"So, that crateful of jewels and whatnot is all that is important to you?"

"Crateful of jewels and—" He broke off, realizing that he had stepped into dangerous territory on more than one account. She understood him well enough.

"Is that not what treasure is?" she demanded. "Just objects? To be sure, they are objects of value to someone or other. But let me tell you, sir, I put higher value on kinship and family than on mere *objects* of any kind. And I'll expect my husband to put his family first. The fact is that this ship carries only a portion of a treasure that, as far as either of us knows, has done no one any good since it disappeared nearly a century ago. What would it matter if the Earl of Fife or anyone else took our portion if their taking it would ensure the safety of everyone involved?"

"Sit down," he said curtly, pointing to one of the little benches in the table alcove. "We are going to have some plain speaking, madam wife, and if you think you can refuse to hear me, let me remind you that I now have every right to insist on your obedience. Don't test me on that, because you'll be sorry if you do."

Sidony met his gaze defiantly, then wished she had not. In truth, she scarcely understood her own defiance. She had carefully planned what she would say to him, and she had said it as calmly as she had planned. She had expected him to be surprised, but she had also expected him to understand, especially since he had once agreed that it must be hard always to do others' bidding.

Her reaction when he leaped to debate with her surprised her almost as much as her decision had surprised him. But he was angry now, and she had never meant to provoke him so far. It was as if, with him, she became a different person entirely.

From the first day, he had elicited characteristics from her that she had not known she possessed, and some of them pleased her. But this impulsive defiance was not one of them. Words of apology sprang to her tongue.

Before she could utter them, he snapped, "I said, 'Sit!'"

She sat.

He loomed over her for a long moment, glowering, then slid onto the narrow bench across the little table from her, where he remained silent for a few moments, but it was not a silence she felt compelled to break. She told herself to be grateful that he did not seem the sort of husband who bellowed at one and laid down laws. Her father was like that and had an added tendency to alter those laws on a whim.

At last, folding his hands on the table, Giff said quietly, "This conversation has not gone as I would have wished any wedding night conversation to go, lass, but that is as much my fault as yours. I ought to have known you might be reluctant. I was as impetuous as you say I was, but it was not impulse that took us so swiftly away from Lestalric or St. Andrews. I hope you do see that. If you don't, we can discuss it further. You may always say what you like to me, in private, even about the treasure. Just do not shout at me, and make sure that no one else can hear us."

"I did not shout," she said. "And it *was* impetuous to steal this boat, not to mention its captain and that priest."

A finger lifted from his folded hands silenced her. "I did not steal the priest," he said, "but we can discuss that later, too. First, you should know that your views on the treasure's value are irrelevant. Don't speak," he added when her mouth opened.

She shut it, pressing her lips together to avoid venting her own rising temper. The urge was strong to pound on the table or stand up and walk away. Not that one could do it well in a room so small, but that fact did nothing to reduce the urge.

"Protecting the treasure—every item in it—is a matter of honor for us," he said. "If you know it has been missing for so long, do you also know its history?"

"Do you mean its connection to the Order?" she asked.

"I do."

This, too, fell into the subjects one ought never to discuss, so it was warily, her anger forgotten, that she nodded.

When he remained silent, she said, "I know that the Knights Templar made it possible for men to travel without carrying their valuables. One needed only a letter from one perceptory to another from Scotland to the Holy Land, or nearly any point between, granting him the right to certain funding on no more than a password. I know, too, that because of their many services of that ilk, and others, they amassed a great fortune that disappeared years ago when the French king tried to seize it."

"The Order also protected items of great value for Holy Kirk and heads of state," he said. "So you must understand that where our honor is concerned, little matters but that we continue to protect what we have promised to protect."

Tempted as she was to point out that he had just promised before God to protect her, she held her tongue. For one thing, she knew that he would risk his life, even sacrifice it, for her. She did not know how she knew, any more than she knew why she was sure of other things about him, but so it had been from the first day on.

He was waiting for her to respond.

"I cannot pretend to understand all that men mean when they talk of honor," she said. "But Isobel, Adela, and Sorcha seem to know as much about the treasure as all you men do. They also know exactly what our cargo is, do they not?"

He nodded. "I believe they do."

"Then, now that we are married, will you tell me?"

He grimaced, but the expression was rueful. "Not yet, lass."

She leaned forward, peering into his eyes. "Why not?"

He shook his head. "I do not know you well enough yet."

"If you *knew* me better, would you tell me then?"

His eyes narrowed. "Art bargaining with me, sweetheart? I hope you are not suggesting that if you couple with me, I will tell you all I know."

Heat flooded her cheeks. "I was afraid that was what *you* were suggesting."

He chuckled then. "I'm thinking I've just proved your point and you have proven mine. We need to become better acquainted, lass. One minute I feel as if I can see into your mind and read your thoughts. The next, I feel as if you are doing that to me. But in the end, I know that neither of us can be sure either way. Suppose we spend some time on this voyage getting to know each other better."

She nodded, surprised to find that her relief contained disappointment, too.

He stood up and extended a hand to her.

Warily, she took it and let him help her to her feet.

He put both hands on her shoulders, looked into her eyes, and said, "I hope you will hear me out on what I am about to say."

"Aye, sure, I will."

"Perhaps," he said with a wry smile. "Let me put my best reason first. You suggested earlier that the only way others need know about your . . . your decision tonight would be if I were to shout it to the world. The fact is that, by acting as you apparently expect, I would be announcing it to everyone aboard."

"I don't know what you mean."

"I mean, my sweet tormentor, that if I were to leave now and sleep outside with the oarsmen, or anywhere on this boat save in this cabin—*my* cabin—with you, I'd be telling them all that my bride has banished me from her presence."

The thought of him spending the night in the tiny cabin with her stopped the breath in her throat and set her heart pounding.

Fife was annoyed that they had as yet seen no sign of their quarry, but he and de Gredin had agreed that MacLennan was heading north. Even if they failed to catch him, the earl was as certain as he could be that the key to the treasure lay at Girnigoe. If last year's information was correct and the Sinclairs and Logan knew where the Stone was hidden, it was likely they were moving it now, especially as their cargo was so important that when he'd sent the Dutchman away, MacLennan had risked stealing the *Serpent Royal* to transport it.

It was cold on the water, and Fife was damp, because as fast as the men had rowed leaving Leith Harbor, their oars had splashed a good deal of water on him. Fortunately, since then, the wind had been brisk enough for them to ship the oars.

It irritated him, too, that they'd heard nothing about the girl at St. Andrews.

As they walked to the palace with the bishop, de Gredin had asked if his eminence had had visitors that day, but he denied having received anyone at all.

Fife and de Gredin had made good time from Leith to St. Andrews themselves, and had seen no sign of the *Serpent* in the harbor, just small vessels, two larger ones, a merchantman bearing a Hanseatic flag, and another with a Norse flag at her bow.

When Fife's man had requested the bishop's permission to interrupt their comfortable evening, it was to tell them the Norse ship had left the harbor.

"It sailed not long after we beached, my lord," the man added.

"Why did you not come and tell us at once?" de Gredin snapped.

Fife said, "What difference can that make? We would scarcely chase it now, even if we wanted to. Why should we care what a Norseman does?"

"Why would any Norseman leave a safe harbor after dark?"

The man who had brought the news looked wretchedly at Fife. "We didna think o' that, my lord. We didna think nowt until a wee while ago when one o' the chevalier's lads said he'd caught a glimpse o' its stern as we passed it earlier."

"Sakes, you'll never tell me it was the *Serpent*!" Fife exclaimed.

"Nay, he didna ken the name," the man said. "But he did notice it has a stern port like the *Serpent*'s, my lord, with crosspieces that form the shape of an M."

"The *Serpent*'s crosspieces do form an M," Fife agreed. "But, surely—"

"We must follow at once, then!" de Gredin exclaimed. "If we have any chance of catching sight of them, my lord, we surely want to do that."

Fife wanted to do nothing of the sort. If he could imagine any more horrible death than wrecking one's boat and drowning in the sea, it was doing so on a pitch-dark night with no hope of rescue. But when de Gredin went on to explain to the bishop that some miscreant had stolen the earl's fine ship, Fife could hardly insist that he would rather sleep in a comfortable bed than try to recover it.

De Gredin would likely agree that he should stay with the bishop, and then be off by himself to capture his so-precious treasure and take the Stone as well.

Resigned now to his fate, Fife sent a prayer aloft and tried to get comfortable, realizing only when the man-at-arms serving as his personal attendant told him so that de Gredin had quietly put half of the earl's other men on the second longboat.

Having made his most persuasive case for sharing the cabin, Giff had heard Sidony gasp softly in response, and his body stirred hopefully. From the moment she had denied him, his desire to hold her in his arms—indeed, to do much more than that—had grown so that what he felt now was pure lust, and he knew it. Her shoulders were warm beneath his hands. His fingers itched to caress her bare skin.

He drew a long, silent breath and carefully released her.

"I suppose you could stay for a while," she said.

"I'm afraid they'd expect me to stay all night."

"Every night?"

"To do aught else would denote banishment, for which they would think less of me, or lack of interest on my part, which would—most unfairly—reflect on you."

She shot him a speculative look but said only, "Then you had better stay tonight at least. I suppose I can trust you to keep your word."

His hands went back to her shoulders before he thought, and he said, "You can always trust my word when I give it, lass, but in this matter, I will not swear it, because I am not sure I can trust myself. You are too bonnie, too enticing to a man's lust, and mine is gey strong for you. So take care that you don't tempt me too much. If you do, I'll not want to answer for my actions."

Her eyes widened so much that he wondered if he had frightened her.

Sidony felt a tingling thrill at the thought that she could tempt him so. She had heard bards' tales of women who wielded such power over men but had never dreamed that she could tempt any man to foreswear himself. The feeling was so energizing that temptation stirred to see what would happen if she tested him.

"Don't be thinking that I'll give you a dagger to defend yourself like the ones I'm told your sisters Isobel and Adela carry," he said with a smile. "I can order the men to catch a large salmon, though, and give it to you to use if I forget myself."

She laughed at that, and the tension between them eased.

"I don't need a salmon, sir," she said. "I can always whistle for help if I need it, or scream. You may stay tonight, but I hope you do not expect me to undress for bed whilst you watch me."

"I'd like to do that, right enough," he admitted. "But I'll see to the crew and speak to Wat Maxwell. Don't worry about the lantern. I'll put it out when I return."

He was gone on the words, and having no idea how long he would be away, she quickly took off her doublet and skirt, shook out both without a hope of doing them any good, and hung them on hooks fastened to the wall by the washstand.

The water-filled ewer sat in a deep pocket in the stand, so the motion of the boat could not tip it onto the floor. She carefully poured enough to wet a cloth, then scrubbed her face and arms and behind her ears. Using her finger, she scrubbed her teeth as well as she could, then pulled two thick feather quilts from the kist where she found them, tossed one onto the top bed and spread the other over the linen-covered pad on the lower one and slid in between them, shivering in her shift.

One could not call such a bed comfortable, and she tried to imagine Fife sleeping on it. Doubtless his manservant would have piled it with eiderdowns first to make his lordship a nest, but with the thin pad that pretended to be a mattress under her, she was certainly more comfortable than when she had wakened in her prison under the floor. And she was sleepy enough, she thought, to sleep on a rock.

She had almost dozed off when the click of the door latch brought her wide awake. "Is that you?" she called, drawing the quilt to her chin as the door began to open. Realizing anyone could answer yes to such a question, she bit back a giggle.

He opened it just wide enough to step inside, shut it behind him, and said, "Were it anyone else, he'd be taking his life in his hands, and well he'd know it."

She experienced that thrill of feminine power again. She did not believe for a moment that he would kill a man whose only mistake was opening that door, but the fact that he had said he would was heady.

"Where are we?" she asked.

"Between Arbroath and Montrose. We passed Devil's Head a few minutes ago and should shortly be able to make out the two high points of Meg's Craig."

"Faith, I don't know how you can tell. I don't even recognize those names."

"The stars are beginning to peek through, but surely you ken Arbroath."

"I know our famous declaration of independence from England was signed there fifty years ago, but I do not know where Arbroath is."

"We're about two and a half hours out of St. Andrews, traveling at four knots per hour. If this wind holds steady, we hope to make Aberdeen by morning."

"The oars are still up," she said. "I can tell by the motion of the boat."

"We've no need of them with a wind as favorable as this and the clouds breaking, but both are unpredictable. Are you ready for me to put out the lantern?"

Her body tingled with new sensations. He looked immense in the cabin, his head nearly touching its ceiling. "Do you think that bed will hold you?"

He chuckled. "I can put you up there if you'd prefer."

The thought of having to climb up there with him in the cabin, or down again with him in the lower bed, was almost worse than the thought of his lifting her up there in her shift. "I'd liefer stay here," she said, hoping she sounded dignified but certain she'd heard a squeak in her voice that was anything but.

He was kind enough not to laugh again. "I'll take off my boots," he said, "but you might want to tuck back a bit, because I'll step on the edge of your cot to ease onto mine, and this ceiling is not anything like as high as a normal one."

Then, the lantern was out and the chamber pitch black, but she knew when he put a foot on the edge of her cot and hoisted himself to the bed above hers. She lay tense in the darkness, still chilly, trying to relax, tinglingly aware of him above her.

"Do you really fit up there?" she asked a moment later.

"Near enough," he said. "I've slept in worse places."

She tried to imagine what they could be.

The motion of the boat was restful. Eventually it would rock her to sleep, but the moments crept by. He shifted, making the wood creak.

Telling herself to stop worrying about him crashing down on top of her, she wriggled on the thin pad and wondered how the oarsmen slept in the small spaces allotted them between the rowing benches, or on the benches themselves.

Jake had told her there were hammocks they could sling in the underdeck spaces but "none so many," according to the boy, and only when those spaces were not filled with cargo and provisions. Western galleys had no underdecks and carried few provisions, nearly always beaching at night and depending on their men to hunt or fish for their food. Remembering her supper with Jake, she smiled.

She shifted again, certain her hips would be black and blue by morning.

"Still awake?" he murmured.

"I was just thinking," she said.

"About us?"

"About the ship," she said. "You never said how you came to steal it—or its captain. And, although you said your decisions to sail away from Lestalric and St. Andrews were not impetuous, can you say the same about stealing the ship and its captain, or stealing the priest? How can you do such things? Especially steal a ship. I should think that would be an impossible feat for one man alone."

Smiling, Giff said, "At the time it seemed the right thing to do, so I did it."

"But the ship did not belong to you! You cannot just take things, any more than Jake should. You told him so and even wanted him to repay your shilling."

"The difference is that I needed both a ship and a way to slow Fife down. He had learned about the Dutch ship I'd hired and sent it on its way. I'd point out, too, that had I not taken this ship, you'd still be a pawn he could threaten to force our capitulation. Doubtless that was his intent when he ordered your abduction."

"Do you know, I don't think he did order it," she said thoughtfully. "Not that he would *not* have done so had he known he could, for he did try to arrest Adela last year to force Rob's hand. But recall that when de Gredin captured me, Fife was searching Isabella's party. How could he even have known I'd be on the ridge?"

"One could suppose that the same spy that told Fife about Isabella's plans somehow learned about your plan to ride with Lady Clendenen to meet her."

"Was there really a spy?"

"Aye, but he was at Roslin," he said, remembering.

"I did not see anyone else I know with de Gredin," she said.

"It doesn't matter," he said. "Fife could not have known you would be there, because no one expected you to ride so far. De Gredin must have seized the chance when you provided it. I wonder if Fife knows even now that you were aboard this ship. Aye, sure, he does. You heard de Gredin order his men to tell him."

"You have not said yet about taking Fife's ship," she said.

He grimaced, but she deserved an answer. "You will probably call it impetuous, or impulsive, even reckless and foolhardy."

"You do frequently seem to behave so," she said.

"In troth, men have called me all those things from time to time. But I have found that in the midst of chaos one can always find at least one moment of opportunity. I look for that moment and seize it when it comes."

"And that is what you did with the ship?"

"Aye, sure. I did not think about its being Fife's ship. I just saw my chance when I realized that, besides the captain and Jake, only two men were aboard."

"But you abducted Captain Maxwell and Jake, too!"

"I asked Maxwell to swear fealty to me, as I would ask

any man in such a case. He did so, because I also vowed to protect Jake. Had I put them ashore and Fife got hold of them, he would hang them both for the loss of his ship."

She said nothing to that.

He let the silence lengthen, then murmured, "Still awake?"

"Aye."

"Do you understand now why I sometimes act as I do?"

Sidony did not answer. She liked listening to him, and it was clear that he believed he had done the right thing. But something bothered her, and she was not sure she should tell him. Men, in her experience, did not like their actions criticized.

"What is it, lass? You're burning to say something more to me. I can feel it."

"Just, it was only luck that I was aboard this ship, so it is unfair to suggest that what you did was right because of my being here. Moreover, to have found yourself without a ship at the last minute seems like dreadfully bad planning for so important a venture, one that others had been planning for almost a year. Even with great treasure at stake, do all men simply wait for that moment of opportunity?"

Her stomach tightened in the silence that followed, but his voice remained reassuringly steady. "No matter how carefully one plans, something always goes amiss, and the likeliest time for error is at the worst possible time. With our cargo already on the move, I had to act fast or the whole venture would have failed."

"I do see that," she said. "But others have said things,

too, you know. They seem mostly to say them about you in jest, but one does wonder all the same."

"When you know me better, mayhap you will cease to wonder about me, but you may always say what you like to me and ask me anything, anytime."

"*Any* time?"

"Any time that we are alone like this," he said firmly. "Now, go to sleep."

She smiled and shut her eyes. The previous day had been terrifying, but she felt safe again. Even on the hard bed, she plunged into sleep, deep and dreamless.

When morning came, she awoke to find herself alone in the cabin.

Giff stood atop the aft cabin, peering into the distance behind them. Puffy white clouds billowed to great heights in the sky, warning of worse weather ahead. They were south of Aberdeen yet, but he thought they could make Peterhead by dusk.

He could see no sails behind them, and to be sure, the strong wind had given them good speed, but for all that he hoped Fife's lack of courage on the water had kept him in St. Andrews, he had a nagging hunch that the hope would prove false.

Wat Maxwell, having given up his bed to Father Adam, had been up all night, in command, and Giff had been confident leaving him in command. Not only did he feel instinctively that Maxwell was trustworthy, but he knew that although the Sinclair oarsmen would obey Maxwell's orders, they would not hesitate to wake him at once if

Maxwell issued any unacceptable command such as a surrender to Fife.

Before climbing atop the aft cabin, Giff had sent Maxwell into the forward one to get some sleep, brushing aside his protest that the priest had not yet arisen.

"Doubtless he enjoys the chance for a lie-in," Giff said. "But he cannot sail this ship, and you need rest or you'll be no use to me. Roust him and get to bed."

So Maxwell had gone.

Giff turned and scanned the rowing deck for one of the smaller oarsmen. Most were long-limbed men with powerful legs and backs because, being Sinclair men, they were fine warriors as well as oarsmen. Finding one he thought would do, he caught the man's eye and beckoned, then climbed quietly down off the cabin in case the lass—his beautiful, stubborn bride, he thought with a smile—still slept.

"Aye, sir?" The wiry oarsmen gazed at him through candid gray eyes.

"Blegbie, isn't it?" Giff said.

"Aye, sir, Ned Blegbie."

"How do you feel about climbing the mast, Ned Blegbie?"

The man grinned. "Nobbut a wee cat's stroll, sir."

"I agree, but it is lowering to morale for a ship's master to have all the fun, so take yourself as high as you safely can and shout if you see any sail behind us."

Still grinning, Ned Blegbie shinned nimbly up to the yardarm. Then, using the halyard loops, he climbed until his head was just above the masthead.

"I could do that, easy."

Giff looked down to find Jake beside him, watching Ned Blegbie.

"You'd better not let me catch you," he said sternly. "And don't tell me your father lets you, because I won't believe it."

"Nay, he caught me starting up once and pulled me back. But I'm no' afraid."

"*Have* you done it?"

"Aye, sure. A couple o' the men as were aboard afore ye took the ship, they dared me to, one night whiles me da' were sleepin'. They promised me a farthing if I touched the masthead. I told 'em I'd do it, but no' for a farthing, so they said they'd give me a ha'penny, and they did. It were gey easy."

"Those men can be glad they are no longer aboard this ship," Giff said. "Have you no chores to do this morning?"

Jake sighed. "I'll do 'em, then. Ye needna put yourself in a thunder-pelt." His gaze shifted to a point behind Giff. "Are ye really married to her now?"

"I am," Giff said, turning to see Sidony in the aft-cabin doorway.

He smiled at her and got a winsome smile in return.

"Sir!" Ned Blegbie shouted. "Two sails, aft t' steer-board!"

Fife was cautiously hopeful. He had ordered the men to erect a canvas shelter for him at the bow of the longship, to protect him from any rain that might come or from too much sun if they ever saw the sun. Moreover, according to de Gredin, the *Serpent* was just an hour ahead of them. Fife couldn't be sure, himself. He did see a ship on the horizon, but it was too far away for anyone to be sure, and he said so.

De Gredin said, "There are few ships of such a size in these northern waters. I'll be very much surprised if it is not the *Serpent*."

"Then tell the lads to put on speed so we can catch up to her," Fife said.

"If you insist, but she is heading the right way," de Gredin said reasonably. "They won't know us, so if we don't threaten them, they've no need to elude us."

Fife agreed, but only because it had occurred to him that to claim the Stone of Destiny for himself might prove difficult even if they did find it in the *Serpent*'s hold. To be sure, the *Serpent* was his and he would have liked to think he could claim the Stone on that basis alone, but MacLennan would fight to keep it.

Also, de Gredin wanted the treasure and would surely assume that the Stone was part of it. He might not care one way or another about keeping it, but he would surely see its worth to Scotsmen determined to keep it in Scotland, and he could demand the treasure as its ransom. And whether the Templars agreed to pay a ransom or not, the Stone would be of no use to Fife in de Gredin's hands or in theirs.

Moreover, not only did Fife have only twelve men of his own, but he had come to realize that although he outranked de Gredin, he was by no means in command of the longships or the men rowing them.

And de Gredin had promised that more ships would soon join him.

Chapter 17

"To the oars, lads!"

Sidony heard Giff shout the words as he motioned Ned Blegbie to descend. She watched as Giff moved swiftly about, giving orders to the men. When he sent Jake to "man" the compass, she smiled at Jake's air of importance as he obeyed.

From that moment through the rest of the day, Giff paid her little heed. She ate salt beef and a roll at midday, and talked with Father Adam, but when the priest began asking questions she felt ill equipped to answer or that seemed too personal, she excused herself and returned to the aft cabin to nap.

Supper included hard rolls and a stew of salt beef and flour dumplings in thin gravy that, despite rolling waves, the men had cooked over a fire pot without mishap.

Giff sat with her to eat the hasty meal but otherwise continued to keep his mind on the sea and the longships following them. Then, to her surprise, an hour before sunset, he took the ship into a bay, dropped anchor, and sent the coble ashore with a number of archers. Then he climbed the mast himself to watch the open sea.

The coble returned in an hour with jugs of fresh water and game bags, and they weighed anchor. When Sidony retired to the cabin at last, Giff put his head in to say, "I'll be along soon, lass, but I won't stay long. Once we reach Peterhead, I'll want to keep a sharp eye on our course, because we'll have seventy miles of open sea before us with no land in sight as we cross the Moray Firth. To miss Sinclair Bay and end up in the Orkneys, or worse, would utterly ruin my reputation."

Since she had no fear that any such thing would happen with him in control of the ship, she just smiled, then prepared quickly for bed and got in to wait for him.

"Why did we stop in that bay?" she asked when he entered.

"Because I couldn't stomach that stew again. Tomorrow we'll have rabbit."

"But what if Fife had caught us?"

"Aye, well, that was another reason. Those galleys are faster than this ship, but they stay about an hour behind us. I wanted to see if they'd stop, too, and they must have, because they are back there now, just as before. They seem to be watching us, mayhap thinking we're daft enough to lead them to the treasure."

She liked listening to his voice. When he said they needn't bother with a lantern, she agreed and asked if he was really concerned about their course.

"Nay, for the stars are peeping out, but the weather's trying hard to brew a storm. Hugo would say I'm a fool not to put into shore until dawn, but the plain fact is that I don't trust Fife, and the sooner we make Girnigoe, the better I'll like it."

They talked about nothing in particular until Maxwell rapped on the door and said they had passed Cairnbulg Point. Then Giff bent down, kissed her too swiftly, and left. The next morning, the skies were dark again, cross-winds blew, and no one could doubt that the storm that had threatened for a sennight would strike soon.

Giff believed the storm would hold off long enough for them to reach Girnigoe, but the dark hours of the night had tested his skill. The turbulent clouds had parted often enough to track a few stars, and the compass held steady, but when day broke with still no sign of land, he hoped he had not miscalculated badly.

Rabbit stew at midday raised his spirits, but it was hours more before Blegbie, on the masthead, sighted land ahead and shouted the welcome news. Then he added, "Them ships be a-closing their distance, sir, and there be a half dozen more o' them!"

Learning that they were not all longships, Giff signed to Maxwell to follow him to the forward cabin, banishing the priest without ceremony as they entered.

"Let's see that rutter again," Giff said as he unrolled a map on the shelf provided for the purpose. Confirming the detail he had recalled, he said, "We'll let them get as near as they like, then cut in close round Noss Head soon after dusk."

"We've almost two hours till then, sir. We'll be cutting it *gey* close."

"I mean to, but if we time it right, Fife and his reinforcements will have other concerns to occupy them whilst I make my landing and confer with Prince Henry."

"Aye, I see that," Maxwell said, casting his own glance at the rutter. "If I may ask ye, how long d'ye mean to stay at Girnigoe?"

"Just a day or two to replenish stores; then I'll be taking our cargo west."

"I expect ye dinna mean to leave Jake and me at Girnigoe, or do ye, sir?"

"I'll need you, Maxwell, and I expect you'll want to keep Jake with you."

"Aye, sir. The lad were so afraid o' losing me after his mam died that I promised I'd keep him with me. I've kept me word till now, but I dinna like the sound o' what lies ahead, what wi' this storm coming and all," he added.

"Prince Henry would look after him if we asked him to," Giff assured him.

"That'd be kind o' him, but I'm right against breaking me word to Jake."

"We'll see, then."

It occurred to Giff that doubtless Sidony should also stay at Girnigoe, but he found himself profoundly reluctant to leave her there.

Heaven only knew when he'd be able to return and collect her.

More than that, she was his now, and he did not want to part with her.

The wind grew more contrary, setting the sail aflap as fast as it refilled the canvas, so that the men at the braces had all they could do to control the yardarm.

The water grew rougher, the waves higher, and darkening clouds sped from the west only to collide with darker ones racing from the east.

Sidony, well wrapped in Fife's voluminous black wool cloak, watched as the clouds tried to pile one atop another. Towering, puffy white ones and billowing gray-to-black ones, all at different levels, seemed to fly in all directions.

The waves, too, were contrary, and the nearer they drew to the headland, the more contrary they grew, until the sea looked like a great pot stirred by a madman.

Giff paused in his continuing rounds to say, "Art cold, lass?"

"No, sir, I love the wind, but I gave up trying to keep my head covered."

He grinned. "This blow doesn't frighten you, then."

She shook her head, unwilling to tell him that his presence reassured her. "How close are those other boats now?" she asked.

"They're gaining, because they're lighter on the water than we are, but we'll reach Girnigoe by nightfall."

She did not want to think about Girnigoe. She had met Prince Henry of Orkney more than once, but she had never met his countess. And since, married now or not, she could not imagine any woman approving of her voyage aboard a ship full of men, she did not look forward to meeting her.

But two hours later, the *Serpent* rounded Noss Head to enter Sinclair Bay.

~

Giff marveled, as he had before, at the magnificent bay stretched before him. Six miles wide at its entrance, the bay's semicircular shoreline, which was bold and rocky everywhere else, subsided for four miles to low sand hills against a backdrop of impressively sheer precipices. Innumerable deep fissures, or "goes," penetrated them, creating gloomy caves or deep, watery chasms open to the sky. And here and there isolated pillars of sandstone called "stacks," resembling tall pickets of land, thrust skyward from the turmoil of the breakers.

"Sir Giff, me da' said to tell ye them ships be nobbut a half hour ahind us."

"Thanks, Jake." As they continued around the headland, Giff watched for the castle as he measured the rhythm of the rapidly ebbing tide with an experienced eye, grateful that Henry kept observers posted to warn him of approaching vessels.

A mile west of the headland, Castle Girnigoe, chief stronghold of the ancient Earls of Caithness and the Sinclair family, loomed on a bold, tonguelike peninsula of land a hundred feet above the southeast end of the bay.

Girnigoe's main tower stood fifty feet and five stories high, and its curtain wall, where it fronted on the sea, stood at the very edge of the craggy precipice. At the foot of that precipice, a steep-sided goe wide enough to shelter a good-sized boat ran in deep behind the castle's high, tonguelike perch.

What came into view on Giff's left, in the shelter of the deeply curved inland face of Noss Head, he admired even more—four of Henry's galleys, well manned.

Ordering the sail down, Giff directed his oarsmen toward the goe.

The wind had dropped significantly as they rounded Noss Head, but the rolling waves remained contrary, and the rock-girded inlet left no room for error.

He prayed that the capricious winds would not decide to blow straight at them from the north or northeast until the ship was safely inside the goe. The Pentland Firth, where storms raged more dangerously than elsewhere and currents and winds often changed direction in a blink, lay less than ten miles away.

He spared a thought for the ships pursuing them, hoping their captains knew naught of the Caithness shoreline. If they but followed where he had led, he could perhaps avoid a battle in the unpredictable bay. Clearing his mind of such thoughts, he focused it on his oarsmen and the impending landing instead.

"It is so beautiful here, so stark and crisp," Sidony said, her voice startling him out of his concentration on his narrow target.

"It is," he murmured, throwing her a quick smile and wondering as he often had since he'd met her just what it was about her that calmed him so one moment and then shoogled up his internals, as Jake would say, the very next.

"Do you know Countess Jean?" she asked. Her voice was quiet, but a note in it caught his attention.

With another quick look, he saw the strain that disturbed her usual serenity.

"Don't fret, sweetheart," he said. "She won't bite you. Henry won't let her."

"Women don't need to bite to hurt, sir."

Still watching closely, knowing he was on course, he put an arm around her shoulders and drew her nearer. "She won't hurt you either, because *I* won't let her."

~

He held her tight, and she drew strength both from him and from his words as she gazed in fascination at the sheer pillars of rock with seawater boiling around their bases. Her worry about the countess slid away, replaced by puzzlement as the sheer wall ahead of them drew too rapidly closer.

She was more accustomed to beaching boats, and the sandy beach some distance away to the right looked as if one could beach nearly any boat there, albeit perhaps not high enough to be safe from a storm-driven tide.

But the unwelcoming pillars and sheer rock dead ahead of them looked far more dangerous. She had every confidence in Giff, but . . .

"Are we not going to hold water soon and drop anchor?"

He chuckled. "Nay, lass, we'd have a time with her if we did. Look there, just ahead now, and you'll see an inlet with a landing like the boatsheds we call *nousts* at home, with rings and narrow wharves on each side to hold her. You can see Henry's men waiting now, too. They'll see that she stays safe overnight."

"What of Fife?" she asked.

"I'm hoping he and his lads will be kept busy, any that make it this far."

She glanced at the four galleys, apparently lying in wait in the lee of the headland, and thought she understood him.

The boats that had been following still had not come into view when Giff directed men on the bow to cast lines to those waiting and shouted, "Hold water, lads!" Calling quickly for them to ship their oars, he kept a close, measuring eye on the flanking rock faces as the ship drifted perilously between them. Others aboard the ship cast more lines to men waiting on either side to catch and secure them.

The ship eased to a stop in surprisingly calm water.

Henry Sinclair, Earl of Orkney—tall, broad-shouldered, and still Viking fair at thirty-six—strode grinning to welcome them.

The plank went out, and stepping onto it, Giff offered a steadying hand to Sidony as she followed. When she reached the landing, he released her to shake Henry's hand, saying, "All's well. Fife's right behind us, as you may know, but I've married the lass—the priest is yonder—and I'll tell you about it all presently."

Henry greeted Sidony warmly, and if he was shocked to see her or to learn of her marriage, she saw no hint of it. Leaving Captain Maxwell and Jake to supervise the men, and taking Father Adam with them, she and Giff followed their host up a narrow, precipitous flight of steps cut in the solid rock, through an archway at the top that opened into a walled forecourt, where they faced Girnigoe's main tower.

Jean, Countess of Orkney, received them on the dais at the west end of the huge, vaulted great hall, where a bow window overlooked the darkening land mass west of the castle. The countess, a plump, comfortable-looking young woman as fair as her husband, relieved Sidony's mind by greeting them as warmly as he had and expressing only delight upon learning of their marriage.

"But you must be exhausted," she said to Sidony. "I always am after a sea voyage, and to have arrived here so quickly from Leith! You must not have set a foot to the ground until you arrived here!"

Sidony acknowledged the truth of that statement with a laugh, saying, "And if Sir Giffard hadn't held on to me, I'd have tumbled right into the water, coming up your steps.

I vow, it felt as if each one of them lurched as I set foot on it."

"And so it always is, aye, but the sensation passes off quickly. Come now, for I know the men want to talk as they sup, so I'll show you to your chamber myself. It grows late, so I'm thinking you won't want your supper here in the hall but will want a bath, a light meal in your chamber, and then a comfortable bed for the night."

Gratefully, Sidony agreed and asked her if perhaps she had a robe to lend her, explaining that she had only the clothing she stood in to call her own.

"My dear! But how came that about?" Hearing the explanation as they went up to the third floor of the tower, Jean exclaimed and assured Sidony that she would provide whatever clothing she needed. "Not that we're at all the same size, my dear, for I've a few inches more than you in all directions, but we shall make do."

The chamber to which Jean showed her opened off a gallery with narrow arched windows that revealed only blackness beyond. But as oil-burning cressets suspended at each end of the gallery lit the passage, she could not see enough to tell if the storm clouds that had threatened were breaking up or thickening.

"I'll have them bring your supper straightaway, and a tub as well," the countess said. "The lads can fill it whilst you eat. You need not hurry, either, because it will be some time yet, I'm sure, before Sir Giffard joins you."

"Joins me?" Sidony heard the squeak in her own voice.

Her hostess smiled. "I'd not dare put him anywhere else to sleep on what must be the first night you've had to enjoy each other's company in real privacy. But I'll send my woman to you with something pretty to wear after your bath."

She went, leaving Sidony to stare at the large bed that dominated the chamber.

Henry turned Father Adam over to his chaplain with assurance that he would arrange his return to St. Andrews on one of his ships. Then he ushered Giff to the high table, saying, "We'll put up privy screens, for we'll be eating alone and thus can talk freely. Jean will see that Sidony gets a bath and anything else she needs."

Giff's body stirred at the thought of Sidony in a bathtub, but Henry diverted him after telling a gillie to set the screens, by saying, "What happened to your tail, Giff? The last report I received had them closing in behind you."

"If they do come into the bay, how dangerous would that be?" Giff asked.

Henry shrugged. "Girnigoe is impregnable, and my boats should keep Fife civil. If he demands entrance here, pretending his father's royal banner gives him that right, I'll allow it, but he'll bring no more than six of his men in with him."

"He has twice as many boats as you have below. I cannot name three lairds in Lothian who would support him, let alone six, and I know of none on the east coast with more than one boat. However, the two longboats fly French banners."

"What of de Gredin?" Henry asked, frowning. "He was in this business last year before I brought him here, and claims connections both to France and the Pope."

"Aye, and he is still in it," Giff said. "He captured Sidony and stowed her on Fife's boat. I stole the boat and found her, which is how we came to be married."

Clearly shocked and a little amused as well, Henry demanded the whole tale. So, as they ate, Giff told him everything, omitting only certain private details.

Reassured that Sidony had suffered no great harm and that the Stone was safely aboard the *Serpent*, Henry expressed astonishment at de Gredin's renewed relationship with Fife. "Those other ships must have come from de Gredin, then," he said at last. "Can he really have got them from his holiness?"

"I doubt the longboats belong to the Pope. Vatican ships always carry cargo. As to the others, they may be warships. We've seen little more than their sails."

"But why not stop you at sea, then? You say they've kept their distance."

"Fife cannot have full control of those ships," Giff said. "Moreover, he may not have risked letting de Gredin think we have the Stone. Fife may not quite believe it himself, come to that. But if he needed de Gredin to follow us and de Gredin cares only about the treasure, my guess is that he hopes I can lead them to the whole thing."

"In any event, you will stay here until we can think what to do about them," Henry said. "That landing can be reached from land only through the castle, and as few as four men with pikes or lances can defend it against anyone trying to approach it from the sea. But we dare not move your cargo until Fife leaves."

"I'll stay a day for my lads to rest and to load more stores, and I'll need one of your rutters with details of the Caithness north coast," Giff said. "But I mean to leave before dawn the day after tomorrow."

"Don't be daft, lad. It is raining already, and the storm

that's about to erupt will turn the Pentland Firth into a churning cauldron and keep it so for days."

Giff grinned. "Can you think of a better way to stop Fife?"

"You've eighty miles to go betwixt here and Cape Wrath," Henry reminded him. "You'd be lucky to get five without foundering, and even if the Fates let you make it past Cape Wrath, the storm could follow you right down the west coast."

"I won't mind if it does," Giff said. "Storms energize me, Henry, and Fife fears them. Moreover, no captain from France or Rome is likely to know these waters well enough to risk following us into that cauldron you've described."

"You'll leave Sidony here, of course."

"I don't know yet," Giff admitted. "I mean to ask her what she wants to do."

"You cannot take her with you on such a trip!"

"We'll see. She says she is tired of others always making her decisions."

"Well, she cannot make this one. Your plan is too reckless. Not only would you endanger everyone aboard, but you've forgotten the importance of your cargo."

"Nay, I have not. But I have faith that St. Columba will protect us on this voyage if on no other, Henry. That cargo I carry is sacred, after all, and the omens have been good. A man either believes in them and in his own course, or he fails."

After that, Henry reserved argument and changed the subject, demanding news from home, but Giff knew he would hear more before leaving. So, an hour later, when one of Henry's men reported that five of the pursuing ships had run aground on the long shoals off Noss Head over which the *Serpent* had skimmed on the rapidly ebbing tide a half hour before them, he took the news as yet another strong omen of approval.

Bidding Henry good night, Giff accepted a jug of brogac, another of claret, and two silver goblets as a wedding present. Then, recalling the image of Sidony in the tub, and eager to discover if other portents he had noted might also favor him, he hurried to find the bedchamber that he was to share with her.

He was halfway up the stairs when the image of his lass in the tub altered to one disapproving of what she had called his impetuosity. Henry had been less polite, calling him reckless, just as Hugo had before him.

Giff disagreed with all of them. To be sure, he had great respect for Henry and Hugo. He cared about the lass, too, and was coming to like her more each day. But she scarcely knew him yet and knew even less about how to ensure victory.

So why, he wondered, did her words linger so clearly in his mind?

Sitting by a cheerful fire on a pile of large, stuffed, embroidered cushions, bathed, well fed, smelling delightfully of lavender from the fine French soap Countess Jean had provided, and wearing the countess's lace-trimmed cambric shift and soft yellow velvet robe, Sidony heard the latch and drew a quick breath.

When she saw that Giff had two jugs and as many goblets, she decided she would feel less vulnerable on her feet and stood up in Jean's slippers to face him.

He stopped in the doorway and stared at her, the expression on his face bringing a flush of heat to her cheeks that seemed to spread all through her. Jean's own maidservant had attended her, had even washed her hair and brushed it dry at the fire. Soft and silky, it spilled over her shoulders and down her back to her waist.

He whistled low and said, "You, my lass, are a sight to steal any man's heart."

Though pleased, she nonetheless nearly reminded him she was not his lass, until she recalled that before God's Holy Kirk, she was. That thought and the sight of him recalled her to her vows and to the fact that she found her marriage less disturbing and more acceptable each time she clapped eyes on him.

His widening smile increased the strange sensations he always stirred in her.

Stepping inside, elbowing the door shut, he said, "You had that robe from Jean, did you not?"

"Aye," she said. "She has been most kind, but it is a trifle large."

"You look like a child wrapped in its mother's clothes."

"I am *not* a child," she said indignantly.

"No, sweetheart, I can see that. Is the water in that tub still warm?"

"I don't know," she said. "It has been sitting some time now, but I'm sure you can find someone to bring you more hot water."

"I don't want to wait," he said, his expression openly hungry now.

The look set her nerves atingle with warning and something else that made her hesitate to say more. But she gathered her wits long enough to say with grave dignity, "If you want to bathe, sir, I can walk in the gallery whilst you do."

"Nay, lass, you'll help me. 'Tis a wife's duty, after all, and you vowed—"

"I know what I vowed, and there was naught in it about baths!"

"There was something about obedience, though. You seem resistant, so doubtless you want practice." He handed her the goblets. "Hold those," he said.

Watching him warily, she obeyed. He poured from one jug into each goblet. It was not wine. Sniffing it suspiciously, she said, "Is this brogac?"

"Aye," he said. "Have you never tasted it?"

She shook her head.

"Well, I'm going to have my bath, and you can sit and watch me and sip your brogac. I'll even tell you a bard's tale or two to pass the time, if you like."

"Very well," she said, seeing naught to lose by obeying such a request.

Giff set the jugs on the low stool by the hearth where she had put his brogac and watched as she curled up on her cushions like a kitten, goblet in hand. She was too far from the stool to set the goblet on it, and setting it on the floor from her deep nest of cushions would be difficult. Satisfied, he tested the water. It was tepid, but it smelled deliciously of her soap, and the fire had kept it from turning icy, so it would serve well enough. He would prove to her that he was not reckless, but he would also prove that she ought to remember warnings when he issued them.

The bruise on her chin had faded, and her cheeks were rosy from her bath.

He burned to touch her, but as he pulled off his clothing,

he turned away when an unfamiliar voice of forethought whispered that he might otherwise frighten her. Then he sank into the tub, picked up the ewer beside it, poured water over himself, and soaped himself all over. Dripping water and soap, he smiled at her.

"Have you ever helped bathe a man, sweetheart?"

She shook her head. "My father says it is not a fit task for a maiden."

"Even a maiden can bathe her husband. You may help me, if you like."

Shifting in a way that told him his words had stirred sensations through her body that she was trying to ignore, she said, "You said you'd tell me a bard's tale."

"We could do both." He dipped the ewer to refill it.

"I'd rather just hear the story," she said, sipping her brogac and making a face. "This is very strong, I think."

"One grows used to it, and 'tis the drink of the Isles, but if you do not think you can tolerate it . . ." He paused, saw her sip again, and thinking things were going well, he said, "I know many Highland tales. Is there one you'd like to hear?"

"Aye, there is," she said, taking another sip.

"Which one?" he asked as he bent forward to pour water over his head and rinse the soap from his hair.

"I want to hear how you came to believe that if a person loses the right moment to do something, he will never find another."

He stopped moving with one hand still on his head as the past surged up and chilled him to the bone.

Ruthlessly suppressing the flood of memory, he said carefully, "'Twas nobbut an old French proverb I once heard: 'All the treasures of the earth cannot buy back one lost moment.' My father said it, and I took it to heart."

"What moment had you lost to make him say that to you?"

The memory swept through his mind again, stronger than ever. Setting down the ewer, he drew a deep breath and let it out. Then, measuring his words, he said, "I do not want to talk about this tonight, lass. 'Tis nowt."

She leaned forward, hands cradling the bowl of her goblet, unaware that her robe gaped enough to show the soft mounds of her breasts and her deep cleavage. Her hair spilled forward, too, a glowing, palely gilded sheet of silk in the firelight.

"It cannot be nowt," she said softly. "I've seen a sad look sometimes cross your face without cause, and you speak of lost moments too often for it to be nowt to you. Whatever happened must have been dreadful."

He had never felt so vulnerable, so unmanned. But when he looked at her and saw the gentle intensity in her eyes, he wanted to tell her, to explain. The thought that he *could* tell her felt strange, and he could think of no easy way. He feared that her gentle, understanding demeanor could too easily turn to repugnance.

Her gaze held steady, her manner remained serene, and her trust in him flowed from her in waves, assuring him that he could say anything to her. Even so, he knew what he risked, and he knew, too, of only one way to say it.

"I killed my brother," he said and, to his shock, felt tears spring to his eyes.

Dashing them away, aware that he sat in rapidly cooling water with wet strands of hair hanging over his face, he reached for his goblet, meaning to drink it dry, but she was there before he could lift it, and she held on to it firmly.

"Wait," she said. "I would hear the rest first. How old were you?"

"Eleven," he said curtly. "Lass, I cannot sit like this and talk of such things."

As if he had not spoken, she said, "How old was your brother?"

"Thirteen." He realized she meant to have the tale, and having begun, decided to tell it quickly. "He taunted me. I don't recall what he said, but he made me angry, then ran, saying I couldn't catch him. Duncraig sits on basalt cliffs above the sea. I'd played there the day before and fallen into a crevice, a small one but enough to trip a careless lad and make him look foolish. I knew he was heading for it but not how near the cliff it lay. I had that moment to stop him, but I hesitated. And he was lost."

"He fell?"

"He . . . he tried to jump it, stumbled, and plunged to the rocks below."

A tear spilled down his cheek and he shivered, eleven years old again, seeing the spirited, beloved boy who had never aged beyond thirteen vanish before his eyes again as he had on that terrible day.

Chapter 18

Sidony wanted to weep with Giff, but she knew that no man would thank her for encouraging or even noticing his tears. She had also seen him shudder, and although she felt sure that a memory had caused it rather than a chill, she pushed his goblet into his hand and said, "Here, drink this. It will warm you."

As he drank, she stood up, taking more care than when she had flown off the cushions and dropped her own goblet to the hearthrug at the sight of the tears in his eyes. At the time, she had meant only to offer comfort, but the same instinct that warned her now against letting him know she had seen his tears had warned her then that she must make him tell her the rest.

It was a wonder, though, that in her haste, the countess's robe had not tripped her and sent her flying into the tub with him. The image nearly made her smile.

"Art trying not to laugh at me, sweetheart?"

"I was thinking about how near I came to treading on this robe and pitching myself headfirst into that tub with you," she said, turning toward the bed. "The countess sent a robe of Henry's for you, too. Her woman put it here on the bed."

She heard water splashing and, turning back, saw that he had got out of the tub. He faced the hearth, dripping, and rubbed his head hard with a towel. His body gleamed golden in the fire's glow and that from the cressets.

Walking up behind him, having all she could do not to stare the whole way at his taut, well-shaped buttocks, she held up the robe, saying, "Put your arms in."

He obeyed and turned to face her with the robe still open, but when she began to step back, he dropped the towel, caught her shoulders, and pulled her close. Her head fit just below his chin.

She hugged him back, hard, muttering, "You will catch your death if—"

"I have never told anyone else."

"Is that why you've stayed away from Duncraig for so long?"

"My father sent me soon afterward to foster with my uncle at Loch Hourn."

"Because of the accident?"

"I'm sure he blamed me. Sakes, I blame myself. Had I shouted . . ."

"Why did you not?" she asked when he remained silent.

"It happened so quickly, but I had time, because I remember thinking he'd look a fool when he fell into that crevice."

"Is that why your father blamed you?"

"I never told him that part," he said. "He asked what happened, and I said Bryan was running and tripped. I said it happened all in a moment, and that's when he said the bit about nothing bringing back lost ones. So I knew."

"But you must have gone home to visit during your fostering."

"Aye, sure, but he was gruff and distant, so in time I stopped. My uncle taught me about boats and gave me one of my own. Then I went to Dunclathy."

She would have asked him more, but he straightened and said, "Enough talk of the past, lass. I want to get into bed and hold you. Will you let me do that?"

She looked into his eyes. "Aye, if you like, but you wanted to seduce me before. That's why you plied me with brogac."

He smiled ruefully. "Aye, I did, but in my favor, you should know I was fool enough to tell Henry I'd let you choose for yourself if you'd go with me or stay here."

"Certainly I'll go with you," she said. "I'm your wife. Even if I were not," she added, "you said before that if I did come with you, you'd take me to Glenelg."

She knew by the way he looked at her that, whatever he had said to Henry, he meant now to persuade her not to go, even to forbid it, so she said quickly, "We can talk about that later. Now, however, I agree that we should go to bed."

Giff watched her walk away from him. Despite the voluminous robe, she moved with a fascinating grace that he could happily watch forever. But why had it been so easy to tell her about Bryan's death? He had expected rejection, but although his confession had saddened her, it had neither shocked nor repulsed her.

Snuffing the cressets, and setting her fallen goblet on the wee stool beside his, he followed her to the huge curtained bed, taking the robe from her when she slipped it off, and laying it across the end of the bed. The lacy shift she wore was also too large for her. She seemed unaware that it revealed most of her charms as she climbed into the bed and scooted to the far side.

He took off Henry's robe and cast it atop hers, then climbed in and lay on his back beside her. Raising his right arm, he eased it to the pillow behind her.

"Come here and let me hold you," he said.

Without protest, she snuggled into the curve of his body with her head on his shoulder. Her hair felt like silk, and her body was even warmer than he had expected, or else his own was colder from his bath than he had thought.

They lay silently for some time before he realized his body had no intention of cooperating with his decision to suppress his lust for her and just hold her.

She snuggled closer, turning enough so he could feel the soft curve of her breast, clad in cambric, against his naked chest.

"You're still cold," she murmured.

"Nay, then, I'm not," he said. "You're as good as a hot brick to warm a man." When she chuckled, he added somberly, "I feared you would think less of me."

"Why should I? Why should anyone? You were only a bairn with no ability to persuade a lad two years older than you of anything, any more than I could sway my sisters. There are many things I do not know, but I do know children," she said firmly. "How could you have known he'd go over the cliff? You had not done so."

"Nay, but I was not running. I'd never have been so—"

"So daft?" she suggested helpfully. "Is your father also a Scottish Templar?"

The non sequitur startled him, but he said, "Aye, sure, 'tis why he sent me to Dunclathy. With all you've heard, doubtless you know many of us trained there."

"I did think so, since nearly everyone I know seems to be a Templar and all of them know Sir Hugo and his father. I presume they are all men of good sense, too."

"Aye, sure, but if you mean they are never reckless, as I am—"

"I did not say that," she said, laying her soft palm on his chest and shifting slightly as if to get more comfortable.

"Sweetheart, if you keep doing that, I won't answer for my actions."

"Why?"

"Shall I show you why?"

Sidony's pulse began to race, because his voice had sounded different as he asked the question. It was lower in his throat and its vibrations resonated through her, igniting her desire and making her feel hot all over.

Her mouth was dry, and she hesitated, until it came into her mind that she might be losing one of those moments he had so often talked about. Still, she could not decide. Her hand seemed to have decided for her, though, because it continued to stroke him, pressing harder and moving more easily across his broad chest.

He caught her wrist in a hard grip, coming onto his right side as he did. "If you are teasing me, sweetheart," he said, his face close to hers, his voice a near growl, "you will learn how dangerous that can be. I want to claim you as my wife but not if you remain unwilling. If you keep doing such things, I'll take it to mean that you *are* willing, but I'd rather hear the words from your lips."

Her fingers twitched on his chest.

"Well?" he said, his patience clearly on a thin tether.

"Aye," she said then, licking dry lips. "If you want to, I . . . I'm willing."

The words were barely out before his mouth came down hard on hers.

He still held her wrist, and his body pressed her into the mattress.

To her astonishment, hers responded by pressing back.

His lips were hot against hers and demanding, but when he released her wrist and put his hand instead on her breast, stroking it as she had stroked his bare chest, he stirred fire wherever he touched her, even through the lacy cambric. And when his thumb slid over her nipple, she heard herself moan in response.

"I want that shift off you, sweetheart." He did not wait for an answer, but she did not protest, and the shift was soon gone. In taking it off, he also pushed away the covers. And after he tossed the shift aside, he gazed down at her.

The glow of the dying fire lit his face and body, and his hungry expression awoke a craving in her that she had not known she could feel. From the first, she had felt comfortable with him. More than that, she had argued with him and spoken her very thoughts to him in an easy way that she shared with no one else.

When his gaze traveled from her breasts to the joining of her legs and back up to look steadily into her eyes, she said in a demure way that was also new to her, "Art still wishful never to have married, sir?"

He shook his head, then said with a wry smile, "But I shall still make the very devil of a husband, madam."

"You are the first to call me so," she said and then gasped as he began to toy with her breast again.

He tickled the nipple, then took it gently between his lips, and laved it with his tongue in a most extraordinary way, sending jolts of fire through her with every lick. His left hand slowly stroked her belly, moving lower and lower. When it reached the juncture of her legs, he claimed her lips again, licking them gently between kisses, then pressing his tongue between them into her mouth.

The interior of her mouth was warm and silky soft, and Giff wanted to explore every inch of it, and every other inch of her. She tasted sweet and fresh, and her small, slender hands were moving on his body, touching him lightly, exploring the texture of his skin, tickling hairs on his chest and belly. Fingertips skimmed one of his nipples, sending another wave of lust through him.

His loins ached, but if he wanted to disprove her belief that he was always impetuous, he could not let her drive him to an early release.

He caught the hand on his nipple, kissed its fingertips lightly, then shifted himself over her, pressing her hand into the pillow as he eased himself down to suckle her breasts again. Releasing the hand he had held, he stroked her arm up to the shoulder, then stroked her side to her hip, shifting again to caress the insides of her thighs. At last, cupping her mound, he eased a finger between her nether lips.

When she stiffened, he released the nipple he was

tonguing to say, “Easy, lass, I just want to prepare the way. Do you know how men and women couple?”

“Aye,” she murmured. “I’ve heard my sisters talk, of course, and Sorcha once told me ’tis much the same as the way most animals couple.”

He doubted that animals felt the same passions people did, but he said only, “If you don’t understand or don’t like something, tell me. Coupling should be enjoyable. The first time is not always so, though. You should know that, as well.”

As he talked, he moved his finger, finding the spot where she was most sensitive. When she moaned and opened her legs wider, he claimed her lips again, thrusting his tongue between them. With each kiss and stroke, his passions mounted until he could wait no longer and eased himself into her. He heard her gasp and tried to give her time to adjust to him, but his own needs urged him to get on with it.

He moved slowly at first, holding himself back, but the urgency grew as her channel began to pulse and the heat rose within her.

Sidony gasped when he began to move faster. His lips still held hers captive, and his tongue filled her mouth. Then his head came up and he pushed into her more deeply. In that moment, everything in her focused on the sensations pouring through her body, on the aching, the heat, and the fullness of him within her.

His face, barely visible in the dimness of the embers’ glow, had contorted as if he, too, felt pain but was too intent on his passion to care. He drove harder, faster, and deeper, until she feared the force of it would split her in two.

Then new sensations began to build, and she felt herself throbbing against him. He was breathing hard, plunging in faster until he pounded against her, threatening to crush her. At last, his rhythm shifted to shorter, speedier bursts and stopped.

He had exhausted himself, for he lay atop her, still breathing hard but replete and heavy. He was still inside her but no longer pulsing or filling her till she ached.

"Can you breathe?" he murmured near her left ear.

"Not easily."

With obvious effort, he moved off her but kept an arm across her ribs just below her breasts. "Better?" When she nodded, he said, "Did I give you much pain?"

"Some, but I never knew anyone could feel like that."

"I thought you said your sisters talked."

"Aye, but it was just talk. I know they enjoy coupling, but I suppose one has to feel the feelings for oneself to understand."

"I'm falling asleep, sweetheart," he murmured. "We'd better get cleaned up."

They did so, and he helped her clean the blood from her thighs. There was not a great deal of it and, to her relief, only a spot or two on the countess's sheet. It bothered her more, when they returned to bed, that he had no sooner kissed her and settled close to her with her head on his shoulder than he fell asleep. And snored.

She lay beside him, wondering if a man could give his wife a baby the first time, or if it took an accumulation of attempts to do so. The next thing she knew, it was morning, and Giff was standing in Henry's dark blue robe, telling the lass who had come to light cressets and a new fire that he wanted more water.

Giff saw Sidony turn over, yawn, and sit up, clutching covers to her breasts, and wondered if she had had second thoughts about her decision to bed with him.

The winds were shifting. He could tell because they had changed from their steady, low howling through the night to roaring gusts. He had no doubt that when the maidservant returned with his water and lit the fire, it would smoke.

Sidony looked wonderful. She had not put the countess's shift back on but had slept beside him naked. And now her beautiful, silken hair spilled over her bare shoulders and down her back. She had not taken time the night before to plait it and put it in a net, and he wondered how she had kept from entangling herself in it.

His own hair probably stood out as if he were in a stiff wind. He would not worry about it now, though. He'd get Henry's man to look after it later.

"Good morning," she said.

He smiled as he replied. Her voice did things to him. It was musical, as if someone had figured out how to tune a voice like a harp. He could never say such a silly thing aloud to her, of course, but that was what it was like. He had always been partial to harpists and to the lute. He carried his own lute aboard the *Storm Lass*.

"You are up early," she said.

"I want to see how Fife and de Gredin have been faring. Henry said they lost several of their ships, so they'll have to decide what to do with their extra men."

"They won't have drowned?"

"Sakes, no," he said. "The reason they ran aground is that just off Noss Head a wide field of shoals surfaces quickly in an ebbing tide. Maxwell's rutter noted them, and I recalled them from other visits. But Fife's ships followed where we led and were coming fast enough to ground some of them before they could see them and stop. How much we hurt them depends on the damage they incurred, though. There's a wide sandbar, too, and if they hit only sand, they'll be in the bay now."

"They won't attack the castle!"

"Wouldn't do them any good," he said. "That long tongue it sits on acts as a more effective deterrent than Roslin's land bridge. Only one pair of horsemen at a time can approach. They cannot capture the landing in the goe for a like reason. Even if they could, it would do them no good, because of the stairs. You saw them. Guards at the top could pick off likely invaders one by one if need be."

"So what will they do?"

A rap at the door heralded the maidservant with his water, so he waited while she put it on the washstand, then said they'd do without a fire and dismissed her.

"That chimney's bound to smoke with wind careering around as it is," he said. "As to Fife, Henry said de Gredin must have had a good look round here last year and found no treasure, so 'tis likely they think we'll be heading to Orkney. Sithee, Henry made a point of keeping de Gredin close to him there."

"Is it in Orkney?"

"Sakes, I don't know, and I must go." He kissed her swiftly and was gone.

Sidony watched him go, wondering if he had spoken the truth. She did not think he would lie to her, but how could he not know where the treasure was hidden if he carried part of it aboard his ship? Did he mean to leave his cargo with Henry? If he did, why was he heading on west, and why—with Fife going to Orkney and the treasure safe—would Henry think it a risk for her to sail with Giff to Kintail?

Not long afterward, Morag, Jean's waiting woman, arrived. As plump as her mistress, she carried a pile of clothing draped over her arms, from which the countess had said that Sidony was to choose as many as she liked.

"Countess Jean did say these be things she wore when she were slimmer, m' lady. They be still too long, she said, but I can quickly hem any ye like. She said, too, that she'd be that grateful to ye did ye stay on here for a few weeks to visit."

"I shall thank her for her kind invitation," Sidony said, suspecting that Giff or Henry had suggested that Jean issue it to keep her at Girnigoe.

Accepting Morag's assistance while she tried on the garments, and assuring her that she had no need of a fire, Sidony spent the next hour trying on and selecting what to keep. When Giff returned, she was standing on a stool, wearing a sleeved surcoat of warm pink cameline over a kirtle of pale green-and-gray striped silk.

Morag had hemmed the kirtle and was pinning up the surcoat hem to reveal a fashionable inch of the kirtle's hem below it. The kirtle's sleeve ends touched Sidony's knuckles and thus also showed, because those of the surcoat stopped at her wrists.

Giff paused in the doorway with the same look on his face she had seen the night before when he had walked in to find her in the countess's robe.

"Thank you, Morag," Sidony said, her gaze locked with her husband's. "If there is more yet to do, you may attend to it later."

"Aye, madam, but I can easily hem this surcoat wi' what pinning I've done. Be there aught else ye'll want to keep?"

"Nay, I have plenty now. The countess has been most generous," Sidony said, stepping down and letting Morag slip the surcoat off. Her own attention was still on Giff, as she tried to read his expression.

He reached out to stroke the pink cameline as Morag passed him, but neither he nor Sidony said anything more until the maid had gone and the door had shut.

"I hope you don't think this gown makes me look like a child," Sidony said.

From her low-curved neckline to her hips, the green-and-gray silk fit like a second skin, outlining her soft, round breasts and the gentle flare of her hips, and emphasizing her small waist. A girdle of four linked silver chains spanned her hips at the widest part and fastened with a jeweled buckle just a tantalizing few inches above the joining of her legs. From the chains' long ends, tiny gleaming silver balls dangled just below her knees and clinked when she moved.

"Well?" she said.

"You don't look *anything* like a child," he said. "I like

that pink thing you had on, too. 'Tis as soft as a kitten. I'll want to stroke it often when you wear it."

"I like it because it is warm and because it does *not* belong to Fife."

"How does that come off?" he asked, indicating her kirtle.

"About a thousand tiny hooks down the back, but do not think you are going to get it off me right now," she said, stepping hastily back and putting up her hands. "I have been dressing and undressing ever since you left, and I'm starving."

"You haven't yet broken your fast?"

"Nay, I never even thought of it after Morag came in."

"Then we'll find you something. The stairways are icy cold, so you'll want a shawl or something till we get to the hall. It is smoky there but warm enough."

She fetched a cheerful yellow wool shawl that the countess had sent along with the rest of the garments, and draped it over her shoulders.

"Did you learn what happened to Fife's ships?" she asked.

"Three that went aground sank. One suffered serious damage. The longships, being more easily maneuvered, hit only sand and came off easily, and the two that were farthest back missed the shoals altogether. So there are still four, and a fifth may rejoin them. We doubt they'll try anything violent with Henry's boats at hand, but Fife may drop a coble in the water and demand entrance under his royal banner."

"Will Henry let him in?"

"He said he'd let Fife and six of his men in, but no more. So far, no one has asked." Shoving a hand through his hair, feeling confined, he turned to the window shutter and opened it a crack to breathe as he added, "I have one more thing to say."

"What?"

"I have changed my mind," he said. Then, because his reluctance to face her went right against his belief that the success of any decision required full commitment to that decision, he closed the shutter, turned back, and gave her a straight look. "It is just too dangerous, sweetheart. I'd be a damned, irresponsible fool to take you along."

Calmly, she said, "So, then, what you told Henry was untrue."

"Sakes, who do you think called it reckless and irresponsible? Henry doesn't want you to go. He'll be pleased that I've seen reason."

"So, your word is untrustworthy only when the matter concerns me?"

"I never told *you* that I would let you decide."

"No, you just said you had told Henry that you would. So if Henry had told me, he would now discover that, thanks to you, he had lied to me, would he not?"

"Stop this!" he snapped.

"Or what? You'll beat me? That is what Hugo always threatens when Sorcha defies *his* dictatorial nature. I don't think he has ever done so, however."

"Hear me well, madam, for I do *not* make empty threats," he said grimly, angry now. "As you have seen for yourself, when I want to do a thing, I do it. So do *not* try me any further in this."

Her chin came up. "I also do what I say I will do, sir. I am your wife, and as far as I can tell, there is no more danger in what lies ahead of us than in what threatened us all the way from Lestalric to Girnigoe."

"You have not seen that storm raging out there," he said. "Look at it!"

And with that, he jerked the shutter open. The effect was not what he had hoped, however, because he had forgotten that for the past hour, the strongest gusts had come from the north and west, their fierce power breaking against the landward side of the castle. To be sure, outside the window the sea raged, but from the third story of a fortress a hundred feet above the water, its impact would seem small to her.

"I have no fear of any storm when you are controlling the ship," she said. "I know that if you say you can do it, you can. It is not even raining."

"It was pouring earlier," he said. "And it will pour again. In any event, the strength of that storm is irrelevant. I am your husband, and you will do as I say."

"Very well, but when you do come to fetch me, if you ever do, you will take me to my father's castle. I'll not stay with a man who doesn't want me with him."

He clenched his fists and said through his teeth, "I *do* want you. Don't you see? You could be killed, either by the storm or by Fife's lot if they catch us."

"Then don't let them catch us," she said. "You must decide, for it is indeed your right, but I won't change my mind. I don't want to stay here in safety, fearing all the time you are gone that you have disappeared under fathoms of water or been killed by Fife and de Gredin, not to mention having not the least notion how long I should wait to hear any news, one way or the—"

"Enough, Sidony!"

"Nay, I am your wife now in *every* way. If I do not have the right to be with you until we have a home of our own, then I do not want to be with you at all."

Hands on her hips, chin still thrust forward, she was just daring him to put her across his knee. And for the life of him, all he wanted to do was to grab her, hug her, strip that clinging silk dress off her, and take her back to bed.

Sidony saw the look in his eyes, and when he stepped toward her, she stepped hastily backward, clapping her hands protectively over her backside.

He stopped, made a sound like a growl low in his throat, then turned and went out, slamming the door behind him.

Drawing a long breath and letting it out, she picked up the shawl that in her rage she had let slip to the floor, rearranged it, and waiting only a minute or two to let him get well ahead of her, she followed him downstairs to the hall.

Fife had awakened on damp, uncomfortable shingle in the wedge-shaped bay where they had beached the longships. It was still raining then, and he ached all over but was glad to be alive. As if the landless stretches of the Moray Firth had not been terrifying enough, to see the damage wrought when they had hit the field of shoals off Noss Head had been enough to make him retch until he could barely stand.

The lead longboat had just scraped the top of a huge sandbar, but the second boat, only minutes behind, had stuck fast on another part of it. Then they had heard the horrible screeching of ships striking rocks that they themselves had missed.

Men had drowned, screaming for help. They had rescued many, but the three ships that had struck hardest on the rocks had sunk before they had got everyone off. They'd turned back south then, where men from ships that had avoided the shoals reported that the wedge-shaped bay could provide shelter for them all.

So they had beached the longships, anchored the others, and set up tents against the rain and the threatening storm. Fife had taken the first opportunity to seek his tent, and when de Gredin had brought him wine, he had drunk it gratefully and for a wonder had slept deeply. Now, his head ached, and he had a raging thirst.

A call to the man who had slept outside his tent achieving nothing, he got up to wake the fellow. No one was there. In fact, he did not see any of his men.

De Gredin had taken to giving them orders, something to which Fife knew he would have to put a stop. So, seeing the chevalier standing by a small fire they had managed to start under a protective ceiling of canvas, he strode to join him there.

Before Fife could speak, de Gredin greeted him cheerfully, saying, "You'll be pleased to know, my lord, that the ship now at Girnigoe is indeed the *Serpent*. Men I sent ashore with the first boats got a look at it and say it is moored in an inlet with sheer cliffs all round it. My lads can easily look down on it from the landward side, so we'll know if MacLennan tries to unload cargo, but apparently, the only access to the castle is up steep, narrow steps, so I doubt they can unload there."

"Gratified as I am to hear that," Fife said stiffly, "I

would like to know what you have done with my men. You seem to think they are yours to command, but—"

"I am afraid they are no one's to command, my lord," de Gredin interjected. "Unfortunately, all of your men drowned in the disaster yestereve."

"That's impossible," Fife said. "I know that some were on your other longship, and several were with me. One was sleeping right outside my tent."

"Aye, it was very sad to lose them all so," de Gredin said.

The chill Fife felt was no fault of the weather.

Chapter 19

Giff found Henry standing before the great hall fire, apparently oblivious to smoke billowing in great gusts from its chimney. The vaulted ceiling was high, and the smoke drifted upward, but it stung Giff's eyes and made breathing a penance.

"They're at Wick Bay south of Noss Head," Henry said. "There's good shelter for them there. Our bay is open to winds coming from the north or east, except here, where the inlet behind the headland provides some protection."

"You've set men to watch them?"

"Aye, sure, just as I'm sure Fife has ordered men to watch us here."

"I won't worry about his, although if you want to send your lads hunting, I won't object. Capturing one or two of his men might tell us more than we know now, such as whether Fife has reason for allying himself with France and Rome in this business, other than to exploit de Gredin's treasure hunt in aid of his own effort to undermine the vast powers of the Sinclairs and Logans, and others of their ilk."

"We might well learn something," Henry said. "But I've no wish to increase Fife's enmity by seizing his men. He's made it clear these past years that he not only resents my Norse title but wants to weaken every powerful clan, thinking thereby to increase Stewart power. 'Tis well known that he did all he could in the Borders to undermine Douglas. But if Fife demands hospitality, I'll feel obliged to provide it."

"If he were a fellow Highlander, perhaps, but he's not," Giff said.

"Our rules of hospitality do not reserve it only for Highlanders."

"Aye, sure, but if you think you can trust that lot of villains inside—"

Henry's chuckle silenced him. "Rules of survival supersede all else, Giff. Come to that, mayhap we should invite Fife in. It would keep him closer, easier to watch."

"Do as you like, but stay *that* invitation till I'm gone," Giff said brusquely.

Henry's eyebrows shot up. "Have I offended you, lad?"

Giff grimaced. "Nay, but my lass put me in a temper. I told her she must stay here, but she declares she won't. And, in troth, Henry, I don't want to leave her. She tells me she would hate not knowing my fate until someone deigned to reveal it to her. Sakes, I cannot blame her, especially when I doubt she would be in any more danger on the ship, even in a storm, than she has been with that lot chasing us."

"What of your own judgment whilst she is aboard?"

Henry asked, frowning. "Would you act the same to save the Stone? What then, if Fife does catch you?"

"She said I should see that he doesn't," Giff said.

Henry laughed, and suddenly Giff was able to see the humor, too. He saw something else just as suddenly, a way he might further protect the Stone.

He might have shared that thought with Henry, particularly as it ought to allay *some* people's fears of his so-called recklessness. But he had no wish to debate the newborn idea until he'd considered it more, if then. In any event, Sidony walked in from the stair hall just then, looking serene and perfectly at home as she moved toward the dais, where a basket of rolls and a pitcher of ale still sat on the table.

Taking a roll, she deigned at last to note their presence, smiling as she made a slight curtsy in Henry's direction. "Good morrow, my lord. Your countess has been very generous. I have enough garments now to clothe me for a year."

"I'm sure you are welcome to them, lass. Did you sleep well, or did last night's fierce winds and crashing seas disturb you?"

"I slept well, thank you. That bed is most comfortable, although it did not rock me to sleep as the one aboard the *Serpent* does," she added with a gleam that told Giff if not Henry that she knew where Henry meant the conversation to go.

Henry persisted. "A ship is scarcely the safest bed during a storm. Our Pentland Firth is particularly noted for its storms, and this one will certainly grow worse."

"My husband promised to provide me with a proper home, sir," she said with her demurest smile. "I mean to see that he does so as soon as possible."

Giff's idea stirred again with a simple adjustment and took firmer shape, for what protected the Stone might also provide protection for Sidony. He said, "She is right, Henry. I did say, after all, that she could make this decision for herself. And I do not think Fife and his lot will catch us if we can get safely away in the darkness."

"Sakes, but it's madness to go out on this bay when you won't be able to see your hand before your face," Henry objected.

"He's sailed in the dark these past two nights," Sidony pointed out.

"I do know that neither this bay nor the firth is at all like being on open sea well away from the coast, Henry," Giff said before Henry could point out the same thing. "But I've a good compass and a fine partner in Maxwell. And once we round Duncansby, I do know the firth and its habits well enough to get us safely to Cape Wrath and then southward." Just how far south they would all go, he did not say.

"But what if they do follow you?" Henry asked.

"If they do, and it's still storming, they're mad," Giff said. "They'll perish on the Boars of Duncansby or the Men of Mey, for they won't be expecting either hazard. For days, they've kept us in sight and done what we've done. I doubt anyone on those ships kens the firth waters as you or I do, so if I can steal a full day's march on them, I'll make Cape Wrath easily. Sithee, they cannot know where I'm headed."

"Fife may guess," Henry warned. "There are few choices if he learns you've not gone to Orkney or stayed here. All he needs to do is stop at one village or another and ask if the *Serpent* has passed by. Ships, even my own, do not so commonly sail west in these waters that folks won't take notice."

Giff was watching Sidony, whose eyes shone bright with expectation. He said, "You still mean to go with me, sweetheart?"

"I do," she said firmly. "What are the Boars of Duncansby?"

They left not long after midnight while the sky and all around them was pitch black, and raging winds whistled around the castle walls. Every now and then, an inquisitive gust darted in from the sea to sweep right up the precipitous stairway.

Not having quite trusted Giff to wake her, Sidony had awakened twice with a start, fearing to find him gone. But he had shaken her from a deep sleep at midnight and told her to dress if she truly wanted to go.

She was grateful now for the countess's warm cameline surcoat, although she wore it under Fife's thick wool cloak. Giff had put that around her himself, insisting not only that she would keep warmer, but also that it would conceal her better than the pink surcoat. It was her own thought that Fife's cloak could get as dirty as it liked and would thereby protect the soft surcoat. She reflected sadly that the latter would not feel as soft or look as pretty by the end of their journey as it did now, but Giff liked the feather-soft fabric, so perhaps he would buy her more of it.

In the shelter of the castle forecourt and on the stairway down into the narrow goe, one did not feel the brunt of wind or rain because, like the tongue of land on which Girnigoe sat, the goe ran almost parallel to the Caithness landmass. But on the narrow wharf, the wildly churning sea suddenly became a terrifying roar of chaotic, thunderous crashes of waves against the outer wall of Girnigoe's perch. Without light, tied to both walls of the goe, the *Serpent* became no more than a denser, noisier piece of the all-encompassing blackness. But its struggle to free itself from its moorings stirred nearby air and made the darkness all the more menacing.

The ties held, and Maxwell's voice came to her from close by, "I'm right here, me lady, and if ye'll take me hands, I'll help ye step aboard."

Giff steadied her as she gripped both of Maxwell's hands, but the boat did not want to stand still, and it took the efforts of both to get her aboard. Immediately she slipped on the wet rowers' bench, and to her annoyance, Giff just stepped over the gunwale onto the same bench, still holding her arm. She landed awkwardly on her feet in the room between benches, but he stepped down beside her without letting go. He slipped an arm around her then and drew her close beside him.

"I'll take you to the aft cabin, sweetheart, so come onto the gangway with me, but take care there, and hold tight to me. It is rolling a little now, but you'll grow used to it if you can make yourself relax and try to anticipate its movements."

Rolling a little!

Easy for one who had lived on boats for years to say, but she had spent many hours on them, too, albeit not in any storm like this one.

"Why have you no lights here?" she asked. "Surely, no one could see us, especially as you and Henry said that Fife's boats are not even in this bay."

"He will have watchers on the headland and elsewhere,

who need only discern a glow to grow suspicious," he said, his voice louder than before. "We'd as lief they not see anything to make them wonder about us."

"Here, me lady, take hold o' me shoulder," Jake said, materializing out of the darkness on a bench to her right. "I can help ye."

Gratefully, she accepted, and with him beside her and Giff on the gangway ahead of her, by the time they reached the cabin, she had found some of her balance.

"The tide is ebbing," Giff said as he opened the door. "I want to make the other end of the bay well before flood, so we can pass the Boars safely and speedily enough to get beyond the Men before it ebbs again. As it is, it'll be a near thing."

He and Henry had explained that the Boars of Duncansby and the Men of Mey were the Scylla and Charybdis of the Pentland Firth, violent agitations that the sea produced at each end of the narrowest part of the firth, where the currents that ran in opposing directions collided, with sometimes cataclysmic results. Huge breakers, they said, would jet up as from a boiling cauldron and tumble over each other in utter frenzy. Men had seen them rage even when the rest of the firth was calm, but they behaved particularly badly, Giff said, during a big storm.

Her eyes were growing accustomed to the blackness outside. She could make out shapes and tell the difference between solid, stationary ones and tossing, wild ones, but she felt as if she were entering a cave when she went into the cabin.

As Henry had warned, she could not see her hand in front of her face.

"I don't suppose you'll let me have a lantern in here when the door is shut."

"Nay, lass," Giff said. "We'll have no flame aboard this boat tonight. What with—" He broke off, and even through the noise of the wind, she heard the distant grumbling his quick ears had caught before hers. "Sakes, I must get us onto the bay at once," he said. "Jake, help her ladyship to the wee table nook and stay with her."

When the lad began to protest, Giff added sternly, "I shall depend on you to keep her safe tonight, because I cannot stay to do that myself."

"Aye, then, I'll look after her," Jake said. "Ye'll ha' nowt to worry ye."

"Was that thunder?" Sidony asked as Giff turned. "Why do you hurry?"

"It was thunder, aye, but 'tis the lightning it attends that concerns me, for a single bolt over this bay will turn night into day and reveal us to Fife's watchers."

He shut the door on the words, and feeling her way, Sidony sat on the aft-most bench in the table alcove so she could face forward. She doubted the rocking motion would make Jake sick if he sat with *his* back to the prow.

"I'd no' like being in here on my own," he muttered a moment later.

"Nor would I," she admitted. "I'm glad you're with me, Jake."

"Aye, well, wi' two of us, we're bound t' scare off any boggarts."

"Do you worry about boggarts?"

"Och, nay, they're nobbut a nuisance from time to time."

Recognizing the truth, she said, "Shall I tell you a tale my sister Adela used to tell me when I was a bairn and afraid that a bad fairy would steal me from my bed?"

"Aye, sure, we might as well do summat to pass the time," he said.

Sidony told him a tale of water fairies calculated to make him laugh, and as she did, she heard men shout and felt the boat begin to toss more. She could not imagine how they would get it out of the narrow goe onto the teeming waters of the bay, but she soon felt the familiar motion of oars in the water and realized that Henry's men on the narrow wharves were helping by pushing the *Serpent* far enough out for the oarsmen, two sets at a time, to plunge their oars into the water and pull.

The *Serpent* began to feel like a child's toy tossed into a river in spate, for it rose, settled, twisted, and turned like a mad thing, but the running tide soon caught the boat and pulled them away from the shore. The tide would run for six more hours, she knew, and Giff had told her that in the firth, the tide could run as fast as ten miles an hour. The Boars were dangerous only in a rising tide, he had said, but the Men showed their wrath with the ebb, which was why their timing would be crucial.

They had six miles to go before they would round Duncansby Head and pass the Boars, then another eight to St. John's Head and the Men of Mey. She reminded herself of her confidence in Giff and focused her efforts on keeping Jake entertained.

The thunder continued rumbling in the distance, growing closer and louder until its deafening cracks seemed directly overhead. Two sent enough light through the space between the nearby shutter and porthole to see Jake's outline opposite her.

For a time, as the thunder grew distant again, rain pounded down on them and the rocking motion of the boat grew less rhythmic. Experience told her the men had raised their oars and the *Serpent* was riding the waves. The ship steadied, and a few minutes later, Jake got up and went to the door, opening it carefully.

"What are you doing?" Sidony asked.

"Seeing," he replied. "They've put up yon sail. I thought they had."

"In this weather?"

"Aye, sure," he said in a superior, male way. "Me da' does the same thing to gain speed and the like, but Sir Giff be sailing gey close to this wind, I'm tellin' ye."

"Well, shut that door before he sees you've got it open," she said. "Then come back, and I'll tell you another story, or you can tell me one. It is your turn, after all."

Perfectly willing, he soon had her laughing at the antics of a pair of Border brownies who lived with a woman who did not treat them properly. Since Sidony would not have known how to treat them, either, she felt for the poor woman.

Time passed swiftly until, without warning, the ship slewed broadside into a wave, nearly dumping both of them from their benches. Only the fact that she had put a hand to steady herself seconds before saved Sidony from a bruising, if not worse.

"Rough water," Jake said. He attempted his customary, casual tone, but she detected his fear, and her quick concern for him steadied her nerves.

"It will pass," she said. "They call him the King of Storms, you know."

"Aye, sure," he said. "Will I tell ye another—" His words ended in a shriek as the boat tossed again and a crash of thunder shook everything around them.

"Hang on, Jake," Sidony cried. "Grab my hand!"

He gripped her hand, and before she knew what he was

doing, he was beside her, pushed in hard against her, clinging to the table and to her. She wrapped an arm around him and said, "Thank you, I was terrified that I'd be pitched onto the floor."

He did not speak, but when the boat settled and the rhythmic motion of oars began again, he said, "Ye'll be safe now, I reckon, so I'll go back to me seat."

Moments later, the door to the cabin opened, with enough light outside to see Giff as he put his head in. "I don't know if Fife saw us in all that lightning," he said. "But I'm guessing he did, so get ready for a rough ride. We've come the whole way much faster than I'd meant to, so the Men may cause us a wee spot of bother."

"How wee?" she asked, hoping she sounded calmer than she felt.

"The tide is still running hard," he said. "Don't worry; just hang on."

"Do you want to come over here again?" she asked when Giff had gone.

"Nay, I'll do," the boy said. "He said it were nowt. D'ye think the waves fly up as high as he said? I'm thinking that when he opened yon door it looked light enough for a man to see what they look like when we pass by 'em."

"You are to stay right where you are," she said, trying to sound as stern as Giff would. "It is too dangerous to be up walking around. Recall what it was like before, and that was just the storm tossing us about. We'd passed the Boars with no trouble."

"Aye, sure, that's right," Jake said. "Will ye tell the first one, or shall I?"

She agreed to go first and told him another Highland tale, but as it reached its climax, she heard shouts from outside and heard Jake jump to his feet.

"Jake, don't—!"

But he flung open the cabin door, and she saw him outlined briefly in the opening before he looked landward and vanished.

Crying out, Sidony leaped to her feet and plunged across the heaving floor to the open doorway, grabbing the jamb and the door itself when it threatened to slam into her. Hanging on to them both, she looked out and saw that Jake had crashed against the stepped gunwale and was clinging to it, half on the upper step and half on the lower. Her sweeping gaze found Maxwell at the helm, gripping the tiller, his face contorted with anxiety, and Giff at the mast, looking forward as he manned one set of braces and shouted orders to Hob Grant on the other. The oarsmen on the sternmost benches saw Jake's predicament, but each larboard bench held three oarsmen, penned in by their oar, and although the gangway-end man on the nearest bench started to move, the man nearest the gunwale shouted at him to stay put or they'd lose the oar.

Giff's attention was on the sea ahead, and he bellowed for the larboard men to pull harder just as the boat yawed hard to larboard, nearly onto its side.

Waves hurled themselves at them from all directions, and Sidony realized the boat was spinning, as if a whirlpool had caught it. Just as that fact registered, the bow plunged down the back of a huge wave, and she saw Jake begin to slide forward off the higher step of the gunwale toward the oarsmen, or overboard into the sea.

The men, pinned behind their oars, could do nothing to help him.

Maxwell shouted, but the wind swept his words away before they reached her. He looked feverishly about, doubtless for someone to take over the tiller.

Afraid he might let go of it and doom them all, she flung herself toward Jake. If her feet touched the deck, she did not feel it. Her eyes were on him, and she thought of nothing and no one else. From a vast distance, she heard Giff shout, but she dared not look, lest the boy vanish over the side to the sea. She could not let Giff lose him, too.

Water sluiced over her, but its only effect was to make her dive toward Jake, arms outstretched. Her left hand missed, but her right caught an ankle as her left shoulder hit the side. Feeling herself skidding, she managed to wrap her left hand around the same ankle. But the boy was heavy and going over, pulling her with him.

~

As usual under such conditions, Giff had taken a stand where he could concentrate on the water and command the boat. Hob Grant having proved nimble with the braces, Giff told him to man the steerboard ones, while he himself manned the landward set. The first time he had navigated the Pentland Firth, he had hired a pilot at Cape Wrath to teach him its quirks, and he knew that the trick with the Men of Mey was to hold a straight course, because less than a mile separated St. John's Head from the Island of Stroma. With two oceans colliding in such narrows, the tide on its ebb seemed to want to run in all directions. These waters had claimed many a ship, and he did not intend the *Serpent* to become one of them.

The Men were leaping high, the ebbing tide trying one moment to drive the ship backward, the next to push it toward the Caithness shore, with the result that he saw the disastrous eddy barely in time to avoid plunging straight into it. As it was, the *Serpent* caught the whirling edge and wanted to ride it around. He shouted for the lads to pull harder, counting particularly on the larboard side, where he'd placed his twelve extra men to fight the unpredictable current's determination to push them shoreward. The wind blew from the north again, too, but he could still harness it as his best ally.

He heard shouts from behind but knowing he had to get the *Serpent* free of the whirlpool, he bellowed again at them all to "Pull!" before he dared take his eye off the water ahead and glance back.

To his shock, he saw Sidony leaping, skidding, and diving toward the larboard gunwale. Only then did he catch sight of Maxwell's anguished face and see Jake.

"Hold that tiller!" Giff roared at Maxwell, then to the men, he bellowed, "Pull, lads, pull for our lives! Hob, tie off your braces!"

The men were shouting now, all of them, and when he saw that Hob Grant had tied his braces, Giff took a quick wrap around his own cleat to fix the luff. Then, sending up a prayer that the wind would hold, he leaped to the gangway, running, praying he would not slip on its puddled surface. His men could not leave their posts without further endangering the ship, and he was terrified that he would be too late.

She was holding tight to the boy, but Jake was struggling, and the waves were doing their best to rip them both from the boat. In Giff's haste to reach them, he nearly plunged overboard himself, but he caught the rail and grabbed Sidony, then Jake.

Her eyes widened as she looked into his, and no wonder. He was furious and wanted nothing more right then than to throttle her for frightening him so.

Gesturing to the nearest outside oarsman to ease off his

bench and let the two others with him shift to keep proper leverage on their oar, Giff handed the lad to him.

"Get him wrapped in a blanket; he's soaked through. Then relieve Maxwell."

"Aye, sir."

In that moment, the boat lurched free of the whirlpool and steadied. They were by no means out of danger, but they were beyond the worst.

Giff looked at his wife, still feeling the shock of near disaster and still wanting to punish her for terrifying him so. He scooped her into his arms and strode to the aft cabin, noting as he passed that Wat Maxwell was holding his son close.

"He wants skelping," Giff growled at him. "Both of them do."

He did not wait for a response but carried Sidony into the cabin and kicked the door shut behind him, only to realize that he had just shut out all the light, and to recall that it was twice as hard to keep one's balance if one could not see one's surroundings.

"Faith, don't drop me," she said when he stumbled.

"Can you stand?"

"I think so," she said, her tone wary. "What are you going to do?"

"What were you thinking to leave this cabin after I told you to stay in here?"

"Jake wanted to see the Men of Mey," she said. "I told him to stay inside, but I didn't see that he was heading for the door as I said it. He opened it and just vanished. I ran and looked out just as the boat yawed. I *couldn't* let him be swept away." Her words ended in a squeak when he put his arms around her and pulled her close.

"If you ever scare me like that again, lass, I swear I'll take leather to you."

She did not speak, but her arms went around him and held him tight, and he was glad the cabin was too dark for her to see the tears that spilled down his cheeks at the knowledge of how near he had come to losing her.

Although she was as wet as Jake was, Sidony felt warmed all through, and why she should when her husband had just threatened to beat her if she ever did such a thing again and, indeed, seemed still within a hair of doing it now, she could not imagine. But the threat that ought to have stirred fear had sent the strange, warm feeling all through her instead, and she held him as tight as she could.

He kissed her forehead and her lips, and then he said, "I can't stay, sweetheart. I must see how Jake is and be sure we're safely past the last of the Men. We've days yet to go before we reach our destination, but this storm is more wind than rain now. Mayhap we can make camp tonight and dry out a bit."

But, an hour later, two sails came into view behind them, forcing them to press on. The weather began to clear, and except for long hours of calm the second day, the winds remained reasonably favorable. Even the calm helped, because with judicious use of his oarsmen, knowing the longboats were unlikely to have loaded enough provisions for so many men at Wick Bay and would have to stop to hunt or fish, Giff was able to keep going while being certain his pursuers could not keep up.

Dusk had turned to darkness on the third day when they entered a rocky inlet. Shouting greetings and commands to men ashore, Giff ordered his rowers to turn the *Serpent* and back her into a gated *noust* at the inlet's head.

"Where are we?" Sidony asked as he handed her from the boat.

"Duncraig," he said. "Fife will need luck to find us now, and as we had to pass by my home in order to reach Ranald on the Isle of Eigg, I decided that filial duty required me to stop long enough to present you to my parents."

Narrowing her eyes, she said, "Mercy, do you mean to leave me here?"

"I had thought I might, because keeping you with me could confuse matters later," he admitted. "But, as Fife and company have fallen behind, I'll take you to Glenelg tomorrow and leave you safely with your father whilst I carry on to Eigg."

Sidony grimaced. Not only did she not want to face her father if Giff had to leave again right away, but knowing now where he was going, she wanted to see their voyage through to the end.

Fife was miserable. He had realized he was as good as a prisoner to de Gredin from the moment the twice-damned traitor had told him the men in his tail were dead. Nonetheless, Fife had stood firm when he learned MacLennan had taken the *Serpent* into the teeth of the raging storm and that de Gredin meant to follow him.

"You're daft," Fife had snapped when the chevalier ordered everyone to the ships. "Just leave me here then, and I'll seek shelter from Prince Henry."

"No, my lord, you will not. You can be of no use to me at Girnigoe."

When Fife had begun to argue, demanding to know what use de Gredin thought he could be to him anywhere else, the chevalier had gestured to one of his men, who brought him a flask. "Drink some of this, my lord. It will calm you."

"I don't want your drink, and I refuse to board any ship in this weather."

"Choose, my lord. You may drink from the flask, or I will have one of these men render you unconscious. We have no time to lose."

Understanding why he had slept so well the previous night, Fife had drunk the wine and awakened hours later with an aching head, drenched to the skin, and more frightened than ever. The bow of the longship was tossing wildly in the storm, and the canvas that had sheltered him before had vanished altogether in the wind.

When a wave struck him full on, he screamed, grabbing at the nearest of two bow storage lockers that formed benches near the stempost, trying to find a handhold.

De Gredin shouted from surprisingly nearby, "Bind him. He's a nuisance as he is, and if he goes overboard, so be it." He stood against the stempost, straddling the lockers, but Fife had been too frightened of the raging sea to look up and see him.

As oarsmen grabbed him and began to bind his hands, he yelled, "Why are you doing this? Why not just kill me and be done with it?"

"In troth, your royal banner is of more use to me, but I may yet need you, as well. If I do, God will keep you alive for me."

"But why should He? And where are we? Are we nearing Orkney?"

"We do not go to Orkney," de Gredin said. "We go to

the Isles. MacLennan would not have set out in this storm if he were just going to Orkney. He is taking his cargo to the only other man besides Henry powerful enough to set himself against you, the King, and his holiness like this. MacLennan is going to MacDonald."

"But—" Fife stopped, realizing that to a man like de Gredin, Donald's power was all that mattered. The chevalier might not even know of their close kinship. In any event, Fife knew that it would be foolhardy to say anything that might lessen his own value. And, too, it was certainly possible that MacLennan had made the same judgment of the Lord of the Isles.

In any event, he could be sure that Donald would not let anything happen to him, and believed Donald would also be willing to help him secure the Stone.

Chapter 20

Leaving his men to look after the *Serpent*, Giff guided Sidony through Duncraig's strong sea gate, up the hill path to the torchlit courtyard, and across it to the main entrance steps. Two of his father's men escorted them. One of them, Donnie Murchie, was a friend of Giff's from his boyhood days and now captain of his father's guard. Donnie informed them on the way that the laird was away with his boats, a fact that Giff had gleaned for himself on seeing the empty noust.

"You won't see much of the castle's exterior tonight, lass," he said, "but you'll have plenty of time later. We'll find my mother in her solar, I expect, after I see if Duncraig can provide supper for my men."

Donnie said, "As to that, Master Giff, ye'll find that the steward will be pleased to look after your men if ye'll send them up to the hall. Her ladyship likes a late supper, so ye and your lady wife willna go hungry there, either. And if I may take the liberty, sir, 'tis gey pleased we be to see ye've taken a wife at last."

Giff smiled and put an arm around Sidony. "I'm rather pleased myself."

When she looked up at him, her eyes shone in the torchlight, and knowing he would soon share a bed with her again, his body stirred.

Sidony saw the way he looked at her and knew what he was thinking. She looked forward to coupling with him, too, in the hope that she could find a way then to persuade him to take her with him to meet Ranald of the Isles.

When he tucked her hand in the crook of his elbow, she gave his arm a squeeze. He seemed pleased to be home, nodding and smiling at retainers as they went. Inside, he escorted her across a great hall crowded with men-at-arms and servants preparing for supper, toward a short stone stairway in the corner diagonally across from the main stairs. They went as quickly as good manners allowed, pausing only so he could present the steward, Eachainn MacCrimmon, to her.

"Eachainn, this is my lady wife," Giff added, shaking his hand. Assuring him that they could find Lady MacLennan without assistance, he asked MacCrimmon to see to his oarsmen and waited only long enough to hear him promise he would.

"I don't want to announce our marriage here until I've told my mother," Giff told Sidony in an undertone. "Doubtless word of it is passing amongst them already, since Donnie Murchie assumed that we were married the moment he saw us."

Pushing open the door at the top of the short flight, he

stepped ahead of her into the chamber beyond, then paused to draw her to his side.

Sidony saw a plump little lady in a simple russet-colored gown and white wimple, who cast aside needlework in her lap as she came quickly but nonetheless gracefully to her feet from a cushioned settle near the hearth.

Hurrying toward them, she exclaimed, "Giffard, is it truly you?"

"Aye, Mam, and I've brought you a wee surprise," he said, releasing Sidony to embrace his mother.

"Oh, my love, it has been too long!" Regarding Sidony curiously as she hugged him, her ladyship went right on to say, "Do tell me about your surprise."

"This is my lady wife, Sidony," he said.

"Oh, I did hope that was it," Lady MacLennan said, holding out both hands to her. Eyes as dark blue as her son's sparkled with pleasure, and as Sidony made her curtsy, her ladyship's hands beckoned. "Come, let me hug you, child. I am so pleased to welcome you to Duncraig. Giffard, dear, tell them to serve our supper in here so we three can talk comfortably together."

"I will, Mam," he said. "But I hope you'll allow me to set it back a half hour or so. I have duties below, to see my men settled and all. Where is my lord father?"

"Faith, I do not know. He received a message hours ago and was off at once. He may have told Eachainn MacCrimmon whither he was bound."

"I'll ask him. I've already taken the liberty of asking him to feed my men."

"Aye, sure, dearling, you must do as you please. Oh, Giffard, your father will be so pleased to see you when he returns."

"As to that," he said evenly, "I cannot linger, Mam. I am

taking Sidony off in the morning to stay with her father whilst I attend to a most important duty."

"Oh," she said, visibly suppressing disappointment as she turned to Sidony and added, "But who is your father, my dear?"

"Macleod of Glenelg, madam."

"Oh, I thought you looked familiar. I have met your sister Cristina many times, and another—Isobel, I believe her name is. Let me see, she married . . ."

"Sir Michael Sinclair," Sidony said with a smile.

"Aye, sure, but if Giffard is leaving us now for a time, you must sit and tell me all about yourself. I know your aunt Euphemia Macleod, too, of course."

"Do you, madam?" Sidony said as Giff kissed her and ruthlessly abandoned her to the daunting task of telling his mother all about herself.

But no sooner had she obeyed her ladyship's invitation to sit on the settle beside her, than she found her hands warmly clasped again as Lady MacLennan said, "Oh, my dear, I do not know how you contrived to bring him home, but I am so grateful. I do not even mind missing your wedding, although I do think it odd that we never heard the slightest whisper of pending nuptials."

"I'm afraid they did not 'pend' very long, madam," Sidony said with a smile. "Giffard did not forbid me to tell you all about it, though, so I shall."

She proceeded to do so, leaving out only the treasure, the fact that the place of concealment from which Giff had rescued her lay aboard a ship he had stolen from the Earl of Fife, and the true reason for their voyage to the Isles.

However, after Lady MacLennan had exclaimed over the wickedness of a member of the royal family's staging the abduction of an innocent young girl and the wondrous chance that led Giff to discover her whereabouts, rescue her, and find a priest to marry them, Sidony did feel obliged to make one thing clear.

"So you see," she said, "it was through no contriving of mine that we came here. Giff has business in the Isles, and as Duncraig lies near Glenelg, he thought it his duty to bring me to meet you before taking me home whilst he attends to it."

"Faith, I recall now, your father is to marry Ealga Clendenen just over a fortnight from now, is he not? They've invited us to their wedding."

"I hope you mean to attend," Sidony said.

"We certainly do now. Oh, how nice this is," she went on, beaming. "I just wish my lord husband were home. He will be so disappointed if he misses seeing Giffard after all this time. We receive word of him on occasion, but one can rarely call such news as we hear reassuring. My lord fears Giffard is dreadfully reckless and that we shall one day learn that one of his escapades has killed him."

"But I thought—" Sidony broke off, realizing that under the circumstances what she thought would probably be imprudent to mention.

But her ladyship would have none of it. "What did you think, dearling? Prithee, tell me if you know aught of why he has scarcely come next or nigh his home in a decade. You cannot imagine how we all miss him. His sisters are away now, visiting cousins, but they, too, will be dreadfully disappointed."

"I know precious little," Sidony admitted. "But he did tell me that after his . . . that is, that his father sent him away because he blamed—"

"Oh, no, pray tell me it had naught to do with that dreadful accident!"

Sidony nodded. "He said his father sent him away to foster with his uncle because he . . . because the laird blames him for his older brother's death."

"Oh, my dear, I do wish men would talk when things upset them. They even teach their sons to hold their tongues. I feared something like that, but when I dared suggest such a thing to my lord, he dismissed the notion out of hand. How could Giff think such a thing, he demanded, when it had never entered his *own* head? But, sithee, I did think it and so did tax him with it. He told me I was a foolish woman and insisted our son would never be so daft. It just shows one, doesn't it?"

"But if that was not the reason—"

"Don't you see? My husband had kept Bryan at home despite many offers to foster him, and he feared he had spoiled him, because Bryan grew to be as heedless as many now say Giffard is. One had only to say no to Bryan to see him do just what one had forbidden, and my husband declared that should *not* become the case with Giffard. Sithee, he feared, having only the one son left, he would guard him even more cautiously than he had Bryan. Thus, he sent him at once to foster with my brother on Loch Hourn. Otherwise, he feared, he would never let him go at all. And he had already promised him to Dunclathy to train for his knighthood."

"Giff still believes he could have saved Bryan just by shouting at him," Sidony said. "He blames himself for his death."

Lady MacLennan frowned. "I tried to explain to him that they were both just children, that it was naught but a tragic accident. But my husband remained silent in his grief and then sent Giffard away. And the few times he has returned, Giffard has refused to discuss the past. My husband thinks he holds a grudge because he did not want to go to Loch Hourn, but my lord would rather die than admit strong feelings for his son. And, I'm thinking," she added sagely, "that being of the same ilk, Giffard won't thank you for telling me this. We must put our heads together, my child."

"Mayhap it will not be so difficult, madam," Sidony said. "I suspect we need only suggest to each man what the other *may* think. Then, when they meet at Chalamine for the wedding, each will see . . ." She paused, spreading her hands.

"'Tis an excellent notion," her hostess applauded. "Now, I wonder how much longer Giffard will be. I am persuaded that much more than a half hour has passed."

"If you will permit me, I've been cooped up on that ship for a sennight, and I should enjoy a walk down to the noust. I warrant Giff will be so eager to get me back up here that he'll bring me faster than if we sent someone to fetch him."

Lady MacLennan laughed merrily. "Oh, my dear, I know I am going to enjoy having you as a daughter."

Taking that as permission, Sidony hurried down to the hall, outside, and down the pathway to the sea gate. There she encountered a slight delay until she explained that Lady MacLennan had sent her to fetch Sir Giffard to supper.

The guard grinned. "Welcome to Duncraig, Lady Giffard."

Thanking him, she hurried on, only to find the *Serpent* apparently abandoned despite lighted cressets in the noust. Walking around the U-shaped wharf inside it, to the stern of the boat, she saw that its stern port was open and assumed that Giff and the others had gone to fetch provisions to replace those they had used.

"Me lady, what be *ye* a-doing here, all on your ownsome?"

Nearly jumping out of her skin, she saw Jake peeking around the large crate that filled a considerable part of the aft hold. "What are *you* doing here?" she asked. "Where are Sir Giffard and the other men?"

"Me da's forward in the wee cabin, talking wi' a Duncraig boatman," he said. "The others ha' gone wi' Sir Giff to fetch some few things, me da' said."

So, it was as she had thought. "But what are you doing?" she repeated.

"This crate," he said, shrugging. "I were a-wondering what might be in it."

Realizing the crate must contain the treasure they were carrying, she frowned and said, "You haven't tried to open that, have you?"

"Nay, then, I wouldna do any such thing," he said with a virtuous look.

Sidony, having many times seen just such a look on her sister Sorcha's face when Sorcha was up to mischief, said sternly, "What *did* you do?"

"Just put a finger in to feel about some," he said, looking anxiously past her as if he feared someone else might come. "There be a knothole where me fingers can poke through, and what I felt be gey smooth but for places where it feels like summat's carved on it. What d'ye think such a thing could be?"

She couldn't imagine, but curiosity stirred. "Show me where you did that."

"Ye'll ha' to come all inside then," he said, and when

she did, he showed her a good-sized knothole in one side of the crate.

As she put a finger through the hole and felt what he had felt, she also felt the hole's splintery rough edges and looked at him suspiciously. "Was that knot out when you found it?" Seeing the answer on his face, she said, "Jake, you must not snoop about down here. You know what Sir Giff would do if he caught you."

"Aye, but ye willna tell him, will ye?"

She had opened her mouth to swear she would not when both of them heard approaching footsteps. Quickly, they stepped away toward the wharf just as Giff, leading four others, reached the stern port.

"What the devil are you two doing here?" he demanded.

"Your mother sent me to fetch you for supper," Sidony said. "The port stood open, so we came in. I hadn't seen this part before, so Jake was showing me."

Fully aware that she was lying through her teeth, she did not dare look at Jake, but Giff only glanced at him as he said, "I did let time run away from me. I'll lock up this port now, lads, whilst we eat, and I'll send supper down to those of you staying with the ship. When I return, we can finish this."

"I suppose you have been loading more provisions," Sidony said as they left the noust together, followed by Jake, Captain Maxwell, and two others. "I'm sure my father will provide more supplies if you need them."

"Do you think so? I'd be grateful," he said.

"Must you really come back down here after supper? It's late now."

"Aye, sweetheart, I must, but you need not wait up for me. Don't look like that," he added with a chuckle when she allowed her disappointment to show. "If you fall asleep, I'll wake you when I return."

He left directly after supper to return to the noust, and although she enjoyed talking with Lady MacLennan and looked forward to meeting her two daughters, Giff still had not returned when her ladyship announced that it was time to retire.

"You will have but a short journey tomorrow, my dear, but Giffard did sound as if he means to make an early start, so it would be as well to sleep whilst you can."

She showed Sidony to the bedchamber she and Giff would share, made sure she had all she required, including the services of a maidservant, then bade her good night.

Sidony was asleep when Giff returned, but true to his word, he woke her. The interlude that followed was brief but pleasurable, and afterward, she lay contentedly, her head resting in the hollow of his shoulder, wondering what the future held.

"What were you really doing in that hold?" he murmured.

She tensed as guilt flooded through her. "I . . . I told you."

"Nay, sweetheart, it's no good. You jumped as if I'd shot you with an arrow."

"Aye, well, but if I tell you—"

"No bargains, lass. I'm content now, but if you don't tell me, I shall soon be angry, and you don't want that."

No, she did not want that, but her concern was not for herself.

"I'll tell you then, but the fault is mine, not Jake's. I wanted to know what was in the crate, and there was a knothole, so I put a finger in."

"Which of you found the knothole?"

"It was my fault, sir."

"So Jake found it. Was the knot missing or did he pull it out? You lied to me before to protect him, lass. Don't do it again."

Her temper stirred. "He is only a boy. Moreover, he is exactly like you are. He takes risks. When he wants to do a thing, he does it, and he does not count cost."

"Then you ought to support punishing him, so he does not grow to be as reckless as you think I am."

"What I think is that Jake admires you and wants to be just like you," she said. "You therefore have a certain duty to provide him with a good example, and that, sir, would seem to preclude punishing behavior that emulates your own."

He was silent for a long moment. Then, matter-of-factly, he said, "And when you lie to me, is there aught to preclude swift punishment for the lie?"

She swallowed hard. The lie had been impulsive, born of her need to protect Jake. She could not remember doing such a thing before, even when Sorcha had flung them both into mischief and their father had caught them. That she was not a liar by nature was hardly an acceptable defense to submit now, however.

He pulled her closer, rising to his side to loom over her. Gently, he kissed her, and just as gently said, "Don't do it again, sweetheart. A man wants to trust his wife."

He bent to taste her breasts, but she fought against succumbing to the sensations he stirred, because relieved as she was, she wanted to know just one thing more.

"That crate does not contain a tumble of jewels and such as I said it did, for its contents felt as smooth as a great slab of marble. Will you tell me what it is?"

"Aye, I will, as soon as I know I've got it safe. For if

I don't tell you, I've no doubt that you'll winkle it out of Isobel or Adela."

"I think they will assume that you've told me when they learn we've married, and I already know where you are taking it."

"Faith, how did you learn that?"

"You told me tonight when you said you'd leave me with my father."

"Sakes, then I'm as bad as the rest. We must all take more care."

She agreed, but his attention had drifted from her breasts to other parts of her body, and she soon ceased to concern herself with anything else.

Afterward, she slept, and it seemed no time at all before he was waking her and telling her to make haste with her ablutions. He had already dressed, and he left at once to break his fast and see to preparations in the noust.

She, too, dressed quickly, choosing the striped silk kirtle and cameline surcoat. Then, leaving her packing to the willing maidservant with orders to send everything down to the ship, she descended to find her hostess alone at the high table in the hall. Privy screens surrounded it, so although others noisily broke their fast in the lower hall, the two women enjoyed some privacy as they talked.

"I've a gift for my son," Lady MacLennan said when Sidony had finished. "I had thought I'd give it to him, but it may be better if you would do it for me." Handing her a cloth bundle, she said, "'Tis a MacLennan banner for his boat. Donnie Murchie told me he seems to have only a Norse flag, and he ought to have a proper MacLennan one to display to any Islesmen who may challenge him."

"I expect the one he had must be on his ship in Galloway," Sidony said.

"He flies a personal banner aboard the *Storm Lass*," Lady MacLennan said. "I'm told it shows just black and gray storm clouds. But you ought to go now, for he said to hurry you. He wants you safe at Chalamine as soon as may be."

Bidding her a warm farewell, Sidony went down to the landing, where she found all in readiness to depart. Jake, busily wiping dampness from oarsmen's benches, shot her an accusing look, telling her he had not escaped a scolding for his part in their venture the previous night.

At the first opportunity, she went to him and said, "Is aught amiss?"

"Nobbut having me ears trimmed back for me," he said grumpily. "I thought ye wouldna tell him."

"I didn't," she said. "He knew when I lied last night, and he asked me if you'd pulled out the knot. One should not expect one's friends to tell lies, Jake, and I should not have told one to him. I will try hard never to do so again."

"Did he carry on like a thunder-pelt at ye, too, then?"

The image he produced required her to suppress a smile, but she managed to say soberly, "He was not pleased with me. But when one does something one ought not to do, the honorable thing is to accept responsibility for it. If you don't want to own up to something, Jake, it is usually because you know you've done wrong."

"That's true enough," he muttered. "Mayhap 'tis also because ye ken fine that soon as ye do own up ye'll ha' a burnin' backside and be up to your ears in chores."

"Do you have a burning backside, Jake?"

He shrugged. "I'd best get back to me chores, me lady. He's a-coming."

He went back to drying benches, and she turned to greet Giff.

He assured her that he'd have her at Chalamine before midday if they could but find horses to hire at Glenelg Bay for the last mile or so to the castle.

They had scarcely entered Loch Alsh from the Inner Sound, however, when they saw two galleys ahead, coming swiftly toward them.

Fearing instantly that Fife had found them, Sidony realized that the two longboats were Isles galleys. She caught Jake's attention and beckoned, then dived back into the cabin to find the banner that Lady MacLennan had given her.

When the boy joined her, she handed him the bundle.

"Take this to Sir Giffard," she said. "Tell him it is a gift from his mam, and he should show it now."

"Be them two boats no' the same ones as near caught us afore?"

"Nay, they are Isles galleys. See how the spray flies from them? They are coming very fast, though, so do not tarry."

Standing atop the forecastle cabin, gripping the forestay, Giff had likewise known that the oncoming boats could not be those of Fife and de Gredin. He watched them carefully nonetheless to judge if they were friend or foe.

"Master," Jake said from behind him. "Your lady said I should give ye this. She said I should say, too, that your mam sent it to ye and to put it up now."

Jumping down to take the cloth from the boy, he shook it out and felt an unexpected surge of pride and gratitude to his mother when saw the familiar red-and-white banner with its nail-pierced heart in the center.

"D'ye ken what this is, Jake?"

"'Tis a war standard."

"'Tis the MacLennan banner," Giff said. "Would you like to come back up with me and help me fasten it to the forestay where those oncoming boats can see it?"

"Aye, sure," Jake said, scrambling up onto the forecastle ahead of him. When Giff was beside him, the boy looked up and said, "Ye're no' wroth wi' me anymore?"

Giff ruffled his already tousled curls. "You deserved the scold, laddie, but I'm gey sorry your da' heard it. I did not mean him to. That business was between us."

Squaring his shoulders and raising his chin in a way that reminded Giff forcibly of Sidony, Jake said, "I were the one at fault, though. Me da' did nae more than what ye'd threatened to do, did I vex ye again."

"That's true enough," Giff said, impressed. "Hold the banner now, whilst I tie these ribbons to the forestay so it can wave freely."

He quickly tied the banner's strings to loops the forestay provided for the purpose. By the time he had finished, the oncoming boats were near enough for him to recognize that each flew the banner of Ranald of the Isles.

"Sakes, what is this all about then?" he muttered to himself.

From below, he heard Sidony call, "'Tis Ranald."

"Aye, lass, but I'd expected to meet with him on Eigg. I wonder what's amiss."

"Must I go back to the aft cabin?" she asked.

"Nay, we've nowt to fear from Ranald," Giff said. "Come to that, we shall have reinforcements now if Fife finds us before I get you safely home."

Turning aft, he raised his hand so Maxwell would

have warning as he shouted, "Weigh enough, lads! Weigh enough!"

~

Sidony loved to watch the oars come up together, their blades all parallel to the water. They made a fine sight with the MacLennan banner flying bravely at their bow.

"Hold water!" Giff roared as Ranald's lead galley swept up to them in fine style. Moments later, the two boats were side by side, just an oar's-length apart.

Two men in Ranald's boat laid a plank from gunwale to gunwale, and like a cat, Ranald of the Isles, despite having four-and-sixty years behind him, leaped onto it and crossed to the *Serpent* as nimbly as a man forty years younger might have.

Oarsmen made room for him to step onto a rowers' bench, and thence to the deck, where Giff met him and shook his hand. "What brings you to meet me, my lord? I'd expected to find you on the Isle of Eigg later today."

"Aye, well, it won't serve, lad," Ranald said. "Donald kens now that ye're coming, so I came ahead to warn ye, but 'tis all I can do. He's commanded me no' to aid ye without he gives me leave after he speaks wi' ye."

"Speaks with me! What manner of trick is this? You swore an oath!"

Ranald held up a hand, silencing him. "I ken fine that ye're wroth wi' me, but as a man of honor, I could not lie to my own liege lord in such a situation."

"What situation?" Giff demanded. "Sakes, my lord, we had an agreement."

"Aye, sure, and we still have one, but ye'd best let me

explain. Ha' ye somewhere more private where we can speak plainly?"

Giff nodded, took him into the forward cabin, and shut the door.

~

"Now, with respect, sir," Giff said tersely, "what the devil is this about?"

"Ye ken fine that Donald's Lord High Admiral of the Isles, Lachlan Lubanach, has created the finest arrangement for gathering news that ever the Isles have seen."

"Aye, so?"

"So, Donald learned thus of a ship flying the Norse banner that had entered his waters, pursued by others bearing the royal banner. He commanded me to join him in confronting you and demanding to know your business here. I told him that ye were friendly and coming to Eigg to see me. But he asked me straight out what business ye had with me. Sakes, but ye'd never expect me to lie in the man's face."

"What exactly did you tell him?" Giff demanded.

"Only that ye were bringing something o' great value for me to protect. He asked who you were, and I told him. I did not mention the Order, for he kens nowt about that, and I told him no more than he asked. Michael said ye'd be the one to tell me what I'd be protecting, but Donald insists that he will see it, whatever it is."

"Well, he won't see it unless you mean to stop us here and betray the Order as well as betraying your sworn word to its members," Giff said.

"I've sworn fealty to Donald, as well, and he is my own brother. Sakes, but I saw to it that he succeeded our father as Lord of the Isles. No man of honor or sense could expect me to defy a direct command from him now. Nor would that have achieved aught but to harden his resolve to intercept ye."

Giff sighed. He could understand Ranald's dilemma, but Donald's knowing even as much about their actions as he did now put them and the Stone at risk.

Ranald said, "I'll tell him nowt but what he asks, though such equivocation stirs guilt in me. Nor will I hinder ye, for he has not commanded either your arrest or that I prevent your departure from the Isles."

Frowning, Giff said, "Then I can return north but cannot go south. Is that it?"

"Aye, if ye mean to escape Donald, ye'd best turn round straightaway and go back to Orkney. Doubtless Henry can aid ye there. Sithee, I cannot—"

"The reason a ship with a royal banner is pursuing us is that Fife is aboard it," Giff said. "The men bringing him are seeking us because they think we have at least a portion of the Templar treasure aboard this ship."

"Sakes, is that what ye have?"

"I won't tell you a thing about our cargo," Giff snapped. "Nor should you expect it. I understand about Donald, but he cannot know what we carry for the very reason that he is likely to tell his uncle Fife. Through Lachlan Lubanach's friends, you must know that Fife wants to seize the Scottish throne when the King dies. You know, too, that Fife is ruthless and that many already believe it is only Carrick's weakness and obvious disinterest in opposing him that prevents Carrick's death now."

"Aye, that is so," Ranald said. "But Parliament still retains legal right to decide the matter, and Donald thinks Fife will persuade its leaders to accept his claim instead of putting Carrick on the throne. Many already think Fife a better man for the job."

"But do you think it the act of an honorable man to aid him in that endeavor?"

"I've no intention of aiding him, but Donald has guessed that Fife commands those ships, and he has forbidden me to engage him in battle for any reason."

"So I'm doubly betrayed," Giff said. "You swore an oath to the Order to put your duties to it above all others," he repeated. "Your father, the first Lord of the Isles, swore the same oath. Do those oaths mean nowt to you?"

Ranald looked away but said nothing, and Giff shook his head. "I do see your dilemma," he said. "I hope you see mine. Pray, do not tarry in returning to your ship."

It occurred to him then that it could not hurt to plant the thought in Ranald's mind that had been muttering in his own for some time. "You ought to know," he said, "that I am not persuaded that Fife does command the boats that chase us."

"Faugh, wherever Fife is, he is in command. How could it be otherwise?"

"Because none of those other ships are his," Giff said.

"We heard he'd had a fine one built."

"Aye, but this is it," Giff said.

"This boat we're on now? This be the *Serpent Royal*?"

"Aye, it is," Giff said. "I . . . well, I borrowed it because he sent away the ship I'd hired at Leith. Also, I'd hoped to make it impossible for him to give chase straightaway, but someone speedily provided him with ships to come after me—a total of eight altogether. It does seem unlikely to me that a man able to supply such ships would answer to Lord Fife. Suggest that to Donald whilst you're about it."

Hearing shouts, they went back outside, and Giff saw that whatever Ranald decided to say to Donald, he could say very soon.

In the distance, from the south, a large flotilla headed straight for them.

Chapter 21

Giff and Ranald shouted orders to their men, and both ships turned quickly, with oarsmen on one side backing water while those on the other pulled hard. Within minutes, her sail full, the *Serpent* was heading back toward the Inner Sound.

As they emerged from Kyle Akin, the narrow passage between Loch Alsh and the Sound, Giff knew that men on watch at Duncraig could see them but would not realize they were under pursuit. And when they did, there would be naught they could do, because without a galley in the noust, they were stuck where they were.

Others might also see, but if Donald had sent for MacLennan of Duncraig, he had sent for other nobles, too. In any event, one could not expect any Islesman not threatened by the Lord of the Isles to attack him or to defend anyone under his attack.

"Will Donald pursue us?" Sidony asked, startling him out of his thoughts.

"I don't know," he said, trying to sound confident.

"I think not. Ranald will do what he can, and he wields strong influence with Donald. I think he'll persuade him that I'm no threat, and they'll let us go in peace. I'm more worried about Fife."

She was looking past him, and her expression suddenly changed. Turning, he saw two ships emerging from the shadow of an islet at the narrowest part of the Sound.

"Those are Fife's longships, aren't they?" she said.

"Aye," he said, and for the first time since the earliest days of his training, he felt fear that chilled him to the bone, fear for her. The longships were too close to allow him to return her to the safety of Duncraig.

"If Duncraig is impregnable . . . ," she said.

"There's no time now, sweetheart." He fought to sound calm.

"Not even to get us all inside? I ken fine that you want to protect the . . . the cargo, but surely all these people are more—"

"When I said 'no time,' lass, I *meant* the people. Remember, those ships are lighter than ours and much faster. Moreover, the wind is coming at us broadside, which also favors them. They would be upon us before we could get this ship into the noust, let alone get all of us into the castle."

"Then, what—"

"I need to think, not talk," he interjected. "I want you to go into our cabin with Jake and bolt the door. When the fighting starts, I want you both to get into the hold where I found you, pull the trap shut, and stay there until I come for you."

"No, I'll not—"

"You will, or when this is all over, I swear I'll teach you

to obey me in a way you won't like," he said fiercely, terrified by the images flitting through his mind.

She did not say another word, just turned on her heel and walked away.

Although he wanted nothing more than to call her back to him to hug her, hold her tight, and assure her that everything would be all right, he watched her instead until she remembered Jake and called the lad to her.

Satisfied that they would be safe as long as he won the forthcoming battle, and trying to persuade himself that neither Fife nor de Gredin—if by some horrible mischance *they* won—would have cause to harm either Sidony or Jake, he turned to issue orders to Maxwell and the men.

"What's this, then?" Jake demanded as Sidony bolted the cabin door. "I dinna want to stay in here. I want to see what happens. Sakes, I'm old enough to fight, too, if they need me," he added stoutly.

The top of his head barely reached her shoulder.

She said calmly, "I'm sorry, Jake, for I'm sure you're right. But I know that if they do start fighting, I'm going to be scared out of my senses. I'll need you then, and Sir Giff very kindly said I could keep you with me because you did such a good job looking after me before, during the storm. Still, if you want to go and tell him that you'd rather fight, you must do as you think best."

Jake stared at the bolted door as if he could see through it, grimaced, and turned back to say casually, "I expect I'll stay then, so ye needna fear nowt."

Deciding it would be best to get the worst out at once,

she said, "He did say that when the fighting starts we should hide in that wee hold where you found me."

Jake's eyes grew big. "Nay, then, there's boggarts down there!"

Feeling much the same way, if not utterly revolted by the thought of returning to that dark, uncomfortable hole, Sidony said, "We need do nothing until they do start fighting. Mayhap we will feel differently about it then."

"Nay, then, we will not," Jake said firmly, glowering at the trapdoor. Then, abruptly, his gaze shifted to the open porthole over the table. "D'ye think I can see them ships from yon hole?"

"Not that one," she said. "I've not tried to look out, but they were off the larboard side before, and that hole is on the steerboard side. Also, your da' may see you there if he looks back."

"Nay, for he'll be a-watching o' them ships," Jake said. "But one o' the oarsmen might see me, I expect. Still . . ." He looked at the other port, over the washstand. The stand itself was only a shelf big enough to hold the basin, with a pocket to hold the ewer. When not in use, the basin hung on a hook beside it.

Sidony said nothing. In truth, she wanted to know what was happening as much as he did. The logical thing was to open the cabin door, but she wanted neither to bring Giff's wrath down on the two of them nor to distract him from the forthcoming battle just as, or when, it transpired.

"Could ye look out that one?" Jake asked. "Ye're taller."

She opened the shutter and latched it to the wall. "I can see straight out," she said. "But, with the shelf in the way as it is, I'm not tall enough to see much ahead."

"Can ye boost me up there?" he asked. "I could look out if ye'd hold me."

She was not sure the shelf would hold him, but she could hear a commotion now, with Giff's voice roaring "Weigh enough," as others shouted in a din of unrecognizable voices. In the end, curiosity outweighed caution.

"I'll try," she said. "Take care, though. It may be too weak to hold you."

She made a cup of her hands and let him step into it, but as she straightened to lift him, the shouting grew louder and, with a cacophony of scraping, crashing noises, the entire ship jolted to a halt and shuddered, flinging them both sideways.

Jake had his hand on the rim of the porthole, so when Sidony let go of him to keep herself from crashing into Fife's kists near the door, the boy was able to push himself away from the shelf and land with astonishing lightness on his feet.

As Sidony straightened, she saw the bow of a longship gliding alongside and quickly moved to shut the shutter.

"Did anyone see you?" she asked.

"Nay, nor I didn't see any o' them," he said indignantly. "What were ye thinking to let go o' me all in a blink like that?"

"I couldn't help it, but they mustn't see either of us, Jake. Only think if someone decided to threaten us in order to make Sir Giff give them this ship."

"Ye're no' going to make me get into yon hole," he said.

"We'll open it," she said. "Then if we do change our minds—if someone tries to kick down the door . . ." She let him fill the rest in for himself.

Nodding, he moved to open the trap as pandemonium erupted outside.

Until the last moment, Giff had harbored a faint hope that Fife and de Gredin would hesitate to attack in MacDonald's waters, but the two longships had flanked the *Serpent*, coming right alongside her, barely giving the men time to ship their oars. Then, using grappling hooks, the enemy began lashing the boats together.

Giff's best warriors were at the bow, swords already drawn. As he drew his, he saw that others had bows and arrows, stones, whatever they had thought to bring aboard as weaponry. But, in truth, he knew they would depend more on their swords and hand-to-hand combat. They were not his own lads, but they were Sinclairs and thus utterly proficient, and he knew they had trained just as he and his men had.

His sword at the ready, he moved swiftly onto a bench, fighting his way steerboard toward what had been the lead longship, looking for Fife or de Gredin. He had cut down three of the enemy without seeing either of their leaders.

Rob, who was one of the finest swordsmen he knew, had said the earl was a fine one, and Michael had warned him not to think de Gredin would be any less. Seeing neither man, he wondered if they could be on the second longship.

Men kept coming, keeping him busy, but his own lads were holding their own. Seeing Hob Grant engaged against two from the second longship and Wat Maxwell wielding his sword like a fiend against two others, he grinned, thinking back to all the earlier concerns about Maxwell's trustworthiness.

Even heavily outnumbered as they were, Giff's men had one big advantage in that their gunwales were three feet higher than the others. As long as they could keep most of the enemy on their own ships and diminish their numbers, they had a chance.

Sitting on the lower bed, covering her ears against the din, and staring at the floor in an attempt to calm her nerves, Sidony sensed movement to her right and looked up to see Jake on the table, his wiry body halfway through the porthole.

Leaping to her feet, she grabbed him and pulled hard.

He slithered back inside, his eyes alight with excitement. "They be fighting summat fierce, me lady, and I can near touch yon stempost. Ye should see 'em!"

"Did anyone see you?"

"Nay, they be looking to nowt save other men's swords or fists. Arrows and stones be a-flying, and they've lashed the boats together, this side at least. I'm guessing the other is the same, and they jump about from boat to boat."

"Did you see Sir Giff?"

"Aye, he dropped about ten o' their lads wi' just a few strokes o' his sword."

"Ten?"

"Mayhap no' so many as that, aye, but a fair lot o' them. I'm going to look again . . . unless ye want a peek yourself," he added with visibly reluctant generosity.

She did want to look, but she shook her head. If the

enemy saw Jake, they were unlikely to act, but if any of them saw her . . . She shut her eyes at the thought.

Returning to the porthole, Jake slid his top half out again, but a moment later, he popped back in. "Me lady, his lordship's yonder."

"Do you mean Lord Fife? We know he is there."

"Aye, but he's lying all folded up by one o' their bow kists, which is what I'm a-looking down at, ye ken. He looks like a bairn hiding when his da's got a belt in hand. Sithee, his arms be over his ears, only . . . I think his hands be tied together."

She had heard men speak of Fife's cowardice on the water, but she had never heard any suggest that he was a coward in battle—a bad tactician, yes, but a skilled and formidable swordsman. Doubtless, to be in the thick of such pandemonium with one's hands tied would terrify anyone, but stirring up sympathy for Fife was difficult.

"We can do naught to help him, Jake. Perhaps you should come back inside."

"Did I no' tell ye I can near reach their stem? If ye'll steady me, I can get to him. By me troth, I can. He were kind to me. I dinna want them villains to kill him."

"They may kill you instead. Did you think of that?"

"Aye, sure, but nae one's looking, nor will they care if they do. Every one o' them be too busy amidships now, looking out for hisself. I'm going to help him!"

He turned back and was two-thirds of the way out before she collected her wits, but as she grabbed one leg, he got the other foot on the rim of the porthole.

Remembering how heavy he was, she realized as he pushed forward that if she held him she could lose him. Letting go, she scrambled onto the bench instead, meaning to help all she could, but she dared not put her head out as he had. She could only watch as he leaped to the stempost of the longship and scrambled down.

When he landed she could still see his upper half, so doubtless he had jumped down onto the bow locker he had mentioned.

He looked back then and pointed. It took a moment to grasp his meaning, but she realized he was pointing toward the cabin door and could not get back in any other way. He vanished seconds later, clearly confident that she would help.

Fife had never known such terror. It had been frightening enough to wake up and find his men all dead and himself in the clutches of a madman, for surely de Gredin had to be mad to have done all he had done. But his men were no mere mortals, either, for no mortal could have rowed as hard or as long as they had and still stand to fight the way they fought now.

Lying there by the forecastle storage locker, helpless, with the odor of smoke from a hastily covered firepot assaulting his nostrils, his only hope was to make them all think he was just another dead body in the gory chaos erupting around him.

"Me lord, be ye dead or still a-breathing?"

The youthful voice sounded close to his head. Easing away the arm covering that ear and then that eye, he found himself looking at young Jake Maxwell.

"Bless us, what are you doing here, lad?"

"I'd ask ye that, too, me lord, but I'm thinking we'd best get away from here afore we chat. I've me wee knife if ye'll let me at them ropes."

Fife did not argue. Getting away sounded like an excellent idea, especially as he had no idea what had happened to his sword and had no other weapon to defend himself. As it was, a stray arrow or rock could mean the end of him.

He could scarcely believe that none of the men fighting wildly around them were paying either of them heed. But the lad remained as cool as if he were in a cottage somewhere about to have his supper.

When Fife was free, Jake said, "Ye can get onto the *Serpent* just yonder easily enough by climbing up from the longship's gunwale and over hers. I think her ladyship'll let ye into the master's cabin then, and I'll be along directly, m'self."

Keeping low, Fife moved with alacrity toward the gunwale. Most of the fighting had moved amidships and sternward, and if anyone noticed him, he saw no sign of it. Even if someone did, nearly everyone would recognize him and as he was unarmed, none were likely to concern themselves with him.

Stepping to the longship gunwale, he leaned forward to grab the first step of the *Serpent*'s and hoisted himself up and over.

When he saw Captain Maxwell lying near the helm, clearly injured or dead, he hesitated briefly, then hurried to the cabin door and knocked on it.

~

At the first rap, Sidony shot the bolt back and lifted the latch. Seeing only Fife in the doorway, she said anxiously and without ceremony, "Where's Jake?"

Fife looked back and said, "I thought he was right behind me. His father is hurt, yonder. No, don't go out there, mistress. We can accomplish naught thereby, and someone might decide we'd make fine hostages."

"But Jake!" When she tried to push past him, he stopped her.

"He'll come if he's coming, for he's a brave lad. I don't know what kept him, for no one heeded us whilst he released me. But we cannot count on that now."

He stepped inside, and as he did, she whisked past him, disgusted with him and thinking only that if Maxwell was hurt, Jake might refuse to leave him.

As she stepped outside, Jake jumped over the gunwale from the longship and ran toward her, casting anxious glances forward as he did and muttering, "Get ye within, me lady. Sir Giff will flay us both if he sees us!"

He hadn't seen his father, and knowing in that instant that Fife had been right to insist they keep out of sight of anyone who might think a hostage could aid him, Sidony grabbed Jake by the arm and hauled him back into the cabin.

She said, "I was looking for you, you wretched bairn. What took you so long?"

"I were just tidying up so they wouldna think o' his lordship right off."

"Bolt that door again, will you, lass?" Fife said from the table nook. "I'd as lief we receive no unwelcome visitors."

Obeying but knowing she would be unwise to trust him no matter how badly he'd been treated, she said warily, "How came you to be tied up as you were?"

"They killed all my men at Wick Bay after some of our ships grounded," he said. "Since then, I've been a prisoner on that longship. I should tell you whilst I can that I had naught to do with your abduction, my lady. De Gredin simply seized what he saw as an opportunity to further his own cause. You see, although he told me he serves the Pope, apparently he serves other, much more villainous masters."

Surprised but still wary, she said, "He told you that he serves the Pope?"

"Aye, he sought my aid to help him restore something his holiness believes belongs to him. De Gredin's group has been looking for it now for many years, and I agreed to help them in the hope of finding a sacred item that I've been seeking."

"I see," she said, believing he spoke of the Templar treasure in both cases but knowing she could not say so in front of Jake—or indeed, at all—and wondering why Fife had called it sacred.

"Those men are killers, Lady Sidony, every one of them. De Gredin told me each of his men will die for him or for their terrible organization. If one of them failed to obey him, de Gredin would kill him without compunction. I thought I was a ruthless man, but these—they call themselves 'assassins.'"

"I've never heard that word before," she said.

"'Tis an old word from the Crusades, de Gredin said. It refers to a group formed to kill heads of tribes or states that displeased its leader. Since the only way one could get close enough to kill such powerful people was to die in the attempt, they were, and still are, promised great rewards in heaven just for trying. If they win today, I fear we are all doomed. They will not care that you are a lass or that I am who I am. Bless us, though, I should be out there with a sword in hand."

"Don't be daft," Sidony said. "Both sides would believe you their enemy."

"Are you looking for me, *monsieur*?"

Whirling, sword slashing upward, Giff deflected a savage blow before he recognized de Gredin behind it. The man had come upon him from behind, taking advantage of the exact moment that Giff dispatched an opponent, to attack him.

"You should have killed without warning me first," Giff said, leaping to the attack with a daring thrust.

Parrying it with a blow hard enough to make Giff's sword ring, de Gredin said, "Ah, but that would be unsporting, would it not? And I do so enjoy *le sport*."

A shout from the bow raised other shouts, and Giff heard Hob Grant's voice above the others, bellowing, "Ships ahead, sir!"

De Gredin glanced forward, and Giff took his moment, bringing his sword up under the other man's with all his strength and sending it into the sea.

"Yield," he snapped as de Gredin looked at him. Instead the man leaped at him, but Giff ducked, lowered his blade, and with the sword's hilt still in one hand, threw both hands up and heaved de Gredin into the sea, as well.

All around him, men were looking at the ships heading toward them from Kyle Akin. One was well ahead of many others, and he narrowed his eyes, trying to make out the leader's banner, hoping it was Ranald and not more trouble.

The banner was white. The device was red, a heart with a nail piercing it.

The MacLennan banner.

Sidony heard all the shouting but could make out no clear words.

Fife, still clearly recovering from his ordeal, sat on the aft bench with his forearms on the table, apparently contemplating his folded hands.

Jake stepped on the other bench and put his head out the porthole.

"Is that how the lad came to find me?" Fife asked Sidony.

"Aye," she said. Then, realizing that she had not been treating him with the respect he doubtless expected, added hastily, "my lord."

He gave her a wry smile. "My enemies would think this dreadful voyage no more than a salutary lesson for me. I'd not blame you if you were one of them."

She thought it better not to reply to that.

Jake pulled out of the porthole. "There be ships coming, hundreds of them!"

"Hundreds?" Sidony said doubtfully.

"Aye, well, more than I've ever seen at once afore."

"'Tis Donald then," Fife said. "De Gredin will not wait to meet him with only two longships. The others he had all sank or wrecked in the storm."

"Coo, the first one be a-flying a banner like ours from Sir Giff's mam," Jake said. "And them what attacked us be a-fishing one o' their own out o' the sea."

Sidony had grabbed the bolt with one hand and the latch with the other before she recalled Giff's threat to teach her obedience in some dreadful way if she and Jake did not hide themselves in the horrid little hold until he came for them.

As she hesitated, Jake said, "The one they fished out be the man as did come to the harbor wi' ye that day, me lord."

"De Gredin," Fife said in a near growl. "I hope he drowns."

"Aye, well, he might yet," Jake said. "They be pulling him onto the boat ye was on, and they've untied it from this 'un. I think they'll all be a-going now."

Heavy pounding on the door made Sidony jump, but she threw the bolt and opened it to Giff. Catching her in his arms, he pulled her close, murmuring against her hair, "Mighty quick with the door for someone hiding under the floor, my lass."

"Aye, sir," she said. "Jake said that de Gredin fell into the sea and that the lead ship bears the MacLennan banner. Is it your father?"

"Sakes, it is well nigh every man in the Isles, I think, but my father is in the lead. What the devil is *he* doing here?" He pushed her aside and stepped between her and Fife, who had come to his feet.

"*Pax*, MacLennan," the earl said, extending a hand. "Although you don't know it yet, I owe you a debt of gratitude, because de Gredin was holding me prisoner. Had Jake Maxwell not cut me free, I'd still be tied up on de Gredin's longboat."

"I see that I'm going to want to hear this tale," Giff said with a look first at Jake and then at Sidony that boded well for neither. "Just now, though, my lord, if you truly want to express your gratitude, I'd ask you to come with me to the stern hold. This way, and quickly, if you please."

Clearly curious, Fife followed him. Sidony and Jake followed, too, and she saw that both ships flanking the *Serpent* had pulled away. The one on the larboard side was in difficulty, having plainly sprung numerous leaks, but as its oarsmen yelled for help, de Gredin's ship pulled rapidly away, raising its sail as it went.

Giff motioned to two men to follow him and Fife, and shouted to Hob Grant, "Keep an eye on the men in that sinking boat and pull out anyone who needs help. Where do you think *you* are going?" he added sternly, looking at Sidony and Jake.

"With you," she said firmly.

"Aye," Jake said just as firmly.

Giff hesitated, then said with a gesture, "Jake, your father was injured, yonder. Men are seeing to him, and he said he just clouted his head, but you—"

He got no further, for the boy had spun on his heel and dashed away.

"Come on then, sweetheart," Giff said. "My lord, I am Giffard MacLennan, and this is my lady wife, who is the daughter of Macleod of Glenelg."

"I know who you are, Sir Giffard. Where are you taking me?"

"To see what I believe you have been hoping to see," Giff said.

Sidony nearly gasped in her astonishment, but she followed them silently down into the stern hold, to the crate that had interested her so at Duncraig.

Giff told the two men who had followed them to open the stern port.

"Good," he said, peering out. "Men can see us as clearly from de Gredin's longboat as from Donald's flotilla. My lord, we'd be glad of your help with this."

"What do you mean?" Fife demanded. "What do you mean to do?"

"To push it into the sea," Giff said. "It's served its purpose, and as I am now a married man, I do *not* want the world hunting me to see what I carry on my ship."

"But—"

"You there," Giff said to one of his men. "Open the crate so his lordship can see for himself what it contains."

Without a word, the man grabbed a pry bar and detached the lid.

Sidony, already biting her tongue, now held her breath.

"Bless us, but this is just rubble!" Fife exclaimed.

"Aye, sir, and I mean to tip it into the sea. Have you any objection?"

She exhaled, glad she had managed not even to squeak in protest.

"None, if it contains only what I can see, but where is the—?"

"This is the only large crate aboard," Giff said. "You have my word that it is all we carry that might interest you, but you may search the ship for yourself if you like. As I said, I'd like to end this farce here and now. Will you help me?"

"Then it was a damned ruse," Fife said with a grimace.

"Call it whatever you like," Giff said. "I'm told that you and your men spent most of the past year making nuisances of yourselves to annoy a number of folks. Is it any wonder if some of the victims of that harassment saw fit to pay you back?"

"But what will you accomplish by pushing it into the sea?"

"Thanks to your pursuit, Donald has also taken interest in my cargo—"

"Bless me, we thought you were taking it to Donald!"

"I had no such intent," Giff said. "But, knowing you were after us, he came to meet us, determined to see it. I turned back when I saw him, so doubtless he now thinks much as you did. If he sees you help me push it overboard, he is less likely to go on believing such stuff, whilst de Gredin will think I'm dumping it to spite *him*."

"I'll help," Fife said. "Mayhap de Gredin will return and try to retrieve it from the sea. If his men want to die serving him, let them, or let Donald hang them all."

Sidony said nothing, but she knew now why Giff had sent Jake away. The lad would have had no cause to conceal his shock at seeing only rubble in the crate.

"Fasten that lid down," Giff told the man with the pry bar. "They are close enough to see what spills out." A short time later, with a great splash, they sent the crate to the bottom of the Sound, then shut and locked the stern port.

As they made their way topside again, Giff said to Fife, "'Tis a fine ship, my lord. I expect you'd like it back again now."

Fife winced. "I should hang you for stealing it, but in troth, I don't want to spend any more time on the water than I must to get home," he said. "Also, as I said before, I do owe you a debt of gratitude. Mayhap, you and I and Donald can draw up an accord that would allow you to keep her here in the Isles to serve Scotland."

"Fair enough," Giff said. As they stepped into the open again, he saw that his father's longboat had come alongside and the laird was boarding the *Serpent*. "Are you acquainted with my lord father, sir?"

Before Fife could reply, MacLennan strode forward and gripped the hand Giff extended, only to pull him into a bearlike embrace. "Sakes, lad," he said, "ye could ha' knocked me down with a broom straw when I saw yon banner."

"I was surprised to see you, too, sir, leading all the others. I'd thought—"

"I ken fine what ye thought, for your mam's told me time and again, and I'm thinking we were both fools. But I were the worse one, for ye were but a lad and I ought to ha' known better. As for being in the lead, I warrant Donald will say a word about that, but when Ranald told us ye meant to rescue his lordship here—"

"Rescue!" Fife exclaimed. "You *knew* de Gredin was holding me prisoner?"

"I believed it likely," Giff said, thinking it more tactful under the circumstances to avoid mentioning that, even so, he had not thought for a moment about rescuing Fife. Therefore, he added only, "I knew you did not command your own ship, and we had seen de Gredin with you. Logan of Lestalric and the Sinclairs having dealt with him before, it seemed likely that he had played you false."

"I see," Fife said. "It is not my nature to act in haste, but he said he served the Pope, so I believed he had good cause to do all he had vowed. I have since come to wonder if he ever had aught to do with his holiness."

"We may never know the answer to that question," Giff said.

Ships from the Lord of the Isles flotilla now surrounded them, and for a time they kept busy helping haul victims of the sinking longboat from the sea.

"Coo, look there," Jake shouted from near the helm, pointing at a billowing black cloud on the northern horizon. "Them villains must ha' tipped over a firepot."

Moving with Fife and Sidony to stand by Jake, Giff

looked closely at him, then back at the smoke. "Looks as if more is burning than a tipped-over pot."

"Aye, but fire on any boat be gey dangerous. Me da's always saying that."

"So he is," Giff agreed. "Those men will have a long swim. The Sound is about seven miles wide at that point, and they're in the middle of it."

Fife's face turned chalky. "Sir Giffard," he said, "I owe more than ordinary gratitude now, as that lad clearly saved my life. He once told me he'd like to be a ship's captain one day. If you will swear to see to his training, the *Serpent* is yours."

Jake's eyes grew wide. "Ye'd do that?"

"I *am* doing it," Fife said. "You're a fine lad and deserve a fine reward."

"But I—"

Sidony clapped a hand to Jake's shoulder, saying, "Remember your manners, Jake. Say thank you to his lordship, and we'll go see how your father is doing."

Giff touched Fife's arm. "My lord, Donald's boat is drawing up. I'm sure you'll want to go with him. We'll hand our prisoners over to him, as well, and he will do as he pleases with the survivors of that fire yonder, if there are any."

"I doubt there will be," Fife said. "De Gredin drove them so hard getting here, that I cannot think how they fought as well as they did. Then rowing away . . . Faith, they cannot have much strength left, no matter how well trained they are."

He left at once to greet his nephew, and Giff engaged himself for the next hour in the business of thanking Donald and the others, and getting ready to depart. At last, he rejoined the small group at the stern to find Maxwell sitting with one arm bound and a bandage round his head but otherwise looking nearly fit again.

Dismissing the men who had aided the captain, Giff looked from Sidony to Jake and said, "Let's have it now, lad. How did that fire start?"

Jake began to shrug, thought better of it, and achieved a wary but innocent air instead as he said, "Me da' would call it sheer carelessness."

"What would *I* call it?" Giff asked sternly.

To his surprise, the lad's expression cleared. "Aye, sure, I ken that fine," he said. "Ye'd call finding live coals by a storage locker full o' tarry oakum the right moment t' snatch for doing what needed doing."

When Sidony choked on a bubble of laughter, Giff put a strong arm around her shoulders and said firmly, "You will come with me, my lass."

Ignoring Maxwell's chuckles and Jake's visible bewilderment, he urged her inside the aft cabin, shut the door, and, grinning, took her in his arms.

"Now *this* is snatching the moment," he said, holding her tight, savoring the way she melted against him, and knowing he would love her forevermore.

Epilogue

Castle Chalamine, Glenelg, a fortnight later

A fire roared on the hearth in the castle's great hall, but Giff, slipping quietly in through a nearby side door, doubted that any but one of the company gathered there could hear it over the din of chatter. Certainly no one had noticed him yet.

With Macleod of Glenelg's wedding to Ealga Clendenen two days past, and most wedding guests departed, only the family remained. But as rapidly as the Macleod sisters seemed to produce children, the family alone was larger than most Highland clachans. Only two dozen or so were scattered in groups throughout the hall now, though, without the bairns: the seven Macleod sisters and their husbands; Hector Reaganach's twin brother, Lachlan, and his wife, Mairi of the Isles; Macleod, his bride, his sister the lady Euphemia Macleod; and Giff's own family.

As Giff moved toward his unsuspecting target, Lady Adela turned her head and saw him, but when he raised a finger to his lips, she turned back again and resumed her conversation with her new stepmother, who was sitting beside her.

Lady Cristina also glanced toward him but turned away naturally as if to intervene in the friendly argument going on between her huge husband, Hector Reaganach, and Sir Hugo Robison. Heaven knew what this latest debate was about, but Giff did not care. His attention shifted back to his target.

She sat near the fire with her stitching, as much out of the conversation as she always seemed to be in large company, and as usual, the others still tended to behave as if she were invisible. He did not understand yet how they could. His own gaze sought and found her in any room without thought on his part.

It had astonished him, too, to see how quickly she had returned to being Silent Sidony, as if her kinsmen's behavior ruled her own. He knew better, but he also understood now that she was content, even comfortable, amid the sort of conversational chaos that engulfed them now. Fortunately, she was as comfortable at Duncraig, if not more so, and had already made a good friend of his mother.

He touched her shoulder, hoping he would not startle her, but when she looked up and smiled the way she smiled only for him, he knew she had sensed his presence already and welcomed it.

Putting a finger to his lips again, he nodded toward the nearby doorway. Without a word, she set aside her stitching, rose gracefully, and followed him until he stood aside to let her precede him to the stairway.

He shut the narrow door and strode after her, but when she looked back over her shoulder with a smile, picked up her skirts, and hurried up the stairs, he caught her at the first landing. Standing a step above him, she was face-to-face with him at exactly the right height to kiss, so he did.

"I knew you would come for me," she said, putting a soft hand to his cheek when he let her breathe.

He kissed her again, lightly, but when she would have turned away again, he held her where she was. "How did you know that I would come for you, madam?"

She chuckled. "I saw you slip away when Hugo walked up to Hector, so I supposed you saw your opportunity and took it."

"I created that opportunity," he said. "I muttered something about finding the garderobe and fled before they could engage me in another of their interminable discussions of who should have done what, and when, on some field of battle."

"Are we escaping them?"

"For an hour or so," he said. "But I do want to return to Duncraig tomorrow when my parents do."

"I told Adela you would."

"Adela? Has she taken up the reins here, then?"

"Aye, sure," Sidony said. "She cannot help it, and Ealga does not mind. She said Adela has taught her a great deal in the sennight since they came up from town."

"I don't want to talk about them," he said, turning her about and giving her a gentle nudge. "I want to make love to my wife."

"'Tis a good thing, then, that Adela arranged for us to have a private room," she said, looking back at him. "Except for my father and Ealga, everyone else is packed women with women, men with men, and bairns with bairns."

"Being newly married has its advantages," he said, leaning past her to open the door to their blessedly private chamber. "This is just one of them," he added as he shut the door and bolted it against the castleful of inquisitive bairns.

"You still have not told me what you did with the Stone of Destiny," she said. "This would be a good time, don't you think?"

The look on his face told Sidony that she had stunned him, which was as good as an admission.

Recovering, he said evenly, "What makes you think I had the Stone?"

"Lord Fife called it sacred and spoke of the treasure separately, as something the Chevalier de Gredin wanted. I wasn't sure, though, until we came here. Nay," she added hastily when he frowned. "I did not overhear anyone else talking, nor ask them to tell me, but I did just casually mention the Stone of Destiny to Isobel and Sorcha, and Sorcha said we ought not to discuss it at all, so I knew."

He shook his head at her. "Rob is right. Keeping secrets is devilish hard. We'd all do better to forget all about it and hope that everyone else does, too."

She just looked at him.

With a sigh, he said, "Very well, I suppose you ought to know that it was, in good part, your doing. Sithee, despite all that you, Henry, and the others had said to me about my being too reckless, it wasn't until you insisted on leaving Girnigoe with me that I realized I had been, especially where you were concerned. In troth, I did not want to leave you at Girnigoe, but I knew I could not take you with me to meet Ranald. In thinking how best to take precautions for your safety, I realized I could take like precautions with the Stone. 'Tis why we went to Duncraig."

"So it is at Duncraig?"

"Not exactly," he said. "Nor does that matter. Just know that it's safe now. The men who aided me have served my family all my life, and their ancestors served my ancestors. I mean to tell only Rob and Henry what I've done."

"But I want to see it," she said.

"Mayhap you will one day," he said. "One day all Scotland will see it, when the world is at peace and all men who would do evil lie at the bottom of the sea."

A peaceful Scotland sounded wonderful, but she did not think the world would ever be without evil men. Not while men continued to lust for power and wealth, and were willing to kill anyone who stood in their way or whose opinion they did not share. A chill touched her just to think of such men.

"Hold me," she said.

"Gladly." He drew her close, his touch warming her as always. A moment later, dulcetly, he added, "I'll even help you take off your gown, my child."

Stiffening, she said, "I have told you before, I am not a child."

"I keep forgetting," he said with a teasing smile as he kissed her. "Come to bed and prove that to me again, sweetheart."

She went willingly, and minutes later, naked in bed with him, she responded to him as she had from the first time he had kissed her.

His every touch sent waves of warmth through her, but he could do the same with a look from across a vast great hall or with a certain tone of voice. And when he *wanted* to stir her, as he did now, he had many methods and seemed always to be finding new ones. In minutes, he had her squirming, hot, and wet with passion.

She knew he liked dominating her in bed, so when he moved atop her and eased gently into her, she expected matters to go as they had before. Instead, with a mischievous grin, he rolled to his back, carrying her with him so that she straddled him. Then, still grinning, he pushed her upright, saying, "I've wanted to do this since the first time I saw you on a horse, lass. Let's see how well you ride me."

Although she felt awkward and oddly exposed at first, she soon found that she enjoyed the position and delighted in pleasing him as well as herself. In time, as their passion increased toward its climax, she found herself under him again and soon, gasping, achieved her release. His came but moments later.

As they lay back against their pillows, she snuggled close to him, content.

"It is good to be home again," he murmured.

"Sakes, Chalamine is not our home."

"Sweetheart, my home is wherever you are. We belong."

"Aye, we do. Your mother wants us to stay at Duncraig, though. She said we could have the entire north wing to ourselves if you're willing."

"I know she did, and I'm eager to go home," he said. "If you wouldn't mind, though, I'd like us to take our meals in the hall with everyone else."

"Is that for my sake, because you'll be away again for long periods?"

"Nay, love. I'd miss my bonnie, demanding wife too

much. 'Tis because I have already lost too much time with my family. Are you ready to try riding again?"

"Sakes, are *you*?"

"Aye, sure, I am," he said, hugging her. "Sithee, I never knew before how much I could enjoy being put on my backside."

Dear Reader,

I hope you enjoyed *King of Storms.* When I read that St. Columba was known by that title because he could tame the wildest seas, I knew I'd found the title for this book. Finding a hero for Lady Sidony, who had been little more than her sister Sorcha's shadow before, and thus invisible otherwise, proved harder.

Sidony needed a man strong enough to startle her out of her habit of shadowing others, so at first Giff resembled Mel Gibson's character in *Lethal Weapon,* but he soon developed his own characteristics. I wanted a man willing to help her find her true self, rather than one who wanted to mold her to suit him.

I also wanted him able to make her see that she was her own person with her own opinions, because like many youngest children in large families, she thought she had to try to be like the sisters born before her, and had come to forget (or had never yet realized) that she could just be herself. However, I did *not* want Giff to do all the teaching, because Sidony had been observing folks all her life and had much that she, too, could teach. *King of Storms* grew from those seeds and others.

For those of you curious about what later became of the Earl of Fife, he went on to become High Chamberlain of Scotland from 1382 to 1407. In 1389, deeming his father, the King, too old and infirm even to rule by proxy, he orchestrated his own election by the nobles as Governor of Scotland. The Earl of Carrick having suffered a crippling kick from a horse that further weakened his health and resolve, the nobles likewise agreed that Fife should be guardian of the kingdom until Carrick recovered or until Carrick's eldest son, David, was able to assume the throne.

Therefore, when Robert II died in 1390 and Carrick succeeded as Robert III, Fife simply continued to rule. In 1397, when Parliament met, Fife was created Duke of Albany (from Albania, believe it or not, which was the ancient name of the country between the Firth of Forth and the river Spey in the north). At the same time, his nephew David was created Duke of Rothesay, a title Prince Charles bears today. These new titles comprised the first introduction of the ducal title in Scotland.

The opinions of Fife expressed by the Sinclairs, Sir Hugo, Rob Logan, and Giff are opinions well documented among the nobility of the period. Moreover, in May 1402, the Scottish Parliament declared that the Duke of Rothesay, Carrick's son and rightful heir to the throne, had died of natural causes after being arrested and imprisoned by Fife. To say that most of the country refused to accept those "natural causes" is to put it mildly, especially after Fife demanded and received a full pardon from that same Parliament for himself and his co-conspirators.

Carrick died in 1406, and his second son and now heir (later James I) was sent to France but was captured by the English on the way and held hostage in London for years. Fife ruled as regent until his own death in 1420. Thus, although never King of Scots, he effectively ruled the kingdom, one way or another, for forty years.

As for the adventures of the Earl of Fife in this book, can anyone wonder that he never mentioned them to any historian? I'm sure that if anyone asked him about that particular absence from Edinburgh, he said only that he had taken it into his head to visit his nephew Donald and attend the wedding of a distant kinswoman.

For those of you always curious about my sources, the information about and the description of Leith Harbor comes from many, but one of the most interesting and detailed is *The Story of Leith* by John Russell on the Web at http://www.electricscotland.com/history/leith/index.htm.

Details of galleys, longships, and other vessels derive from numerous sources as well, but primarily from *The West Highland Galley* by Denis Rixon (Edinburgh, 1998). Models for the *Serpent Royal* were the Isles birlinn and the Norse "esnecca" or "snekkjur," which boasted both sail and oars and carried cargo, unlike the usual west Highland galley, which carried no cargo other than extra oars, canvas, ropes, and minimal provisions and water for its crew.

Again, primary description of the Stone came from *Stone of Destiny* by Pat Gerber (Edinburgh, 1997).

For more about the Templar treasure, I suggest again the following sources: *Holy Blood, Holy Grail* by Michael Baigent and Richard Leigh (New York, 1982); *The Temple and the Lodge* by Michael Baigent and Richard Leigh (New York, 1989); *Pirates & the Lost Templar Fleet* by David H. Childress (Illinois, 2003); and *The Lost Treasure of the Knights Templar* by Steven Sora (Vermont, 1999). For more about the Assassins, see *The Assassins* by Bernard Lewis (London, 1967).

As always, I'd also like to thank Beth de Guzman, vice president and editor in chief of Warner Books; my terrific agents, Lucy Childs and Aaron Priest; my wonderful editor, Frances Jalet-Miller; and everyone else at

Hachette Book Group who contributed to the creation of this book.

If you enjoyed *King of Storms*, please look for *Border Wedding* at your favorite bookstore in March 2008. In the meantime, *Suas Alba!*

Sincerely,

http://home.att.net/~amandascott

About the Author

Amanda Scott, *USA Today* best-selling author and winner of Romance Writers of America's RITA/Golden Medallion awards, *Romantic Times*' Career Achievement Award for British Isles Historical, and *Romantic Times*' Awards for Best Regency Author and Best Sensual Regency, began writing on a dare from her husband. She has sold every manuscript she has written. She sold her first novel, *The Fugitive Heiress*—written on a battered Smith Corona—in 1980. Since then, she has sold many more, but since the second one, she has used a word processor. More than twenty-five of her books are set in the English Regency period (1810-1820); others are set in fifteenth-century England and fourteenth-through-eighteenth-century Scotland. Three are contemporary romances.

Amanda is a fourth-generation Californian who was born and raised in Salinas and graduated with a bachelor's degree in history from Mills College in Oakland. She did graduate work at the University of North Carolina at Chapel Hill, specializing in British history, before obtaining her master's in history from San Jose State University. She is a fellow of the Society of Antiquaries of Scotland. After graduate school, she taught for the Salinas City School District for three years before marrying her husband, who was then a captain in the Air Force. They lived in Honolulu for a year, then in Nebraska, where their son was born, for seven years. Amanda now lives with her husband in northern California.